THE DRAGON PORTAL SERIES

SHADOWS AND TWILIGHT

BOOK 4

JAMIE A. WATERS

Shadows and Twilight © 2022 by Jamie A. Waters

Cover Art: Deranged Doctor Design
Editor: Novel Nurse Editing

ISBN: 978-1-949524-28-4 (Hardback Edition)
ISBN: 978-1-949524-26-0 (Paperback Edition)
ISBN: 978-1-949524-25-3 (eBook Edition)

Library of Congress Control Number: 2022907347
First Edition *August 2022

THE DRAGON PORTAL SERIES

To Kill a Fae
By Blood and Magic
Facets of Power
Shadows and Twilight
Dance of Wings
Forest of Secrets

Chapter One

"*D*on't go that way, Dagmar!" a woman shrieked from the hallway. "The cave trolls are—"

A resounding crash sounded outside the door to Sabine's bedchamber, but she didn't look up from her letter. The tone of this missive needed to be perfect. Somehow, she needed to convince everyone that her absence from the Unseelie court was temporary.

Balkin, her beastman protector, had already warned that some prominent families were suggesting they install their own proxy to rule in her stead. Since she had no intention of giving up her throne, she was suffering through another afternoon of writing letters.

Gods, fae politics were a convoluted mess. She'd prefer an outright assassination attempt any day.

She needed a strong statement to add, to encourage the rest of the Unseelie to fall in line. If they believed she had plans in motion that could benefit them, her people would hesitate to strike out against her. Some plots took centuries to come to fruition. Sabine didn't intend to wait that long to return to her homeland, but buying herself even a few months would help. Tilting her head, she studied the message, desperately needing inspiration to convince her people she was trying to subvert her father's machinations.

"Crap on a crystal, Dagmar," a woman complained from outside Sabine's bedroom. "The cave trolls are mopping. Didn't you see the warning crystals? They're lit up like it's the solstice! You're supposed to be a household manager now, not giving them more work to do!"

Sabine straightened, her mouth curving in a wicked smile. If inspiration crashed outside the room in the form of cave trolls, it was a good idea to put them to use. Cave trolls not only maintained everything in the dwarven city of Razadon but they also doubled as an inventive and resourceful spy network. Fortunately, they were now beholden to Sabine.

Putting her quill to the parchment, Sabine wrote, *"As a gesture of my goodwill, I shall send a trusted emissary of the dwarven community to your household."*

"Sorry, Mum," Dagmar said in a muffled voice. "I'll fix the crystals later. I've got an important—"

Babda's exasperation was evident when she shouted, "No! Don't you dare move! I don't care if there's a soapy cave troll in your face. Wait until I reset the crystals, or the cave trolls will start climbing the walls. I'll never get them out of the chandeliers. And what in the name of Grobdar's beard is a goat doing in the embassy?"

A goat? Sabine shook her head in bewilderment and dipped her quill in the ink again. If she'd learned anything over the past week, it was that Dagmar was bringing another "urgent" message for her to handle. She needed to finish this letter before some random dwarven noble wanted to petition her about the cost of mushroom exports to Faerie. A faint headache bloomed behind her eyes. Fae and dwarven bureaucracies were more soul-sucking than being chased by the Wild Hunt.

Dagmar's reply was muffled. There was another crash and a squeal, followed by pounding footsteps. From the sounds, Sabine guessed the goat was about to make another break for it.

"Not that way, Bombady! You'll let the goat out!" a tiny pixie voice called. "Oops. There goes the other bucket of soapy water. Gotta move faster than the goat, Bombady. Shake off those suds and let's go!"

"No! Don't shake! Aieeee!" Screams filled the hallway, followed by more running footsteps.

Sabine continued writing. *"The illustrious cave troll Bombady is eager to serve any of my father's Seelie subjects as you see fit. His skills are varied, especially when it comes to household tasks. I trust in your discretion and handling of this important matter."*

She grinned and signed her name with a flourish. From what she remembered about the cunningness of the Rivinath family, they would have no trouble determining which Seelie household to target. With any luck, the cave troll spy would pick up a few snippets of information in his travels. At the worst, he'd cause mischief and mayhem among Sabine's enemies. Cave trolls were too much of a novelty for the fae to kill outright. Besides, they were as skilled as the pixies when it came to getting out of trouble—and getting into it.

Sabine picked up a small vial of glittering pixie dust and sprinkled it over the parchment. She blew gently to dry the ink before carefully rolling the missive. Humming a wordless melody, she ignored the muttered curses coming from the hall. Without missing a beat, she affixed her wax seal and infused a trace of magic to seal the letter. No one except the recipient would be able to read the enchanted ink, and the seal prevented anyone from attempting to open it without serious backlash.

"If I weren't already impressed by you, I would be now," Malek mused aloud from the far side of the room. "I think I've read the same paragraph fifteen times in the time you've written at least a dozen letters."

Malek's voice pulled her out of her reverie, more than the commotion outside. Sabine turned in her chair to catch a glimpse of the dragon shapeshifter lounging on the bed. He captured her gaze, the force of his look enough to make her heart skip a beat. Every time she looked at him, warmth and undeniable need rushed through her.

"Any time you'd like to trade places, let me know," she said, giving him a teasing smile.

She took the opportunity to study his golden features, captivated by the way the light struck him. His dark hair had been tied back away from his face, revealing striking blue eyes that always saw far too much. Even while relaxed, there was an air of power about him, a staggering reminder he was a dangerous predator who could easily crush his foes. Part of her was drawn to the sharp edge of violence contained within him. She suspected he was one of the rare few who wasn't intimidated by her magic or her title.

As though sensing the direction of her thoughts, Malek's gaze heated with a fire that warmed her from within. He put his book aside, a heavy crystal-faced tome he'd acquired from the dwarven archives. The dwarves had been uneasy about his presence in their city after he'd revealed his true nature. Out of respect for their fears, Malek had elected to remain in the embassy over the past week, with only brief trips into the heart of the city. Most of his time had been spent searching for information about the artifacts needed to seal the Dragon Portal.

The thought squelched some of the flames of her desire.

Sabine glanced down at the glowing golden marks on her wrist and barely resisted the urge to touch the signs of her newly acquired magic. A chalice, a pearl, and now a hammer decorated her skin. Each of the three emblems represented a different magical race: the fae, the merfolk, and the dwarves. The goddess Lachlina had infused power into mystical artifacts to seal the portal and prevent the war between the gods and dragons from spilling out into the world. Now that the portal seals were failing, the war that had nearly decimated the world threatened to consume them again. They needed to find the rest of the artifacts soon. Unfortunately, it meant Sabine was absorbing powers no fae had ever been meant to wield.

"I need a break from these translations," Malek said and rose to his feet. "Would you care to join me and perhaps clear your head for a bit?"

Sabine hesitated and then sighed, glancing at the stack of letters waiting for a response. She could no longer see the deep mahogany color of her desk or the whorls of silver that served as its only decoration. Was someone sneaking more letters onto her desk without her realizing it? The pile had multiplied since that morning.

"I *should* take a break, but I'd hoped to clear some of these tasks first. Once we leave Razadon, it'll be more difficult to communicate with Balkin or the rest of my people in Faerie."

"I know messages are easier to send and receive while we're occupying this pocket of Faerie, but I thought Balkin installed a new administrator to help you."

She nodded absently, thinking of her beastman protector back in her homeland. "He did, but the Unseelie throne has been vacant for ten years. The Council of Eight has been handling some of the tasks, but there's still a backlog."

With a small flash of light, a new letter appeared on top of the pile. Sabine muttered a curse. Faerie was sometimes a little too helpful. Apparently she wasn't sorting her mail fast enough, and the collection plate in the main hall was full again. She picked up the newly delivered letter, not recognizing the flowery script with its graceful slopes and curlicues.

Temper flared within her as she scanned it. "Turnips? Of all the outlandish requests. Why on the goddess's green earth would anyone care about the color of *turnips*?"

"What?"

She waved the letter in the air and said, "Lady Orga'Vennils prefers wearing robes of purple, since it's one of their house colors. She and the rest of her household are convinced that the Toshar family are growing purple turnips as a slight. They're petitioning for all turnips to be made into a non-offensive color."

Malek chuckled. He crossed the room toward her, not quite stalking but almost prowling. Every step made her heart beat a little faster, and a small thrill went through her. Gods. He really was a beautiful man. She tossed the letter onto her desk and focused on the charismatic dragon instead. To the underworld and back with the Vennils and Toshar families. They could choke on their damn turnips.

Malek leaned against her desk, a small, sexy smile teasing the corner of his mouth. He crossed his arms over his chest and nodded toward the door. "We could always release a horde of cave trolls into their turnip garden."

Sabine tilted her head, a small smile playing upon her lips as well. The idea had merit.

Malek grinned and said, "I'm afraid Lady Orga'Vennils will need to suffer a bit longer with purple turnips. From the sound of it, we're about to be invaded." He leaned in close, his voice conspiratorial. "Care to make a wager? My money's on some dwarven noble who wants the new queen to settle an argument about the best lunar cycle to harvest power crystals."

Sabine wrinkled her nose. "I was guessing mushroom exports."

Malek thew his head back and laughed. The sound was enough to lighten her heart. She took Malek's extended hand, allowing him to help her stand. He drew her into his arms, and she leaned against him for a moment, enjoying the way his heated fire magic trailed over her skin. She pressed her hand against his chest and looked up into his striking blue eyes. His gaze immediately heated, and he tucked a lock of her silvery hair behind her ear, then trailed the back of his fingers down the side of her face.

Another crash sounded from outside. Sabine caught sight of a gray-and-white goat charging down the hallway.

"Follow that goat!" Blossom shrieked, zipping down the hall after the goat and leaving a glittering trail of pixie dust in her wake. Two small creatures reminiscent of blue hedge-hogs with spindly arms and legs sprinted after the pixie.

"It's not too late to hide," Malek whispered next to her ear, sending a small shiver through her. "If we ask nicely, Faerie might seal the door for a few hours. We could sneak over to the room with the heated spring before anyone knows we're gone."

Sabine made a noise of agreement, recalling the events from the night before, when she'd been able to get lost in him for several hours. The embassy boasted its own private spring, fueled by heat from the underworld. It was delectable and so very tempting, especially with her dragon at her side.

She looked up at him and asked, "Do you think we'd still have an embassy left if we disappear again?"

He threaded his fingers through hers and brought her knuckles up to press a kiss against them. "It would be worth it for a few hours alone with you."

She softened against him and wound her arms around his neck, responding to the heated promise in his eyes. He ran his hands up her side, sending a rush of desire through her. Each touch and caress from him stoked her need into a fiery inferno that caused her blood to hum.

Dagmar stumbled into the room on a platform of soapy water. She grabbed at the doorframe with her free hand, stopping her momentum with a wobble. In her other hand, she clutched a dark box against her chest tightly.

"It's too late. We've been invaded," Sabine whispered and reluctantly pulled away from Malek.

He chuckled and placed his hand against her lower back. Leaning close, he said, "Only temporarily. I intend to finish this when she leaves."

His hand caressed her back, warming her with his power through the thin material of her dress. She trembled, recalling the skill of those clever hands. Gods. She was tempted to send Dagmar away before even letting her house manager speak. This dragon had completely bewitched her.

The dwarven woman snapped to attention, her red braids swinging from the abrupt movement. Soapy water slid down her face and dripped from her clothes, puddling on the floor. The absurdity of the situation struck Sabine, and she struggled to keep her face neutral. Dagmar had been receiving additional lessons in court protocol from her mother, but there were still a few challenges to iron out. Fortunately, Dagmar likely wouldn't need to travel to Faerie for several years yet—and Sabine hoped she wouldn't bring the goats.

Babda followed her and said, "Dagmar! What in the world do you think yer doing? Yer grandda would be rolling over in his tomb if he saw this. You better get down on this floor and help me clean up this mess."

Dagmar rolled her eyes. "Grandda isn't dead, Mum! He's down at the pub getting sloshed."

"He'll wish he were dead if he saw what you've done to the fae queen's embassy."

"Mum! It's an urgent message! I'll clean up the mess later." Dagmar held up the small box, shaking it hard enough to make a loud rattle.

Sabine winced. The crystal boxes forged by the dwarves were strong, but Dagmar was giving it a powerful beating.

Behind her, Babda threw up her hands and exclaimed, "Soapy water all over the queen's royal chamber, and I get sass! The Faerie queen will fire us before the month's up. Centuries of stewardship down the drain, all because we can't keep goats out of the embassy."

Babda pointed her finger at the soapy cave trolls gathered in the hallway and said, "We're going to need reinforcements. All of you, spread out. Let's find the goat and clean up this mess. We don't have all day!"

A chorus of chittering filled the air, and a mob of blue creatures followed the retreating dwarven woman. Dagmar cleared her throat and straightened.

"Queen Sabin'theoria, I bring an urgent message from Councilwoman Astrid," Dagmar said, taking a large wobbly step into the room. Her green eyes widened when her legs slid out in front of her. She yelped.

Malek leaped forward and grabbed Dagmar, catching her before she fell.

The crystal box flew out of her hand and into the air. Dagmar gasped as it landed on the ground, the lid flying off and somewhere under Sabine's desk.

Dagmar paled. "Astrid's gonna kill me."

"Your cousin likes you too much to kill you," Sabine said and walked over to collect the box. She knelt and picked it up, halting at the sight of the small stone that had fallen to the ground. Sabine swallowed, a tendril of unease wrapping around her.

She picked up the stone and stood, staring at it. It was unremarkable as stones went, except for the splash of blood coating the glowing rune etched on the bottom.

"It's another memory stone, isn't it?" Malek asked.

Sabine nodded and turned toward Dagmar. "Did Astrid's messenger say anything when they delivered this?"

Dagmar clasped her hands together. "It arrived in the city less than an hour ago. She viewed it and called for her fastest runner to bring it here. She said the stone recorded an incident that happened recently, shortly after you claimed Atlantia as part of your domain."

Sabine froze. The Seelie side of her family had forced her into exile more than a decade ago, and Sabine had done her best not to reveal she was still alive. Unfortunately, in her efforts to save a merfolk woman, Sabine had been forced to claim her birthright: the title of Unseelie queen. She'd announced to the world she was now a power to be reckoned with, but the truth was, she was ill-equipped to handle such a declaration. Compared to the rest of her people and their remarkable power, she was little more than a child.

Malek frowned. "Someone else was murdered, weren't they?"

Sabine took a shaky breath, running her thumb along the glowing rune. Several Unseelie had been murdered over the past several months, and the numbers were increasing.

"It's likely," she admitted. "I need to view the memory to find out. I suspect this is my father's twisted idea of a coronation gift. This death will probably have some special meaning for me."

"Considering that he still wants to kill you, this could be a trap. You're not fully recovered yet, Sabine. If you have to rely upon your magic for any reason while you're in this memory, you may not have the strength to return."

Sabine frowned. "I can't delay. If Astrid sent a runner so quickly, this is a time-sensitive matter."

"I'm going with you then."

Sabine looked up at him and nodded. She'd nearly died a few short days ago, after being shot with a crossbow bolt made from cold iron. It was only through Malek's love and the gift of his power that she'd survived the attack. While she was growing stronger every day, too much magical exertion fatigued her. Dwarves had little magic of their own and the memory stone had already been observed once. She'd need to infuse a measure of her power with the stone to strengthen the memory, not only to view it but also to escape. If she faltered, either Malek or Bane had the ability to strengthen her magic. Malek could help her up to a point, but it was better to have both nearby.

Thinking of her demon protector, Sabine turned back to Dagmar and asked, "Where is Bane?"

Dagmar's eyes widened. "He's in the training room with Rika. Do you want me to get him for you?"

Sabine hesitated and then shook her head. "No. Leave them to it. He's helping Rika test out more dwarven weapons to see which ones suit her best. He should be able to monitor my lifeforce from there. He'll find me if he senses I'm in trouble."

She wasn't in a hurry to go head-to-head with Bane again. He still wasn't pleased she'd made the decision to remain in the relative safety of Razadon for the next month instead of immediately venturing to the underworld to secure her position among the demons. Sabine wanted to be as strong as possible before she faced the demon king in his den. Kal'thorz had already proven he would challenge her limits, both in deeds and words.

Bane had begrudgingly agreed, taking the opportunity to turn one of the empty embassy rooms into a training area for

Rika. He was determined to teach the young seer not only how to master various weapons but also how to utilize her magic as a weapon. Sabine had been enjoying the training sessions too. It had been too long since she'd practiced her weapon skills.

Sabine clutched the stone and looked up into Malek's eyes. "If you're joining me, you'll need to wear your warding medallion."

Malek nodded and retrieved the necklace from the small table beside their bed. He fastened it around his neck and adjusted the metal to rest against his skin. His power immediately muted, including the faint scent of burning leaves that always surrounded him.

Sabine brushed her fingertips against the cool metal, marveling at how a witch could hide such powerful dragon magic behind such a small object. She couldn't sense anything from it.

Malek's arm wrapped around her waist, his expression grim. "I'm ready."

Sabine took a deep breath and gathered her magic around them. Running her thumb along the rune etched into the stone, she infused her Unseelie magic into the pattern to unlock its secrets. The memory stone glowed, then became brighter and brighter. With a flash, the bedroom faded away, and they fell into the memory.

Chapter Two

Sabine blinked rapidly, trying to clear her vision.

Majestic trees reached from the earth to brush the sky, spreading their fingers outward in a sheltering canopy of dark greens and silvers. The thick, rough ridges of the bark had traces of the silvery magic that had given them life. As the wind rustled the leaves and infused the air with their power, the tree's song resonated within her.

Magic was everywhere, connecting her to the land and embracing her soul. There was only one location that felt like quite like this, the Silver Forests of Faerie.

A brief flash of elation rushed through her at being back in her homeland, even though this was only a captured memory. She didn't recognize this part of the forest, but that wasn't surprising. Faerie was vaster than anyone knew, constantly changing as it saw fit.

She wasn't sure why the dwarves had cast their memory stone in this remote part of the forest rather than closer to one of the cities. Under most circumstances, it wouldn't record more than some wildlife or possibly a passing hunter.

It made her wonder how many of these stones the dwarves had hidden.

The last six memory stones she'd viewed had also recorded events that had taken place in the Silver Forests of Faerie. Either her people held a monopoly on unsavory happenings that needed to be recorded or the dwarves had an unhealthy obsession with her people. She was betting on a little of both.

On the surface, everything appeared peaceful. Sunlight dappled through the leaves of the Silver trees, but the edges were harsher somehow. It was almost as though the shadows had retreated from this area and taken with them her biggest source of power. The normal sounds of birds and other forest creatures rustling through the foliage were also strangely absent.

Flashes of light pulsed from beyond the tree line. They were at the edge of Faerie, and these Silver trees were part of the land's magical defense. Crouching low, Sabine reached over to brush her hand against Malek's arm. She quickly wrapped a shroud of glamour around him to better obscure his identity. The trees were sentient, and even in a recorded memory, they were well aware of the dangers of dragonfire.

In this place between memory and dreams, neither Malek nor Sabine were safe. While their physical forms remained within the embassy in Razadon, they were still vulnerable while encased in the vision. If one or both died here, their physical bodies would be affected as well. One careless misstep and everything they'd been working toward would be lost.

"Will-o'-the-wisps," she murmured in a low voice, gesturing toward the lights.

"Are they dangerous?"

"Not exactly," Sabine said quietly. "They're the souls of fallen pixies. They're omens of death, meant to light the way to the realm of the afterlife. They won't harm us, but their presence means someone will die."

"I'm guessing we're supposed to follow them?"

Sabine nodded. Motioning for Malek to stay close, Sabine led him through the trees toward the lights. Moving silently through the forest had been instilled in her since birth, but it was taking more effort than necessary to mask their presence. Normally the magic of the forest was quick to obey her unspoken commands.

"Something's wrong with the magic here," Malek whispered, echoing her thoughts. "This isn't like the other memory stones we've seen. The forest feels almost... angry."

She glanced at the dragon shapeshifter by her side, disconcerted he'd sensed the maliciousness in the air. The magic was as thick as syrup, but only someone of fae descent should have been able to sense its intent. Part of her wondered if their shared blood bond allowed him to draw upon her innate gifts. With a brush of her power, she checked his warding medallion and her glamour to ensure he wasn't revealing himself. Nothing was penetrating his protections. Malek wasn't the cause of the forest's restlessness. But still, something wasn't right. The weight of eyes upon them made her skin prickle with awareness.

Leaning close to Malek, she murmured, "We're being watched. Someone's manipulating this memory beyond what the stone should have recorded. Step lightly. We may be in more danger than I expected."

He gave her a curt nod and fell silent, his hand straying to the hilt of his sword. It likely wouldn't do him much good here, but Sabine didn't tell him that. She couldn't be sure what magic was at work in this place. Dreamweavers and memorywalkers weren't always content to simply observe. Intent was a large part of magic, and Malek's sword might help focus his strength if it was needed.

Sabine continued to move forward, listening to the soft sound of Malek's footfalls crunching the leaves behind her. He moved quietly enough for being such a powerful predator, but the dragon shapeshifter was out of place in the Silver Forest. The boundaries of the memory were larger than she expected. Someone had expended a great deal of magic to expand this pocket of Faerie.

Malek grabbed her arm to halt her progress. In a low voice, he whispered, "I smell blood."

Sabine froze. In the other memories they'd seen, some of the Seelie fae had murdered those of the Unseelie. They'd all been different races—trolls, orcs, and even a goblin. Sabine had never arrived after the death had already occurred. The memory stone was supposed to act as an anchor, recording only moments that evoked the strongest emotions or magic. If someone had already died in this area and the stone was still recording, it didn't bode well for her and Malek.

She took a deep breath, inhaling the heady scent of the forest where she'd grown up. Reaching beyond it, she focused on slight nuances. A faint whiff of a distinct metallic scent carried on the breeze, like rusty nails or something rotten.

She glanced at him and murmured, "It doesn't smell right."

"No. It's both old and new blood, but I'd swear it's from the same source. The layers are overlapping somehow, like blood has repeatedly been spilled in the same place."

Sabine frowned, unsure how such a thing could be possible. "Corruption? Or a hunting ground?"

Malek hesitated. "It doesn't feel like the corruption we experienced in Razadon, but anything's possible. Perhaps someone was trying to use blood magic and it didn't work right."

Sabine frowned. A misguided dwarven woman had tried

to recreate the magic of the gods. Her attempts had killed countless innocents and endangered many others. Sabine had nearly died bringing her to justice. She wasn't eager to repeat the experience.

If someone was using blood magic here, it might explain the expanded boundaries of the memory. Corruption or not, the land must be trying to reject the blood offering. Something had happened here that went against the laws of nature. Otherwise, the forest would have embraced the magic and absorbed its power.

"Do you know where it's coming from?" she asked, trying to determine the direction. Layers of magic were masking her ability to get a good reading. She couldn't risk opening herself more to the forest without making them both vulnerable.

Malek gestured toward a dense grouping of trees to the east. "That way."

Sabine arched her brow, surprised by his ease in cutting through the magic of her people. Alarm bells sounded in her head. Malek might be the apex predator, but this forest shouldn't speak to him so easily. The dragons had nearly eradicated her people centuries ago, and even now, the hatred between the two groups ran deep. This could be a trap, one carefully designed to target Malek.

A strange awareness rushed through her and caused her skin to pebble. She pushed the invasive magic away and gripped the memory stone in her hand tightly. Someone had been trying to read her thoughts or emotions. Sabine needed to be more cognizant of her mental shields, or she could lose the man she loved.

"It's the memorywalkers," Sabine whispered. "The blood scent is overlapping because they've accessed this memory several times. Every time they fuel their magical working, they have to perform a sacrifice. They're forcing the land to relive this foul magic repeatedly. Faerie isn't happy with what they're doing."

Malek scowled. "Neither am I."

No matter how many times the memorywalker had come here to observe and wait, Sabine's instincts warned her that they were here at her father's behest. If they could trail the memorywalker back to his or her patron, she'd have definitive proof of who was responsible for the murders. It might be enough to sway the Council of Eight in her favor.

After moving in the direction Malek had indicated, Sabine stopped at a tightly clustered group of trees. The dense foliage was barring the way. She pressed her hand against a nearby tree trunk, hoping the memory would respond to her request. Threading her magic through the bark, Sabine's shoulders relaxed as the branches moved aside to allow them to pass.

It had worked, but Sabine had the impression the watchers weren't pleased. The coldness of the eyes upon them sent a chill through her, but she tried to remember the watchers weren't truly here. Like her and Malek, the memorywalker's physical form was ensconced in the real forest, back in Faerie. It was only their mind and magic that had crossed over to this in-between realm, making them as vulnerable as her and Malek.

"Try not to kill them," she whispered, her hand tightening around the stone. "If we can get close enough, I can temporarily sever their ability to return to their physical body. It might be our only option to question them. But be careful. Any harm you cause will have an effect on them in the real world. Too much damage will cause their mind to give out, and we'll lose them."

Malek nodded, and his hand tightened on his sword. He motioned toward the pulsing lights in the distance and frowned. They were larger somehow, as though the magic was building in potency.

Sabine narrowed her eyes on them. Instead of being solid white, they were flashing in soothing colors of green, blue, and purple. The resonance of the lights didn't match the power she sensed from the memorywalker.

The stone in her hand warmed, pulling her toward the lights. Sabine hesitated for only a moment. Something or someone else was the reason behind this memory, and they were far more dangerous than any memorywalker who had been ordered to observe.

Sabine nodded at Malek and slowly crept toward the anomalies. The memorywalker would have to wait. The wisps of light were emitting calming influences of magic for some reason. Whatever or whomever they were trying to calm was likely the reason she'd been brought here. If she didn't learn what she could before the memory ended, she'd lose her chance to find out who was killing the Unseelie.

Sabine stepped lightly upon the ground, discomforted by the increasingly unwelcome feel of the land. Whatever had happened here had set the forest on edge. The leaves rustled in agitation, and Sabine cast her gaze upward. The trees immediately stilled, but she understood the warning. Faerie was responding to her presence, but it wasn't safe for her to be here.

She pressed her hand against a nearby tree in a reassuring gesture before continuing toward the lights. The pattern was rhythmic, nearly hypnotizing. Almost without realizing it, she began timing her steps to correspond with the flashes. Sabine slowed her pace, refusing to succumb to the spell, but continued to move forward. With each step she took, the lure tightened. Sabine paused repeatedly to unravel the weavings around her and Malek before moving forward again.

A vine snaked out from a bush and wrapped around her

ankle. Sabine halted her progress. Grabbing Malek's hand, she pulled him down behind some flowering bushes to break the memorywalker's line of sight.

"*Va deshein,*" she murmured, brushing her fingertips along the vine to indicate she understood its warning. It tightened for a moment and then loosened its grip, but it didn't release her. She wasn't in a hurry to pull away. The connection to the land strengthened her internal shields.

She took a deep breath, focusing on clearing any lingering mind fog from the magical calling. Whoever was controlling the will-o'-the-wisps was more skilled than she'd expected. She was able to withstand it, but anyone without the potency of a strong bloodline would fall victim to their weaving. There was a tremendous amount of power being utilized, almost as though it were a group of fae working in tandem.

"We can't cross that boundary," she whispered, pointing toward the tree line where a faint shimmer cast upward from the land. "If we do, we'll leave Faerie's realm. The normal rules of magic won't apply."

Malek frowned. "I'm assuming that would be bad?"

She nodded. "We'd be outside of the memory and unable to return to our physical forms. It would leave us at the mercy of a memorywalker to bring us back, and I doubt they'd have such noble intentions."

"Imagine that," Malek said dryly. "Since we have no intention of lying down and dying for them, what's the plan? Can we break the memory?"

"We have to wait until it ends," Sabine said, glancing at the vine still wrapped around her ankle. Their crouching in the bushes seemed to ease some of Faerie's discomfort. Sabine pressed her fingers into the soil at her feet, sending a small tendril of reassuring magic into the land.

Malek leaned forward to watch the lights. In a low voice,

he asked, "The other murders didn't happen so close to the edge of the forest, did they?"

Sabine shook her head. "Most of Faerie's creatures prefer insulating themselves deep within the heart of Faerie. We're too close to the human villages for them to feel comfortable."

Malek muttered a curse. "I was worried you'd say that."

Sabine inhaled sharply at the sight of a young woman racing up a hill toward the edge of the Silver Forest. The hood of her cloak had been thrown back, and her dark hair cascaded behind her as the wind whipped it away from her face. Her skin was nearly the same golden color as Malek's, and her brown eyes sparkled in the morning light. She laughed while the colorful will-o'-the-wisps danced around her. She couldn't be more than sixteen or seventeen years old, nearly the same age as Sabine when she'd fled her home.

The girl was too focused on the mesmerizing lights to realize she was being lured toward the forest. It was a trap—a clever and insidious snare. Sabine knew what that girl saw, surrounded by the colorful globes. Each of her dreams hovered in midair like unfulfilled wishes, if only she grasped ahold of them.

Malek's shoulders tensed, and he murmured, "She's human, not Unseelie. Why would they create such an elaborate trap to kill her? She doesn't have any magic."

Sabine didn't respond immediately, her mouth suddenly dry. There was only one reason this particular victim had been chosen. The girl's features were all too familiar, from the shape of her eyes to the slant of her nose. Malek was right; they didn't intend to consume her power like they had from the other victims. Her death was meant to serve a different purpose.

Placing her hand on Malek's arm, she whispered, "She's not like the others. She's a message."

Malek's brow furrowed, and he turned back to watch the girl racing up the hill. Her breathless and innocent laughter filled the air, a sharp contrast against what was coming.

Sabine took a shaky breath, mentally willing the young woman to turn away from the forest. It was no use. She didn't even hesitate before stepping across the magical barrier. Like a shockwave through Sabine's body, her skin prickled at the uncomfortable feeling of an outsider violating the sanctum of Faerie.

The will-o'-the-wisps must have confused the girl and hidden the forest from her view. No one who lived anywhere near the Silver Forest willingly entered without fear of dire consequences. The fae were feared by most humans for good reason.

Mist rose from the ground to envelope her, the first of the warnings to trespassers. Normally, if she intended no harm or the intrusion were accidental, Faerie might consider simply turning her away. But because she'd been lured, the forest hesitated.

It was her undoing.

Sabine pushed away the revulsion, forcing herself not to intervene. This was a memory. She needed to focus on the details and remember as much as possible, no matter how heart-wrenching. The girl's life had been stolen before Sabine and Malek had ever stepped foot in this place.

"It's so beautiful, like heaven collided with the forest," the young girl said, her eyes staring in wonder at the boughs of the Silver trees. Flowers surrounded her, their jeweled petals shimmering with magic and filling the air with their perfume. She spread out her arms and slowly spun, the magic in the air dusting her golden skin with power.

Malek scowled. "She looks like Rika. I'm guessing that's not a coincidence."

"There aren't any coincidences when dealing with the

fae," Sabine murmured, her heart sinking at the realization her father must have been spying on them. She hadn't protected her friends well enough, just like she hadn't protected the other murder victims.

Rika hadn't been traveling with them for long. It had been less than two months since they'd first met the human seer, but someone must have alerted Sabine's enemies—namely her father—about her young charge.

Sabine had expected him to be more concerned about Malek. After all, he was a dragon. Rika was a seer, powerful in some ways, but she was still a human. She'd barely begun to embrace her talents.

Seers possessed the ability to negate glamour and other magic with barely a thought. Besides the gift of foresight, they had the power to walk into the Silver Forest and past Faerie's defenses without consequences. Harmful magic didn't always work on them, but they could be killed through mundane means.

Sabine's hands curled into fists. While other seers were hunted down and killed on sight, she wouldn't allow such a thing to happen to Rika. She'd made a promise to protect the young seer, and she'd do everything within her power to honor that oath.

Rika wasn't a threat to the fae, especially since she had sworn a blood oath to serve Sabine. Perhaps it would have been wiser to hide her affection for Rika. But spending just a few hours with her had made such a thing impossible. It was their closeness that Sabine's father or his minions had likely decided to prey upon. Sabine's beastman protector, Balkin, had often warned that friendships and close ties were liabilities.

Rika's doppelgänger leaned over to smell one of the wild roses that grew on the outskirts of the forest. The petals were a deep blue, the edges tinged with silver dust. The roses could kill with a prick of their thorns, but magic from the will-o'-the-wisps had temporarily neutralized their poison. Sabine scanned the forested area, searching for any sign of the people who had been present in the previous murders. They always struck as a group, but the forest was still strangely quiet.

The vine that had stopped Sabine tightened around her ankle, tugging sharply. Sabine stilled, feeling another set of eyes on her and Malek. Someone else was observing the memory, besides the memorywalker.

The will-o'-the-wisps glowed even brighter, their soothing colors shifting to more alarming and bolder colors. Sabine inhaled sharply, catching sight of distinctive seams of power. These weren't will-o'-the-wisps. They were fae wrapped in illusion magic.

Their glamoured forms shimmered until they appeared as their true selves. Five fae circled the young girl, their faces obscured to hide their true identity. They were masked with both magical illusions and billowing cloaks that swallowed their features. If Sabine tried to rip apart the illusion while in someone else's memory, she risked unraveling the entire thing.

Sabine's hands curled into fists, but she forced her body to relax and keep her expression neutral. They were still being observed. Sabine had no intention of revealing how deeply this scene affected her. If her father was behind it, which she suspected, it was likely his way of eliciting a response. Sabine had no intention of giving him the satisfaction.

The fae continued to circle the girl as though they were assessing livestock. Shocked horror had stripped away and replaced her earlier expression of wonderment. The fae could weave illusions to beguile and charm, but these had decided to prey upon her nightmares. The girl had likely just realized the stories and warnings were true. She was destined to become Faerie's plaything.

Malek's jaw hardened. He muttered something under his breath, too low to hear. Sabine glanced at him, but he was focused on the fae. The barely restrained fury in the dragon's gaze sent a shiver down her spine. Bringing him here had been a mistake.

The girl screamed. She turned and tried to run toward the forest's edge, but a wave of an assailant's hand halted her progress. With a rumble, the ground burst upward and encased the human's feet in thick, wet mud. With a strangled cry, she thrashed and pulled, trying to break free of her earthen restraints.

"What unremarkable looking creatures," an unknown man mused in the musical language of Faerie. "Ears stunted. Eyes the color of dung. They hold little allure beyond a passing novelty. A pet?"

"Please don't hurt me," the girl begged, her eyes filling with tears. "I didn't mean to enter your forest. My family always leaves the required offerings at the edge of the trees. I swear I meant no harm!"

"Will you beg, child?" One of the fae, a woman as far as Sabine could tell, stepped forward. She reached out, her cloak shifting enough to reveal the etching of a sun on her wrist.

Sabine started. It was her father's symbol. Only his closest advisors and courtiers had that emblem infused into their skin. It was both a mark of power and a sign of favor, a designation highly coveted by those at Seelie court. This was the confirmation Sabine had been seeking. Her father was behind these murders. Even though she'd suspected it, it was still a blow to her heart. He would try to destroy and kill everyone she loved, to punish her.

"Please," the girl pleaded, tears spilling down her cheeks. "I'll do anything. Don't kill me!"

The sun woman grabbed the girl's brown hair and yanked it hard. The girl cried out in pain, the sound echoing through the forest. She cut a fistful of the girl's long hair and shoved her back. The girl wavered but didn't fall, still imprisoned by the ground.

Lifting the hair, the sun woman studied it briefly before she tossed it to the earth. With a sneer, she said, "Hair like animals. No magic. Nothing of consequence. Nothing but blood and meat."

Malek started to rise, but Sabine grabbed his arm and shook her head in warning. He narrowed his eyes but turned back toward the scene.

Sabine followed his gaze, back to the group still circling the girl. Another man, wearing a dark emerald-green cape, had moved close to the girl. There was an unremarkable silver band around his wrist, but Sabine couldn't identify any other distinguishing marks. His cloak and glamour obscured too much of his true appearance.

He held up his hands. In a melodic voice infused with power, he proclaimed, "A debt is due, human. You have trespassed here, and your life is forfeit. We shall drink of your soul in the same manner of all Good Folk, as we have for generations. Only then shall the debt be settled."

The man's voice sent a shiver of fear through Sabine. His voice was vaguely familiar. Her time in the Seelie court had been minimal, especially once her Unseelie magic had surfaced. She couldn't recall where she knew him from, except to know she'd encountered his power before.

The mists grew thicker, and Sabine's stomach lurched. This wasn't a blood sacrifice like the other murders. This was surgical excision of a foreign invader. Faerie hadn't claimed this girl or offered her protection. She had crossed the protective boundary, and these fae had claimed bloodrights against her for invading their homeland. It didn't matter that they'd tricked her. Since they couldn't lie, the fae had become masters at exploiting loopholes.

The man's blade caught a flash of sunlight, and the girl screamed in fear. Sabine looked away, unable to watch what was about to transpire. Each cry from the girl pierced Sabine's heart and wounded her soul. A wave of nausea rose swiftly. She'd been away from court life for far too long. She'd forgotten the almost casual brutality of its courtiers.

Malek's nostrils flared, his skin glowing with barely restrained power. Sabine's eyes widened, terrified he'd lose control. If he shifted, the forest would turn on him. He'd be at the mercy of the memorywalker, and she'd be powerless to aid him.

She grabbed his arm, the touch nearly searing her with his heat. Ignoring the pain, she tightened her grip and forced him to meet her eyes. In a fervent whisper, she urged, "No! Not here! You can't help her, Malek. It's a memory. She's already gone."

Malek's skin flickered while he battled to regain control. The girl's screams weren't making it easy on him. Sabine moved her hands upward and pressed them against his face. She continued to hold his gaze, silently urging him to keep his power in check.

She wrapped more power around herself and Malek, changing their image silently so the watchers wouldn't see what was happening between them. Rumors had already likely reached her father that Malek was a dragon, but Sabine didn't want to confirm anything. Giving the fae any information about Malek would endanger him, and without his scales and dragonfire to protect him, Malek was vulnerable in his human form.

Sabine cupped his face and kissed him softly, needing him

to recall himself. The heat emanating from his skin slowly cooled, but it hadn't dimmed the flames of vengeance in his eyes. The girl's screams had been reduced to feeble whimpers, which was almost worse. When a sick sucking noise filled the forest and the sharp metallic scent of blood and human waste tainted the air, Sabine's heart fractured.

If given the opportunity, her father would do the same to Rika.

Malek wrapped his hands around her wrists and pulled her closer. "I want you out of here, Sabine. You don't need to see more of this."

Sabine swallowed, desperately wanting to flee. She had no desire to get close or witness what was happening to the girl, but it was the only chance they had to discern a weakness in her father's games.

"I need to stay," Sabine said softly, unable and unwilling to allow the girl's sacrifice to be in vain. "Will you remain here for a few moments? I won't be able to mask you while I'm trying to penetrate their glamour. It will tear yours aside."

Malek took a deep breath and nodded, but his expression was pained. The look of murder in his eyes mirrored the same in her heart. She'd destroy every last one of these people for this.

"No more than fifteen steps away, Sabine. I'm not willing to risk your safety, not for anything."

Sabine hesitated and then nodded in agreement. It wasn't the time to argue. Malek's control seemed to falter whenever she was threatened. She couldn't risk it here.

She bent and brushed her hand against the vine still clinging to her ankle. It unwrapped itself and slithered back into the bushes.

Squaring her shoulders, Sabine walked toward the fae who were butchering and feasting upon the young girl. Blood spattered the fallen leaves on the ground and the bottom of their cloaks. Another wave of nausea rose swiftly, and Sabine had to force herself to keep moving forward. Schooling her features into the expressionless mask she used to wear at court, she approached the group.

She tried to focus on the individuals rather than the grisly scene. Based on their body language and physiques, there were three men and two women. With each step, she studied them for identifiable features not hidden behind layers of glamour. Her people had spent centuries receiving markings of power upon their skin, either as a way of cementing an alliance or because they needed to harness their talents. If she could get a glimpse of another of their skin etchings, she might be able to trace it back to the artist.

With a wave of her hand, Sabine sent a small probe of magic outward. It fractured, its pulse sent into a nearby tree. She bit back a curse. Their images continued to flicker. Different faces were layered over one another and shifted to obscure the wearer's identity. She wove together another more substantial magical probe, but sparks flew outward before it penetrated.

She narrowed her eyes. Her magic should have pierced some of the illusion, especially with the power boost she'd received from the goddess and the three portal artifacts she'd absorbed. It was almost as though these fae had a secondary illusion masking their own personal glamour, similar to how she was hiding Malek. Sabine's inability to remove their glamour was one more indicator her father was responsible for this. The Lord of Illusions had earned his reputation over the centuries.

The sun symbol on the woman's wrist was the only visible marker. Sabine was too much of a skeptic to believe it was an accident. It was possible someone was attempting to frame her father, but the simplest explanation was far like-lier. No. Her father wanted her to know this had been done at his command. Many of the fae, including her father, still believed she was the hapless girl who'd fled Faerie ten years earlier.

The truth wasn't quite so simple. She might have been inexperienced compared to most of the fae, but her time with the humans had taught her a great deal. Every moment had been spent behind a glamoured shield, pretending to be one of them. But her magic could only hide her appearance. She'd also had to learn how to adopt her accent, change her walk, and mask her mannerisms without relying on her power.

The insight gave her pause. Her other senses might offer a clue to their identities where her magic was failing. She'd already recognized the green-cloaked man's voice, but there was another sense she hadn't considered.

Closing her eyes, she stretched out her hands and tried to determine where the illusions began and ended. The sunlight warmed her skin, and she used its power to brush her fingertips against the edges of their Seelie magic. It had the same resonance as her father's power—or as close to what her memory of him entailed. It had been ten years since she'd seen him in person, but far longer since she'd been welcome in his presence.

Sabine focused on her other senses. Their footsteps crunched upon the fallen leaves, and the sickening sucking noise of things she didn't want to focus on filled the air. She took a deep breath, fighting down the revulsion of the sharp metallic scents of the girl's blood and terror. Beneath it was the distinct scent of cinnamon and lilac. That was it—the clue she'd been searching to find.

Sabine paused and tilted her head, committing the nuances of the scent to her memory. The wind moved in a fragile whisper, caressing Sabine's skin and through her hair like fingers. It was the confirmation she needed. Faerie wanted her to remember this. She opened her eyes. The scent was emanating from the sun woman. Her magic was steeped with cinnamon and lilac, like a wine that had been allowed to ferment too long.

The girl's screams had long since stopped. Once they had each taken what power they could wrest from her human soul, they rose as a group, fused together by the commonality of the gruesome act they'd just performed. Without a word, their images shimmered back into wisp forms, and they faded from view. A moment later, Sabine felt the memory-walkers retreat from their silent observation, likely to report their impressions to their master.

Sabine squeezed her eyes shut, feeling her emotional shields crumble. All that was left was the violence of the memory. Her knees were weak, and she knew she was on the verge of collapsing. She took a steadying breath, not wanting to remain in this place a moment longer than necessary, but her task wasn't yet done.

She reached for Malek through their bond and felt him emerge from his hiding place. He walked toward her, but she didn't look at him for fear it would break her. She was barely holding it together.

Pressing her hand against the blood-soaked ground, she said, "By blood and magic, I swear your death shall be avenged."

The wind blew again, rustling Sabine's hair in acknowledgement of her promise. The lock of hair that had been cut from the girl lay in a pool of blood and gore. Sabine brushed her fingertips along the girl's hair, the once beautiful nutmeg shade now matted against the ground. The fae had been right; there had been no power to imbibe from her death, but each moment of her life had been a treasured gift to someone who cared for her. There was power in that love, even if her people could only sip its essence.

"I'm so sorry I couldn't protect you," she whispered, wishing she could give the girl's family answers. Any contact would only endanger them. If Sabine's father discovered how much living among the humans had changed her and how much she'd grown to care about them, he'd use it against her. He'd systematically raze human cities to the ground if he thought it could bring Sabine out of hiding. Part of her was tempted to give him what he wanted and step into the light. How many more innocents had to die before he gave up on his vengeance?

"Sabine," Malek murmured, pulling her to her feet. He stared at her blood-soaked hand, his jaw clenching tightly. His blue eyes met hers, and Sabine saw the barely restrained fury brewing under the surface. "I'll kill every last one of them for putting these shadows in your eyes. But that's nothing compared to what I'll do if they dare touch you or Rika. I'll burn their city to the ground and everyone in it."

Sabine took a shaky breath, her hand tightening on the memory stone she still held. "On that, we're in agreement. I don't know their intention, but I'm going to do everything within my power to ensure they won't be able to do this to anyone ever again."

Chapter Three

*S*abine released the magic tying them to the memory
stone and opened her eyes to stare into Malek's.
She blinked rapidly, scanning the bedroom to ensure the
magic had completely dissipated. The heavy wooden furniture, with its ornate carvings, the dark blue and silver
accents, and even the silvering vines trailing up the wall,
were indications they were safely within the Faerie embassy
in Razadon.

Her gaze fell upon the desk where she'd spent several
hours that day composing letters. The political games and
intrigue that had demanded her attention a few minutes ago
now seemed meaningless compared to what they'd just
witnessed—the life of a girl taken far too soon.

Sabine stared at the blood-spattered memory stone in
disgust. "That was my father's idea of a coronation gift—
advance warning that he intends to come after Rika next."

Malek's arm tightened around her, and he pulled her
close. She leaned against him, needing the comfort and
strength he offered. In a voice as unyielding as stone, he

promised, "We will not allow him to hurt Rika or anyone else."

"Is Rika really in danger?" Dagmar took a step forward, her clothing still dripping on the floor. The dwarven woman shuffled forward, her eyes wide with fear. Dagmar and Rika had become close since they'd arrived in the city. "King Cadan'ellesar can't touch her here, can he?"

Sabine flinched. Hearing her father's name was like being blasted with a bucket of ice water. There were other Seelie lords on the Council of Eight who harbored no tender feelings for her, but few were as powerful as her father. Even Sabine wasn't sure the extent of his abilities. Part of her was tempted to lock down the embassy, but that would convey the depth of her fear. She couldn't show weakness, no matter how terrified she was of the Seelie king.

"Not if I have any say over it," Sabine said and walked to a crystal panel embedded into the wall. She pressed her hand against it and infused her magic into the device, connecting with the heart of Faerie.

The embassy in Razadon, like all pockets of Faerie, possessed its own awareness. Fae scholars had debated for centuries about why Faerie did certain things, like allow a forest to grow where none should exist or rearrange rooms or entire residences on a whim. No one ruler or anyone controlled the decisions of Faerie. The relationship between the fae and Faerie was symbiotic. Sabine could make a request, but it was ultimately up to Faerie whether to act upon her wishes.

"I swore an oath to protect the seer, Rika of Karga," Sabine said in the musical language of her birth. Each word was steeped in magic, as it was far easier to communicate with Faerie this way than in the common tongue. At her words, Malek's gaze sharpened on her. He'd learned a great deal of her language at the hands of his fae grandmother. It had been one of the things that had first piqued her interest when they'd met.

Faerie's magic swirled around Sabine, its power tasting like a question. An image formed in her mind of a dark-haired girl wielding a small sword and battling a demon. Her hair was pulled back in braids, and they swished through the air as she danced in accordance with the steps Bane called out. The teenager's face was full of determination as she tried to counter each of the demon's moves.

Sabine smiled at the realization that Faerie had been watching Rika and Bane. It had been curious about her companions since they arrived. "Yes, that Rika. I believe she's in danger, and I risk being forsworn if I fail to protect her."

Faerie didn't respond, waiting for Sabine to continue. She swallowed, trying to decide how to frame her request. She couldn't point fingers or make accusations without confirmation. The magic could easily turn against her if she wasn't careful.

"I need information to determine where or how an attacker plans to strike at Rika."

Magic flowed up her arm and enveloped her, sifting through her memories like fingers flipping through pages. It lingered over the events she'd witnessed in the memory stone.

Sabine shivered, but it wasn't from the cold. There was almost a clinical type of detachment to Faerie's assessment. After several moments, Faerie withdrew from her mind.

Sabine waited, but Faerie remained silent. Sabine withdrew her hand and lowered her head in defeat. Maybe the land knew nothing, but it was far more likely that it wasn't willing to help. She'd hoped the land's curiosity about the newcomers might have offered an incentive to keep them alive.

"Did Faerie tell you anything?" Malek asked, taking a step toward her.

Sabine turned around to face him and shook her head. "No."

"Then we'll protect ourselves another way, Sabine. We will not let this stand."

His fierce determination helped bring clarity to her thoughts. She needed to take action. Now.

Gesturing toward the small pile of letters she'd written earlier, Sabine said, "Dagmar, I need you to send these correspondences right away. You'll also need to let your mother know we're moving up our timetable. Coordinate with Balkin to determine whom he thinks we should target first to maximize our potential for acquiring any relevant information on our enemies. I want the cave trolls and pixies installed at their homes and spying by the end of the month."

Dagmar's eyes widened, and she hastily nodded. She scooped up the sealed letters and said, "I'll take care of it. No worries! We won't let those stinky Seelie hurt our friends. Want me to let Rika know you need to speak with her?"

"Yes. I need to see Bane too. It can wait until they're finished with their training, but I don't want them leaving the embassy until they've been alerted to the danger."

"Got it!" The dwarf turned on her heel and scampered out of the room.

Malek turned toward Sabine and asked, "How safe is Rika while we're here? Can your father infiltrate the embassy?"

Sabine hesitated, remembering the portal that had opened to allow the Huntsman to enter. Once, she would have said no one could step foot inside the protected area without her allowing it, but now she knew differently.

"I don't know. My father's resources are more extensive than mine. I just wish I knew what he was planning. I can't fight a battle I know nothing about. I'm not even sure he's the one behind the threat."

A wind kicked up in the room, filling the air with a strong scent of flowers. Malek spun around, his hand going to his sword.

Sabine inhaled sharply, watching as an ancient cabinet in the corner of the room rocked back and forth with a groan. The vines dangling from the ceiling reached down and brushed the top of the cabinet with their leaves. Two small red crystals emerged from the front of the cabinet, creating a magical handle where none had previously existed.

She blinked at it. The cabinet had been sealed since they arrived. Dagmar and her family had been searching the archives for the ritual required to open it, but they hadn't found anything yet. Sabine had forgotten about it, since there were hundreds of other tasks that had required her attention over the past week.

"That's different," Malek muttered, his brow furrowing. "I'm guessing there wasn't a ritual. You just needed to ask Faerie to open the door?"

"I asked for information on how to protect Rika," Sabine whispered, crossing the room. The cabinet was nearly black with silver veins running through it, the effect caused by a demon spilling their life's blood on a fallen Silver tree. Only someone from her line could open it without succumbing to the poison imbued in a demon's blood.

Sabine placed her hand on the delicate crystal knobs, infused a trace of magic into the locking mechanism to nullify the demon blood, and opened the cabinet.

The scent of her mother's floral perfume filled the air. Sabine's eyes fluttered closed as memories flooded through her. Thoughts of Queen Mali'theoria had once made Sabine recoil in fear, but now, she couldn't help but wonder how much she'd misunderstood her mother. A pang of regret filled her, but she pushed it aside and focused on the rows of bottles and small wooden containers.

"It looks like herbs and potions," Malek said with a frown, leaning close to the cabinet. "It reminds me of Esme's shop, where she sold those teas."

"Be careful not to touch the wood or anything inside the cabinet. I'm not sure if the individual bottles are warded. This is a bloodlock cabinet, tied to my specific bloodline. My magic will prevent me from accidentally tripping any security measures my mother had in place, but your proximity might confuse it."

Malek nodded and took a step back, still close enough to assist her if she encountered a problem. Turning back to the cabinet, she focused on the individual vials and containers filled with a combination of herbs and liquids.

The bottles toward the front had been labeled with her mother's familiar script. Some of the ones tucked farther back appeared much older, and many promised to contain extremely rare reagents. Even in her wildest dreams, Sabine had never expected to find such bounty anywhere except in the most protected vaults in Faerie.

"That one has your family's colors," Malek said, pointing at a long cylindrical vial near the front. It was deep blue and sparkled with flecks of silver.

Sabine lifted the labeled vial and held it up to the light, marveling at how the shimmering twilight liquid had kept so well over the years. A soft wind caressed her skin, and Sabine's eyes widened.

With a reverent voice, she whispered, "It's lendolian oil. How can this be?"

"It's what?"

She spun to face Malek, clutching the vial to her chest.

"Faerie's given us a way to protect Rika by offering one of her greatest blessings. This is how we can find out the information we need."

Malek frowned, his expression skeptical. "Tell me you don't have to drink it."

She smiled and shook her head. "No. We're going to scry for information. I should be able to trace the memorywalker's magic. They could lead us back to the person who sent them to observe us."

"If it helps protect Rika, I'll do whatever it takes. What do you need from me?"

Sabine's gaze softened. If she lived thousands of years, she might never again find such an ally or easy acceptance. Unable to resist him, she kissed him lightly and then handed him the memory stone. "Can you collect the crystal bowl on the dresser and the pitcher of water? You can put them on the floor, along with the memory stone."

When he walked away, Sabine turned back to the cabinet. On the bottom shelf was a familiar wooden box. The twin to it had been displayed in her mother's rooms in the Unseelie palace back in Faerie. It had the ability to cleanse wayward magics from sensitive instruments and to prepare the seeker for using high magic.

Sabine swallowed back her memories and placed the vial of lendolian oil inside. From another shelf, she collected a bough from a Silver tree and a silver ritual knife. They went into the box too.

It was a simple undertaking she was about to perform, but caution was necessary. A trace of residual magic from another working could affect the outcome of her scrying. Rika's life was far too important to leave anything to chance. Sabine closed the box and brought them to the bowl and pitcher Malek had already placed on the floor.

"I need a moment to connect with the land," Sabine said, gesturing toward the bowl on the ground.

Malek's brow furrowed, but he inclined his head and stepped back.

Sabine sat in front of the bowl and placed the box beside her. Her palms were growing damp from nerves. She'd thought about doing this countless times over the years, but without Faerie's protection, she hadn't been able to risk it. Now that she was in the relative safety of the embassy in Razadon, she had a chance to not only find out how to protect her people but also to catch another glimpse of her homeland.

Placing her hands over her mother's box, she closed her eyes and said, "By blood and magic, and by my rights to both, I ask you to cleanse and purge the contents from all foreign magics. No harm is intended, and no harm is sought. I entrust the land to be my guide beyond the boundaries of sight."

A soft breeze flowed over her and through her hair, caressing her with ancient magic. The rich and earthy undertones of the forest filled her nose. Her heart soared at Faerie's touch. The land had responded to her request.

"Sabine? Are you all right?"

Overcome with emotion, Sabine took a shaky breath and nodded. Until she'd left the human city of Akros, she hadn't felt Faerie's presence in ten years. It had always been with her, but she'd been forced to deny her heritage to remain hidden from her father. The grace and beauty of the land reached out to her again, bringing with it a sweeping, undeniable joy.

Tears sprang to her eyes, and Sabine lowered her head in respectful acknowledgement of Faerie's approval. The land didn't communicate with words, but with emotion or sensation. Its touch was an embrace, as loving and protective as a mother when holding her child for the first time. When the wind finally ceased its gentle caress, Sabine opened her eyes and looked upon the box in front of her. It was encased in a soft glow, a remnant of the power Faerie offered.

"Faerie has given her blessing for this scrying," Sabine said softly, still feeling the touch of the magic as she lifted the lid of the box. "I believe she'll help us find the information we seek."

Malek leaned against the wall. "I hope you're right but be careful. Your father is also tied to the land. I can't fathom why he'd seek Rika's death."

"I don't know," Sabine admitted. That was the crux of her concern. "I thought maybe he was trying to lure me out of hiding. He's made no overt threat against Bane, who has been with me much longer. Nor did he directly try to target you."

Malek considered her for a moment. "Both Bane and I have sworn to protect you, not the other way around. You strive to protect both of us out of love, not because of a sworn oath."

Sabine paused in surprise. "You believe my promise to safeguard her is the reason she's a target?"

"The Wild Hunt seeks out those who are forsworn or oath-breakers," Malek said to remind her and then gestured toward the box. "What's involved in this ritual? You normally do a blood sacrifice to harness your magic."

Sabine lifted the simple black cloth that had once belonged to her mother and laid it on the ground. "Most of what you've seen me do has been using my raw power. I haven't had the resources or time to perform some of the more nuanced forms of magic. That's what I'm going to attempt now."

Malek arched his brow. "I've seen you perform some

remarkable feats. It's hard to imagine anything requiring more power."

Sabine smoothed the wrinkles in the fabric. "This will require very little magic but more focused concentration."

"I'm intrigued. What's the cloth for?"

Sabine placed the box on top of the cloth and said, "Rituals can be another type of magic, but it's mostly about focusing your intentions. A barrier between the components and the land helps set the parameters. Otherwise, Faerie might decide to intervene. Our agendas don't always coincide, even if she's offered her blessing. The cloth is simply a request to not interfere."

Malek nodded. "I've heard that. My grandmother had one that she brought out on rare occasions. It was green with silver edging, and she said the color reminded her of her home and made it easier for her to connect with the land."

Sabine carefully placed the bowl on top of the linen, listening to the warmth in his voice. Malek often spoke fondly of his fae grandmother. They had captured her during the war between their people, but Malek claimed she'd fallen in love with his grandfather and had elected to remain in the Sky Cities. The reminder of the long-standing war between their people brought another concern to mind.

Lifting her head so she could meet his eyes, Sabine said softly, "You won't be able to accompany me this time, Malek."

Malek straightened. "I don't think it's a good idea to do this alone."

"Perhaps," Sabine said and lowered her gaze. "I'm not as comfortable with this type of magic. I'll need to concentrate on the ritual portion to ensure I don't misstep. I won't be able to hide your identity and keep myself safe at the same time. Your presence may incite my people to violence."

The admission spoke to some of her deepest insecurities.

Scrying was an elementary ritual, but her expertise was lacking from the years she'd been forced to deny her gifts. Viewing the memory stone was simpler because someone else had already laid the groundwork. With scrying, she would need to depend solely on her own will and magic to merge her consciousness with the vision. One wrong step and she could lose herself in the vision without any way to return.

Malek muttered a curse and ran a hand over his dark hair. "I don't like the thought of you handling this alone."

Neither did she, but this might be the only way to get the information they needed in time to save lives. Sabine withdrew her silver knife and placed it beside the bowl, within easy reach. Next to it, she placed the branch from a Silver tree and the corked crystal vial. Finding the vial of lendolian oil in her mother's belongings had been a stroke of luck. The flowers only bloomed once every decade, and it could take close to a century to amass enough to produce one vial of the precious oil.

Malek sighed. "It's not just the emotional impact on you that has me concerned. You've said yourself that this is unfamiliar magic, and you're still not at full strength after the assassination attempt. At least take Bane with you."

Sabine frowned at him. "Trying to hide a demon from the Seelie would drain my remaining magic. I'm aware of my limitations, but my father orchestrated that memory for a reason. He wanted me to know he's been spying on us." She looked away and stared at the wall, not really seeing it. "Rika hasn't been with us for very long and he knew about her. What else does he know? How many more people will he hurt to get to me? I have to do this, Malek."

Malek crouched beside her, careful not to disturb the cloth. He took her hand and squeezed it gently. "I'm not disputing the necessity of learning more. Your crown might be a weight on your head, but no one said you had to shoulder it alone."

"You make it far too easy to depend upon you for guidance." Sabine managed a weak smile and leaned over to kiss him. "You're right. I'll take Blossom. Pixies are far more accepted in Faerie than demons or dragons. She has enough magic of her own that she can hide herself if necessary. No one will suspect her."

With a flick of her wrist, she sent a small pulse of magic into the air to call Blossom to her. No matter where the pixie was in the embassy, she'd never be able to resist the lure of Sabine's magic.

Malek's eyes lit with appreciation before his expression sobered again. "Good. Now tell me about this ritual and what to expect. At the very least, I can keep watch from a distance and intervene if things go bad."

Sabine nodded and placed the memory stone in the bottom of the bowl. "It's fairly straightforward. This ritual will create a viewing portal into my homeland and allow me to infuse my spirit or essence with Faerie. While we were in that memory, I caught a distinct scent from a woman with a sun marking on her wrist. I believe I can trace her if I use the smell as a marker. If not, I'll seek out the memorywalker."

"I've heard the fae version of scrying is much more powerful than a normal witch's efforts, but I thought both relied on sight. You can track someone by using scent?"

"Mmhmm. The ability to hide smells with glamour is extremely rare. I had to rely upon illusion magic while hiding in the human city. It made me much more aware of sounds and smells. Most of my people have never had to concern themselves with such things."

Malek gave her a wry grin. "Their ignorance is your gain?"

Sabine's lips twitched in a smile. "Something like that. At

the very least, I believe it's our best chance to learn something. Faerie wouldn't have suggested it otherwise."

Her thoughts drifted to the other memory stones the dwarves had given her. There was a strong possibility that the number of murders exceeded the ones captured by the dwarven stones.

Every Unseelie death had been an execution. She just didn't understand *why*. Until recently, she'd thought the fae had achieved an uneasy truce between the light and dark courts. Her father might want her dead, but what he was doing would take her people to the brink of a civil war. Had her absence for a mere decade upset the fragile balance between Seelie and Unseelie? She had to be missing something.

"Why haven't you tried to scry before now?"

Sabine frowned at the question. As a general rule, her people didn't discuss their abilities with outsiders, much less with one of their feared enemies. She knew Malek would never intentionally cause her harm, but caution was still necessary. One careless word could endanger her people. The fae couldn't lie, but he didn't need to know her every reason either. If he knew the true dangers of this magic, he would try to stop her.

"This is a variation of portal magic," Sabine said, settling on a partial truth. "It's risky at the best of times, but without Faerie's blessing, the dangers are compounded. I also couldn't risk anyone knowing I was still alive. I don't have to worry about such things now, but it'll be difficult to see my homeland and know it remains out of reach."

Malek fell silent, as though sensing there was more behind her words. Sabine picked up the pitcher of water and poured some into the crystal scrying bowl and over the memory stone. She stopped when it nearly reached the brim and then placed the pitcher on the ground beside her.

A tiny voice shouted, "I'm here! I'm here! I want to help!"

Sabine looked up to find a colorful pixie flying toward them. Blossom landed on the edge of the bowl, grinning up at her. Her hair and dress were rainbow colored, a testament to the colorful dwarven crystals surrounding them. Blossom's gossamer wings twitched in anticipation, her gaze darting back and forth between the water and Sabine.

Sabine bit back a smile. Blossom must have been on the far side of the embassy to have taken so long to arrive. "Did you herd the goat back outside?"

"Umm…"

Sabine arched her brow. "Is that a no?"

"Wellllll…" Blossom dragged out the word, her wings twitching as she glanced at the doorway.

Sabine frowned at the pixie. "Where is the goat?"

"Playing hide-and-seek with the cave trolls?"

Malek laughed. At Sabine's warning look, he averted his gaze, but a grin still played upon his lips.

"Blossom," Sabine said, not bothering to hide her exasperation. "We talked about this. The dwarves said the goats are outdoor-mountain goats, not inside-mountain goats. You can't let a goat run loose in the embassy! They eat the furniture!"

Blossom threw her hands upward. "They like it here! It's not my fault! Faerie thinks it's funny. She keeps opening pocket portals and letting one run amok while the cave trolls chase it down." Blossom turned toward Malek. "We're taking bets. Odds are three to one that Bombady will catch the goat before Blueboy. You in?"

Malek hid another laugh behind a discreet cough, but Sabine couldn't miss the twinkle of amusement in his gaze— or the way he flashed five fingers at Blossom to place his bet. Her mouth dropped open. Blossom gave him a thumbs-up and grinned at Sabine.

"You both are impossible," Sabine said with a sigh, focusing on the bowl again. "I was hoping you'd accompany me while I scry, Blossom. Bane and Malek can't keep themselves hidden like you can."

"Sure! Sounds like fun." Blossom sniffed the air and leaned toward the corked vial. Her wings fluttered so fast, they blurred together. "You have lendolian oil!"

Malek looked back and forth between them. "The vial? Why is that significant?"

"It makes the potency of the ritual stronger," Sabine said, folding up her sleeves. "Only fae from certain royal bloodlines can harvest the flowers, but the plants whisper to pixies in their dreams. They're the ones who know when the flowers are about to bloom."

"We're really doing this? You're going to uncork it?" Blossom asked, bouncing on the edge of the bowl and causing the water to ripple.

"Yes, but only if you don't spill the water," Sabine said, checking to make sure each of the components was within easy reach. She would only have seconds to complete each task. It had been nearly ten years since she'd attempted a scrying. Even back then, it had been done under her tutor's guidance. If she were honest with herself, she was a little nervous, especially with an audience.

"You won't even know I'm here," Blossom said, leaning down to sniff at the water.

Sabine made a noncommittal noise. "All right. Let me know if the magic isn't resonating properly."

Taking a steadying breath, she tried to calm her thoughts and focus only on the steps of the ritual. *Clarity. Peace. Harmony. Balance.* With each breath, she concentrated, feeling the power building within her. Her skin began to glow with power, chasing the shadows from the room.

Her surroundings faded until only the bowl in front of

her held her attention. Time seemed to slow, her heartbeat along with it. Even noises from remote places in the embassy faded as she stared into the bowl and focused on her breathing.

"I seek," she whispered in the musical language of Faerie. "By will. By magic. I shall See."

Sabine mentally embraced the memory stone, which was acting as a focus. The sharp and bitter memory of the girl's death floated to the forefront of her mind. Focusing again on the building magic, Sabine reached for her knife. From the corner of her eye, she caught Malek tensing, but she ignored him. This wasn't blood magic, and a sacrifice of that nature wasn't necessary. Using her knife, she cut a small lock of her hair and allowed it to fall into the water. The water shimmered for a moment, absorbing the power contained within her sacrifice.

Sabine reached for the vial of oil and uncorked the bottle. The cloying scent of lendolian flowers filled the air, surrounding her with memories of home. The power contained within the flowers was substantial, but the oil was even more condensed. Blossom's wings twitched and she swayed, inhaling deeply of the oil that was like ambrosia to pixies.

A drop of the deep blue liquid was all that was required, and it slid along the surface of the water, forming a barrier between Sabine and the memory stone. She corked the vial and placed it beside her.

Sabine reached for the bough of the Silver tree. The branch vibrated in her hand, reinforcing her connection between her magic and the elemental force contained within the land. She dipped it into the water, allowing the magics to combine. Not once, not twice, but thrice she stirred the water widdershins, taking care not to disturb the focus object at the bottom. The water glowed brightly, indicating its readiness for the next step.

Infusing her breath with the power of her ancestors, she slowly exhaled over the bowl. The water rippled and combined with the existing magic to send traces of her power outward to the edges of the bowl. Flashes of light broke through the ripples, revealing colorful images pulsing in time with the water's movements.

"It's working! I see Faerie!" Blossom cried, pointing toward one of the flashes of light. A forest. Fae running through the trees. Pixies. Beastpeople. The winding and canopied pathways. The ripples were paths branching from the same memory.

When she submerged her consciousness into the portal, the vision struck her suddenly, like a flash of lightning followed by a sonic boom of thunder. Sabine was hurtled down the forest pathways toward the crystal cities of Faerie, on the hunt of the scent. In less than an instant, Sabine caught sight of hundreds of fae and their allies—both Seelie and Unseelie. Some of them stopped what they were doing and looked upward as though sensing her silent observation, while others went about their duties.

The glittering crystal spires of the city called to her. They swirled upward with grace and beauty; the sunlight acted as a prism to cascade a rainbow over the winding pathways. She caught sight of the ancient libraries and the schools of learning as she chased her quarry. In the distance, she saw the heart of the city, where the Council of Eight met to govern the lands. She ignored all of it, in pursuit of the sun woman. Behind her, she sensed Blossom keeping pace with her.

"Where are you?" she muttered, the smell of cinnamon and lilac teasing her senses. She turned down another path and deeper into the city, chasing the elusive scent.

The gleaming heart of the Seelie court seemed to rise as she approached it, a crystal-and-marble palace that shone with its own light. It chased the shadows and stood as a beacon of light, even though many who belonged to the Seelie had nothing but darkness in their heart. At the large double doors to the Seelie court, some invisible force halted her.

She was swatted away from the gates like a bug, the illusion shattering. With a muttered curse, Sabine blinked and shook her head, trying to ignore the pain behind her eyes. She was back in the dwarven city. With a muttered curse, she focused again on the area in between the ripples.

"Sabine?" Malek asked, taking a step toward her.

She held up her hand to indicate she was unharmed. She'd been so close. The woman was definitely tied to the Seelie court.

Sabine plunged into the ripples once again, looking for an alternate way to find the woman. Even if she couldn't reach her directly, there had to be someone else who might reveal something.

Sabine leaned over the scrying bowl and blew on the water again, infusing it with another burst of power. The ripples flashed, and Sabine was again thrust into Faerie.

"This way, Sabine!" Blossom cried, pulling Sabine into another ripple. Sabine's eyes widened. She'd forgotten the affinity the pixies had for the Seelie. If anyone knew the ins and outs of the Seelie court, it was Blossom. Trusting her companion, Sabine circled the palace entrance and followed Blossom over the walls and into one of the Seelie gardens.

Aware that her presence could capture the attention of some Seelie nobles, she reached for the lendolian oil and allowed two more drops to fall on the surface of the water. It should be enough to hide her presence. Blossom was also staying nearby, so Sabine used the pixie's influence to better mask herself.

Catching a whiff of the sun woman again, Sabine chased the scent down the crystal-and-marble hallways. Flowering vines climbed the walls, while dazzling crystals cascaded from the ceiling on a wave of magic as delicate as a butterfly's wings. She'd played here with Rhys as a child, and like most things in Faerie, it hadn't changed. It was a place full of light and color, where magic infused the air with its intoxicating scent. It was stunning and utterly captivating, provided no one looked too close to see the blood staining the floor or the scratch marks from victims who had sought their escape.

Neither doors nor walls barred her in her semi-corporeal form. Sabine burst into a lounging room with a sprawling terrace. There, the scent of cinnamon and lilac was nearly overwhelming. Sabine spun, searching for any sign of the woman. Plush cushions in soft pale colors had been artfully arranged on the lounging beds, while low tables offered a place to serve refreshments. This was a parlor, and one that was well used if Sabine was any judge. They had likely just missed the woman.

The sounds of voices and laughter beckoned from a nearby balcony. The image wavered slightly. Sabine blew on the scrying water again and approached the balcony, which overlooked one of the palace's many gardens. Even if the woman she sought was gone, Sabine might be able to discover her identity through her associates. Balkin had plenty of resources he could use to find out information if she could provide him with a name.

Sabine leaned over the crystal balcony to survey the flowering gardens below. Thousands of blooms in every color filled her sight while the sweet scent of their perfume drifted on the air. Cascading fountains peppered the garden, providing elegant symmetry and private nooks with lush fruit trees. Sabine's heart pounded in her chest as recognition slammed into her. When she'd been a child, this garden had been a second home to her.

Shock nearly broke her concentration. Turning her head, she caught sight of only a few other balconies that were grander than the one she was standing on. She was close to her father's private quarters and among some of the most powerful Seelie. She hesitated, warring her desire for information over her need for caution. Her weak efforts at masking her identity wouldn't withstand her father's power.

"Sabine?" Blossom said, bringing Sabine's attention back to the present. "We have to hurry! The magic's fading."

Determination fueled her. Inhaling deeply, Sabine caught the faint scent of cinnamon and lilac from somewhere nearby. It wasn't recent. If Sabine had to guess, someone who knew the woman was strolling through the garden.

"This way!" Sabine urged and leaped over the balcony railing. She flung her consciousness down the pathways, the sound of voices capturing her attention. It wasn't the same as finding the sun woman, but it was a connection. She refused to be forsworn in her promise to protect Rika.

Sabine rounded a corner and froze. Two fae, a man and a woman, stood close to one another. From their body language, the intimacy of these two was obvious. The woman was vaguely familiar, but it was the man who captured and held her attention. Magic swirled around him as the intricate markings on his skin glowed faintly with power. The woman said something to him, and he threw his head back and laughed.

Sabine's eyes welled with emotion as she drank in her brother's image. She hadn't seen him for more than ten years. He'd changed so much, but then again, so had she. He'd gotten so tall, more than she'd expected. Even if the richness of his clothing didn't mark him as the heir apparent, Rhys carried himself with the authority and confidence of someone born to rule. Compared to her, he was a child of the light with golden hair and sun-kissed skin, while she was the daughter of the night's embrace.

"Oh, Rhys," Sabine murmured, blinking back the emotion that filled her eyes. He was no longer the boy she'd once known, but a self-confident and imposing man.

As though hearing her words, Rhys turned in her direction. His lavender eyes, mirrors of her own, widened in shock. "Sabine? By the gods, how—You're *alive?*"

The young woman's face paled. Before Sabine could say anything, a strong and heated wind blasted through the garden. She was knocked off her feet with enough force to steal her breath. Rhys took a step toward her, but the young woman at his side grabbed his arm.

"Your Highness, we must be away! Now!"

Rhys hesitated for only a moment. He grabbed the woman by the hand and pulled her in the opposite direction. Light flooded the garden with a brutal intensity. Flowers that had bloomed vividly mere seconds before were shriveling and dying, turning to dust. If she and Blossom became trapped in this magic, they'd never survive.

Blossom squeaked and shouted, "Sabine! Break the magic! He called the sun!"

Sabine inhaled sharply and tried to back away from the scrying. Something held her fast. She was here somehow, trapped between realities. She was dimly aware of her body still in the embassy in Razadon, but somehow a metaphysical bridge between that pocket of Faerie and this one had formed. It was no longer solely under her control.

"Blossom! Run!" Sabine shouted as wind whipped through the garden. The sun was getting even hotter, her blood boiling from within. Bushes and trees lost their leaves in a heated blast, curling on the ground and withering. She might not be able to backtrack to the forest, but she had to escape from the Seelie court before the wind or sun touched her. Sabine tried to pull back, retreating from the garden and back into the mysterious woman's rooms. With a wave of her hand, she barricaded the door to the balcony. It wouldn't stop the wind for long.

Sabine tore down the hallway, leaping over furniture and startled servants. The wind was relentless, flinging fae and their servants aside. Those unable to withstand its assault collapsed as the wind scalded the air and made it impossible to breathe. Blossom screamed and then disappeared from existence.

"*Malek!*" Sabine mentally shouted, trying to reach him through their bond. Magic poured out of her, and the ground trembled beneath her feet. Columns toppled, the walls collapsing around her. She gasped as terror set in. She was going to die here, in the land of her birth and surrounded by enemies.

It was too late to escape. The wind was upon her. It slammed her against the wall, smothering her power. Sabine coughed and choked, clawing at her neck, trying to escape whatever magic was strangling her. It was blistering hot but not yet scalding. If it hadn't been for Malek's shared protection of dragonfire, it surely would have killed her instantly. Even so, it was still building, and her eyes watered from the oppressive heat.

Her chest burned from lack of air, and she tried to shove her magic toward whatever power was killing her. It was too strong. Nothing in her arsenal had prepared her to fight against a summoned windstorm. There was nothing tangible to battle, nothing to grip or ward against. If she had been physically present instead of her consciousness, she might have had a chance. Darkness edged into the corner of Sabine's vision, a sign of her losing the battle.

No! She had to keep fighting. Sabine flung out another thought toward the dragon she loved, wishing she'd had more time with him before her life was cruelly stripped away. Her father's laughter echoed in her ears as she succumbed to the darkness.

It was too late. She'd failed them all.

Chapter Four

"Sabine!" Malek roared, diving toward her. He yanked her away from the scrying bowl, pulling her into his arms. The walls trembled, and furniture continued to shake around them. He shielded her with his body, watching as the contents of her desk crashed to the floor. The water in the scrying bowl sloshed back and forth, spilling over the sides.

"The bowl, Malek! Gotta knock it over!" Blossom shrieked, trying to use her weight to push down on the edge of the scrying bowl. Malek shot his hand out and flipped it over. Blossom squeaked as water went everywhere. The shaking stopped abruptly.

"Sabine! Talk to me!" Malek urged, a wave of panic gripping him at the realization she wasn't breathing. Her skin was as cold as ice and quickly turning blue. He pulled her against himself, but she didn't open her eyes. The goddess markings on her wrist had been glowing with a golden light, but even those were dimming.

"Breathe, Sabine. Dammit, I will not lose you!" He cupped the back of her head and kissed her, breathing his dragonfire into her. It had saved her life before. He had to trust it would heal her again. The alternative was unfathomable. She was his heart, his soul, his everything. He wouldn't lose her to whatever magic sought to steal her away.

Sabine coughed and choked, blinking open her lavender eyes. Malek's breath rushed out of him in his relief. She was alive. He clutched her tightly for a moment and then leaned back, searching for any sign of injury.

A dark imprint was wrapped around her slim neck. He could make out individual details, almost like handprint. His jaw clenched, fury ripping through him. He'd destroy anyone who'd dared touch her.

Lifting his head, he scanned the room for potential threats. Except for Blossom, no one else was there. Malek scowled at the toppled bowl. He'd never heard of magic that allowed physical harm over such distances, but the fae had many secrets. He should have refused to allow her to attempt such unfamiliar magic without him. He wouldn't make that mistake again.

He trailed his hand along her cheek, needing to touch her to reassure himself that she was safe. She still hadn't fully recovered after she'd been struck by the iron bolt. That threat had been narrowly subverted, but Malek knew it wouldn't be the last one.

Ever since she'd claimed her throne, the risks to the woman he loved had grown. He hadn't considered the possibility she could be attacked in their private quarters while he stood a handful of steps away from her. The thought of stealing her away and hiding her in the Sky Cities under the protection of his dragon clan was more appealing than ever.

"They were trying to kill her, Malek!" Blossom exclaimed, her rainbow-colored hair plastered against her head. The pixie was soaking wet from the scrying bowl. She otherwise appeared unharmed.

Sabine was the only one who appeared to have been affected by whatever had transpired. Slender fingers wrapped around his wrist. His gaze flew back to meet hers.

"Water," Sabine whispered, her voice hoarse.

Malek reached for the pitcher still sitting beside them. They'd used most of it for the scrying, but there was enough. He carefully held it to Sabine's lips, steadying the pitcher so she could drink. She swallowed and then sat up, wincing when she gingerly touched her throat.

"Who did this to you?" Malek asked, his voice coming out harsher than he'd intended. He took a deep breath, trying to rein in his instincts. Every part of him screamed for retribution.

Sabine opened her mouth to speak, but her eyes welled with tears at the effort.

Blossom's wings fluttered, their tips tinged with red. She lifted into the air and said, "Bane can heal her. I'll get him!"

Malek gave Blossom a curt nod. It might have been faster to carry Sabine, but he couldn't risk moving her until he knew what was wrong. Lifting the pitcher again, he angled it so she could drink. In a gentler voice, he said, "Take it slow. You don't need to say anything."

She drank a little more while Malek cradled her. The idea of anyone laying a hand on her was anathema to him. He'd never met anyone like her in all his travels, and the thought of a world without her in it defied all reason. The dragon within him was ready to burn the Silver Forests to the ground if it would keep Sabine safe.

Malek buried his face against her hair, breathing in the scent of night-blooming flowers that always seemed to surround her. It was enough to calm the worst of his rage.

Blossom darted back inside the room and landed on top of the upturned bowl. She'd returned faster than he'd expected. "Demon incoming! He was already running here."

A loud roar from the hallway made the walls tremble again. A demon with skin the color of pitch burst into the room, the silver shine from his horns reflecting off his gleaming skin. His eyes had also turned pure silver, a sign he was either consumed with power or entering battle lust.

Malek's arms reflexively tightened around Sabine as he angled his body in front of her. He didn't believe Bane would hurt her, but it would take a few minutes for him to realize Sabine was safe.

"Bane," Sabine whispered and sat up further. Bane's chest was heaving, and he was staring at Sabine as though she were the only oasis in a desert.

"Not yet, love. Give him a minute," Malek said quietly, grateful when she leaned against him once more. It spoke to Sabine's pain that she didn't insist upon rising. Malek narrowed his eyes at Bane. If he didn't get ahold of himself, Malek would have to put the demon down—and it would only hurt Sabine more.

The sound of running footsteps echoed from beyond the hallway. Rika burst into the room, stumbling to a halt near the door. Her dark hair was braided away from her face, and a light sheen of sweat coated her skin from her recent training session.

The fae couldn't have chosen someone to better represent Rika. He'd known the murdered girl had a similar appearance, but the comparison was staggering.

Rika's face paled, the knife in her hand clattering to the ground. "Is—is she okay?"

"She will be," Malek said, still cradling Sabine in his arms. He turned toward Bane. "She needs healing, but only if you can keep yourself in check."

Bane growled at him. After another minute, his eyes reverted to their normal amber. It spoke to the remarkable shift in their dynamic that Bane had relaxed. Even a month ago, the demon would have assumed Sabine was in danger from *him*. The time might still come when Malek and Bane would be on opposite ends of a battle, but it wouldn't be today.

Bane's gaze landed briefly on the upturned bowl and other items Sabine had used for the ritual. His expression darkened, and he glared accusingly at Malek.

"Give her to me," Bane demanded, reaching out his clawed hand. "You obviously cannot keep her safe."

Malek held Bane's gaze. "Until I know what magic caused this, she will not leave my arms. It was only my dragonfire that brought her back. Something was choking her."

Bane hesitated for a moment before giving Malek a curt nod. He knelt in front of Sabine.

"Forgive me, little one," Bane murmured, placing his clawed hand around her neck. His eyes flared to silver, and Malek tensed at the vulnerable position. Sabine simply wrapped her hand around Bane's wrist and closed her eyes, her trust in the demon unquestioned.

A thin trail of silver magic moved from Sabine and snaked up Bane's arm. It surrounded him, and his skin glowed softly. A moment later, a dark shadow slithered over Bane's skin and enveloped Sabine in its embrace.

Malek was uneasy about any foreign magic right now, but Sabine knew what she was doing as far as Bane was concerned. No matter what issues Malek had had in the past with the demon, there was no one else he trusted Sabine with more than his former enemy.

Sabine relaxed in Malek's arms and sighed. "It's enough, Bane."

The demon released her neck, and his eyes flickered back to amber. He sat back and narrowed his gaze on Sabine. "What befouled magic did you evoke in here?"

"It was yummy goodness until Sabine's dad got mad and

trapped her with the lendolian oil," Blossom said, sitting in the puddle of water. She threw herself onto the ground and rolled in the water, coating her rainbow-colored dress with remnants of the magic.

Sabine frowned at her before turning back toward Bane. "We were scrying for information. My father somehow broke the covenants of scrying magic and was able to pull me farther into their reality." She stared down at the bowl and shook her head. "I hadn't thought such a thing was possible. He somehow trapped me with my magic. I didn't realize what had happened until it was too late."

"And the earthquake?" Bane demanded and stood.

Sabine blanched. "It happened here too? I thought it was only in Faerie."

Malek frowned. "Your goddess marks were glowing. It stopped as soon as we knocked over the bowl. You must have caused an earthquake in both locations."

Sabine inhaled sharply and ran her fingers along the symbols on her wrist. "It was worse there. I—I hadn't real-ized I was the cause. I thought it was my father's magic or some Seelie defense."

"The goddess's influence over you continues to grow," Bane muttered, pacing the length of the room. He stopped near Rika and snatched the blade off the floor.

"If you wish to live, little seer, you will take better care with your weapons," Bane said sharply. Holding the hilt outward, he thrust the knife in Rika's direction. "This is an extension of your arm. If you lose your weapon, you will lose your life. Never surrender it, not for any reason. You will eat, sleep, and bathe with this weapon until it becomes a part of you."

Rika's mouth turned downward in a determined frown, and she nodded. "It won't happen again, Bane."

He gave her a curt nod and resumed his pacing. Sabine

sighed and squeezed Malek's hand. He stood and helped her to her feet. She was steadier than she had been, but he didn't move away. Her skin once again had returned to its normal healthy glow, but there was hesitation in her movements. Something had shaken her, more than her injury.

Malek ran his hand down her back and asked, "Are you sure you're all right?"

Sabine nodded. "I am, but it was a near thing. I won't make that mistake again."

"Indeed you won't," Bane snapped, still prowling from one end of the room to the other. "What in the bowels of the underworld possessed you to walk yourself into a Seelie trap?"

Sabine took a step toward Bane and pinned him with her glare. "Do not issue orders to me, Bane."

"Then use some common sense!"

Malek considered intervening, but he couldn't fault Bane's anger, especially when his own was equally as fierce. Sabine had taken an unnecessary risk. He crossed his arms over his chest and remained silent.

"Common sense?" Sabine asked in exasperation. "The only danger should have been allowing our enemies to spy on us while the viewing portal was open. I took precautions to counteract that possibility by asking for Faerie's protection. I weighed the risk against the necessity for information and deemed it acceptable."

"Your logic was flawed. You knowingly created an opportunity for your enemies to capitalize on your inexperience. That's unacceptable."

Sabine muttered a curse about high-handed, stubborn demons. Gesturing at the capsized bowl and ritual remnants on the ground, she said, "Councilwoman Astrid sent another memory to us. A group of fae murdered a human who looked like Rika."

Rika gasped. "That's why Dagmar said I shouldn't leave the embassy?"

Sabine nodded. "You're safe here, but I don't want to take any chances." Turning back toward Bane, she said, "My father's been watching us since we met the merfolk. That recorded memory was a warning, both to me and to the dwarves. I will not be forsworn in my oath to protect Rika."

Bane glanced at the scrying bowl, his lip curling in disgust. Blossom was sitting in the middle of the mess, dipping her fingers into the spilled water and licking off the droplets. The pixie's eyes were unfocused, a wide smile plastered on her face. She was obviously enjoying herself.

"Did you ever stop to consider this was your father's plan?" Bane asked. "You've essentially declared your greatest weaknesses are your traveling companions. You walked into his trap like a foolish child without a thought to the consequences and compounded the ways he can strike at you."

"You would have done the same," she snapped, her eyes flashing with anger. "I refuse to sit here and do nothing while he targets those I care about."

"Then act smarter," Bane retorted. "If you die, we're all lost."

"That's enough," Malek ordered, refusing to let this argument continue. "Sabine made a decision based on the information she was privy to at the time. It was a mistake, but it's done."

Sabine fell silent and rubbed her temples. "No, Bane's right to chastise me for my arrogance. He often tells me the harsh truth I need to hear. My inexperience is a liability we can't afford. I should have let him know before I attempted to scry for information. Blossom helped me infiltrate the Seelie palace, but I knew she couldn't pull me out if I ran into a problem."

Bane grunted in acknowledgment and leaned against the

wall. "Then perhaps you should dry off the pixie before she drinks herself into a stupor. Otherwise, she won't be sober enough to share her insights."

Malek glanced at the toppled crystal bowl and spilled water. Blossom was giggling and lying in the middle of the puddle, making melted snow pixies by spreading her arms and legs in rapid motion. His mouth twitched in a grin. Leave it to the pixie to find some levity in an assassination attempt.

Sabine blew out a breath in exasperation. "Blossom, what do you think you're doing?"

"I waited to drink the water until you were done with it," Blossom said with another giggle.

Sabine scooped up the pixie. Her expression was stern, but Malek couldn't miss the humor dancing in her eyes. "I should have known you wouldn't be able to resist."

"There was so much magic!" Blossom protested with a grin. Her expression sobered a moment later. "I think your dad used your brother to set another trap for you. Rhys was surprised to see you, just like you were to find him there."

Sabine's expression turned thoughtful. "I think you might be right, Blossom."

"Who's Rhys?" Rika asked.

"My twin brother," Sabine said, turning to stare at the wall with a faraway expression. Something about the vulnerability in her eyes tugged at Malek's heart. For all her raw power, he suspected her estranged brother was her greatest weakness, not Rika or anyone else. And that was far more troubling than a mere assassination attempt. If rumors were to be believed, her brother was determined to claim Sabine's crown for himself—at any cost.

Chapter Five

"My brother might not be as culpable in the assassination attempts as we thought," Sabine explained. She hadn't wanted to believe Rhys wanted her killed. His surprise helped give credence to that possibility.

"Do not make assumptions of the Seelie prince's innocence until you have proof," Bane warned, crossing his arms over his chest. "Balkin was convinced your brother summoned the Wild Hunt after you at least once. No matter what you might wish, your presence is a threat to his ambitions. He wants your throne. You should consider him a threat and take steps to ward against him."

Sabine didn't respond right away. Some Faerie Elders had been convinced that once she died, Rhys would inherit her Seelie power. She didn't know if Rhys believed their rhetoric, but he now had confirmation that she still lived. If Rhys truly desired her power and wanted to test their theories, he might be inclined to renew his efforts in hunting her down. Her mother had warned her about the possible threat her brother posed, which was part of the reason Rhys had been exiled from the Unseelie court.

Unable to remain still, Sabine paced. Bane's suggestion to acquire proof was sound, but how to find it was another matter. Was it simply blind hope that made her want to believe Rhys's possible innocence? Nothing in her brother's demeanor had indicated deception or malice.

Sabine blew out a breath, realizing her father's trap had left her feeling more unsure than ever. Perhaps that had been his intention. Mistakes were far too easy to make when plagued with uncertainty. Fortunately, she'd been blessed with companions who had tremendous insight and skills. She'd be a fool not to rely on their wisdom, especially when she was so conflicted about her path.

Determined not to make the same mistake again, Sabine lifted her head to regard the dragon who had captured her heart, her fierce and loyal demon protector, the young seer who was braver than she realized, and the valiant pixie whose small size didn't diminish her strength of will in the slightest. Together they were stronger than if they stood alone.

"I erred earlier and badly," Sabine admitted quietly. "I allowed my emotions to cloud my judgment and didn't consider the ramifications of my actions. If it weren't for you, I wouldn't have survived. What I do and the actions I take affect all of us." She fell silent for a moment, remembering her brother's surprised expression. "I don't believe I can be objective about Rhys's involvement. I'll need to rely on all of your insight and guidance. I can't promise to heed your advice, but I will consider it."

Blossom's eyes widened. "You're not supposed to apologize to us, Sabine. You're a queen. It's against the rules, isn't it?"

Sabine managed a half-hearted smile. "Right of birth

doesn't mean I'm infallible. Besides, I think we've already thrown out court etiquette. We're all in newly charted territory, and you're my friends. With the exception of Balkin, I trust everyone in this room above all others. My father's had centuries to hone his skills and has likely spent most of my life plotting my demise. I'm just not sure about our best course of action."

Rika worried her lower lip, glancing at Bane for guidance. Bane's expression was shuttered. Sabine knew he would consider everything carefully before sharing his opinion. It might be minutes or days from now, but the demon would likely have considered and rejected hundreds of plans before then.

Blossom appeared more stunned at Sabine's admission than anyone. It wasn't every day that a lesser fae was asked to advise about matters involving royal families.

Malek, on the other hand, was another matter. The dragon shapeshifter was studying her carefully, as though trying to gauge her emotions. Sabine held his gaze and waited. Except for Bane, he likely had the most insight. He'd proven time and again that he had experiences that dwarfed her own.

After a long moment, Malek said, "I'm not as familiar with the intricacies of Faerie politics as you, Bane, or Blossom. I'm still of the mind that you would be safest in the Sky Cities, where my clan's magic can protect you from harm until you're strong enough to face your father."

Strangely enough, the thought didn't terrify her the way it once had. It was a possibility, but the Wild Hunt was still waiting outside the dwarven city. The only way out was through the demonic underworld, which offered a host of new problems. She still wasn't sure her magic had replenished itself enough to risk facing the demon king. But hiding in the Sky Cities wouldn't eliminate the greater threat.

"And what about the portal?" Sabine asked, taking a step toward him. "Every day we delay, the seals grow weaker. If the gods are allowed back into this world, everything we know and love will be lost. We can't allow that to happen."

Malek took Sabine's hand and squeezed it gently. "Then we need to find the next artifact and put an end to the portal threat before facing your father. The dwarven archives indicate each of the first races were entrusted with the keys to seal the portal." He turned her hand over, revealing the markings that the goddess Lachlina had etched upon her wrist. "You hold three keys already. We only need to find the last two. Based on everything I've learned over the past week, once we locate all the artifacts, the path to the portal will open to us."

Sabine's eyes widened. "That's why we haven't been able to determine the portal's location?"

Malek nodded. "I believe so. The artifacts act as a type of lodestone. The combined powers sealed the portal, but it also hid the entrance to safeguard its secrets. If the seals fail before we acquire the artifacts, we won't be able to stop another war. Only the gods can create a new seal, and they've all been long gone from this world."

"Except for Lachlina," Sabine murmured, trailing her fingertips along the markings. The golden glow was faint, but Sabine swore there was a persistent heat in the location where they'd been etched.

The tips of Blossom's wings darkened to a faint red. Before Sabine could ask what was bothering her, Rika asked, "If we can't find the artifacts in time, can't Lachlina create a new seal?"

Sabine shook her head. "No. Lachlina betrayed the other gods by giving us the knowledge to seal the portal. When she did, the other gods stripped her powers and had her imprisoned. For the most part, she's beyond our reach, except for her sparse communication through either Blossom or my marks. We *must* find the rest of the artifacts. That has to be our priority, more so than anything my father is planning."

With a renewed sense of urgency, Sabine turned toward her demon protector and asked, "Your people possess one of the artifacts, don't they?"

Bane considered her for a long time. "My people guard their secrets closely, little one. If you wish to seek their answers, you will need to embrace your birthright and claim your superiority over the most powerful of the demons."

A sliver of fear wrapped around Sabine's heart. The test to claim her place among the dwarves had nearly killed her. She wasn't sure she was strong enough to survive whatever the demons had planned. If Sabine's mother had lived longer, she would have instructed Sabine in how to complete the underworld trial necessary to claim her throne.

Bane shook his head. "It is imperative you forge an alliance with my people and soon. I suggest you wait only long enough until you have recovered from this latest misadventure before claiming your place. Only then, and with our armies at your back, will we have the power to march on Faerie and destroy any who would oppose you."

Rika paled. "You're talking about war?"

Blossom squeaked and dropped the small leaf she'd been using to dry her hair. "You can't unleash the demons on Faerie! You're going to squish the pixies! Barley's going to be turned into a pancake! My whole family will be eaten!"

"I'm *not* going to allow them to be eaten or squished," Sabine said with promise and then turned back toward Bane. "I won't have the blood of innocents on my hands, Bane. A demonic uprising would result in hundreds, if not thousands of casualties. Besides, the Seelie aren't united in their desire to have me executed. I'd rather not burn all my bridges if there's any way to avoid it."

Malek nodded. "If eliminating the threat against Sabine were that simple, she would have the aid of dragons to support her. We aren't united as a people, but there are several clans who owe my family favors. I would call them in to keep Sabine safe."

"What?" Sabine stared at Malek, shocked by his offer. She'd never considered the implications of her relationship with Malek beyond the two of them. Balkin had once suggested such a thing, but Sabine had never intended to manipulate his feelings to such an end.

Malek threaded his fingers through hers and kissed her knuckles. "This is what I've been trying to tell you, love. You aren't alone. You've secured the alliance of the merfolk and the dwarves, but through me, you can call upon several dragon clans for assistance or protection. There aren't any lengths I won't go to protect you."

Sabine's eyes softened as she gazed up at him. Once again, he'd given her the gift of security and safety she'd been lacking for so long. It was a wonder she'd ever considered him to be her enemy. In only a few months, he'd come to mean more to her than she had ever imagined possible. He'd become her strength, confidant, lover, and friend.

Pressing her hand against his cheek, she sent a wave of magic over him and said, "I hadn't really considered all the alliances we've made. Perhaps our situation isn't so dire as it once was."

He pressed his forehead against hers. "I'm not planning on letting anything happen to you, Sabine—not to you or anyone else we care about."

"The pixies are your allies too," Blossom said, flying to the ground and folding the leaf into a cup. She tried to siphon up some of the spilled water from the floor. "We may not be as big as the dragons, but I bet there's a lot more of us than them."

Sabine smiled at Blossom. "You've already taught me to never discount the aid of the pixies. You've saved the day more than once, my dearest friend."

Blossom beamed at Sabine, her pixie dust turning to a warm golden color before she turned back to her task.

"The dragon is giving you a false sense of security, Sabine," Bane said, crossing his arms over his chest again. "Use his allies, but do not depend solely upon them."

Sabine frowned. "What do you mean? You know Malek would never hurt me."

"No, I wouldn't," Malek said sharply, a trace of temper in his eyes as he glared at Bane.

Bane ignored Malek and focused on Sabine. "Your father's spies have likely already heard of Malek's presence. He knows you've made inroads with the dragons. He will use your people's fear of them to drive a wedge between them and their allegiance to you."

Sabine paled. No matter how much she might care for him, many of her people would always equate Malek as nothing more than an ancient evil that needed to be scoured from the land. Her father would absolutely capitalize upon this knowledge to discredit her. She could lose everything.

"Shit," Malek muttered and scrubbed his hands against his face. "Bane's right. Everyone in Razadon knows I'm a dragon. If there are Seelie spies here, then we've lost the element of surprise."

Sabine swallowed her dread and said, "All right, Bane. You knew I'd reject your first suggestion outright. I would never enslave my people or slaughter them simply to secure my throne. Now tell me the advice you really want me to take."

Bane's lips curved upward. He gave her a nod of approval and said, "A weapon may remain in its sheath, but its presence is still a powerful deterrent against your enemies."

Blossom wrinkled her nose. "Is that a weird demon riddle?"

Sabine frowned. "No. I believe he's suggesting that I use the *threat* of the demons to force my father to back off."

Bane inclined his head. "You've been recovering in the relative safety of the dwarven city for the last few days. During that time, you've dabbled with the dragon and played armchair politics that have little to no bearing on the current climate in Faerie."

Malek's eyes narrowed.

Bane ignored him and continued. "Now that you've asserted your intention to rule, leave the administrative tasks to others. Focus on honing your strength. Once you're battle-ready, descend to the underworld and cement your alliance with my people. With the threat of the demons at your back, your father will hesitate to strike out against you."

Sabine didn't respond right away. She'd thought handling some of the individual requests might give her more insight into the current political climate, but most of the letters she'd received had been trivial. Most fae were reluctant to put their true concerns in written correspondence, which could easily be intercepted. At the least, she could safely forgo reading about the color of turnips. But battle-ready? Gods. She couldn't hope to survive the combined strength of the Seelie, but the backing of the demons would give her father pause. It might be the reason why he'd been trying so hard to kill her—before she enlisted the underworld's aid.

"My father must be growing desperate," Sabine murmured, the words resonating as she spoke them. "He can't afford to have me secure an alliance with your people. The demons are the army of the gods. My people may be stronger with magic, but not even we could withstand your combined might. The only reason my mother fell to my father was through treachery and deceit—another clever trap of his."

Malek ran his hand down her arm, sending a light trace of his heated power over her skin. "But unlike your mother, you have strong allies who will remain at your side. We know he intends to harm you, and we'll take steps to ensure that *never* happens. From what you've said, your mother suspected possible treachery but never had confirmation."

Rika looked at Bane and asked, "I thought it was just humans who were afraid of the demons. If your people are so powerful, why haven't they taken over? I never saw a demon until you came to Karga."

Bane's eyes flashed silver briefly before reverting to amber. He crossed his arms over his chest and didn't respond.

Rika frowned at him and then turned toward Sabine with a questioning look. "Did I say something wrong?"

Sabine paused, knowing the subject was delicate. "She needs to know, Bane, especially since we're going to be traveling to the underworld."

Bane grunted and then made a gesture to indicate his acquiescence. Fortunately, Malek remained silent, but his eyes had sharpened on Bane. Blossom was busy dipping her fingers into the small puddle of water and licking the droplets off.

Sabine turned back toward Rika and said, "The demons were created by the gods to protect this world and wage war against its enemies. They were, by far, fiercer and more skilled than the gods had anticipated. Millions died at their hands, and the gods began to fear the demons would set their sights upon them and challenge their right to rule. They banded together, shackling the demons to the underworld. With blood and magic, they sealed them underground, and only with blood and magic can they return to the light."

Rika's eyes widened. "Blood and magic? That's what you say when you do major magic."

Sabine nodded. "Yes. Magic is integral to my people. The fae are the caretakers of this world, and the royal families were entrusted by the gods with great power. Outside of the gods, we alone have the ability to anchor the demons aboveground."

Rika frowned. "But what about demonic possession and summoning them? I heard stories back in Karga about how people could do that. It's why the guards would kill anyone who practiced magic or had ties to it. They weren't willing to risk an uprising."

Bane growled, causing Rika to take a step back. "No innate magic is required for a human to forge a pact with a greater demon. Your people were ignorant fools. I hope you do not intend to repeat their mistakes by repeating such falsehoods."

Rika winced. "I didn't mean to offend you, Bane. I'll choose my words more carefully."

Bane harrumphed.

Sabine smiled at Rika and said, "Demonic possession is a rare and highly coveted talent among the demons, similar to how only fae from certain bloodlines can perform some types of magic. Even then, there are some... limitations to such power. All magic requires a cost, and possession burns out the host quickly."

Rika nodded in understanding.

"Tell me more about your scrying," Bane said, pushing away from the wall. "What prompted your decision to travel to the Seelie court?"

Sabine frowned, recalling the murder of the innocent human girl. "One of the fae in the memory stone smelled of cinnamon and lilac. I followed the scent marker into the Seelie court, hoping to learn the individual's identity. She wasn't in the room where the signature ended, but I caught something else that led me into the garden. That's where I discovered Rhys."

"I recognized the room we were in," Blossom said, folding her leaf into a hat and placing it on her head. "Pixies aren't allowed in that part of the palace, but the gardenia emblem on the walls means those quarters belong to King Cadan's current mistress and her retinue."

Sabine straightened as she considered the implications. "Are you sure?"

Blossom nodded and wrung out the bottom of her water-soaked dress. "Yep. All the pixies know about the symbol. We always try to figure out ways to sneak into that part of the palace so we can steal some flowers from her garden. It's one of the rights of passage in being a pixie. You can't get caught."

Needing time to think, Sabine picked up the fallen memory stone and placed it back in the box. Malek placed it on the nearby desk and then collected the fallen scrying bowl while Sabine picked up the rest of the items she'd used for the ritual. She cleaned them with the black cloth and placed them back in the bloodlock cabinet.

"I'll need to send a message to Balkin detailing what happened. He might learn something about the identity of my father's mistress. At the very least, he'll need to curtail rumors before my people believe my father bested me."

"It won't do much good," Bane said, his voice gruff. "Even though you survived, you'll lose standing among the fae for this latest episode."

Sabine inwardly cursed, knowing he was right. "Balkin might help spin it somehow. I can't afford to alienate more of my people or have them believe I'm too weak to hold my throne."

"If nothing else, at least it's a lead," Malek said, setting the pitcher back on the dresser. "Take your victories where you can. An hour ago, you didn't have this much."

Sabine nodded, but she wasn't convinced. "Perhaps. But if this was a cleverly designed trap, I'm just not sure we can trust anything we witnessed in either the memory or the scrying."

"Good," Bane said in approval. "You're learning."

Rika straightened. "Do you want me to ask Dagmar to send your beastman a message? They've been corresponding as part of her new lessons."

Sabine managed a smile and nodded at her. She gestured toward the memory stone box and said, "Send this box with the message. Dagmar will need to use the same coded phrases we've been working on and avoid any mention of Astrid. I won't endanger any of our allies by naming them outright."

"Got it," Rika said, picking up the box and holding it tightly against her chest. She beamed a quick smile at Sabine before heading out of the room.

Sabine's smile faded, uncertain about the best way to protect Rika. As a human seer, Rika was safe enough here in the embassy, but Sabine couldn't remain here much longer. Once more fae arrived in Razadon, now that the city had been reopened, the chances of spies infiltrating the embassy would rise. Sabine and her friends needed to be away before that happened. And based on what Bane had said, their next journey would take them to the underworld. She shuddered.

"It's good that you gave her the task," Malek said, gesturing toward the door where Rika had disappeared. "Rika wants to be of more use to you. She's been asking about more ways she can help you."

"It's sometimes hard to remember she's a seer with her own abilities and not an ordinary human," Sabine admitted.

"I promised to protect her, but it feels like I'm putting her in more danger by keeping her close."

Sabine rubbed her throat, still feeling the effects of her father's magic. Even though Bane had healed her, it would be a long time before she forgot the feel of her father's hand around her neck. She had to remember it wasn't only her life at stake. Bane, Blossom, and Rika were all depending on her. Even Malek needed her help if they were going to ensure the Dragon Portal remained sealed.

Blossom flew over to land on Sabine's shoulder. "We won't let anything happen to her, Sabine. We'll all protect Rika. Besides, she's learning how to defend herself. That's why she's training to fight with Bane."

Sabine turned toward Bane. "How is the training going?"

"For all her efforts and strength of spirit, the seer is a human and as frail as one," Bane said gruffly. "But I agree with the dragon and the pixie. She will likely never be a master-at-arms, but the training will give her much-needed confidence. You need to assign her more tasks so she may temper her abilities and strength into becoming a formidable weapon. You will need her in the coming days."

It wasn't just Rika. They'd all need to focus on building their strength if they were going to survive what was to come.

Straightening her shoulders, Sabine said, "I think it's time we focus on the training you think I'll need to survive my encounter with the demons."

Bane's eyes shone silver. "Then let's begin."

Chapter Six

The demon roared.

The walls shook, and a frisson of fear wrapped around Sabine, threatening to steal her will. Demons preyed on fear, a lesson she'd learned well over the years. Pushing aside the useless emotion, she held her ground. She wouldn't show Bane any signs of weakness.

She withdrew her dagger from its sheath, the familiar weight no longer offering its usual confidence. Such mundane weapons were woefully inadequate against one of the most powerful demons in the world. His size dwarfed even the largest of humans, both in height and in physique. But it was his large curved horns that made him distinctive, even among his kind. Bane's horns were both a formidable weapon and also a sign of his elevated status within the underworld. He had the advantage both in years and in physical strength, but she wasn't about to submit.

The best defense is a good offense.

Her lips curved in a smirk, and she tilted her blade to catch the light. "Shall we dance?"

His eyes flashed to silver, either in bloodlust or harsh

amusement. Sabine wasn't sure which option was better. Gods. Taunting him was likely a mistake, but bravado could be used as a powerful weapon if wielded well.

A bluish light flickered along his skin, a sign he was tapping into his substantial magic. His skin was darker than the deepest pitch, more of an absence of light than any true color. Not even the glow from the crystalline lanterns touched him. It was almost as though the light was afraid to embrace the darkness.

Sabine crouched, the dagger an extension of her hand as the demon charged toward her. After waiting until he was nearly upon her, she sidestepped. Her foot lashed out, trying to trip him. He anticipated the move and twisted his large body with far more grace than she'd expected.

Bluish magic burst from the tips of his claws, and Sabine dove to the side. The burst of power slammed into the wall, leaving a distinctive char mark. The smell of sulfur and burning metal filled the air. Sabine swallowed back the bitter taste of fear the scent evoked. If she were human, such a strike would have killed her.

She darted forward again, using her agility and quickness to her advantage. She sliced outward, feeling the knife slide between his ribs. Thick black blood dribbled downward against his skin.

"First blood," he said with a growl. "Come, little fae. If you wish to dance, I'll spin you around."

"Sweet talker," Sabine retorted, unsheathing a second blade by feel alone. With a battle cry, she rushed toward him and slid down, angling for a low strike. His clawed hand encircled her wrists, and he tilted it backward with a cry. Her knife clanged to the stone floor. She kicked out and pushed off the floor, leaping backward.

He rushed her again, using her stolen knife against her. She blocked and parried, but he was faster and had centuries of training over her. She continued to retreat, knowing he was trying to box her in. Sabine feigned a stumble, and the demon's hesitation was his undoing. With a well-timed thrust, she sliced the tendons of his wrist, disarming him. The knife clattered to the ground.

He roared again. His poisoned claws slashed outward, and Sabine jumped back, but not before they hit his mark. Pain lanced through her midsection, almost exactly in the same spot where she'd injured him.

Poison surged through her bloodstream, and her magic fought against it. A fine sheen of perspiration broke out along her skin. For most, an injury from this demon's claws would be a death sentence. As it was, even she would eventually weaken until she struggled to hold her weapon. She had to end this soon or buy some time to burn the poison out.

Jumping into the air and away from him, she sent a burst of magic outward, using the wind to fuel her speed and height. Victory would be hers, even if she had to cheat to ensure it.

The demon launched upward, wrapped his arm around her waist, and slammed her against the padded floor. Her breath exploded out of her at the jarring impact. It was a wonder he hadn't broken her ribs.

The demon growled. "No magic."

Sabine glared at him. It would be impossible to beat him relying only upon her weapon skill. He knew that. What in the world was he hoping to teach her if she couldn't rely on her strengths? She paused, suspicion threading its way through her thoughts. He couldn't be trying to push her into asserting her will over his, could he?

She arched her brow. "Are *you* dictating to *me*, Bane'umbra?"

Bane's lips curved upward in a hint of a smile. "You're the one under me, little one. Until you hold a position of power,

I shall dictate to you as I see fit." He paused, his eyes roaming over her with salacious intent. "Or you may surrender to me, and I'll take whatever reward I choose."

Sabine narrowed her eyes. Pressing her hand against Bane's chest, she shoved a blast of power into him. He flew upward. With a flick of her wrist, she slammed Bane into the wall.

Springing to her feet, Sabine's hand tightened around her dagger. "You dare too much, Bane."

"And you need to remember who you are," Bane retorted, his eyes flashing silver as he grabbed her discarded knife from the ground. "There are no rules in combat. Honor means nothing if you are dead. Skill is good, trickery is better. Utilize all the weapons at your disposal or give them to someone better suited to wield them."

"Dammit," she muttered, jumping back and narrowly escaping his strike. She should have kicked the weapon aside or taken it out of play.

"Sloppy," Bane snapped, lashing outward with both the blade and his claws. "What are you going to do, little fae? Will you die or be a queen in truth?"

Sabine continued to retreat, narrowly avoiding his strikes. Bane was right; she'd been sloppy. Mundane weapons were well and good, but they weren't the source of her strength. She wasn't pretending to be human anymore.

She dodged and parried, but he was still faster and stronger. Her skin glowed as power built within her. Her silvery braids whipped across her face as she kicked out at him. He sprung backward, his expression taunting.

"The Wild Hunt will pursue you if you step outside the dwarven city," Bane said to remind her, lashing out again with sharpened claws.

She stumbled and then rolled to the side, springing up again.

"Your family wants you dead."

Thrust, thrust, parry, parry. His strikes were coming quicker now. Her dagger took on a sheen of power as her magic flowed along the blade.

"Enemies at every turn if you cannot defend yourself."

Sabine muttered a curse and sidestepped again, her footwork falling into a familiar pattern. Her breathing was coming heavier as her magic continued to fight against the poison. She needed to end it soon.

Bane darted toward her again, his claws swiping out. She inhaled sharply and leaped away. "Concentrate, Sabine! You have less than two months to prepare before you must face my brethren in the underworld or forfeit your claim. Will you be predator or prey?"

"I am Queen Sabin'theoria of the Unseelie," she shouted, blocking another attack and spinning away from him. "I will *never* be prey."

Thrusting out her hand, Sabine expelled her magic in a shocking blast. Bane was thrown into the air. With another swipe of power as biting as any blade, she disarmed him and pinned him against the wall. He fought against her hold, his furious gaze promising vengeance. In this, she was supreme. She would *never* surrender.

Sweeping Bane's abandoned weapon into the air with another blast of power, she jabbed it against his chest, directly below his heart. A trickle of blackened blood appeared where it pierced his skin, dribbling down his chest. Bane's eyes flashed to silver, and he roared again. Sabine clenched her fist, and his roar cut off abruptly as she silenced his voice.

She stalked toward him and demanded, "Do you yield?"

Bane blinked, his eyes immediately reverting to their normal amber color. Understanding his unspoken acquiescence, Sabine released her hold and lowered him to the floor.

Her hands shook as she sheathed her knife and turned away from him. It was a deliberate move that not only demonstrated trust but also gave him time to curb any lingering battle lust.

A stack of folded linen cloths, armor, and an assortment of weapons had been neatly arranged on a single table on the far side of the room. Other than a nearby weapon rack, it was the only furniture in the room. The dwarves had said they'd never seen this training room in the embassy until they'd arrived. The magic of Faerie often moved things around or modified rooms to suit the inhabitants' needs. Once they departed, the room would likely change again.

She picked up a cloth and patted her face to absorb the purged poison. When she finished, she tossed it into a container to the side so it could be burned later.

A wave of dizziness flowed over her, and she blinked back the fatigue that threatened. She couldn't afford this weakness. If she was going to protect her friends, she had to master this lesson and quickly.

Sabine lowered her head and took a steadying breath. Her braids fell forward in a silvery curtain, and she noticed the blood-soaked tatters of her shirt. She touched the edge of the deep claw marks and winced. She needed to change out of these clothes before Malek saw the evidence of her injuries.

"You've improved, but you lack finesse," Bane said, retrieving the fallen weapon from the ground. He checked the integrity of the blade before placing it on the table with the other weapons. "Your magic needs to be as sharp as your blade. Each strike must be made with surgical precision."

Sabine lifted her head and frowned at Bane. "Malek's going to lose his mind if he realizes you're not pulling your strikes. Have you ever considered simply telling me your lesson instead of beating it into me?"

Bane chuckled and approached her. "This method

ensures you will embrace these tactics rather than simply repeating instructions back to me. Besides, I enjoy yanking on the dragon's tail. Since you've forbidden me from killing him, this is the next best thing."

"I won't allow you to continue antagonizing him."

"Good. Then you'll be motivated to learn faster," Bane said and slid his hand under her ruined shirt. Sabine wrinkled her nose at him but remained silent. As much as she might want to argue the point, Bane was skilled at pushing her beyond her normal limits. She never would have survived hiding among humans for ten years if it hadn't been for him and his brother, Dax.

She hissed out a breath as he brushed against her injury. Bane's skin glowed with a bluish light. She gritted her teeth as he knitted her skin back together, not leaving even a trace of a scar. Most demons couldn't heal, but Bane was an anomaly. He had the rare ability to manipulate someone's lifeforce, which had made him skilled beyond measure as an assassin. Thanks to their blood bond, his magic allowed him to reverse most of her physical injuries. Unfortunately, it wasn't pleasant. All magic required a sacrifice, and he used her pain to fuel his power.

Bane wrapped his arm around her waist, drawing her closer. He was gentler than she expected, and she'd missed sharing this intimacy with him. With a sigh, she leaned against him and allowed his magic to envelop her. Sabine pressed her hand against his bare chest and sent her own magic outward to embrace him. Her skin shone as Bane siphoned off her power, infusing it with his aura to heal himself.

She waited for him to pull away, but he continued to caress her skin. His claws lightly traced the marks of fae power that had been etched upon her skin years ago. It reminded her of the way he used to touch her when she had still been in hiding in the human city of Akros. She'd had to stifle so much of herself simply to survive.

His gaze roamed over her as he murmured, "I will never tire of seeing you without human glamour, little one. You belong to the magic of the night's embrace, not cities reeking of sickness and refuse."

She looked up into Bane's amber eyes and smiled. The light from the crystalline lanterns surrounded him like a nimbus, never touching his skin. He was made of shadows and darkness, his terrible beauty and strength a captivating sight to behold.

Her smile faded as memories, both bitter and sweet, engulfed her. She'd been remiss in her obligations to him over the past few months. He rarely made demands upon her, and she needed to be more cognizant of his needs. She was his lodestone, allowing him to freely travel outside the underworld. But with everything that had happened, she hadn't been able to share as much magic with him as she should.

In a soft voice, she asked, "What do you need from me, my protector?"

Bane's expression turned guarded at her ritualistic words. Something had been bothering him over the past week, ever since the dwarven councilwoman had tried to kill her. It was more than his concerns over her deepening relationship with Malek. She was trying to be patient and not pry, but the increasing distance was worrying her.

When he didn't respond, she sighed and infused her touch with more magic. She ran her fingertips along the place where she'd cut him. His arm tightened around her, and his eyes flashed to silver before returning to their normal amber color. He accepted her magical offering willingly, but he didn't ask for more. Whatever was going on needed to be addressed soon. His emotions were too close to the surface, which could spell disaster for a demon. They were volatile on the best of days.

"Hi," Rika said from behind them. "I thought you might want a drink after your training session."

Bane lowered his hand and took a step away from Sabine, shattering the moment. Burying her concern, Sabine turned and smiled warmly at the dark-haired teenager at the doorway. Rika had begun wearing her hair in braids, in a similar style to how Sabine wore hers. Even her clothing had been modified to resemble Sabine's wardrobe, with leather pants and a form-fitting top that laced up the front. It allowed more freedom of movement in combat rather than the dresses often worn at court.

Rika walked toward them, holding out drinks that were cold enough that the glasses had begun to sweat. One benefit of staying in the dwarven city was their access to the cool mountain streams and even ice harvested from the top of the mountains.

Sabine accepted the glass and took a long drink of the sweet, fruity beverage. Rika held out another glass to Bane. He considered her for a moment and then took the glass, then downed it before he placed it on a nearby table. Sabine wondered if Rika realized the compliment Bane had offered her. Demons didn't trust easily. Taking food or drink from someone without assessing it first was one of the highest forms of respect.

"You're next, little seer," Bane said, gesturing toward an assortment of weapons piled in the corner. "Select your weapons and prepare to defend yourself."

Rika's eyes widened. "Again? But we just trained this morning!"

"Do you expect your enemies to wait around until you're refreshed?"

Rika's mouth dropped open. She darted a glance at

Sabine, a question on her face. Sabine shrugged to indicate he had a point. Bane could be a harsh taskmaster, but he was an effective teacher.

At Rika's hesitation, Bane scowled and said, "Arm yourself or prepare to fight with your innate gifts. You have five minutes to prepare."

Rika rushed toward the weapons and armor. Bane couldn't heal Rika, so additional protective measures had to be taken. Under Bane's direction, the dwarves had created some lightweight armor for Rika to wear. The biggest obstacle had been finding suitable power crystals that offered both healing and quickness yet wouldn't interfere with Rika's seer abilities.

From the weapon pile, Rika selected two knives that were longer than the ones Sabine had used. In a battle against an opponent who was larger, quickness and speed were critical. Her weapons and armor were designed to allow for such movement, but Rika was still becoming accustomed to the added weight. Part of her training was her getting used to wearing and fighting in it. For the first two days, Bane had made her wear it nonstop, even while she'd slept.

Once she was equipped, Rika faced her instructor and adopted a fighting stance. Bane assessed Rika with a critical eye, making minor corrections to her positioning. Sabine sipped her iced drink and watched, impressed by how much Rika had learned in less than a week. Bane was determined to use every minute of their time in Razadon to train them.

"Sabine! Sabine!"

Sabine turned to see Blossom flying into the room. Immediately, Sabine held out her hand to give Blossom a place to land.

The pixie crashed into her palm, landing face first in dramatic fashion. She panted, her shimmering wings twitching and spreading twinkling pixie dust. Blossom rolled over, her hair spread out across Sabine's palm. Sabine's mouth twitched in a smile. Blossom had been experimenting with minor glamour again, if her glittering rainbow-colored hair tipped with pink and purple was any indication. Even her dress matched the sparkling kaleidoscope of colors.

"Messenger. Here." Blossom panted, her foot hanging off the side of Sabine's palm. "Goat. Escaped. Not my fault."

Sabine wasn't even going to begin dissecting Blossom's statement. Jiggling her glass so the broken ice made a tinkling noise, Sabine said, "Take a sip, catch your breath, and then explain."

Blossom sat up, her eyes wide. "Is that... weebo juice?"

Without waiting for a response, Blossom perched on the edge of the cup and took a drink. When she'd had enough, she wiped her mouth with the back of her hand and grinned. "So, so good. I gotta harvest some of those seeds so we can plant them when we find a new garden."

Bane looked over at them and frowned. "If you're going to keep the bug around, she needs to learn how to relay messages properly."

Blossom put her hands on her hips. "I'm not a bug!"

Sabine sighed. "Blossom, tell me about the messenger. Is this related to the goat? I thought you'd already caught it."

Blossom jerked her head up. "Oh. Um, no. They're two different things." She held up one finger. "There's a representative from the underworld here with an urgent message from the demon king. Malek told me to find you and Bane right away. The dwarves look like they want to skewer him."

Sabine frowned. The previous messages she'd received had been in the form of missives or elaborate gifts. Each one had been more ostentatious than the last, and the trap embedded in each was growing in complexity. Bane had taken over receiving them on her behalf while she'd been recovering.

Before she could ask about the messenger, Blossom held up a second finger and said, "This is a different goat, and he's a little sneaky. Faerie's helping him escape. The cave trolls are trying to catch him, but he's really fast. Dagmar's mom might be a little upset because the goat knocked over tonight's dinner. Watch out for four-legged soup prints and a dwarf wielding a rolling pin. Maybe go the opposite way so you don't get knocked over."

Sabine's brow furrowed. The goats were part of Razadon's defense since they had the unique ability to see through fae glamour. "Blossom, how do these goats keep ending up in the embassy?"

Blossom flew out of the room and yelled, "It's not my fault!"

Rika giggled and then clamped a hand over her mouth. Sabine blew out a breath. It was definitely the pixie's fault. A demonic messenger and a panicked goat. Great. The assassination efforts of the Seelie would have to wait until she handled this latest disaster.

Bane gestured toward Rika and said, "Remain armed. You will accompany Queen Sabin'theoria to meet this representative. One step to the right and behind her to protect and defend. Keep your weapon at the ready."

Rika snapped to attention and nodded. Sabine headed for the door with Rika trailing her, her armor creaking slightly from its newness.

"If this is a demonic messenger, you need to change," Bane said, pressing his hand against her back and steering her away from the main sitting room.

Sabine glanced at her blood-splattered shirt and nodded. "It doesn't exactly scream queen of the Unseelie."

"On the contrary. There is no greater allure for a demon than the promise of royal fae blood. Change quickly. I'll join the dragon in keeping an eye on the representative. Our rivalry will have to wait until your potential enemies have been dealt with."

Sabine blew out a breath and headed for her bedroom, with Rika on her heels. If someone had arrived with urgent news from the underworld, it wasn't anything good.

Chapter Seven

*S*abine adjusted her crown and smoothed her dress. Unlike the fabric of the more formal gowns worn at court, its soft and delicate material was lighter in weight and perfect for entertaining at home. The color was a deep blue, the shade reminding her of the sky at twilight. Silver threading had been intricately woven into decorative patterns, swirling up from her hem like smoke. The dress had been waiting on her bed when she'd arrived in her quarters, another offering from Faerie.

"You don't want to wear the gorget the demon king sent you as a gift, do you?"

Sabine glanced at Rika, who was still poking through her jewelry box. Kal'thorz's priceless gift was still in its box, on her dressing table. It was a stunning piece of workmanship, but Sabine wasn't sure about the demon king's motivations behind such a gift.

"Do you believe I should?" Sabine asked, curious about Rika's impressions.

Rika wrinkled her nose. "It's pretty, but there's something creepy about it. Bane didn't like you wearing it either.

Besides, it's just a messenger. You probably don't want to show them your favor."

Sabine smiled, pleased Rika was getting a better sense of politics. "I agree. Why don't you select something that you think is suitable?"

"Maybe something from the dwarves, since we're staying with them," Rika murmured, opening another drawer on the table.

Messenger or not, Sabine knew whoever had been sent would report every detail back to his or her king. Sabine studied her reflection in the floor-length mirror with a critical eye. Her skin was still too pale. Using a trace amount of glamour, she hid any traces of the fatigue that had been plaguing her. It would have to do. She couldn't afford to show weakness.

Besides weapon training, Rika had also been practicing her seer abilities, which allowed her to see through glamour. Her efforts were still hit or miss.

"Can you see through my glamour?" Sabine asked, taking the jeweled silver bangle from Rika's outstretched hand. She slid it onto her wrist. Each precious stone was actually a dwarven power crystal, embedded with protection magic. Rika's choice was perfect, both complementing the gown and giving a nod toward their hosts.

Rika squinted and then nodded. "Yeah, but it's a lot harder to see through your illusions than Blossom's. You're not going to hide your markings?"

Sabine shook her head. "Not when meeting with a representative from the underworld. My skin etchings are a sign of power. We're going to need every advantage."

Motioning for Rika to follow her, Sabine left her bedroom suite. She headed down the hallway leading to the main sitting area frequently used for guests. She'd taken enough time to make it clear she didn't act on Kal'thorz's command. So consumed with composing her thoughts, she hadn't noticed her surroundings. She halted suddenly, nearly causing Rika to crash into her.

Malek was leaning against the wall at the entrance to the sitting area, his arms crossed over his chest. It wasn't an accident that he'd positioned himself to intercept her before she could fully enter the room.

At the sound of her footsteps, Malek straightened. Her magic hummed at the sight of him. His hair was pulled away from his face, the inky darkness contrasting with the golden hues of his skin.

She started to smile but stopped at the intensity in his expression. His blue eyes held a warning rather than the warmth and affection that usually filled them when she was near. Sabine arched her brow at the dragon shapeshifter, trying to bury her misgivings. If Malek was on edge, she had reason to worry.

He was wearing more weapons than earlier, and his shoulders were fraught with tension. From his body language, he wasn't happy with Bane, the messenger, or possibly both.

"What's wrong?" she asked quietly, so as not to be overheard by their guest.

"Keep a full body length between you and the creature," he murmured and took her arm, sending a tingle of awareness through her at his touch.

Creature? Sabine frowned at his choice of wording and then quickly schooled her features. Squaring her shoulders, she nodded at Malek to indicate she'd heed his warning.

Placing his hand on the hilt of his sword, Malek led her into the room, where Bane and the messenger were waiting.

Sabine nearly missed a step at the sight of her demon protector. Bane was in full demonic mode. His eyes were silvered and his claws extended, as he towered over a small, hunched, goblin-like creature. Behind him were several dwarven guards, who were waiting to deliver the messenger straight back to the underworld.

Fascinated, Sabine moved closer to get a better look at the scrawny misshapen thing. She'd never seen its like before. It was the size of a tall goblin, reaching almost to her shoulders, but that was where the similarity ended. Goblins usually had lumpy, grassy-green skin, but this creature's skin was reddish, wizened, and wrinkled. Two small nubs, like emerging horns, jutted out of its head, making it appear almost like a minor demon left out in the sun too long.

"It's a fire imp," Malek whispered next to her ear. "Bane wanted me to tell you they're tricksters, assassins, and occasionally, messengers. Let's hope he's not a gift."

Sabine's misgivings deepened. If she had a choice, she'd take the elaborate gifts and magic scrolls from the demon king—even if most of them were traps. Something about this creature worried her.

The fire imp twisted and rubbed its hands together as it stared up at Bane. Its long black tongue slithered out and then darted back in, almost like a snake. Bane growled at the creature. It dropped to the ground and flattened itself with a whimper. The tongue didn't emerge again.

Sabine straightened her shoulders and stared at the fire imp. She wasn't sure how this creature was connected with Kal'thorz, the demon king.

"Be respectful, or I will end you," Bane warned, glaring at the creature. "Speak, and know you address Queen Sabin'theoria of the Unseelie."

The fire imp stared at her from its prone position on the floor. Its amber slitted eyes were overly large, and Sabine felt almost unclean being scrutinized by such a creature.

"I has messssssage."

The fire imp hissed out the words, making Sabine

wonder if he could have snake blood in his background. He crept forward, his tongue darting out in Sabine's direction as though tasting the air for her magic.

Bane grabbed the imp and threw him back to the ground. He leaned over the imp and pressed his clawed hand against its neck. "The messenger will speak. Now. Or I will remove your head from your neck."

Its tongue disappeared again. The fire imp blinked its serpentine eyes at Sabine. She watched in fascination as they began to glow with a golden light. When the imp spoke, his voice was high-pitched and far more cultured. Sabine would swear it was now speaking at the behest of a woman. She'd known some demons could possess living creatures, but she'd never seen it in practice.

"King Kal'thorz Versed, most feared and admired ruler of all the underworld, extends an invitation to the illustrious Sabin'theoria of the Unseelie. Sabin'theoria and her companions are hereby invited to the underworld as guests of honor to attend an upcoming trial by combat, which will commence three days from now."

Sabine frowned. "What trial?"

A third eyelid slid over the fire imp's gaze. "Dax'than Versed has been accused of treason."

All the blood rushed from Sabine's head. Dax was being accused of treason? When she'd heard he was back in the underworld, she had thought Dax might have been in trouble. But treason? He was far too smart to get caught up in something that would get him executed.

Sabine glanced at Bane for guidance, but his expression was shuttered. The similarities between this trial and the one Bane had endured couldn't be a coincidence. Two brothers, both with a death sentence hanging over their heads in less than a week? Bane had been falsely accused by the dwarven council, which had been resolved at great personal cost to Sabine.

Bane grabbed the fire imp and hauled him upright. "You've delivered your message. Return to your liege."

The fire imp looked up at Bane with eyes that still glowed. "I have a message for you as well, Bane'umbra Versed. You have been summoned."

Fast as lightning, the imp jerked forward and bit Bane's hand. A flash of red light pulsed around Bane for a moment and then disappeared. The demon roared and swiped out with his clawed hands, tearing out the fire imp's throat. He threw its body aside and into the wall. With a sickening thud, it slid downward into a crumpled heap, leaving a smear of blood down the wall. Its body burst into flames.

Sabine stared in shocked horror, watching as Malek grabbed a pitcher off the table. He tossed the contents over the burning fire imp. With a sizzling sound, the fire extinguished. A stream of smoke rose from the body, filling the air with the harsh and acrid odor of burned skin and hair.

Rika gagged and stepped backward. The young seer's face was ashen. Sabine waved her hand, sending a sharp wind through the room to dissipate the stench.

Stepping in front of Rika, Sabine blocked her view and gestured down the hall. "Go find Dagmar and tell her that we have a… *situation* that needs to be cleaned up. We'll also need to make arrangements to leave right away. Dagmar and her mother will need to coordinate with my representatives in Faerie during our absence."

Rika swallowed and nodded. Without a word, she turned and ran down the hall to find the household manager. Sabine hoped Rika would manage to compose herself during that time.

Sabine dismissed the guards back to their posts. The moment they were gone, she walked toward Bane. She reached out to take his hand to inspect the injury, but he pulled away from her.

"This bite does not require your magic to heal."

"Don't be difficult," she said, holding out her hand toward him. "Or I'll pin you against the wall again and look anyway."

Bane gave her a disgusted look and held out his hand. She took his clawed hand in hers, studying it closely. There appeared to be puncture marks on his hand, similar to those of a snake bite. A faint sulfuric and metallic scent tickled her nose.

She leaned closer and relaxed her eyes. A faint reddish glow surrounded the wound, almost like an intricate webbing or net. Lifting her gaze, she asked, "Is it poison or magic? It's almost as though it's both."

Bane didn't respond.

Malek walked over to her and said, "I believe our taciturn friend received a summoning mark."

"A what?"

Malek frowned. "Among my kind and some lesser dragons, a bite is infused with magic to fulfill a specific purpose. Sometimes it's used to bind someone's magic or to summon an adventurous child back home. I suspect Kal'thorz wants his wayward son to return home—and bring you with him."

Sabine looked up at Bane. "Is that true?"

Bane glared at Malek before focusing on her again. "Kal'thorz grows impatient. That you're so close and remain out of reach vexes him. Since the demon king is unsure about your affections for my brother and has heard about your efforts to free me here, he offered an incentive for you to attend him sooner."

Sabine narrowed her eyes. "I don't care much for being manipulated. If left untreated, what will the bite do to you?"

"The fire imp's venom was cursed by a powerful sorceress. It has blocked my access to your magic. If I do not return to the underworld to receive the cure within a week or destroy the source, I will fall into bloodlust. Without your magic tying me to the surface, I will either kill anyone who crosses my path or be forced back into the underworld."

"This is unacceptable," Sabine said, clenching her fists.

Bane and Malek exchanged a look but didn't say anything.

Sabine spun around and paced, her fury growing with every step. "This is the equivalent of an act of war. That pompous, arrogant, self-proclaimed king thinks he can try to harm my advisor without consequences? I'll tear the underworld to pieces before I allow this to pass."

"You're glowing," Malek said gently.

Sabine ignored him, not caring that her skin markings were shining with power. If she didn't take a stand, it would announce to the world that she was merely a hapless girl who couldn't hold her throne. It was one thing to be attacked by her father and the Seelie court. That feud had been going on for generations. But she hadn't anticipated this newest threat. She had to act swiftly and decisively, or her people would be in danger.

She flung out her hand and said, "Dax is under Balkin's protection, and my beastman is sworn to my service. By default, Dax is mine to pass judgment upon! This demon king has not only threatened the life of two of my subjects, but he has the audacity to launch an attack in my domain of all places. He bit you!"

She finished her diatribe in a shout, curling her hands into fists. Magic was still building within her, threatening to be unleashed.

"Don't be foolish," Bane said, his eyes flashing silver again. "This is what Kal'thorz wants, which is all the more reason to resist. The moment you step foot into the underworld, you will be playing into his hands. You're still weakened from the assassination attempt, a fact he likely knows and intends to exploit. I will go alone to face Kal'thorz and answer his summons."

"I will not lose you," Sabine snapped. "Don't tell me you'll scamper off to the underworld for this cure while I stay here hiding in the embassy. It will not happen, Bane."

Bane looked affronted. "Demons *don't* scamper."

Sabine waved off the comment. "You and I both know he'll keep you there until I show up. I won't allow anyone to hurt the people I love. What kind of queen will I be if I allow my people to be threatened or harmed on my watch?"

"As much as I hate to admit it, she has a point," Malek said, turning toward Bane. "I know you have concerns about her traveling to the underworld on Kal'thorz's terms, but we can't ignore this. You're her strongest Unseelie ally—and the best one to advise her in navigating the politics. If something happens to you, Sabine will be in a weaker position than she is now."

Bane was quiet for a long time. "I cannot protect you there."

Sabine sighed and approached him. She lifted her hands and pressed them against his chest. "I know there are things you've kept from me. Out of respect for you, I've tried not to pry. When you're ready, I'm willing to listen."

Bane lifted his clawed hand and touched her cheek. The last time he'd looked at her that way was when she'd cried over him when he'd been imprisoned. He'd captured her tears then, treasuring them for the emotion it held.

He stared at her now with the same sort of wonder and puzzlement. Sabine's gaze softened. Demons felt things more deeply than they wanted to admit, but emotion wasn't a weakness. It was a precious gift that deserved to be honored and protected.

"There are many things I am forbidden to discuss," Bane said after a long interval. "My oaths are binding and have not diminished with our blood bond. While we are in the underworld, I am a demon first. Until you bind the demons to the Unseelie throne, I will be limited in my ability to aid you. Only then will your authority supersede my father's rule."

Sabine nodded and lowered her hands. She could work with that.

"What do you know about Dax's trial? Why is he accused of treason?"

"He staged a coup and attempted to murder my father. The trial is nothing but a farce. Dax had been slated for execution years ago."

Sabine's mouth dropped open. Before she could respond, Dagmar flounced into the room, her red braids swinging. She was followed by a guard and three of her cousins, who were armed with buckets and mops. Dagmar skidded to a halt, her green eyes wide at the sight of the dead fire imp still smoking in the corner.

"What'd you do? Have a barbecue because the goat ruined dinner?"

Sabine turned toward her house manager, still trying to wrap her head around what Bane had told her. Rika trudged in behind them and made another gagging noise.

Dagmar turned toward Sabine and wrinkled her freckled nose. "Um, don't take this the wrong way, but I think the meat's gone bad."

Sabine rubbed her temples. "It's a fire imp. We'll need to dispose of it. I also need to make plans to travel to the underworld right away."

Dagmar nodded. "Ah, yep. Fire imp. That's right. They're impossible to cook because they just erupt into flames. They're either raw or burned, no in-between. Shame too. They'd probably be pretty tasty."

Dagmar's cousins giggled and carted their mops and buckets to the dead imp. Sabine tried to recall their names but gave up. It was impossible to keep up with all of Dagmar's second and third cousins twice removed. After a time, they were all "cousins."

Bane walked to Rika and spoke quietly to her. Rika nodded and replied in a voice too low for Sabine to overhear. At least her color was better now, and she didn't appear distraught over the fire imp.

"Mum's going to reach out to Balkin and let him know about your trip once they catch the goat," Dagmar said, directing her cousins with expansive gestures. "She's called in the aunts to cook dinner. Might be another hour before they whip something up."

"That's fine," Sabine said, no longer feeling the slightest bit hungry.

"Self, where did you put that other thing?" Dagmar muttered, patting her pockets. With a grin, she pulled a note from her back pocket with a flourish. "Here it is! Sneaky little sucker."

"What is it?" Sabine asked, taking the rolled parchment from Dagmar's outstretched hand.

"It's from Astrid," Dagmar said, referring to the dwarven councilwoman who was one of Dagmar's many cousins. "She said one of her people in Faerie sent an urgent message less than an hour ago. Her fastest messenger delivered it while you must have been cooking the imp."

Malek moved closer while Sabine unrolled the parchment. Her face paled as she read the message and then held it out for him.

Earthquake in Seelie court. Severe damage. All dwarves evacuating to Unseelie side or returning home. Trade suspended. Lines have been drawn. Talk of war. Official notice from Faerie incoming.

Gods. What had she done? Sabine lowered her gaze to stare at the goddess marks on her skin. The golden glow was constant now. She'd absorbed too much power in a short period of time. This was why the Elders marked a fae's skin. Each skin etching harnessed her power to allow her time to learn the full scope of her abilities. Before skin etchings were common, some fae had leveled mountains or created giant craters by a blast of wayward magic.

She handed the letter to Bane. He quickly scanned the message, his expression grim. Turning back toward Dagmar, Sabine asked, "Have we heard anything from Balkin?"

"Aye," Dagmar said, lowering her eyes. "Balkin suggests you declare this an intentional strike against your father. The Seelie court is in an uproar and demanding blood."

Sabine didn't reply. If she stepped out on the path to return home, the Wild Hunt would take her life. The Huntsman had already warned that way was closed to her. Plus, with Bane's and Dax's predicaments, she had to journey to the underworld. She needed the backing of the demons now more than ever, and her companions had just slaughtered an official demonic messenger.

Bane growled and crumpled the paper. "You must secure the alliance with the demons now. There's no alternative. This will end in bloodshed, one way or another."

Sabine nodded. "We'll make the arrangements to depart immediately. My mother has a few magical items stored here that we may want to take with us. There are also a few rare weapons in the armory that will be of use. We likely won't be returning to Razadon in the near future."

"The dwarves will stand with you," Dagmar told her.

"Unfortunately, what we need more than anything is the

element of surprise," Bane said. "With the Wild Hunt still lingering outside Razadon's gates, we'll need to take the underworld entrance beneath the dwarven city. My father will know the moment we cross into his kingdom through Razadon's entrance."

"Why does that matter?" Rika asked.

"The moment we enter, we'll be surrounded by those loyal only to Kal'thorz. He'll use that opportunity to separate Sabine from her allies." He turned toward Sabine. "You cannot appear weakened in front of him. Kal'thorz's spies have likely heard about what happened in Faerie. He'll take advantage of the precariousness of your position."

Sabine blew out a breath and rubbed her temples. It was imperative they secure this alliance, no matter the cost. If she could throw Kal'thorz off balance, she might have a chance. "Are there any other entrances to the underworld we can use? One that isn't well known?"

"That's not a bad idea," Malek said. "Perhaps Blossom can check with the cave trolls. They know the tunnels better than anyone."

A wind swept through the room, and the earthy scent of the forest filled the air. Sabine inhaled deeply, breathing in the power of Faerie.

The wall on the far side of the room shifted, its appearance becoming almost fluid. A silver sheen coated part of the wall, creating a mirrored effect. It had the appearance of liquid metal flowing over that one area. Sabine stared at it in wonder. The last time she'd seen such a thing had been when the Huntsman had created a portal to their reality. It was beautiful but beyond dangerous.

She took a step toward it, wondering if it was Faerie or the Huntsman who had given her a way out. The Huntsman had saved her life, but even that had had a cost. She wasn't sure if the price of this doorway was one she was willing or able to pay.

The strong scent of sulfur filled the air, and Bane's eyes flashed to silver. "That's a portal to the underworld."

The floor at Sabine's feet trembled and wavered. Malek grabbed her around her waist, spinning her around and putting himself between her and a hole forming in the floor. Sabine leaned around him, her eyes widening as two lumpy pieces of silver fabric no larger than her hand pushed through the opening. The ground trembled again, and the floor reformed beneath what appeared to be twin cloth pouches. They were fastened shut by large gold buckles that sparkled in the light.

Sabine's eyes widened. "They're traveler packs."

Malek kneeled and picked up one of the pouches. Sabine reached over and traced the runes inscribed on the buckle. It unfastened and opened, filling the air with the scent of a moonlit meadow.

Malek peered inside and said, "All of our belongings have already been packed, along with some extra items: clothing, weapons, and rations. They're all tiny beyond belief. How is this possible?"

Bane frowned and picked up the other. He opened it using the same gesture Sabine had used. "I've heard of this, but I've never seen it in practice. Such magic is only found among the fae."

Sabine touched the soft fabric, feeling the tingle of magic on her fingertips. "They're rare. It's said they're offered as a gift from Faerie when a traveler is preparing for a quest. The pouches can be opened by only the people in the traveling party, which makes them secure from would-be thieves."

Rika leaned around Bane to look inside. "Do the items get big when you pull them out?"

Sabine nodded. "Yes. They compress when you repack

them. It looks like Faerie understands the urgency of our mission."

"No," Bane said, shaking his horned head. "We do not know where that portal leads. There are places in the underworld more dangerous than you can imagine."

Sabine hesitated, uncertain about dismissing a gift from Faerie. The land could take it as a slight. No one knew how or what motivated Faerie. Its magic was wild, untamed power that centuries of fae scholars had attempted to study without fully understanding how it worked.

Shouts caught Sabine's attention. She spun and saw a goat race into the room, followed by half a dozen cave trolls. On top of the largest cave troll and at the forefront of the pack was Blossom. With a loud whoop, she fluttered her wings and shouted, "Onward, Blueboy! After that goat!"

The goat's eyes were wide with panic. He ran as though he were being chased by demons. On that thought, Sabine's eyes widened. She opened her mouth to shout a warning, but it was too late. The goat had run directly through the portal.

Blueboy screeched to a halt at the edge of the barrier. Blossom yelped and flew over his head, directly into the portal. The pixie was gone.

Chapter Eight

"Blossom!" Sabine shouted, rushing after the pixie.

Bane grabbed Sabine around the waist and hauled her against his chest. "No. It's too dangerous. We must not act rashly."

"We have to save her!" Rika cried.

"Blossom's a creature of Seelie magic," Sabine said, unable to tear her gaze away from the portal. "She can't survive without ties to the light."

Bane's arms tightened around her. "And what if this is another trap by your father? The bug will not die in seconds unless she runs into the mouth of a demon, and even then, she'll probably be hacked up from the indigestion she causes."

"He's right about a possible trap. Wait a moment," Malek said, approaching the glowing portal with the traveler's pack still in his hand. "She may come back through the portal."

"Not if it's a one-way doorway," Sabine said, staring at the portal with the hopes of seeing Blossom return. "Most of these doorways are activated by magic or runes. If it's fixed in the underworld, it's likely her magic won't be compatible.

I don't believe my father is responsible for this. I've never heard of any Seelie who can manipulate a doorway to the underworld."

"Perhaps, but you should still consider the consequences of taking an unknown path," Bane said, his clawed hand pressing against her stomach. "Will you sacrifice all your people to save one Seelie creature?"

Sabine jerked her head upward at him and narrowed her eyes. "Every life is precious, no matter how small or how they're aligned. I may not be able to save everyone, but I refuse to be the type of person who isn't willing to try."

"Your ideals will get you killed," Bane muttered.

"No," Sabine said, shaking her head and pulling away from him. "My ideals give me purpose and focus. My friends and loved ones give me the strength to meet my obstacles head on. Blossom offered her life for mine without hesitation when the Huntsman demanded a sacrifice. I won't abandon her now."

"Saving a pixie is the equivalent of opening a vein to feed a mosquito." Bane huffed and fastened the magical pouch to his belt. "Very well. I'll go to safeguard you from foolishness, not to protect the bug."

Sabine squeezed his arm in appreciation. "And to find a cure for you." She didn't mention they also needed to save Dax and secure the blasted alliance with the demons. Plus, something was wrong with her magic. She hadn't meant to create an earthquake. These foreign abilities needed to be properly harnessed, or she risked endangering more people.

Turning toward Dagmar, Sabine said, "It may be some time before I see you again, my friend. I'll send word to Balkin when I'm able. You can let him know everything that transpired." She paused, remembering her beastman's displeasure about her alliance with the pixies. "It might be wise to omit the part about the goat… and Blossom's involvement."

Dagmar nodded, still looking worried about the doorway. "Got it. I'll use the coded messages you taught me."

"Rika, grab that plant," Malek said, gesturing toward a small plant with bursts of red-and-yellow flowers sitting on the table. "I'm assuming there are no flowers for Blossom in the underworld."

Rika nodded and scooped up the small potted plant, then tucked it under her arm.

"Bane, put your hand on my shoulder," Sabine ordered, studying the swirling metallic sheen on the wall. "Remain in contact with me when we pass through. The portal is probably already keyed to our destination, but odd things can happen before we reach the other side."

Bane did as she instructed and said, "Once we're through, stay behind me. Until we know what we face, I'll lead the way."

Taking both Malek's and Rika's hands, Sabine stepped into the portal and pulled the seer and dragon shapeshifter with her. Magic was unpredictable, and she wasn't willing to risk Rika's seer abilities interfering with the direction of the portal. Sabine should be able to offer some added protection to Bane and Malek through the bonds they shared with her.

For a moment, she was suspended in gray nothingness. A tingle of magic coated her skin. It was the same feeling she'd had after stepping through the long-forgotten doorways in Akros, a remnant from a time when the gods had walked this world.

There was no need to breathe in this space. They were at one with the universe, in a place in between life and death—a place that held the promise of creation and the destruction of life. It was power in its purest form.

She gathered her companions in her thoughts,

surrounding them with a protective shield of magic. It was too easy to lose oneself in this in-between place without a guide.

Rika was fluid, like water flowing through her hands. It made sense since magic didn't always work around seers. She bubbled Rika quickly and then moved on to Malek.

His essence roared like a burning flame, scalding to the touch and capable of unfathomable destruction. She instinctively recoiled, realizing with shocked horror that Malek had the power to burn through the nothingness and destroy her with the barest of thoughts.

He wouldn't. Malek loved her. Of that, she was certain beyond all doubts. And it was through his love that Sabine could protect and shelter him. She dove toward him, surrounding him with her love. Water would extinguish his light, and air would suffocate him. Only by softening the edges of his internal fire could she protect both herself and the dragon she loved. He sensed her immediately, his flame dimming to prevent her from harm. She smiled inwardly and pulled him closer, allowing the banked ember of his power to warm her from within.

Bane, on the other hand, was tied to her on another level through their blood bond. She didn't have to seek him out; he simply was there, in her thoughts. Unlike Malek, Bane was the absence of flame, the coal where flames originated. She sent out a pulse of magic, trying to deepen her tie to him.

The fire imp's venom infecting Bane surged upward, trying to push aside her power. No! She wouldn't allow this to stand, not here, not in this place where magic ruled supreme. With grim determination, she struck, piercing through the magic to penetrate the darkest part of Bane's essence. He was true nothingness, a complete absence of light.

She sent her light into him and heard the echo of a scream in her mind. She didn't know if it was her, the sorceress who twisted the curse, or Bane. It didn't matter. She wouldn't lose him. She struck again and again, pushing more of her light outward. Only through brightness could the shadows around Bane deepen. He clawed his way toward her, the shadows allowing him a foothold to navigate the path with her.

Exhausted, Sabine pulled back and focused on the nothingness. Time didn't exist in this in-between place. They could have been here for minutes or decades, and it would still be the same. Even so, she couldn't linger. Things hunted in the in-between, and they were drawn to life essences the way a shark scented blood in the water.

Gathering her strength, Sabine searched the nothingness for a trace of Blossom's essence or for the edges of the doorway Faerie had created. The echo of power was faint, a miniscule ribbon of light, like a dimming candle flame. Using her will to direct their destination, she pushed everyone through the opposite side of the barrier and landed lightly on the rocky ground.

A blast of heat greeted them, and the ground rumbled beneath their feet. The sharp tang of burning metal hung in the air and coated her tongue. Sabine coughed and blinked rapidly, trying to adjust her eyes to the dark surroundings. She held out a hand and summoned a light source.

Her eyes widened at the sight of Bane standing beside her. Sabine took a step forward, drinking in the image of the fearsome and haughty demon. Bane had changed, almost as though he'd sloughed off his own glamour to reveal his true appearance. The night's shadows had always encompassed him, but it appeared as though a fire had lit him from within and was contained only by his skin and strength of will. The deep vibrant red color of his skin now gleamed with power while his horns shone with a silver light, reflecting the silver color in his eyes.

Unable to resist, Sabine touched his gleaming red arm and felt his magic pulse against her fingertips. Her own Unseelie power flared to life, and her skin glowed like moonlight, reacting to his nearness. She stared up at him, realizing for the first time that she was truly seeing him and everything he was. He was power incarnate, an arrogant prince of the night whose magic had returned in full.

"Why didn't you tell me?" Sabine asked softly, her heart hurting with the knowledge he'd denied the truth of himself for so long. She'd been in hiding for ten years, but he'd been doing it for much longer. It was no wonder he often commented about hating her glamour when he was hiding similar secrets.

Bane gazed at her, some unnamed emotion in his eyes. "I cannot be as I am and still remain with you on the surface, little one. I choose to remain by your side as your chosen bloodsworn general."

"Oh, Bane," she murmured, wishing she'd understood the extent of his sacrifice. Staying with her and denying this part of himself must have been unbearable. It was the equivalent of cutting off one of your limbs.

She still didn't understand why he'd accompanied Dax to the surface all those years ago. Dax might have been exiled, but Bane had refused to speak about his reasons for leaving the underworld. Whatever it was had to be important for him to cut off his ties to his strength.

"You both look like pure magic," Rika whispered, staring at them awestruck. "Sabine, even your crown is glowing."

"This is why Sabine had to live among humans and couldn't hide among your people," Malek said with a frown. "Your magic calls to hers. Her family would have known she was still alive."

"Indeed," Bane replied, still watching Sabine.

Sabine lowered her hand, but her glow didn't fade completely. She considered reining it in, but it helped cut through some of the shadows her light source didn't touch. Sabine looked around, trying to get her bearings and searching for any sign of Blossom. The portal behind them was gone, revealing only a cave wall.

The cave didn't look entirely natural. Or at least, it was unlike anything Sabine had ever seen. The walls were solid black, but flecks of crystal broke through the darkness like stars. Her summoned light source made the crystals sparkle and shine as though fractured diamonds were embedded within it. It was beautiful, but there was something odd about it. Sabine couldn't put her finger on what exactly bothered her about the walls.

It appeared as though they were at some sort of waypoint, with multiple tunnels branching in different directions. Blossom could have traveled down any of them in a blind panic.

Sabine started to call for Blossom, but Malek clamped his hand over her mouth and drew her against himself. Sabine froze. In the distance, she heard a low scuttling noise, like hundreds of creatures moving along the rocky path. Rika whimpered and scrambled closer to them.

"Shh," Malek urged next to her ear before removing his hand from her mouth. "Something awakens."

In a low voice, Bane said, "The dragon is right. I can feel something in the distance stirring. It's not a life force but something else. Sentient."

"What is it?" Sabine asked quietly, trying to recall some of the feared creatures that lived in the depths of the under-world. "A revenant?"

"No. It's doesn't feel like one of the animated corpses," Bane said with a frown. "I'm not familiar with this area of the underworld, nor the creatures lurking here. These rocks are different from the ones in our common tunnels or even our cities. We could be days away from reaching the heart of the volcano."

Rika's eyes widened. "A volcano?"

Bane gave her a curt nod. "Yes. The volcano is the lifeblood of the underworld and where the demon king claims his home. Like a heart that beats, the core of the volcano sends out its pulse throughout the caverns to all parts of the world."

Sabine scanned the ground in front of them, but she didn't see any sign of a pixie. "As soon as we find Blossom, we'll head to the heart of the volcano."

Malek frowned, his hand tightening on the hilt of his sword. "Does the demon king know we're here?"

"Kal'thorz can sense my location if he focuses on me, but it's unlikely he yet knows we've crossed into his realm. It's better to keep it that way for as long as possible. We must get around whatever creatures are in our path and approach the city on our own merit to prove ourselves as worthy adversaries. Only then will Sabine impress upon him her own cunning and resourcefulness."

"Can you sense him or the direction of his city?" Sabine asked, counting six different tunnels they could travel. Each looked nearly identical. Her light source illuminated the area where they were standing, but it couldn't penetrate the darkness beyond the tunnel entrances.

If Bane didn't know where they were, they might have a bigger problem than she'd expected. While her magic had affected him while they were inside the portal, pushing past the fire imp's bite had taken a great deal out of her. She didn't trust that she could break the magical hold on Bane again, especially in this realm. It was imperative they hurry and find a cure for Bane before he succumbed to madness.

"If I attempt to sense Kal'thorz directly, it will alert him to our presence. There should be markers in some tunnels that are only visible to my people. We will try to rescue your pixie, but I'm not willing to compromise your safety, Sabine. No matter what, we must secure this alliance."

Malek touched Sabine's arm. She looked up into his blue eyes and saw his concern and determination. "Bane's right. I know how much Blossom means to you. She also means a great deal to me, but your safety must come first. If you fall, the portal will fail. Everyone's lives will be in jeopardy."

Sabine didn't respond. There was no point. It would destroy something inside her to abandon her friend, but she couldn't risk millions of lives by allowing the war between the gods and dragons to scorch the world again. But she wouldn't sacrifice Blossom easily. She'd do everything in her power to find the mischievous pixie and then make sure Blossom didn't chase any more goats through portals.

Bane looked around the cave and frowned. Gesturing toward her light source, he said, "Extinguish your light. It acts as a beacon to the creatures of the dark."

Sabine did as he asked. The world plummeted into darkness, except for Bane's silver-and-red glow and her own skin, which shimmered softly.

Bane pressed his hand against the wall, and the wall lightened. Each of those small glittering crystal specks was somehow reacting to Bane's magic. Sabine's power pulsed in response, and she had the sudden realization that she could also affect the lights. Something about this place called to her on some level she didn't fully understand, even more so than the dwarven city. It was eerily familiar, but she could have sworn she'd never seen anything like this place.

"Wow," Rika said, still holding the small plant tucked under her arm. "It's even prettier than the dwarven caves."

"Blossom can't create a light," Malek said with a frown.

"I'm guessing she would have followed the goat. The ground is too rocky to see any tracks. Would she have traveled far in the darkness?"

"If she glamoured herself like a glowbug, yes. There's another way I can locate her," Sabine said and reached out with her senses. There was a slight tug on her magic, but it was weak. Pushing aside her worry, she pointed toward one of the tunnels. "I can sense her magic that way, but it's fading fast. We need to hurry."

"Stay behind me," Bane said and moved forward. "Do not leave the glittering path, or the creatures who prefer the darkness may decide to lay claim to a bit of flesh."

Malek pressed his hand against Sabine's back. "I'll keep an eye out behind us."

Sabine nodded, his comforting presence offering more relief than she expected. Rika's arm tightened around the small plant while her other hand gripped the hilt of her short sword so tightly that her knuckles turned white.

Sabine followed Bane down the nondescript tunnel. The path stretched out before them in an endless black ribbon, broken only by the small silver crystal flecks that sparkled like stars in the night sky. With each step she took toward the small flicker of Blossom's magic, a strange sense of déjà vu filled Sabine.

The rocky floor beneath her feet began to change and shift. She could see an image in her mind, overlapping the truth of what was in front of her. It was almost as though decorative stepping-stones had once been placed here. They were gone now, but some part of Sabine warned they still existed somewhere in time and space. What she was seeing was possibly an echo of what once had been there.

There was a pattern to the mosaic, and Sabine altered her steps to follow the flow of the stones. A beguiling song rose within her, like distant drums beating a steady rhythm in time with her steps.

Bane halted abruptly and whirled to face her. "What have you done?"

She blinked. "What?"

"You are aligning my heartbeat with your footsteps."

Her brow furrowed, and she shook her head. Bane had always been able to read her life force, but she'd never had such an ability. She could only sense him in the same way she could Blossom.

She looked at the ground, but it was once again simply rock. "I thought I saw carved stepping-stones. Walking upon them was almost hypnotic, like listening to a song." She lifted her gaze to stare at the walls. They were smoother than the ones in the previous tunnel—and achingly familiar. "This place feels alive somehow, like magic that's been asleep too long. It calls to me."

Bane moved closer to her. In a low voice that carried a hint of urgency, he asked, "What did you see?"

"Patterns," she admitted, hearing a pulse in her head. "There were lines and sloped images that were infused with power. The floor was once made from some sort of stone or tile. For a moment, I could see how it once was."

Malek frowned. "It looks like a rock floor to me. I don't sense anything."

Rika worried her lower lip. "Me neither."

"Nor do I," Bane said, a flicker of worry crossing his features. He swept his gaze along the ground and then up the walls. "There are places in the underworld where the veil…" He shook his head. "We need to find the pixie and leave this area."

Sabine frowned at him. "You suspect something?"

Bane hesitated. "I will not speak of such things until I have confirmation. In the meantime, I would ask you to avoid connecting with the essence of the underworld. There are darker magics here that even my people are reluctant to disturb."

Malek moved closer and pressed his hand against her back. Sabine blinked as the sudden fog that had been plaguing her disappeared. The sound she'd been hearing was gone. Now she heard faint scuttling noises as creatures, possibly in the walls, moved around. From farther away, the faint sound of water rushing reached her ears.

She looked up at Malek and asked, "When you touched me, it went away. What did you do?"

His brow furrowed, and he glanced at Bane. "Nothing intentional. Is this why you suggested before that I remain close to her while we're here?"

Bane's expression became pensive. "No, but your magic may mitigate some of the effects from this place. I don't know why Faerie brought us here, but I don't like that Sabine is being affected. This place has an echo to it."

Blossom tugged at the edges of Sabine's mind. The pixie's magic was flickering like a dying ember. Sabine's eyes widened, and she pointed straight ahead. "Hurry! Blossom's in trouble!"

Bane turned and headed back down the corridor, moving at a faster pace. Sabine avoiding looking at the hypnotizing floor and focused on her destination instead. Some part of her warned that if she didn't find Blossom in the next few minutes, the tiny pixie wouldn't survive.

Chapter Nine

Sabine raced down the corridor, following Bane. Behind her, Malek's and Rika's footsteps kept pace with them. In the distance, she caught sight of a faint glow on the ground ahead.

With a burst of magically enhanced speed, Sabine rode an air current until she reached the glowbug lying on the ground. She scooped up the tiny creature, its body limp and unmoving. Its normal golden glow was tinged with gray, as though most of Blossom's pixie dust had already been exhausted. Pixies didn't die; they simply faded away.

"Blossom," Sabine whispered, unable to hide the tremor in her voice.

Rika gasped. "No! She can't die! You can save her, right?"

Malek muttered a curse and placed his hands under Sabine's to keep them steady. "Let me help."

Until that moment, Sabine hadn't realized she was shaking. Relying on Malek's strength to keep her from dropping Blossom, Sabine held one of her hands over her and sent a surge of magic over her glamoured figure. The glowbug's wings twitched slightly and then went still again. It wasn't enough.

"Fight, Blossom," Malek urged, his tone filled with fierce determination. "Open your eyes, and I'll take you soaring in the skies like a dragon."

Tears streaked down Rika's cheeks, her breath hitching on a sob. Sabine sent another stronger burst of magic over Blossom. Her wings flickered and then fell limp.

"Bring the plant closer," Sabine said, motioning for Rika to place the flowers close to Blossom's nose. Between her magic and the plants, she would have expected to see more of a response.

"She's still fading," Sabine muttered, trying to think of a way to lure her back from the edge. She needed a stronger tie to the light. If there was a way she could open another portal, she could send Blossom back to Faerie.

Malek frowned. "When you were injured back in Akros, you nearly died because you were keeping your glamour up. If Blossom's doing the same thing, she's expending magic she can't afford to lose."

Sabine's eyes widened. Of course. With renewed determination, Sabine gathered her magic within her.

The mechanics of the glamour used by pixies was different than what Sabine used. Centuries of relying upon their illusions to survive had honed the pixies' ability into one of the strongest forms of magic found anywhere in Faerie. While Sabine could craft skilled illusions that were virtually undetectable among the fae, she was an anomaly. Most fae either lacked the interest or the ability to craft such intricate masks.

Sabine sharpened her magic in her mind, forging it into a tool like the edge of a knife. Using her fingernail as a focus, she slid the sharp edge of the magic as close to Blossom's skin as she dared. She leaned in closer, careful not to injure the pixie while she sought the barely perceptible gap where Blossom's true appearance met her illusion.

With a sigh of relief, she slipped inside and pierced the pixie's glamour from within. Blossom's figure shimmered for a moment and then the illusion fell away to reveal the pixie's true appearance.

Blossom's blonde hair spilled out across Sabine's palm. Her normally luminescent skin was gray and ashen. Her eyes were closed, her body still limp and unresponsive. Sabine's breath hitched. Pixies were such fierce yet fragile creatures. Blossom must have panicked and burned too brightly, desperate to find a way out or a source of magic to sustain her.

"Is—Is she going to be okay?" Rika asked, leaning closer to Blossom.

Sabine hesitated. There might be a way to save her, but it could also change Blossom into something… more. Pixies were lesser fae. Their capacity for magic was great, but it could never equal the power of the sidhe, the royal fae. If she tried to force Blossom into accepting more potent magic, it could change her very nature.

If there were consequences down the road, they'd have to deal with it. She wasn't going to lose Blossom.

She turned toward Malek and said, "I need you to prick my finger. I can't put Blossom down to do it myself. My connection to this plane of existence is the only thing currently sustaining her, but it won't last long."

Malek nodded and withdrew his knife.

"Blood magic? On a pixie?" Bane demanded, his eyes flashing silver. He glanced at Malek and Rika before focusing on her again. "You offer too much, Sabine. A pixie cannot understand the magnitude of this sacrifice."

Sabine met his gaze, knowing what he was reluctant to say in front of their audience. Some magic wasn't exactly forbidden, but it was highly discouraged. The beastpeople and kumili races had stemmed from a magic like Sabine was about to attempt.

"She's not just a typical pixie, Bane," Sabine said, cradling Blossom in her hands. "She's the leader of my spy network, one of my advisors, and someone who has proven both in deeds and words that she is worthy of this gift. What she makes of it in time will be her choice."

Bane glared at her for a moment and then turned away, scanning the hallways for approaching enemies. His silence spoke volumes. He might not care much for pixies as a general rule, but Blossom had proven herself to him. Sabine doubted any other pixie had commanded the respect of a demon.

"Which finger?" Malek asked, cupping her hand.

She curled her fingers under, exposing only her index finger. With almost surgical precision, he pierced her skin. A drop of blood welled to the surface.

With a silent prayer to whatever gods might be listening, Sabine allowed one drop to fall on each of Blossom's wings. Her blood intermingled with the glittering pixie dust, smearing across Sabine's palm. Blossom's wings began to glow, but she didn't stir.

Infusing her breath with the power of her ancestors, Sabine leaned down and said, "By blood and magic, and by my rights to both, I gift you this power to use as you see fit— no ties to me or mine, beyond those gifted from love and friendship."

Return to me and live, she ordered silently, her blood carrying the command through Blossom's body. Sabine's skin shone more brilliantly than moonlight as power surged to the surface. Her markings flared with silver and gold, and the air surrounding them charged with electricity. Her hair lifted from a magical wind that filled the cavern with a tidal wave of power.

Sabine's light surrounded the pixie, enveloping her in silver and gold. Blossom's body lifted into the air, propelled upward by the magic, and hovered over Sabine's outstretched hand. Blossom arched her back and blinked open her eyes with a gasp. Her wings glowed with the brightness of the sun, moving so fast they were little more than a blur.

Shrieks sounded in the distance, and the scuffing noise in the walls grew louder. Malek leaped to his feet, drawing his sword. Bane crouched, roaring a warning to whatever was approaching. The noise muffled, but there was heaviness in the air that hadn't been there before.

"Any chance those creatures won't attack?" Malek asked quietly, his hand still gripping his sword.

"Don't count on it," Bane said, his eyes pure molten silver. "They won't be able to resist the lure of Sabine's magic for long. Her blood and power have awakened everything in this part of the underworld."

Blossom ran her hands down the front of her rainbow-colored dress and then glanced behind her at her wings. Turning back toward Sabine with wide eyes, Blossom asked, "I'm still here? You saved me?"

Sabine smiled. "Yes. You're still you, and you're still here. How do you feel?"

Blossom darted forward and hugged her neck. "I think I'm good. Really good. Like five taps of honey good. Maybe even more."

Bane harrumphed. "The quiet was nice while it lasted."

Blossom blew a raspberry at Bane and then zipped around them. Rika grinned in delight. Without sheathing his weapon, Malek offered his hand to Sabine and helped her stand.

"Be careful, Blossom," Sabine warned, feeling a little light-headed from the magnitude of the magic she'd attempted. "You'll need to conserve your strength. I won't be able to sustain you until I recover."

Blossom peered over her shoulder at her vibrating wings. "Something's wrong, Sabine! I can't stop moving my wings. Are they broken?"

Sabine winced. "They'll stop vibrating soon enough, but you may have a bit of a power boost for the foreseeable future. It'll sustain you while you're in the underworld, but you may have an adjustment period once we're back on the surface. Try to take it a little easy while your magic equalizes."

Blossom landed on Sabine's shoulder and tugged a lock of her silvery hair. "I saw the Great Garden, Sabine! It had every flower in it! I could spend eternity tasting all the yummy nectar, and there would always be more. I wanted to go inside, but I wasn't allowed."

"What's the Great Garden?" Rika asked.

Sabine frowned. "It's believed to be one of the largest gardens in the in-between realm. It's a remnant from the time when the gods walked the land. Supposedly, it's impossible for pixies or anyone else to visit without the assistance of the gods or their messengers."

Blossom grinned widely. "It normally is. But the portal dropped us in a spot where the veil is thinner. I kept popping in and out, trying to find my way back to you. The goat went a different direction, but I couldn't resist the flowers. They were so pretty, Sabine. You should have seen it!"

Bane's head whipped around to face Blossom. "You passed through the veil?"

Blossom nodded. "It's not usually so easy. Normally, we have to search really hard for the in-between places."

"In between life and death," Sabine whispered, recalling

the last time she'd moved to one of the in-between areas. The Huntsman had brought her back, but she'd had to provide him with a suitable sacrifice to power the magic. If Blossom had truly been in the in-between, Sabine should have needed a stronger pull than two drops of fae blood to bring her back.

Malek frowned and pressed his hand against Sabine's back. "When you were walking down the tunnel, you said you were seeing stepping-stones on the ground. Were you passing through the veil without us realizing it?"

Sabine floundered, wondering if such a thing were possible. "Did I fade?"

Rika shook her head. "No. I didn't see anything different about you."

Bane scowled. "There are some areas of the underworld that are forbidden to trespass. I believe we may have ended up in one of them. We should not linger here. Those creatures will grow bolder the longer we delay."

Sabine nodded. The entire place was making her edgy, and whatever was moving around in the walls wasn't helping. "How do we find our way to the heart of the volcano?"

Bane cocked his head as though listening for something. "The call is faint in this area. That should not be…" He frowned and shook his head. "We continue down this forgotten path. All roads eventually lead to the heart."

"That sounds almost poetic," Rika said, adjusting the plant back under her arm and falling into step behind Bane. "I see magic coating the walls in this part of the tunnel. It looks really old. Do you know what it does?"

"Most of the tunnels in the underworld are lava caves, little seer," Bane said quietly, leading the way down the tunnel. "They can be sealed off and flooded with molten lava to exterminate trespassers. This particular tunnel also has crystals embedded in the wall, which allows me to illuminate our path. Some of the more recent tunnels have sconces lit with fae fire."

Blossom sat on Sabine's shoulder and rubbed her nose. "Can dragons survive lava?"

"Some dragons can," Malek said. "It's not altogether pleasant, but we can immerse ourselves for short periods of time. It requires a fair bit of our magic."

"I want to be a dragon! Sabine, will you make me look like a dragon?"

Sabine arched her brow. "I think you make a much better pixie than a dragon."

Blossom sniffled and itched her nose again. "I do, but I think I'd like to be a dragon for a day. Just to try it."

She sneezed loudly. With a flash of light, Blossom disappeared. In her place was a small dragonfly with golden wings. Her bug eyes turned in Sabine's direction, her wings humming loudly.

Malek arched his brow. "A dragonfly? Not sure if I should be insulted or not."

Bane snarled at Blossom. "Your queen ordered you to conserve your magic. Instead, you waste the gift that she could scarcely afford to offer. If your carelessness causes any harm to her, I *will* eat you, bug."

Concerned something might be wrong, Sabine captured Blossom in her hands. Blossom didn't waste magic when there wasn't a strong source nearby. She might be inquisitive and fun-loving, but pixies harbored memories of the Starving Times. They remembered what it had been like when their ancestors had died during the war between the dragons and gods.

Taking care not to damage Blossom's fragile wings, she said, "I need you to change back, Blossom. We have to keep moving."

Blossom's image wavered, and she turned back into her

normal pixie self. Her eyes were wide with horror. She rubbed her nose and exclaimed, "I didn't mean to do it! Sabine, I didn't mean to glamour—" She sneezed again. With another flash of light, a brightly colored bluebird took Blossom's place. She chirped and flew into the air, flapping her wings in agitation. She changed back almost immediately.

"What's wrong with her?" Rika asked.

Sabine frowned. "Pixies aren't exactly compatible with high magic. Her body may be trying to expel the excess power in the safest way it knows how."

Bane muttered something about crunchy bugs and picking wings out of his teeth.

Blossom sneezed even louder. Light formed around her, shifting her image to a bright blue-and-silver butterfly.

Rika made a strangled noise and said, "I hope she doesn't get stuck like that."

Sabine grimaced. Rika had been accidentally given wings and antenna during a magical mishap. For a while, Sabine hadn't been sure she'd be able to restore the girl's normal appearance.

Blossom turned back to her normal pixie form a moment later. With a loud wail, she cried, "I'm allergic to the underworld!"

"Keep your voice down," Bane said, his voice carrying a hint of steel. "There are already creatures tracking us. We do not need to draw the entire underworld's attention to us."

Blossom squeaked and darted to Sabine's shoulder, burrowing under her hair. Everyone else fell silent and began moving again. Malek's hand tightened on the hilt of his sword, while Rika unsheathed her short sword.

"I'm sorry, Sabine. I really didn't mean to do it." Blossom scooted closer to Sabine's neck. She was trembling hard enough that Sabine worried she might fall. At least she'd temporarily stopped sneezing.

Determined to distract the pixie, Sabine asked quietly, "Blossom, will you tell me about the garden you saw?"

She was partly curious about the garden but even more so about Blossom's ability to penetrate the veil. In ancient times, when the gods had still walked the world, she'd heard some fae and other creatures had possessed such a gift. If Blossom knew how it was done, it could open all sorts of possibilities for the future.

Blossom tugged lightly on Sabine's hair as she braided. The action often soothed the pixie. "I only got to see it through the gate. He told me I wouldn't be allowed to leave the garden if I entered by myself."

"You spoke with someone at the garden? Who? Another pixie?"

"The Huntsman," Blossom said with a grin. "He said he'll let me visit the garden if you accompany me. Can we go, Sabine? Pretty please? I saw this really pretty blue-and-gold rose near the entrance. I've never seen a flower like it before."

Sabine tensed. The Huntsman? She knew he had the ability to navigate the in-between, but why would he warn Blossom away from the Great Garden?

The Huntsman's interest in her activities and those of her friends was worrying. He was outside of normal fae society —and something far more powerful and ancient than she understood. He was the leader of the Wild Hunt, the bogeyman of Faerie, and stuff of nightmares. He'd saved her life, even though he'd been tasked with ending it. She had nothing to offer him, no great power or ability that accounted for his interest. And there was the small music box he'd left her as a gift…

"That's not going to happen," Malek said, his expression darkening. "Sabine's not leaving this plane to step into the in-between again. She nearly died last time."

Bane narrowed his eyes. "I agree."

Rika looked up at Sabine and said softly, "The Huntsman saved your life. Maybe he needs to talk to you again, but he can't come to you for some reason."

Sabine frowned. "There are scarce few places in the world where the Wild Hunt can't trespass. Razadon is one, but the Huntsman proved he alone could enter the heart of the dwarves' mountain. I believe the Wild Hunt can enter the underworld."

"They can," Bane replied. "It does not happen often, but I have seen the riders myself. They do not, however, pass the boundaries into Harfanel."

"All the more reason not to linger," Malek said quietly.

The scuttling noise was growing louder, as though the creatures in the darkness were growing bolder. Bane growled loudly, his eyes flashing silver again. The noises quieted, but not nearly as much as earlier.

Blossom whimpered. "I really don't like this place, Sabine. Are we there yet?"

"Perhaps by the time you finish braiding," she murmured, reassured slightly when Blossom tugged on her hair again.

The tunnel path and walls were changing from the coarse rock. They were smoothing out, offering hints of the tiles Sabine had seen earlier. A deep sadness filled Sabine with each step, but she wasn't sure why. It felt as though something important had been abandoned and lost.

Sabine stepped lightly, avoiding the broken mosaic tiles on the ground. The patterns were similar to the ones she'd seen in her earlier vision. Perhaps Blossom wasn't the only one who had almost slipped through reality.

"What exactly happened when you saw the Huntsman, Blossom? Did he show you where the veil was thin?"

"Nope. That was an accident. He was waiting for me at the entrance to the garden. He said all pixies try to go there before they fade from the world. I told him I wasn't ready to fade, but he just smiled." In a softer voice, Blossom muttered, "I might have yelled at him. He made me mad."

Sabine whipped her head toward Blossom and whispered, "You *yelled* at the Huntsman?"

Blossom nodded. "You still need me. I can't fade yet. There's too much to do. We have a world to save, demons to dust, and honeycakes to eat. But the garden was so pretty behind the gate. I asked him if I could take just a quick peek."

Sabine blew out a breath. "I see."

"He said no." Blossom sighed. "That's when he told me he would allow it, but only if you accompanied me into the garden. I tried to tell him you didn't know the way. He said you could find it in your memories. I wasn't sure what that meant. Then he told me it was time to leave. You were calling me back to you."

Memories? Some fae, particularly those of the royal families who held the purest bloodlines, could tap into their ancestors' collective memories. That could possibly explain how Sabine had seen the vision. If one of her ancestors had walked this path before, she could have overlaid the image with one from her archived memories.

Sabine stepped around a chunk of rock that had dislodged from the wall, scratching her ankle on one of the crystals jutting out from the wall of the narrow passage. She stumbled, but Malek grabbed her arm to steady her. She threw him a grateful look. In addition to the missing tiles, something had caused a great deal of damage to this tunnel.

A loud howl pierced the air. It was coming from somewhere behind them.

Bane muttered a curse, his eyes flashing silver. "Hellhounds. They've begun their hunt. One howl to acknowledge. Twice in pursuit. Thrice when they locate their target."

Something screamed. The scuttling noise grew louder again. A light smattering of dust fell from the ceiling.

Malek pointed in the direction they were heading. "We need to find a more defensible position. Now!"

"Run!" Bane shouted. "The hellhounds will destroy anything in their path. We need to make sure we keep those creatures between us and them. At the very least, it may slow them down."

Chapter Ten

They raced forward, no longer mindful of their surroundings. From behind them, the screams of dying creatures pierced Malek's ears, while the smell of blood and carnage hung heavily in the air. Another howl pierced the darkness, followed immediately by another scream. The creatures were drawing closer.

"That's the second howl! We've got movement!" Blossom yelled, flying to land on top of Sabine's head. She gripped Sabine's crown tightly and shouted, "Faster, people! Put your backs into it!"

"I'm going to swat you, bug," Bane threatened.

"Not with how slow you're running! I thought demons were supposed to be tough. You'll be hellhound lunch if you don't move!"

Unsure of whether they were running directly toward danger, Malek fought to suppress instincts that demanded he stay and fight. Predators didn't run away. Only the knowledge that Sabine was in danger allowed him to retreat. Dragons *always* protected their mates.

Rika stumbled on one of the fallen tiles, nearly dropping Blossom's potted plant.

"You okay?" Malek asked, grabbing her arm to steady her. While the rest of the group could navigate well in low-light conditions, Rika didn't possess preternatural vision. The glow from the walls wasn't bright enough to cut through much of the darkness at the speed they were running.

"I've got her," Sabine said, flicking out her wrist. A band of power surrounded Rika, keeping her upright as they ran.

Claws scraped along the rocky ground behind them. They were running out of time. Malek's blood hummed as his power surged to the surface. He couldn't shift in such close quarters without risking harm to anyone else. Fortunately, his magic could also be used to supplement his hand-to-hand combat skills. As long as these creatures bled, they could die.

The tunnel ended abruptly. A large cavern was in front of them with a set of large black doors that were sealed shut. Dark red and silver runes had been etched into the doors, while words in some unknown language had been carved overhead.

They skidded to a halt. Bane cursed in a harsh, guttural language.

Blossom lifted into the air. "Those words at the top are written in the Old Language. Can you read it, Sabine?"

"The Hall of the Gods," Sabine whispered, her face paling. "This is the entrance to…" She shook her head as though to clear it. "I've heard stories, but I didn't realize it still existed." She reached out, pausing before she came into contact with the stone doors. "The wards are more complex than anything I've seen."

"Can we get it open?" Malek asked, glancing back toward the tunnel. The creatures were nearly upon them, and they were sorely outnumbered.

"Not without divine intervention," Bane said with a growl. "The Hall has been sealed since the Harbinger of Nightmares abandoned this realm millennia ago. There are multiple protections safeguarding its secrets."

Rika frowned. "There's magic covering the runes on the doors. It's slippery. I can't seem to look directly at it. The magic doesn't *want* me to see it." She cocked her head. "It reminds me of your glamour, Sabine."

Sabine's eyes widened. "Glamour? It makes sense, as an additional layer of security. Can you tell where it begins?"

Rika nodded and reached out, gesturing toward a small area beside the doors. Sabine lifted her hand again to trace the edge of the magic. She hummed, the wordless song a haunting melody. Her magic shifted from silver to gold as the glamour reacted to her tune. A moment later, the doors changed ever so slightly. The runes sharpened in appearance as though they were no longer out of focus.

Blossom cheered. "You did it! I can see the warding now."

Sabine smiled. "We both did. Faerie wouldn't have sent us in this direction if we didn't have a way to open the doors. Now we need to find a way to unlock the rest of the protections."

Another scream from something dying drew Malek's attention back to the tunnel. His hand tightened around the hilt of his sword. "We've got company. There's not enough space here for me to shift without bringing down the tunnel."

"Then prepare to fight," Bane said, his silvered eyes turning to stare at the dark tunnel. "The hellhounds are part of the Hall's defense. They're driving those creatures to us. They won't stop until every living thing in their path is dead, including us."

"Stay close and fight defensively," Sabine said to Rika.

Dozens of large arachnoid creatures scuttled forward. They were nearly the size of wolves. Their exoskeletons were a deep black color, while yellow ooze dripped from their fangs.

"Spiders?" Blossom shrieked. "Spiders shouldn't be that big! What kind of garden do those suckers live in?"

Malek sliced through the first one, leaping back as one of its sawtooth legs tried to swipe at him. He spun toward the next, narrowly missing a spat of the yellow ooze it had shot at him. Using his magic to fuel his strength and speed, he took the head of the creature.

"Watch their venom," Bane warned, swiping his claws down one of the arachnoids' necks.

Sabine threw shimmering orbs of condensed power. Each one burst apart, expanding like a magical explosion to cut down dozens of creatures at once. It was effective, but Malek wasn't sure how long she could keep up the attack.

"Die, evil fiends!" Blossom shrieked and darted in between their legs, tripping the creatures as they tried to catch the pixie. One after another, they toppled over and then scrambled back to their feet.

Rika shouted a battle cry and lifted her short sword, hacking at the legs on the creatures Blossom targeted. Malek grinned at their teamwork and turned his attention toward the nearest attacker. He quickly cut it down before facing the next, each one brandishing its sharpened legs.

A creature struck out at Malek, but Sabine shot her hand out and speared the creature with another burst of magic. His gaze met hers, and in that moment, the connection between them flared to life. Love and undeniable need surged within him, mirroring the emotions in her eyes.

Sabine gave him a teasing smile. "Try not to die, will you? I have plans with you later."

"I wouldn't dream of disappointing you," Malek said with a grin.

"A dragon that can die from a spider bite isn't much of an

ally," Bane said, piercing his claws through an exoskeleton. "You'll be the laughingstock of the underworld."

Malek snorted. Demons and dragons might have been natural enemies, but he'd begun to begrudgingly respect and even enjoy bickering with Bane. The demon had a dry sense of humor, but his loyalty toward Sabine was undeniable.

One of the creatures screamed at Rika, spitting yellow ooze in her direction. She dove to the side, screaming when the goo made contact. Malek brought down his sword, slicing the creature in two before kicking another away from the seer. There was no end to them. They kept coming.

Sabine grabbed Rika's wrist, pulled some moisture from the air, and sent a pulse of cool water over the seer's skin. Rika gave her a curt nod before turning back to the fight, bringing down her sword on another creature.

Sticky yellow goo coated the ground, filling the air with a harsh and bitter stench that burned his eyes and the back of his throat. Rika coughed and choked, dropping to one knee.

"Too much venom!" Blossom shouted, her wings fluttering wildly as she darted away from one of the giant spiders.

"We need these bodies cleared," Malek said, cutting down another creature.

A large fireball erupted from Bane's hands and burned the bodies to ash. Sabine raised her hands, whipping the heated air into the tunnel to kill even more of the creatures. Perspiration broke out on Sabine's forehead, and she staggered. Her hand pressed against the wall, but it was obvious she was struggling to remain upright. She was burning out too fast.

"Take what you need from me," Malek called to Sabine. He might not be able to safely use his dragonfire in such close confines, but his magic could help supplement hers.

Sabine nodded and pulled on Malek's power, cutting

down another wave of creatures. The direness of their situation struck him. She never would have weakened him unless she was close to passing out. He attacked another one, killing it cleanly before yanking his sword from the fallen body. It came away with more of the yellow ooze. They must have already killed dozens of them, yet they still came.

More of the arachnids screamed from somewhere within the tunnel.

"I don't think there's only one hellhound," Rika said, perspiration dripping down her face. "It sounds like a pack."

"Keep fighting or die, little seer," Bane said, using his claws to dissect another arachnoid.

"No one is dying," Sabine said and unsheathed her knife. She sliced it down the palm of her hand. A sharp wind blew through the tunnel, carrying with it the scent of old blood and sulfur.

Sabine stepped forward, blood dripping down her fingers. Kneeling, she slapped her hand against the ground and shouted, "*Bela'guardi!*"

The rock wall trembled. Vines burst out of the crystals embedded in the lavastone walls. Sharp, golden thorns jutted from the branches and wove together over the tunnel entrance to form a thick barrier. The spiderlike creatures crashed into it, their sharp legs trying to pierce the thick vines. Every place they cut through, the vines grew back thicker than before.

"It's gold, not silver?" Malek asked, frowning at the sharp thorns that were piercing the hardened exoskeletons. Yellow ooze dribbled out from beneath the vined obstacle.

"I used both fae and dwarven magic," Sabine said and stood, curling her injured hand into a fist. "The hellhounds are fire-based. It won't stand against them, but it'll give us a few minutes to figure out a plan and allow the hellhounds to take out some spiders."

"We need to get these doors open," Malek said, gesturing at the dark entryway that took up most of the wall. The power emanating from them was stronger than he'd expected. He knew instinctively that he couldn't force these doors open, even in dragon form, without causing damage to the foundation of this cavern.

In the distance, an eerie wailing drifted toward them like fog. It grew in volume and intensity until the air was thick with the harsh taint of undead magic. The sound was like claws digging into his skull. Rika cried out, dropping to the ground. Even Sabine staggered, her face pale and drawn. Blossom dove under Sabine's hair, her wings tinged with red.

Malek clutched his head and lowered his sword, trying to remain on his feet as the magic wrapped tendrils of ice around him. His urge to shift was nearly overwhelming. He needed to destroy whatever was approaching. It would steal all their lives if it wasn't stopped.

Sabine waved her hand sharply, causing the vines to grow even more dense. The plaits wound themselves even tighter, blocking the worst effects. Malek took a shaky breath, but the urgency inside him continued to beat against his skin. He *needed* to change.

"Wraiths. They're being called by your blood," Bane said, grabbing Sabine's bleeding hand. "This forsaken curse won't allow me to heal you."

Malek cut a strip from the bottom of his shirt. Dammit. He hadn't realized the bite would prevent Bane from healing her. Without that ability, Sabine would be even more vulnerable down here. "How much does it hurt?"

"It's not a serious wound," Sabine said, the comment typical of a fae's avoidance to admit weakness. They might not lie, but they danced around the razor's edge of truth.

Malek wrapped the bandage around her hand. When he

tied it off, Sabine kissed his cheek and walked to the vined barrier. She plucked several leaves from the vines.

Malek frowned and took a step toward her. "What are you doing?"

"Protecting our sanity," Sabine said, closing her hands over the top of the leaves. She lowered her head, the tips of her ears poking through her hair. Her voice was soft and musical as she murmured words of power over the leaves.

Sabine handed several leaves to each of them. "Put these in your ears. They'll suppress the sound from the wraiths or any other undead creatures."

"Life combating death?" Rika asked, using her thumb to stick the leaves in her ears.

"Exactly."

"If you can't deactivate the wards, maybe the goddess's magic will open the doors," Blossom said, hovering in front of Sabine.

"Possibly." Sabine placed her hand on Malek's arm, the contact sending a light caress of magic over his skin. "Wraiths can't be killed, but they don't like the kiss of metal either. If you can buy me some time, I may be able to break the wards on the doors."

"My sword is yours, as is my magic." Malek covered his hand with hers, the contact helping to suppress the worst of his protective instincts. The marks of power on Sabine's fair skin glowed softly, a balance of both silver and gold. His eyes roamed over her delicate features, taking in the way the blue stones from her crown reflected the light that shone brilliantly from within her. With her silvery hair partially unbound and cascading over her shoulders, she looked like an avenging warrior goddess from the old legends.

Malek grabbed her and hauled her against himself, her lavender eyes widening for a moment as she stared up at him. When he wrapped his heated power around her in a possessive claim, Sabine's body softened against his and her eyes fluttered closed. The dragon within him wanted to roar in victory that she was his. He kissed her deeply, infusing her with more magic to strengthen her innate gifts. He broke their kiss and released her, whirling away to face the first of the undead creatures.

~

"WOW, THAT WAS KINDA HOT, SABINE," Blossom said, landing on Sabine's head.

"Yes, it was," Sabine said, nearly swaying from the power boost. "Now let me concentrate."

Sabine stared at the runes etched into the doors, trying to block out the sounds of battle and muted screams from the wraiths. The language was an archaic form of the Old Language, only taught to those from royal bloodlines or Seelie who were dedicated to serving in the temples of the lost gods. It was the foundation of the words of power, the magic that had been among the sharpest weapons used during the Dragon War.

Focusing her senses, she traced the edge of one of the runes. It was achingly cold, its protection powerful enough to penetrate the deepest layers of her magical protections. She shivered and pulled away, moving to the next one and searching for a weakness or clue to unlock the ward.

Blossom's wings fluttered. "The goddess says she'll open the doors if you'll grant her a favor."

"She's quick to make such promises," Sabine said, glancing down at the marks on her wrist. They were almost always gold now, and the glow was creeping up her arm. She'd been trying to glamour it as much as possible, but she knew her friends had noticed. Her magic had been changing over the past few weeks, becoming more unpredictable.

Falling further into debt with the renegade goddess wouldn't be wise. She had to try to solve this on her own, but she wouldn't allow anyone to be harmed either.

"I think you can do it without her help, Sabine."

Sabine stepped closer to the doors, studying them and allowing the magic to penetrate her defenses. Some of the oldest and most powerful magic required an immersion of self. It was the same principle behind the power of the memorywalkers and dreamweavers. Sabine took a steadying breath... and merged.

A biting chill wrapped around her, like tiny pinpricks of icicles embedding themselves under her skin. She inhaled sharply and pushed aside the pain, needing to lay herself completely bare and allow the doors to determine her worthiness. She hoped her ancestry was enough to grant them access.

"As we will it, so shall we rule," Sabine said, infusing her voice with power as she translated the runes etched into the black doors. "In all things, *Balance.*"

The runes glowed as she spoke the ancient words. She ignored the shrieks from the wraiths and the sharp metallic twang of Malek's sword bouncing off of them. The hellhounds' third howl was close enough to touch, but she couldn't risk breaking her connection with the doors. If she did, the backlash could kill them all.

She moved to the next line and read, "By blood and magic, by land and sea, by the heavens and hells of all the worlds. In all things, *Sacrifice.*"

Light burst forth from the runes, searing Sabine's skin and cutting through the icy coldness that had been gripping her. Sacrifice. The demand ripped through her thoughts.

Sabine yanked the binding off her injured hand and slapped her palm against the doors, fusing her magic into the runes. Drums sounded in her ears. It was the pulse of the land, beating within her. The heat from the runes trailed along Sabine's skin, but she ignored it and forced her consciousness deeper into the magic. It tasted her power, sipping her aura like a fine wine.

"*Sacrifice*," Sabine whispered, closing her eyes and surrendering herself to the magic guarding the doors. "I am Sabin'theoria, daughter of Mali'theoria and great-great-granddaughter of Theoria, First of the Fae and daughter of Lachlina, Bringer of Shadows, and Vestior, Harbinger of Nightmares. I seek entry by rights of blood and magic."

A gong sounded from somewhere behind the doors, its echo cascading through the tunnels. The battle noises faded away. Sabine looked at her injured hand, but it was healed. In its place was a faint gold line on the surface of her palm, but even that was fading.

"You did it!" Blossom cried, clapping her hands together.

Turning, she found Malek with his sword still at the ready, but he wasn't attacking. Neither was Bane. They were both warily watching the hellhounds.

The spiders were dead. The wraiths were gone. The hellhounds had torn through the vined barrier she'd erected. All of them, save one, were lying at the tunnel entrance, watching Sabine and the others with glowing red eyes. The one standing in front was enormous, the size of a small horse rather than a wolf. It reached almost to Sabine's shoulders. Unlike the others, whose fur was dappled gray and shone like moonlight, this one was solid black with a long mane and tail, swishing with a preternatural flame.

Rika leaned back against the wall, wiping the sweat from her face with the back of her arm. "They're not going to kill us, are they?"

Bane grunted. "That remains to be seen. The hellhounds are not only the emissaries of the Wild Hunt. They're also the guardians of the Hall. If they deem our presence undesirable, they'll attack."

The large hellhound continued to stare at Sabine, regarding her with an unmistakable intelligence in his red eyes. This hellhound was *old*, just like the magic that protected this area. He growled softly, but it didn't sound malicious. If anything, it almost sounded welcoming.

He took a step toward her, but Malek moved to stand protectively in front of her. The hellhound's fiery tail whipped in the air, staring at Malek like he might be a tasty morsel to nibble on.

"It's all right." Sabine placed her hand on Malek's arm and moved to stand beside him. She'd expected fear to be the strongest of her emotions, but instead, a strange sense of kinship filled her when she met the hellhound's gaze. Only Balkin, the beastman who had been sworn to protect her from birth, had ever elicited the same feeling.

The hellhound turned his gaze on Sabine. He moved to stand directly in front of her, nearly overwhelming her with the strong scent of sulfur that blanketed his fur.

He angled his head downward in an almost bow, nudging her hand so it rested on the top of his head. She inhaled sharply and then spread her fingers against his silky midnight fur, staring into the depths of his burning red irises.

"*Welcome, daughter of Vestior,*" the hellhound whispered in her mind. "*We have long awaited your arrival.*"

With a loud groan, the doors swung open, revealing the Hall of the Gods.

Chapter Eleven

A long hall stretched out before them. The hellhound nudged her toward the doorway and the darkness beyond it. Sabine held her ground, suddenly wary. Something about this place called to more than her magic. She had the feeling that once she entered, she wouldn't leave unchanged. She just didn't know if it would be for the better.

"Entering the Hall is forbidden," Bane said, eyeing the hellhound beside her. "We will need assurances before entering."

The hellhound growled softly at Bane. Rika sidled closer to the demon, taking care to avoid the hound's fiery tail.

"Not sure we have any other options unless you want to challenge them," Malek said, nodding toward the other hellhounds still blocking the tunnel. They weren't acting in a threatening manner and were deferring to their leader, but that could change in an instant.

"It should be safe to enter if we're with Sabine," Blossom said, tugging on Sabine's hair. "The door wouldn't have opened if she wasn't allowed to go in. Besides, they're not trying to eat us anymore."

The hellhound pushed against Sabine with his large body, more insistent this time. *"You called us with your blood, daughter of Vestior. We have rid the entrance of your enemies. Why do you hesitate?"*

She met its red gaze but only found frank curiosity. "Might I know who I'm addressing?"

The hellhound straightened. *"You may call me Azran."*

"Well met, Azran," Sabine said, tilting her head in greeting. She wasn't sure what sort of acknowledgment was appropriate for a hellhound. "I am known as Sabine to my friends. These are my traveling companions, Malek, Bane, Rika, and Blossom." Sabine gestured toward each of them. "Does the invitation to enter also extend to them?"

Azran inclined his head. *"For this one night, all of you may travel safely through the Hall. However, be warned: None, save the daughter of Vestior, are permitted to cross the threshold to the Well of Dreams. Your oaths will be binding, as are the consequences for violating them."*

"Cool! Mind speech just like the beastpeople?" Blossom asked, peeking through Sabine's hair. "You have my oath! Wells and pixies don't mix anyway."

Rika nodded. "You have mine too. I don't know what this Well of Dreams is, but I won't go near it."

Malek frowned. "Oaths should never be given lightly. What is the Well of Dreams?"

Azran growled softly.

Something flickered in Bane's eyes. "Before the gods abandoned this realm, the Well of Dreams was a place of power. It was said that incomparable magic could be found at the bottom of the well for those brave enough to explore its depths."

"We're not here to expand anyone's magic," Sabine said, shaking her head. "We need to find a cure for you, save Dax, locate another artifact, and secure an alliance with Kal'thorz."

"With the power of the Well, you could accomplish all you hope and more."

Sabine frowned, not liking the calculating gleam in Bane's eyes. "At what cost? I think we have enough to worry about without borrowing more trouble."

"Perhaps, but great power also provides great opportunities. If you are invited to partake, I strongly suggest you consider it. The hellhound has my oath that I will not drink, but I intend to accompany you to the chamber where the Well is housed. I will not trust anyone in the underworld with your safety, no matter what guarantees they provide."

"The demon knows the consequences of violating the sanctity of the Well. We will have his oath not to cross the threshold, or his life. Decide. Now."

A loud, warning growl rumbled from the hellhound. The others rose and snarled. One of them lunged toward Bane, its jaws snapping. Bane extended his claws, but before he could attack, Azran slammed into the challenger, knocking him astride. His massive jaws latched onto the gray's neck. He shook him and then tossed him to the far side of the cavern, slamming him against the wall. The challenger whimpered, crawling away on his belly toward the rest of the pack.

Azran turned his red gaze on Bane and howled, the soul-rendering sound making Sabine's skin prickle in warning. The other hounds took up the call.

"Their magic is changing," Rika whispered, her voice hoarse. "It… hurts."

Blossom squeaked and dove under Sabine's hair. Hugging Sabine's neck, she said, "He's going to summon the wraiths again. Demons can't go near the Well. Pixies can't go in the garden. Don't let him break the rules or we'll all die, Sabine! Make him swear!"

Sabine straightened, prepared to intervene, but Malek grabbed her hand. He pulled her to his side and said, "I suggest you pacify Sabine's new friend, Bane. We only have one way out of here that doesn't involve fighting—and you no longer have the ability to heal your queen."

The hellhound continued to snarl, steam rising from its fur. *"Demon, you will swear, or we will enforce the pact made with the first of your kings."*

Bane's jaw clenched. "I do not hold the ember, hellspawn, nor have I received contradictory orders from my master. For now, I obey Sabin'theoria, my queen and your mistress. If she forbids me to look upon the Well, so be it. That is the only oath you and your kind will receive from me."

The hellhound trotted back to Sabine. When he nudged her hand again, she lifted it and placed it back on his head. At the contact, something inside her eased. She didn't know what ember Bane was referring to, but it probably wasn't the best time to ask.

"I will respect our host's wishes," Malek said, watching the hellhound. "You have my oath I will not approach the Well of Dreams, except to protect the lives of my companions. If I sense any danger or harm to Sabine, I *will* go to her, oath or not." Malek threaded his fingers through hers and lifted her hand to kiss her knuckles. "I have sworn to protect her, and that oath surpasses all others."

Azran bared his teeth at Malek. *"No harm will come to the daughter of Vestior while in our Hall. Our lives are dedicated to safeguarding hers while she is here, but you have our leave to protect her if her life is endangered."*

Malek gave him a curt nod. "Agreed."

"Your companions may enter the Hall, little goddess."

Sabine tilted her head, surprised by the diminutive. Even more puzzling was Azran's more-readily acceptance of

Malek compared to Bane. There was troubled history between demons and hellhounds; she was sure of it.

With her left hand on the hellhound's head and Malek walking on her right, Sabine stepped through the doorway and onto the golden tiles. The six gray hellhounds fell into step behind them, their fiery tails swishing as they walked to create a trail of fire.

The room was enormous, at least half a dozen stories in height. Painted murals lined the walls from floor to ceiling, each so beautiful it almost hurt to look upon them. A tingle from a complex ward dusted her skin when she moved a little too close to one of them. Some of the archivists back in Faerie often used a similar preservative for their more price-less art.

The scenes and locations depicted in the murals were unlike anything she'd seen before. Tall, beautiful, faelike people wearing unusual clothing graced most of the panels. In each one, there were animals that had never walked their world, skies that were the soothing shade of lavender, and odd-looking plants that reflected light like rainbows. Even the weapons were unusual, made from what appeared to be glowing crystals or metals. Some shot lightning or other types of magic.

"Is this a temple?" Rika asked, staring at the chandeliers. Crystal icicles infused with fae-wrought magic dangled from the ceiling to illuminate the room. Blossom flew upward to investigate.

"The Hall of the Gods was said to be a meeting place and forum," Sabine said, her fingers curling into the hellhound's thick fur. "Here, the gods could put aside their differences and make decisions with impunity. Bloodshed was discour-aged within these walls, and old grievances were suspended."

"Yet more lives were lost here than any other place in the

world," Bane said, an odd cadence in his tone. "These golden floors once flowed with blood, and those chandeliers held the intestines of still-living prisoners."

Sabine darted a quick look at Bane, but his face was an expressionless mask. Malek squeezed her hand. He gave her a grim nod, indicating he agreed that trouble was simmering below the surface.

They continued walking through the entrance hall until they reached another set of double doors, which took up most of the wall. With their gargantuan size, no one except maybe a northern giant could hope to physically open the doors. It was another security measure, on the off chance someone managed to penetrate the first line of defenses. The gods guarded their secrets like a jealous mistress.

The doors slowly swung open at their approach. Azran continued to guide them forward, but Sabine noted he automatically slowed his pace if something caught her eye. Although they hadn't yet seen anyone, Sabine didn't have the impression the Hall was empty. It was almost as though if she were to turn her head quickly enough, she might catch a glimpse of someone.

"Are we the only ones here?" Sabine asked Azran.

"*The Hall remains open and available to those of power. We act as a waystation, a junction between worlds. Visitors come, but they can no longer cross the veil to our realm. The Betrayer closed the way.*"

Sabine blinked. Azran spoke in such a way that made her think he knew an alternate history rather than the one she'd learned growing up in Faerie. "Are you saying the Hall also exists outside of our realm?"

Azran chuffed. "*Of course. Vestior and his kin often moved between worlds. You will understand more once you visit the Well of Dreams.*"

Malek arched his brow and gave her a meaningful look. Sabine nodded to indicate she would be careful. She'd already started to slip through the veil once since arriving in the underworld. She had no inclination to repeat the experience.

They entered another room. This one had the appearance of a forum. A large dais was situated toward the front. Behind the dais were towering marble statues, representing some of the different gods of justice, righteousness, and punishment.

Blossom landed on Sabine's shoulder and whispered, "Someone's taking care of this place, Sabine. There wasn't any dust on the chandeliers. I also smelled cleaning wax on the floors. But I didn't see anyone. No footprints. No fur. No feathers. I couldn't find any sign of them!"

"Nor will she," Azran said, despite Blossom's effort to keep her voice quiet.

Blossom bristled, causing Sabine to inwardly sigh. The pixie would take Azran's comment as a personal challenge to locate whoever was maintaining this place. Sabine hoped Blossom wouldn't raise Azran's ire in the process.

Rika yawned, her eyes starting to drift shut despite the novelty of their surroundings. Bane said something to her in a hushed voice. Whatever he'd told her caused the young seer's eyes to fly open. She straightened and marched with overly dramatic steps. Sabine bit back a smile at the tired seer's antics. They'd need to rest soon. Her own fatigue was weighing in the back of her mind.

"You and your followers will be taken to a staging area near the entrance to the Well of Dreams. You may rest there in relative comfort tonight, daughter of Vestior. The Well will summon you once your mind is clear."

Summon? Sabine wasn't sure that sounded good.

"Will you tell me more about the Well, Azran?" Sabine asked, hoping this was part of the reason Faerie had directed them here. *Unless it wasn't Faerie who had opened the way...* The Huntsman also had the ability to manipulate portals, and he'd already shown his hand here—both with Blossom in the garden and in the appearance of the hellhounds.

Azran huffed, smoke rising from his nostrils. "*The Well of Dreams is a repository of knowledge and power. It is both a terrible weapon and an offer of salvation. After you have drunk of its secrets, we will grant your party passage to Harfanel, the capital of the underworld and home to the ember's guardian.*"

Sabine's brow furrowed. Azran's voice no longer had the same echo, indicating he was speaking privately to her. She'd never been particularly skilled at mental communication, but she reached out to the hellhound.

"*While I am honored by the offer to drink of the gods' memories and power,*" Sabine said, struggling to maintain the unfamiliar weight of mind speech, "*I simply seek safe passage to Harfanel. It's my hope to learn more about my heritage once I'm able to return to the Hall.*"

"*You will drink before you leave. Vestior wills it so.*"

Sabine gaped at Azran, the mental thread of communication fraying at her lapse in concentration. Too stunned to be offended by his high-handedness, she sputtered, "You can communicate with him?"

"Who?" Malek asked, glancing at them.

"I believe the hellhounds can speak with the gods the same way pixies can," Sabine said, still reeling from the implications that Vestior was still alive somewhere beyond the boundaries of their world.

He wasn't just her direct blood relative. Vestior was one of the gods who had fought dragons for centuries and disappeared millennia ago. If the hellhounds were his, it was a huge concession for them to permit an enemy dragon to trespass on their warded grounds. Why would Vestior allow such a thing? She couldn't ignore the idea they might be walking into a trap, no matter how comfortable she felt with the hellhound.

"Your companions are safe, provided they keep to their oaths. Vestior is interested in the dragon. He wishes to observe him and the rest of your companions."

Sabine frowned at the hellhound. "My thoughts aren't yours to pick through, Azran. It's rude to spy on people, whether it be their deeds or thoughts."

Azran chuffed with laughter. *"You think loudly, little goddess. Your mind-touch skills are better than you believe. You simply need to visualize your thoughts behind an impregnable shield to make it so."* He bowed his head. *"I will share your comments with Vestior, but he often says, 'A god does not spy. He simply surveys the entirety of his domain.'"*

From the sound of it, she wasn't the first to point out his rudeness. She tilted her head, conceding Azran's point and his suggestion. "And since we're in his Hall, I suppose I can't begrudge him for observing." She sighed. "I'll make an effort to better shield, but in return, I ask that you try not to intrude upon any private thoughts."

"As you will, little goddess."

Sabine closed her eyes for a moment and imagined a dense vined wall protecting her mind. It was the same lesson she'd been taught as a child, but she was sorely out of practice. Once she was sure no wayward thoughts would slip out, she opened her eyes again.

"Sabine?" Malek asked, his expression full of concern. "Perhaps we should return to the tunnel."

She shook her head. If they left, they'd be back in unfamiliar territory, with potential enemies surrounding them. At least Azran and the hellhounds offered them a modicum of protection. If she was going to face the demon king soon, she needed all the strength she could get.

"It's safer for all of us if we remain in the Hall. In addition to Azran noting our lack of privacy here, he was explaining a few things about the Well of Dreams and how it's a place of ritual to unlock additional magic." She paused and then said, "He wants me to drink from the Well before we leave. I'm not agreeing, but I will… consider his request."

"New magic might be problematic," Malek said quietly.

She nodded, not surprised he shared her concerns.

"I like new magic," Blossom said, her wings perking up.

Sabine bit back a smile. "Of course you do."

Azran trotted down another hallway, this one even more splendid than the last. Gold-paneled walls with fantastic imagery surrounded them. Statues of strange creatures that were both beautiful and terrifying had been placed at the entrance to each new scene. Sabine slowed, staring at a mural that sent a cold chill through her.

"Is that the goddess Lachlina? She looks like you," Rika said, pointing at the woman at the center of the image. Unlike the previous versions Sabine had seen, this one was far more detailed and exact.

"Yes, but I've never seen this representation of her," Sabine whispered, pressing her fingers against the goddess markings on her wrist. For the first time since she'd received them, they didn't warm. The goddess was strangely absent within her.

In the mural, a faelike woman was kneeling on the ground, her silvery-white hair thrown back. Her arms were extended in chains, while a group of robed figures surrounded her. At the center was a man who was also cloaked, while a skeletal hand reached out from the folds of his cloth. Purple bands of power shot from his hand, surrounding the imprisoned goddess while she screamed her fury. In the background was a dark circular portal, its appearance reminiscent of a mirror that had been shattered.

"*The Betrayer,*" Azran said with a low growl.

"Your goddess was revered by the dwarves, little one," Bane said, studying the mural in question. "But that is only because she gifted them with great power. In reality, she was a selfish creature and the enemy to many, including the gods and some of the oldest races. Even those who applauded her actions thought her choice in timing was suspect."

"What did she do?" Rika asked.

Sabine studied the image, wondering if this mural depicted the truth of Lachlina's punishment. She'd only heard that Lachlina had been imprisoned for her crimes.

"During a major offensive, and while the gods were otherwise occupied, Lachlina combined several types of magic and infused them into keys that could seal the portal," Sabine explained. "She gave these items to the first races, along with the knowledge of how to use them. It ended the war, but at great cost. The dragons, humans, and other non-native races who remained here became trapped, forever cut off from their home worlds."

Malek frowned. "Lachlina's dramatic efforts stopped the war, but her betrayal wasn't viewed favorably by many."

Sabine lifted her head to meet Malek's gaze. "Do your people view her as an enemy?"

Malek turned to face her and cupped her cheek. He searched her gaze and said, "How they view her has no bearing on how they'll regard you. We are more than our ancestors, more than our history. It's who we are and our actions in the present that determine our future."

Bane snickered. "The dragon's learning how to twist words."

Sabine wrapped her hand around Malek's wrist and gave

him a teasing smile. "Bane's right. You avoid the truth as prettily as the fae now."

He pressed his forehead against hers. "I won't deceive you, Sabine. Some will hate what you represent, but you're *mine*. Many will love you simply for that reason, but I know the rest will follow once they get to know you. No matter how they feel though, I won't allow any harm to come to you, no matter the source."

Sabine placed her hand against Malek's cheek. *"Ta vashein doi.* You hold my heart, Malek."

Azran nudged Sabine gently. *"The hour grows late, daughter of Vestior. If you wish to rest before you are summoned, it would be wise to do so."*

She pulled away from Malek and placed her hand back on Azran's head. The hellhound led them to another set of double doors. These also opened, revealing a chamber where a large table with an expansive buffet had been arranged. It was nearly overflowing with a wide assortment of food and drink. They had placed several cushions around the room, offering visitors a place to relax and eat in peace.

The gray hellhounds took up places around the room. None of them showed any sign of leaving.

"The hospitality of the Hall is open to you," Azran said to everyone. *"Refreshments have been made available. Through the door to your left are your personal quarters, where you may rest and mentally prepare for the Well's bounty. You may explore the Hall as you wish, but none of the sealed doors will abide force."*

"We'll heed your warning," Sabine said, scanning the room again.

"If you have need of me before the Well of Dreams summons you, simply let one of the guards know or call my name aloud."

Sabine nodded, watching as Azran left the room. His absence brought that unsettled feeling back in force. Her skin prickled, and she absently rubbed her arms. She could swear someone was watching them, and not just the hellhounds.

Turning to face her companions, she asked, "What do you think?"

Blossom put her hands on her hips. "I think everyone's wondering the same thing: What exactly do hellhounds consider food around here? They don't exactly strike me as honeycake bakers."

Chapter Twelve

*A*zran's six hellhounds lay on the floor, watching them with glowing eyes. Malek had no idea where Azran had gone or what the hellhound leader was doing. Every few minutes, one of the remaining hounds got up to patrol the length of the room before it returned to its designated place.

Malek studied them for potential weaknesses, just as they'd been doing the same to him and Bane. Their ties to the Wild Hunt made him wary. He wasn't sure why these hounds weren't pursuing Sabine when the rest of the Wild Hunt was camped outside of Razadon, waiting for her to appear.

Using one of the wall fountains, Sabine washed her hands and splashed some water on her face before heading to the table. "They have honeycakes, Blossom. There's also a pot of wildflowers for you."

"Ooooh! Really?" Blossom flew over to investigate. "Hey, Rika, check out some of these pastries. These are like the ones they served in the bakeries in Karga!"

Rika darted toward the table. "Wow. They have something for everyone here. How did they know what we eat at home?"

"It's magic," Blossom whispered loudly. "You know, one of the perks when you work with *gods*."

"Go wash up," Sabine said, pointing at the fountain.

Both Rika and Blossom darted over to get cleaned up before tackling the food. Malek waited until they were finished and then used the cool water to wash away the grime, blood, and sweat from their earlier battle.

Bane ignored the food and headed for the door to their quarters. Malek let him go, knowing he'd check to ensure the rooms were safe. Malek wasn't about to leave Sabine or Rika alone with a handful of hellhounds as guards. Although, every time the hellhounds turned their heads in Sabine's direction, their body language relaxed and tails wagged. They seemed to be enamored by her.

Sabine fixed herself a plate and a glass of wine before sitting on a nearby lounge. She patted the cushion beside her and asked, "Will you join me, Malek?"

Malek kept his eye on the hellhounds as he sat beside her. Rika was still putting together a plate for herself, with Blossom's help. Sabine had divided up her plate so one side was filled with small, delectable pieces of sliced fruits, lightly seasoned vegetables, and fragrant cheeses while the other was piled high with a variety of seared meats.

Sabine absently began eating, but her preoccupied expression made it clear she wasn't truly tasting it. Malek reached over and helped himself to the roasted meat she'd selected for him. Sabine might prefer fruits and vegetables, but dragons were, first and foremost, meat eaters. He took a bite, pleasantly surprised.

He hadn't had scyleton since he'd last visited the Sky Cities. The wily, striped creatures were the size of a fox and difficult to snare, but they were incredibly tasty when cooked with a brief burst of flame.

Rika settled on a lounge chair near them while Blossom perched on the edge of Rika's plate. Rika tore off a small piece from a pastry and handed it to Blossom before popping the rest into her mouth. "Don't tell Dagmar, but this food is better than what they serve in the dwarven city. I was getting tired of mushrooms and barbecue lizard."

Malek made a noise of agreement and took another bite. At least they wouldn't have to dig into their rations tonight. The dried wayfarer biscuits in the bags Faerie had packed didn't look remotely appetizing.

He glanced at the doorway, but Bane hadn't yet reemerged. "Have you given any thought about what you intend to do with the Well of Dreams?"

Sabine took a sip of the wine. "I'd rather wait, but Azran was fairly insistent that I drink from the Well before I leave. I'm not sure if its existence is common knowledge in Faerie or something only the Elders know about. I had never heard of it until today."

Malek frowned. She'd only lived in Faerie for the first seventeen years of her life. It was possible she simply hadn't been told about it, but Malek wasn't sure it was that easy. He'd never heard anything about the Well of Dreams either, and he'd been researching everything related to the gods for years.

"Do you think it'll hurt you?" Rika asked, her brow furrowing.

Sabine nibbled at a small piece of cheese and took another sip of wine. "I don't get that impression from Azran. Something he said makes me think it's similar to my family's wine. Each woman in my line infuses their memories and knowledge into it. With each sip future generations take, our collective magic and understanding of the universe increases."

Malek stared at her. "You believe the Well contains the memories of the gods?"

Sabine nodded and handed him her goblet. "The power boost would help replenish my magic, but I'm not sure about any other effects. Drinking too many memories can create problems, which is part of the reason we renew only either our matriarchal or patriarchal lines."

Blossom licked a drizzle of honey off her fingers. "You should take a big ole drink from the Well."

Sabine looked at Blossom in surprise. "Why do you say that?"

"Vestior's the big guy down here. He ruled the under-world and all the demons, before Lachlina betrayed him. If he's offering you a power boost, maybe he knows you'll need it when you face the demon king."

Sabine leaned back, ignoring the plate sitting beside her. "Perhaps."

The hellhounds all sat up, turning their attention to the door. Bane swept back into the room, scowling at the hounds. They growled softly at each other. Bane stalked to the table and grabbed a heaping plate of lumpy green meat. He sat on a chair and used his claws to skewer his food. His eyes flashed silver when his teeth tore into his meal, his eyes never leaving the hellhounds.

Rika frowned. Abandoning her plate, she grabbed a dinner roll and pastry off the buffet table and brought them to Bane. She held out the pastry to him, but the demon simply narrowed his eyes at her. At his annoyed look, she began telling him about a bakery in Karga and how her grandmother had used to take her there as a special treat. That pastry was one of her favorites, and she really wanted to share part of her world since he was doing the same for her.

She put it on the edge of his plate, beside the meat.

When he scowled at her, she smiled and poked a hole in the dinner roll. She fished a piece of meat off his plate and stuffed it inside the bread. Handing it to him, she motioned for him to eat while she explained how her grandmother used to hide different foods in their bread. It could be a vegetable, some type of meat, or even a sweet treat.

Bane's brow furrowed, but he took a bite of the bread. When he gave her a grunt of approval, Rika flashed him a huge smile. Malek bit back a smile and took a drink of Sabine's wine. At least she'd distracted Bane from trying to intimidate the hellhounds. The hounds had also relaxed, and two of them went back to lying on the floor. With a pleased expression, Rika walked back to her plate and took her seat.

Clever girl. It had only been about a month, but Rika had already learned how to twist a demon around her little finger. Now they just needed to keep her alive so she could continue confounding Bane.

Sabine was staring at one of the murals, this one depicting a scene where a man was in a temple and reaching out to touch a pool of water. Others were slumped over or lying near the water, in what appeared to be in peaceful repose or even death. It had to be a representation of the Well of Dreams.

Malek nudged Sabine's forgotten plate toward her and asked, "What do you know about Vestior?"

The hellhounds' ears perked up, turning in their direction.

Sabine picked up another piece of fruit and resumed eating. "Not as much as I'd like. The ties were recognized, and a few stories were handed down, but my bloodline always focused more on Lachlina. Since Theoria was her daughter, we follow the matriarchal line in my family."

She tilted her head and smiled, the blue jewels in her silver crown catching the light. "Vestior was, or is, Lachlina's mate or husband. It was said that the moment they met, the moon rose in the sky over this world for the first time. On the night they consummated their passion, the magic shared between them was strong enough to steal the sun and cast the world into darkness."

Malek lowered his glass. "Their lovemaking caused an eclipse?"

Sabine smiled, her lavender eyes dancing with amusement. "So the legend goes. On that night, Lachlina was deemed Bringer of Shadows, and Vestior became Master of the Night."

Rika leaned forward. "I thought Vestior was referred to as the 'Harbinger of Nightmares.'"

Bane finished the rest of his food and said, "That's how he's best known after summoning living nightmares to destroy an entire city of frost giants."

Rika's eyes widened. "He killed a whole city?"

"You do not slight a god and expect to remain unscathed."

Sabine studied Bane with a troubled expression. Deciding to interject, Malek asked, "Any issues with where we're sleeping tonight?"

"The rooms are acceptable," Bane said, pushing aside his empty plate. "There's only one way in and out. Anyone who enters our assigned quarters must venture through this room. I have some ideas about setting up a ward once Sabine is finished eating."

Sabine stood and said, "I'll take a look now."

"I'll come too!" Blossom said, flying to Sabine's shoulder.

Malek glanced at Rika. She was still eating. Sabine should be safe enough with Bane, especially if there was only one entrance to the room. He gestured toward his plate and said, "I'll finish up and then join you."

Sabine smoothed her dress and walked with Bane into the back room. None of the hellhounds followed. At least they decided to give them the illusion of privacy.

Rika watched them go before picking up her plate. She moved to Sabine's abandoned spot and sat beside Malek. In a voice too low for anyone to overhear, she whispered, "Something's not right with Bane."

Malek arched his brow. "What do you mean?"

"It's the bite on his hand," Rika said quietly, darting another look toward the door where Bane had disappeared. "Bane always has magic surrounding him, just like Sabine. But ever since the fire imp attacked him, his magic is frayed and sparking. I think he's trying to hide how much it's affecting him."

Malek frowned. "Can you sense anything else?"

Rika hesitated and then shrugged. "It looks like his magic is weakening. In the places where it's thinnest, there's another red layer that's growing stronger. I'm not sure what it means."

"We'll need to get him to the demon king quickly," Malek said quietly, concerned that Sabine still wasn't at full strength. Maybe having her drink from a well powered by the gods' magic would help.

Rika nodded and went back to eating. Malek leaned back and waited for her to finish, still trying to decide whether he should encourage Sabine to drink from the well or rely on her innate gifts. At times like this, he wished Rika's seer abilities were fully working. He could definitely use a strong dose of foresight.

Chapter Thirteen

*S*abine swept her gaze over the communal sleeping area. In the center of the circular room was a large fountain with cascading water. Along the perimeter of the walls were several low beds piled high with cushions. Drapery was tied back, allowing people a modicum of privacy if they wished to sleep undisturbed. Off to the side was a separate door, with a bathing chamber for more personal needs behind it.

Blossom zipped around the room, investigating under cushions and around the hanging lamps. The room was larger than Sabine had expected, but it was easily defensible. With one strong ward on the door, they could all sleep without bothering to assign someone sentry duty.

"At least this room configuration will allow us to stay together," Sabine said, running her hand through the flowing water of the fountain. A trace of refreshing magic coated her skin, and she absently rubbed her fingers together. It wasn't enough to assuage the fatigue plaguing her. Those beds were calling to her.

"Hellhounds," Bane muttered. "They like to sleep in puppy piles and assume everyone else does too."

Sabine arched her brow. "I'm sensing some tension between demons and hellhounds. You're not usually this irritable."

Bane didn't reply. Sabine cocked her head, studying him. She reached for his hand, the one with the imp bite, and examined it. The skin was still angry and red, with growing red marks spreading up his hand and past his wrist. It was getting worse.

She lifted her head to look up at him. "How long?"

"Less than I first thought. A few days at most. The amount of venom was substantial. Kal'thorz chose the fire imp with care."

Sabine frowned and released him. Malek and Rika walked into the room a few minutes later. Rika placed Blossom's potted plant on a low table. With a yawn, Rika trudged up to one of the beds and sprawled across it.

"I called it," she said, her voice muffled from the pillows.

Sabine smiled. "You might want to try taking off your boots first. They still have dried ooze on them from the spiders."

Rika groaned, flopped over, and kicked off her boots. With another yawn, she shuffled to the bathing room to clean up.

Malek unhooked a traveler's pack from his belt and handed it to Sabine. "There's probably something in here for her to wear that's not covered with spider guts. Bane has the bag with our weapons and some of my clothing."

Sabine nodded and thumbed through the pack, noticing Faerie had provided her with several lightweight yet formal robes. She selected some night apparel and personal items for herself and Rika. As soon as she pulled them from the bag, the items enlarged to the correct size. Handing the bag to Malek, she headed for the bathing room.

It had an almost cave-like quality to it, with moss and lichen growing on the walls. They glowed softly, providing additional illumination to the glowing-blue fae orbs hovering in midair. The walls were made from volcanic rock, and the stone tables and benches offered a splash of contrasting color with silver accents. On the far side of the room was a showering area with a cascading waterfall. Small holes in the volcanic floor drained the excess water away and prevented the room from flooding.

Rika stood in the middle of the room, struggling to unhook her armor. Taking pity on her, Sabine put the clothing on a small table with an assortment of perfumed oils. She unlatched the seer's bindings and helped to pull off the protective plates.

Rika shot her a look of pure gratitude. "I think my blisters have blisters."

Sabine made a sympathetic noise. "You'll grow calluses soon enough. I didn't think I'd survive the first month of training with Dax and Bane. You're handling it far better than I did."

"I hope so."

While Rika removed the rest of her clothing and stepped into the waterfall, Sabine took care of her more personal needs. Once finished, she removed her crown and placed it on a nearby table. She'd assumed they would be traveling in more rugged conditions until they reached the demon capital. With the brush she'd brought into the room, she untangled her long hair.

"How long will it take us to get to Bane's home?"

Sabine used a trace of magic to unravel the laces on the back of her gown. "I'll have to find out from Azran in the morning. Probably no more than a day or two. We only have a few days to reach Dax."

She folded the dress and placed it on the table beside her crown before stepping under the waterfall. The water was warmer than she'd expected, likely heated from the volcanic source. She stood beneath the water, allowing it to soothe her tired and aching muscles.

Rika gasped and covered herself. "Those linens! They weren't here a minute ago."

Sabine opened her eyes and saw a stack of drying cloths on a nearby ledge. "Brownies, house elves, or domovoi most likely. Possibly even a goblin, but they're not usually discreet. Blossom's going to be disappointed she missed another opportunity to meet one of the caretakers."

"But they just came in while we're bathing!" Rika sputtered, her eyes wide. She snatched up a drying cloth and wrapped it around her, darting furtive glances around the room.

Sabine smiled and turned around, picking up the scented soap nestled in a small cove. "You bathed with other women in the hot springs back in Karga, no?"

Rika nodded and bit her lip. "But I knew they were there. Whatever snuck in here was practically invisible."

Sabine lathered the soap, wondering if this was human modesty at work. "As soon as we're done and you're clothed, we can try to request an audience so you can meet her."

Rika relaxed slightly, her natural curiosity emerging to the forefront. "How do you know it's a girl?"

Sabine smiled and washed her hair. "Because the alternative would have made you uneasy. If the lemon-and-sugar soap is any indication, our friend is a brownie. They enjoy sweet-smelling things."

"A brownie? Really?"

Sabine finished rinsing the soap off. "When I was

growing up in Faerie, brownies oversaw the entire Unseelie palace. They managed the household, stocking supplies, setting schedules, and handling all the cooking and the cleaning while the gnomes and pixies tended the gardens. The royal fae might rule over the courts, but the lesser fae are no small power."

"Why did she hide from us?"

Sabine smiled and patted her skin with the soft drying cloth. "They're cautious around new people, especially humans. Once they feel comfortable in your presence, and as long as you want to see them, they'll make an appearance."

Rika worried her lower lip and looked around the room. "Then maybe we should wait to ask for an audience. I don't want to frighten them."

Sabine nodded, pleased Rika was willing to respect their privacy. She walked to the clothing she'd laid out and handed a soft but intricately detailed shift to Rika, which was adorned with gold leaves at the bottom. Sabine dressed in a similar one and tied a lightweight robe around her waist.

Taking both the damp towels and their soiled clothing, Sabine sent a trace of her magic over the cloths before placing them on the counter.

"We're leaving them here?"

Sabine nodded. "The brownies caring for this place will take offense if we don't leave this for them. It's a sign of trust that we're willing to leave our treasured belongings in their care. I've offered them a trade of sorts, to keep the balance between us. They'll clean the items and return them to us before dawn."

Sabine headed back out into the main sleeping area and found Bane standing over Malek, while the dragon cleaned his sword. Blossom was curled up under the flowering plant, already sleeping soundly. Pixies, as a general rule, were diurnal. It was a wonder she'd stayed awake this long.

Malek sheathed his weapon and stood. He kissed her lightly and said, "Give me a few minutes to clean up."

She nodded, watching as he headed to the bathing room. Bane walked toward her and asked, "Do you have enough magic readily available to create a ward that will ignore my presence?"

Rika climbed into one of the empty beds, shoved her short sword under her pillow, and watched Sabine and Bane with sleepy eyes. "You're going out, Bane? The hellhounds said we only have safe passage for one night. We need to leave in the morning."

"Someone needs to scout our surroundings and beyond the Hall. I will go, while you rest behind the ward's protection."

Sabine glanced at the door and frowned. She wasn't thrilled with the idea of Bane exploring on his own, but she wouldn't object. Still, he was asking a favor. She was fae enough to press the advantage. "I have enough magic to create the ward, but I'd like some information about this place in exchange for keying it to ignore you."

Bane crossed his arms over his chest, a look of amusement flickering in his expression. "Very well, little one. Ask your questions."

She lifted her head and asked, "Earlier, you said entering the Hall of the Gods was forbidden. Why?"

Bane fell silent, likely trying to decide how much to tell her. As the seconds turned to minutes, Sabine started to wonder if he'd reconsidered. Rika's eyes began drifting shut, but when Bane started speaking, her attention became solely focused on him.

"This place was once called the Hall of Awakening. Before dragons came to this realm, demons were the guardians of the underworld. We protected the Source, the place of awakening where the gods dreamed their dreams of power."

Sabine sat, her body melting into the soft feather down of the cushions on the large bed. Growing up, she'd heard only a few stories about the history of demons. Most of what she'd learned had been from tidbits Dax and Bane had shared, and they were surprisingly tightlipped about their past.

Malek came back into the room, his dark hair damp and curling around his neck. He took a seat beside her, taking her hand in his. The warmth of his magic surrounded her, and she relaxed against him.

Bane ignored Malek's appearance, continuing to stare at the wall with a faraway expression. "As guardians, we were gifted unspeakable authority in the underworld. Our magic rivaled that of some gods. The only condition was that we never cross the boundary into the Hall of Awakening."

Sabine curled her feet under her. "Someone entered the hall, didn't they?"

"Tav'shesin."

Sabine blinked. "The first demon king?"

Bane gave a curt nod. "In the underworld, we have always held as much, if not more, power than the fae. But back then, we also had the ability to travel freely above ground, even if our magical ability was weakened. Tav'shesin believed we could possess the power of the gods, both above and below ground, if we awakened our power the same way as the gods."

Malek ran his thumb along Sabine's hand. "I'm assuming Tav'shesin was caught sneaking in?"

"Details are scarce, but put simply, yes. I do not know if he made it to the awakening chamber or not. He was half dead when he was dumped back in our capital and Vestior announced our punishment."

Sabine knew Vestior had close ties to the demons, but not about the connection to the first demon king. She wondered if there might be some resentment since she was his descendant. It was an unfortunate part of dealing with such long-lived races that they harbored grudges that spanned centuries. "What was Tav'shesin's punishment?"

Bane snorted. "The demons as a whole were banished from above ground, forced to retreat into the darkness. We were stripped of our power, except for one tiny ember known as the Heartstone, which holds the collective of demon souls. As a reminder that we only exist by the will of the gods, our king was entrusted with that ember."

Malek arched his brow. "They didn't kill him for his betrayal?"

"No. The gods were never so succinct with their punishments."

Rika propped herself up on the pillow. "What do you mean?"

Sabine looked at Rika and said, "The gods decided the demon collective would punish Tav'shesin for his transgressions."

"Indeed. My people were so enraged at their fall from power that they dragged Tav'shesin to the deepest part of the volcano. He was chained in mithril, his hands and feet severed from his body. Each evening, he was lashed a hundred times. If he drew upon the power of the ember to heal himself or regrow his limbs, they would sever them again and increase the lashes."

Rika's eyes widened. "That's... That's terrible. How could they do such a thing?"

"They believed death was too quick a punishment, little seer. As long as they suffered from their lack of magic, they were determined to inflict even worse punishment on Tav'shesin."

"Why wouldn't they just kill him?"

"He may have wished for death, but they always stopped

before it reached that point. The gods made it clear that if Tav'shesin died, the flames of the ember would die with him. By striking him down, they would have doomed all our people."

Sabine frowned. "He can't still be alive."

"No. After a century or so of listening to Tav'shesin's screams, the gods relented. They decreed that he could be challenged for the Heartstone, but only by a direct blood descendant. So it has passed with each generation, each son slaying their father for the right to possess the ember and for power over all the demons. Our people cannot survive without the tie to the Heartstone, yet most abhor the line destined to rule them."

Sabine studied Bane, seeing the proud demon in a new light. They had more in common than she realized. She knew how it felt for your own people to despise you simply because of your lineage. "You're related to Tav'shesin, aren't you?"

Bane inclined his head. "Kal'thorz currently holds the Heartstone. While he does, no demon dares raise a hand against him. If they do, the light from that ember will stop shining upon us, and we will cease to exist."

"Then only you or Dax have the power to strike him down," Malek mused aloud.

"To even suggest such a thing is considered treason."

Sabine frowned. "Dax really tried to kill him, didn't he? That's why he's being tried for treason?"

Bane scowled. "I believe I have fulfilled the terms of our agreement. You've been given relevant information, and in exchange, you'll key the ward to allow me access."

Sabine blew out a breath and stood. He'd told her more than she'd expected—and with an audience. Curiosity thrummed steadily inside her, but she wouldn't push. Not now.

She walked toward the door and lifted her hands. Magic rose within her, and she gathered it tightly, then wove a complex netting to protect the entryway. Infusing her thoughts with the resonance of her friend's auras, she modified the webbing to ignore Bane and the rest of her companions.

She affixed the ward, whispering words of power to seal it to the wall, floor, and ceiling. It wouldn't stop anyone from entering through a portal, but they wouldn't be able to walk inside the room without making a racket. Putting a death ward on a door in the Hall of the Gods might not be the wisest decision, even if she had the magic to spare.

"It's done," Sabine said, turning to face Bane. He moved toward the door, but she reached out to stop him.

His skin was cooler than normal, and it worried her. He'd been acting strangely since they arrived, and it had only gotten worse since they entered the Hall. She wasn't sure if he was planning on trying to handle Kal'thorz on his own or if he simply wanted to explore the Hall of the Gods. It was tempting to bind him here, but she knew such action would irrevocably damage the trust between them.

"Separating from the group isn't wise, Bane."

Bane's amber gaze swept over her, a flicker of some unnamed emotion crossing his features. "As long as I'm able, I will always return to you. But you must remember that while you are in the underworld, there are dangers that exist for you, and you alone."

Her brow furrowed, and she took a step closer to him. "What dangers?"

Malek stood and started walking toward them. Sabine's hand tightened on Bane's arm, knowing he would shut down once Malek reached them.

Bane's expression became pained. "Do not ask more of me, Sabine."

Sabine lowered her gaze and took a steadying breath. He was hers but also not. She'd always known that, but it had never been more apparent than since they stepped foot in this godsforsaken place.

Malek stopped beside her. "What's going on?"

"You're charged with her care in my absence, dragon," Bane said, pinning Malek with a look before his gaze softened on her again. "Do not leave his side while you're in the underworld, Sabine. If I'm unable to protect you for any reason, he's agreed to take you, the seer, and the bug away from here. I know you have reservations, but you will find refuge in the Sky Cities. If you cannot bind the demons in an alliance, the dragons will help turn the tide of battle against the Seelie."

Sabine tried to send a wave of magic over Bane, but the slickness of the curse forced her power to slide away like water. She lowered her hand, unable to hide her frustration. "Be careful, Bane. Curse or not, you're *mine*. You will come back to me by dawn, or I'll tear the underworld apart looking for you."

"Sleep well, little one. May your dreams show you the true path of power." Without waiting for a response, he turned and left the room, leaving her and Malek to watch him disappear into the darkness.

Chapter Fourteen

A howl awakened Sabine. She jerked upright, immediately reaching for her knives. In addition to the throwing knives strapped to her thigh even while she slept, she and Malek had also stashed additional weapons beside the bed.

The faint glow from the crystals embedded in the wall gave her enough light to see Malek's still form beside her. His chest rose and fell in the rhythmic motions of a deep sleep.

"Malek," she whispered, reaching for him. She shook him gently, but he didn't stir. She muttered a curse, not liking this at all. He had to be under another enchanted sleep. The last time this happened, she'd received a visit from the Huntsman.

Rika was asleep on a bed not far from them. The seer was surrounded by pillows, her limbs askew and tangled in the blankets. Sabine didn't see any sign of Blossom, but the pixie was likely still curled up around her plant. Bane was nowhere to be found. He either hadn't returned yet or he'd been the cause of the howling.

"You'd better not have done something foolish, Bane," she

muttered, sliding out from the warm cocoon of blankets. Sabine tied her robe around her waist and headed toward the door, the tile floor cold against her bare feet.

She paused for a moment, glancing back at Malek and recalling Bane's warning. Under ordinary circumstances, she wouldn't leave them. But if the magic followed the same pattern as last time, her friends would remain asleep until her business was concluded. Malek was going to be furious when he realized she'd walked into potential danger without him.

Determined to get this over with as quickly as possible, Sabine stepped through the ward protecting their sleeping chamber. The room where the food had been served had been cleared. There was a smaller repast set out, in the event anyone decided they were still hungry, but the most startling sight was the six hellhounds all sound asleep, just like her companions.

Sabine paused, her brow furrowing as her hand automatically went to her knives. If the hellhounds were asleep, who was left guarding the Hall of the Gods? They hadn't seen any sign of anyone other than the brownie, but Sabine knew well what sort of creatures kept to the shadows.

Azran entered the room, his glowing red eyes fixed on her. It appeared not everyone was asleep. Despite Azran's earlier solicitousness, Sabine didn't relax her grip on her dagger. "Why has the Huntsman sent my companions into an enchanted sleep, Azran?"

"*I serve as my master wills,*" Azran replied, his mental voice slipping seamlessly into her mind. "*Your attendance has been requested, Sabin'theoria, daughter of Vestior and the Betrayer, Lachlina.*"

Sabine inwardly winced. As titles went, it left something to be desired. She didn't believe the Huntsman intended her harm simply because of her bloodline. He already knew her origins. She just hoped her connection to her great-great-great-grandfather, Vestior, helped offset some of Lachlina's evil deeds.

"Will my friends be safe during my absence?"

"No harm is intended where none is sought. He simply seeks a private audience with you, Sabin'theoria."

It was probably the best affirmation she could hope to get. Sabine gave him a brief nod to indicate her agreement.

Azran approached her, and she placed her hand on his head. At the moment of contact, she suddenly became attuned to the environment once again. It was almost as though this place had a pulse, a heartbeat. While she was connected to Azran, she was able to breathe it in and allow the magic of this place to fortify her.

Azran led her into the main part of the hall, his fiery tail swishing behind him. Instead of taking her the same direction they'd entered, he turned and headed down a different hallway. Tall granite columns lined the path, each carved with elemental designs. They were paired together, fire contrasting water and earth against wind. It was a reminder of the necessity of balance in all things.

Sabine passed a large mirror that took up an entire wall. The sight of her reflection nearly made her miss a step. She looked different somehow, her markings of power more pronounced against the glow of her skin. Even her hair was different in the image, with gold strands complementing the silver. It wasn't real. It couldn't be.

"It's a reflection of what you are becoming."

"And what am I becoming?"

"Who you were always meant to be."

Gods. Azran was more cryptic than the Faerie Elders. He chuffed, likely in response to her thought. She narrowed her eyes, rebuilding her mental walls. They must have slipped when she'd fallen asleep.

"Forgiveness for any intrusion, little goddess. We do not receive many visitors on this side of the veil. Your insights and thoughts are... refreshing."

Sabine looked away, not wanting to chastise him again. She'd been lonely for a long time while hiding in the human city of Akros, even though she'd had Dax and Bane with her. But her longing to connect with other magical beings, particularly the fae, made the isolation of the hellhounds understandable.

Deciding to focus on something else, she said, "I thought the hellhounds were part of the Wild Hunt. What is your connection to the Hall?"

"Some of our kind run with the Hunt, but a chosen few act as guardians for the Hall. We remain in wait, escorting those who are worthy through the Hall and to the Well of Dreams."

Sabine slowed her footsteps as they passed a huge mural that took up most of the wall. Dozens of gods and goddesses stood in a large chamber, surrounding a glowing pool of water. One man captured her attention, and she froze. He looked almost identical to the Huntsman, with his silvery-white hair and piercing blue eyes. She lifted her hand and traced the image as though it could answer her questions.

"The Huntsman once stood among the gods?"

"It will not do to keep him waiting, little goddess," Azran said, bumping against her side.

Sabine frowned and placed her hand on Azran's head again, falling into step beside him. She passed another mural, but other than giving it a cursory glance, she continued moving. Most of the scenes depicted made no sense, or she had no frame of reference for what they were describing. Part of her wondered if even the most learned Faerie Elder knew what the images represented. She wasn't sure her mother had ever traversed these halls.

Turning down another passage, Sabine tensed at the sight of a demon slumped on the ground in front of an archway.

"Bane?" she exclaimed, pulling away from Azran and rushing to her friend. His head was lowered, his eyes closed. She kneeled beside him and placed her hand on his arm. He didn't stir, but he otherwise appeared unharmed.

She lifted her head to regard Azran. "He's all right?"

"He sleeps, as they all do. This meeting is not for them."

She turned toward the archway and frowned. "What is this place?"

"The Well of Dreams. The demon located it but has not crossed the threshold. If he does, he will die."

Sabine frowned, not liking the idea that Bane was out here and exposed. "I'll go no farther until Bane's awakened and safe from harm."

"As you will." Azran's tail swished, sending a trail of fire through the air. Bane's image shimmered and then faded from sight.

"Where have you taken him?"

"The demon has been transported away from the Well. He has been warned to stay away until your meeting is concluded." Azran's head cocked for a moment as though listening to someone. *"Since it troubles you to have him put to sleep, we shall refrain. He is continuing to explore the Hall."*

Sabine nodded and turned back toward the archway. Something or someone was pulling her in that direction. She lifted her hand, trying to read the energy signature of the power. "I haven't yet decided whether I intend to drink."

"Vestior wills it so."

Sabine narrowed her eyes at Azran. "The Unseelie do not bow to any gods, not even in their Hall."

A brief flicker of steam rose from Azran's nostrils, and his body shook. Sabine arched her brow, realizing he was laughing at her. She frowned and turned back toward the

Well's entrance. Most people didn't survive one meeting with the Huntsman. At some point, she was going to run out of luck. She hoped it wouldn't be tonight.

Sabine took a deep breath and stepped under the archway, feeling a tingle of magic slide over her skin. Unlike normal wards, this one reached deeper somehow, weighing her past, present, and future. Fingers seemed to thread through her hair, tasting the silver strands. It traced her marks of power with an almost searing heat that made her wince. She had the uncomfortable sensation it didn't like the marks on her skin.

Resisting the urge to rub her arms, she pushed through the barrier and into the chamber beyond. Her eyes widened in astonishment. It was a temple, reminiscent of the ones she'd visited as a child in Faerie.

The decorative white pillars contrasted sharply against the black volcanic rock that formed the base and capital of each column. Golden accents married both together, serving as another reminder that balance needed to be maintained.

Carved marble figures lined the walls, each representing a different god or goddess. Their serene expressions looked upon a glowing pool of water in the center of the room. The water itself called to her, its eerie luminescence speaking to some dormant part within her being. A song filled her mind, the melody achingly familiar.

Unable to resist, she approached the water. A light floral scent filled the air, reminding her of the gardens from her childhood. She kneeled beside the pool, gazing into its depths.

The water was completely clear, so she was able to see the grooves from the lavastone on the sides of the Well. It was deeper than she'd expected, and she leaned forward, trying to see the bottom. It seemed to go on forever until it disappeared into inky darkness.

Something glimmered in the depths. Sabine pressed her hands against the cool tiles, trying to get a better look at what appeared to be some sort of small orb. It pulsed in time with her heartbeat, each flare of power like a beacon calling her toward it. The sound of drums filled her mind, beating in time with the object. She started to reach toward the water but hesitated.

Curling her hands into fists, she laid them on her lap. Accepting foreign magic was too risky right now, even if she desperately needed the power boost to protect her friends. The sacrifice necessary to accept such a gift would likely be greater than what she was willing to pay.

"Few understand the true cost of great power. That you hesitate in claiming it only reaffirms that you are deserving of such."

The mental voice startled Sabine out of her reverie, and she lifted her gaze. The Huntsman was cloaked, his skeletal form standing on the opposite side of the well. He regarded her with glowing red eyes, almost identical to Azran's.

She slowly rose, recalling the times she'd seen the Huntsman in the past. Part of her was still terrified of him, but after he'd helped save her life from a dwarven assassin, she was more curious than afraid. She just hoped her curiosity wouldn't be her downfall.

"Why did you bring me here?"

The Huntsman gestured toward the water in front of her. *"The Well of Dreams is a direct link to the ether. Once you absorb its magic, you will be able to harness such power at will."*

Sabine looked at the water, still hearing the orb calling to her. It was *hers*. She knew it with every sense of her being. Still, she hesitated. If she'd already caused an earthquake from the powers she'd acquired, what would this item do?

Fighting her instinctive need to claim it, Sabine said, "I haven't agreed to accept such power."

"You will *accept this as your birthright or risk relinquishing all*

ties to the same," the Huntsman said, withdrawing his skeletal hand into the folds of his cloak.

Sabine stared at the Huntsman, the warmth she'd felt for him dissipating as quickly as a summer breeze. "You've brought me here under false pretenses, isolated me from my allies, and now you're threatening me? I refuse to accept this so-called *gift* until you share with me the cost."

"You dare challenge me?" came the thunderous reply. The walls and ground trembled, stone bits falling from the ceiling. Sabine staggered but remained standing, mentally willing the columns not to fall and crush her. Although, the Huntsman's anger might make her fears moot anyway.

"I dare challenge for my right to my own destiny," Sabine said, meeting his glowing-red gaze. "I will not blindly follow your commands or any other's without an explanation, even should you strike me down in the process."

Silence.

More silence.

Sabine held her ground.

"Very well." The Huntsman's mental voice was soft yet still retained the sharpest hint of an edge.

The wave of relief that washed over her was strong enough that it should have knocked her to the ground.

"No magic gained is without sacrifice, even that which is destined."

Destined? She frowned, eyeing the Well of Dreams with misgivings. It was foolish to keep refusing the Huntsman, and the pull she felt toward the glowing orb was overwhelming. It was taking nearly everything she had to keep resisting.

Too many things didn't add up, including those murals. Something about seeing the Huntsman's image on the way here made her think of another possibility. It was outlandish and highly improbable, but—

"If you will not embrace the magic willingly, the experience will be far less pleasant." With those cryptic words, the Huntsman disappeared from view.

"That could have gone better," Sabine muttered, unsure what she was supposed to do. The orb still beckoned her. If anything, the pull was stronger now that it was no longer competing with the Huntsman's presence.

A howl interrupted her thoughts. Before she could turn, she was shoved from behind. Hard. She floundered, plunging face first into the clear water. Frost pierced her skin, so cold it felt as though she were being burned alive.

It was pure, liquid magic. She struggled and kicked, trying to break the surface, but the water pulled her down as though invisible hands were grabbing ahold of her.

Summoning the magic of the sea, Sabine tried to propel herself upward. It was no use. The merfolk's power was little more than droplets compared to the ocean of power that was the magic of the gods.

Panic swelled within her. Her lungs burned. She could no longer see the light from the chamber above her. Knowing there was only one option left, she reached downward and allowed the Well to engulf her in darkness.

Chapter Fifteen

*S*omething changed.

Sabine wasn't sure what had happened, but the need to breathe was suddenly gone. Instead of water, she was floating in nothingness. She spread out her hands, the ebb and flow of the magic similar to the sensation of when she traveled by portal to a different location. Could she have somehow slipped beyond the veil to the in-between, the bridge between their realm and others? The Huntsman had mentioned the ether, but she didn't know what that was.

Without a focused destination or reference point, Sabine wasn't sure how she was supposed to leave. She tried to focus on Malek, using their shared bond, but she couldn't sense his direction. She pushed harder, but it was no use. Even if he weren't asleep, Sabine wasn't sure her magic was enough to penetrate the protections of this place.

Mentally cursing Azran to the fiery pits of the lowest level of the underworld, she summoned a light in the palm of her hand. It did little to cut through the thick fog. If the Well of Dreams was a portal to the in-between, Sabine was in a place beyond space and time. It made sense. The in-between was the source of all magic and the origins of life. It was the birthplace of the gods.

Sabine sent out a strong pulse of magic to get her bearings. If she could read the echoes to determine where the veil began and ended, she could cross through it to return to the Hall.

A flicker of light below her pulsed in time with her magic. Sabine froze. It must be the orb. But that would mean Sabine was still in the Well and not in the in-between. Or was the Well of Dreams part of the in-between?

Sabine descended, sinking to investigate the orb. Even if she didn't claim it, she might be able to use it to break free of this place. She had the suspicion the Huntsman intended her to take the power into herself; otherwise, he would have given her a choice.

The glowing orb hovered in front of her, its golden light breaking through the darkness. Sabine stared at the shimmering beauty in wonder. It almost hurt to merely look upon it, even as it called to her. In its depths, she saw endless possibilities, like droplets of water falling from a waterfall.

Sabine reached for it, and her hands closed on the pulsing sphere beating in time with her heartbeat. Power surged within her, her skin glowing to match the illumination from the orb.

The detailed skin markings Faerie Elders had spent days carving into her skin flared to life. Something moved under Sabine's skin, and she screamed as the power from the orb pierced her over and over, like thousands of needles being jabbed into her arms and legs. It was everywhere. She couldn't escape the pain or release the orb. Her marks grew, the designs expanding and becoming more elaborate. It was almost as though the Elders had begun painting a masterpiece, but the Well of Dreams was finishing it. What should have taken months or even years was being done in an instant.

Sabine floated limply in the nothingness, unable to focus on anything. When the pain finally subsided to a dull ache, she tried to rally her remaining strength. The orb was gone, its essence having been consumed. While Sabine's magic strummed powerfully within her, she was wrung out and exhausted from the ordeal. A dim part of her knew she needed to leave this place before it was too late.

With grim determination, Sabine reached outward again to locate the boundaries of the veil. Her markings flared to life, eliciting another whimper of pain. The edges of the veil, however, were easy to identify. She had no idea how she'd missed it before, unless the orb had gifted her with the ability to better sense the boundaries of her realm.

She pushed her magic through the opening, forming a doorway. She slipped through and collapsed on a cold granite floor. She lifted her head, brushing her hair out of her eyes, and blinked in surprise.

Hundreds of dark bookshelves, each covered with countless tomes, lined the granite walls. On the far side of the room was a roaring fireplace with flickering flames of blue Faerie fire. The chandeliers overhead dripped with dwarven crystals that had been infused with fae power. The familiar sight was somewhat reassuring. At least she hadn't ended up in one of those strange places she'd seen in the murals in the Hall of the Gods.

"The Elders would fall over themselves if they saw this," she muttered, pushing up from the ground and brushing off her hands.

The problem was trying to figure out where she was. From all appearances, she was in some sort of study, possibly in another part of the Hall. The Huntsman was nowhere to be seen.

A large black desk sat in the center of the room, with the telltale silver swirls that indicated it was bloodlock desk. More cabinets were on the far corner of the wall, made from the same material. The amount of demon blood that had to have spilled to formulate such a macabre collection was staggering.

A mural had been painted in an alcove over the fireplace. This one had not only the Huntsman appearing in his mortal form but also someone who looked a great deal like Sabine—the goddess Lachlina. The Huntsman's creatures were binding a kneeling Lachlina with chains while she glared up at him with eyes full of anger and betrayal.

Sabine frowned, her gaze sweeping the empty room. The lack of windows and doors was potentially worrisome, but she wouldn't panic just yet. If the Huntsman had wanted her dead, he wouldn't have forced her into the Well to accept more magic.

Somewhat reassured, Sabine walked to the nearest book-shelf and ran her finger along the spines of the tomes. They were written in the ancient language of the gods. She picked one up, its heavy weight reminding her of the libraries she used to explore while she'd been living among the humans.

She flipped open the book, the scent of old parchment tickling her nose. The words had been written with a heavy script, the long sloping letters a work of art on their own merit. But it was the content that fascinated her. From all appearances, the book was some sort of scientific study about the amount and type of magic required to develop mental speech among animals.

"Were you taught to read the Old Tongue, as well as speak it?"

Sabine whirled around at the sound of the man's voice, nearly dropping the book from her hands. He'd stepped through a silver portal in the wall, its mirrored reflection swirling with untold mysteries. A moment later, the portal disappeared from view.

The man in front of her no longer bore much resemblance to the skeletal visage, but instead had taken on his true form. He was almost a full head taller than her, with wisps of his silvery-white hair framing a face composed of a strong jaw and finely chiseled cheeks. His ears curved upward like hers, ending at a point. He was more fae in appearance than most of the royals, with his remote and haughty demeanor. His piercing blue eyes were focused on her, a far cry from the glowing red gaze he possessed while wearing the Huntsman's mien. The mural she'd seen earlier made her suspect he was far more than he pretended.

"For the most part," Sabine said, closing the book and placing it on the shelf. "We lose more of the Old Tongue, or Old Language, every year. All among the royal line are taught to read and speak the Old Language from the time they're born, but the words of power are the primary focus."

The Huntsman approached her, his commanding presence making the room feel smaller. "All words are a power unto themselves if used correctly."

Sabine tilted her head in acknowledgment of his truth. "Names also have power."

His blue eyes flickered with something akin to amusement. "Ask your question, daughter."

Reassured by his recognition of their blood ties, she faced the man who was the bogeyman of fae children everywhere. "Should I call you Huntsman of the Wild Hunt? Or Vestior, Harbinger of Nightmares?" She arched her brow. "Or great-great-great-grandfather?"

He inclined his head, a hint of an arrogant smile playing upon his lips. "I have had many names over the years. You may call me what you wish."

Gods—er, god. It was true. She was the descendant of a

still-living god who had, for some reason, chosen to become the feared leader of the Wild Hunt. Sabine took a deep breath, desperately trying to rein in her conflicting emotions. She stared at the man—or god—in front of her. Was she supposed to bow? Hug him? Kneel, maybe? The Elders had never taught her the proper protocol for this scenario.

Family connection or not, Sabine had no intention of kneeling for anyone, especially not when he'd arranged to have her thrown into the Well of Dreams. "It was you, not Faerie, who opened the portal to the underworld. Why have you brought me here?"

"We needed to speak privately, and the Well of Dreams is one of the few places in your realm where others cannot venture. Very soon, you will need to make a decision that will shape the future of your world."

Sabine frowned. "What decision?"

Vestior cocked his head as though listening for something. "We have less time to speak than I anticipated. The dragon, in particular, is deeply tied to you. He senses your absence already, even while he slumbers."

Sabine wasn't surprised. She was becoming more attuned to Malek every day. It made sense that the reverse was happening. She wasn't sure how Vestior was sensing Malek, but it was likely the same way he'd been spying on them since they entered the Hall. "We share a blood bond."

"That will be either problematic or extremely fortuitous," Vestior murmured. "We'll see if he's truly worthy of the gift you've bestowed upon him."

Fear coiled in her belly. Sabine reached out to Malek in her thoughts, hoping he would continue to sleep. At least in his dreams, he was safe from whatever creatures protected the Hall of the Gods.

Chapter Sixteen

*M*alek woke suddenly.

Even in the darkened room, he knew Sabine was no longer with him. He felt her absence like a piece of his soul were missing. For a moment, he could have sworn he heard her voice.

The sheets on Sabine's side of the bed were cool to the touch. She'd been gone for a while. Her shoes were still where she'd left them, indicating she hadn't gone far. He frowned. It wasn't like her to leave without letting him know.

He climbed out of bed, still wearing his pants from earlier. Rika and Blossom were sleeping soundly. He didn't like the idea of leaving them unprotected, but the ward would offer them a modicum of security.

"Dammit, Bane," Malek muttered, pulling on his boots. "You said I couldn't count on you while we were in the underworld, but I didn't think you'd completely abandon us either."

Malek walked over to Rika and tried to rouse her. She mumbled something incoherent and rolled over. He shook her a bit harder. She didn't stir. At the small potted plant on a nearby table, he tried to repeat the gesture with Blossom.

The pixie swatted at his hand and said, "Go back to bed. We're not supposed to be awake yet. You're missing all the good dreams."

"Blossom, Sabine's missing."

Blossom blinked open her eyes and yawned. "No, she's not. She's finding her magic at the bottom of the well. Stupid place to hide magic. It's wet."

Malek straightened in alarm. "What?"

Her eyes fluttered closed, but Malek poked her gently with his index finger.

"Blossom, what do you know? Where is the Well of Dreams?"

"Dunno. Not allowed. It's like the Garden. No-pixie zone." Blossom's eyes started to close again.

"Do you know how I can find it?"

"Music box." Blossom waved him away and tucked one of the leaves around her like a blanket. A moment later, she was snoring softly again.

Malek muttered a curse. When they last spoke, Sabine hadn't shown any interest in absorbing more magic. She was having enough problems with her existing power.

Logically, he knew his reaction to her absence wasn't rational. Sabine was more than capable of taking care of herself. But it didn't diminish his need to ensure she was unharmed. This mating dance would be the death of him if he didn't get her to the safety of the Sky Cities soon.

Malek rubbed the back of his neck. "Dammit. I can't leave her to face this alone."

Turning back to his bed, he grabbed their bag and rifled through it. Blossom had mentioned a music box. He hoped it was in this one with the rest of Sabine's belongings and not with Bane. The only music box he knew about was the one given to her by the Huntsman as a coronation gift. The Huntsman had put them in an enchanted sleep back then too. If this music box was the key to finding Sabine, Malek would use it.

He picked up the small ornate box embellished with precious gems. Each dark-blue stone sparkled brightly, drawing his attention to the golden crown emblem on the top. The box was small, easily able to fit in the palm of his hand. He lifted the lid and allowed the soft music to fill the room, but nothing happened. He slid it into his pocket, unsure how it was supposed to help find Sabine.

Heading out of the sleeping area, he barely spared a glance at the sleeping hellhounds littering the floor. "So much for guards."

At the main hallway, Malek hesitated, glancing in both directions. He closed his eyes for a moment, forming an image of Sabine in his mind. He focused on each detail he remembered: the way the light brought out the silver tones in her hair, the sensuality in her movements, the softness of her skin, and the way she always smelled of night-blooming roses.

She was utterly captivating, but it was her teasing smile and the way her laughter lit up a room that Malek treasured most. In the distance, he felt a distinct pull through their bond.

His eyes flew open. It was fainter than he'd expected and weakening by the second. Malek ran down the hall in the direction he'd felt her. She was in trouble. He knew it with every fiber of his being.

Other than the sound of his boots on the marble tiles, there was an eerie silence in the Hall. He turned corner after corner, unsure where he was going except that he was moving in the right direction.

He slowed at the sight of a mural on one of the walls. A

woman, bearing a striking resemblance to Sabine, was locked in an embrace with a fair-haired man. They were standing in some sort of garden with demons, fae, dwarves, and winged people kneeling around them in supplication. But the couple only had eyes for each other.

"Lachlina," Malek murmured, troubled by the similarities to Sabine. This wasn't the first image he'd seen of her, but it was the most detailed. From the color of her eyes to the shape of her nose, even her bearing made Sabine almost appear closer to a sister than a distant blood relative.

Malek turned away, feeling decidedly uneasy by the image. Focusing again on the woman he sought, Malek continued to wander using the thin connection between them to find Sabine. He passed through several more rooms, each one empty except for priceless artwork.

After what was beginning to feel like a hopeless search, Malek stopped in a large chamber. Tall marble columns went from the floor up to the ceiling. In between each pillar were large clay figurines that looked a little like giants that had been left out in the sun too long. They towered above Malek's height and were at least twice his width. Their arms were long, allowing their knuckles to reach nearly to the floor. Each had a golden glowing symbol etched on their forehead. There had to be at least a dozen in there, and they were all blocking his way.

He started to move past them. As one, their clay eyes opened and shone with a golden light. They each shifted, sending a dusting of clay to the ground. They moved to a defensive position, preventing him from reaching the chamber beyond.

"Turn back, dragonspawn," one of the golems rasped. "You are not welcome here."

Malek withdrew his sword. "I suggest you get out of my way. I'm not leaving without Sabine."

"She has not asked for your aid. You will be destroyed if you approach."

"So be it. You're not keeping her from me."

The golems attacked. They fought with brute strength, not skill. Malek might be a superior swordsman by most standards, but these creatures were elemental. They didn't feel pain and didn't fight by the same conventions of most sentient beings. They had been crafted by magic and made to fulfill a sole purpose, nothing else.

He slashed outward, his sword sliding into the golem's chest with a wet sucking noise. Malek yanked his weapon free and dodged another golem as it reached for him. Mud rose from the cracks between the tiles, covering the injured golem and filling in its injury with more clay.

One of the golems knocked into Malek, sending him staggering backward. The music box fell from his pocket and onto the ground.

Malek retreated several steps to avoid them, striking again and again. They were healing almost as soon as he'd pull his weapon free. Gripping his sword with both hands, he used the bulk of his strength to strike out, severing one of the golems' heads from its body. It fell to the ground with a wet thud.

Another took its place. The decapitated golem reached down, plucked its head from the ground, and replaced it. Mud formed over its neck, making it appear as though it had never been injured.

Malek shouted with rage, feeling the tenuous grasp on Sabine weakening even more. If he didn't get to her soon, he could lose her forever.

Fury rose within him, demanding he destroy anyone who tried to harm the woman he loved. With a flash of light, he allowed his power to fill him. In less than the blink of an eye, he reverted to his true dragon form.

The change seemed to enrage the golems. Instead of remaining on the defensive, they began to attack as one. Malek roared, sending dragonfire throughout the chamber to incinerate his enemies.

Some of the golems leaped on his back, trying to crush him. Others merged together, forming an even larger golem. Malek swept out with his tail, knocking them astride and crumbling the pillars nearby. The room shook. Malek whipped around, breathing more dragonfire on the golems and leaving them nothing more than smoking piles of dust.

When they were all destroyed, Malek returned to his human form, breathing heavily. If he had to destroy the entire Hall of the Gods to find Sabine, so be it. Nothing would keep him from her.

He picked up his fallen sword and the music box. Concerned it might have been damaged during the fight, he lifted the lid. The music played, but something about it was different. The tone was off. Malek lifted it, peering at the bottom. One of the jewels had come loose. Warming his hand slightly with his magic, he pressed the gemstone back in place and sealed it. The music played normally again.

On the far side of the room, the wall shimmered. A large silver portal opened, beckoning him. Malek stared at it in surprise. Every instinct told him Sabine was through there. Still holding the music box in his hand, he stepped through the doorway and into the Chamber of Dreams.

Chapter Seventeen

Sabine clasped her hands together, watching Vestior approach the desk on the far side of the room. For a god, he was more unassuming than she could have imagined. It was a little too easy to pretend he was just another Faerie royal, so much that she wondered if it was intentional on his part.

"Tell me, child. How much do you know about portal magic?"

"Very little," Sabine admitted with a frown. "The fae can manipulate existing portals, but we lack the means to create new ones. Even the locations of the existing ones are a closely guarded secret."

"It is to our regret that even those are still active." He waved his hand. "Continue."

Her frown deepened, feeling as though she were being tested on her knowledge and found lacking. "There are only a handful left that allow us to move over short distances in an instant, and even fewer that are stable. The Dragon Portal once allowed free travel between dimensions. While it was active, entire cities could be relocated in the blink of an eye. It also allowed you and the rest of the gods to use our magic to supplement your abilities."

"Indeed," Vestior said. "We also shared power when we had excess, similar to how the fae expunge their extra magic into the crystals and world itself. What else have you learned?"

Sabine recalled her tutor's lessons and the stories she'd heard over the years. "The war with the dragons was destroying us. The aderyan were gone, the merfolk were divided, the dwarves had retreated to their mountain, and our people were dying. Too much power was being drained from our world." She paused. "Lachlina betrayed you and the rest of the gods to seal the portal and save our people."

Given Azran's comment earlier, Sabine had expected more of a reaction to the mention of Lachlina's name. Vestior's face remained completely neutral, a typical court expression of polite interest and nothing more.

"What has Lachlina offered you in exchange for doing her bidding?"

"She hasn't been particularly forthcoming," Sabine said, rubbing her wrist where the goddess had marked her skin. If Vestior could offer some insight into Lachlina's motivations, so much the better. "Do you know what she wants from me?"

The Huntsman didn't respond right away. He waved his hand at one of the large cabinets, which took up most of the wall. It was a black cabinet with the same silver vined design, suggesting it had also been touched with demon blood. The doors swung open, revealing a large contraption that was moving in place.

Forgetting herself, Sabine walked toward the cabinet and stared in wonder at the device. It was some sort of machine that appeared to be moving of its own volition. She leaned forward, wondering if it was being powered by magic. Thin strands of metal linked hundreds of tiny spinning spheres together, each a different brilliant color.

She reached out to touch one of them but paused before she made contact. "What is this?"

"It is but a brief glimpse into the boundaries beyond yours. Your world, Aeslion, is but one small thread on a larger tapestry."

Sabine glanced at Vestior and then studied the small spheres with renewed interest. "These are all different worlds?"

Vestior gestured toward the thin filament strung between the worlds. "Each is connected by the in-between, and the veil is the protective sheath shielding it."

Sabine frowned and took a step closer. Each sphere was almost like a bead, strung with a thin filament going in one side and out the other. "Which one is Aeslion?"

He pointed at one of the spheres that appeared to be almost falling off the thread. It was a beautiful orb, swirling with soft colors of green, blue, and silver. The effect was hypnotic, but Sabine couldn't escape the sense of wrongness from seeing it tilt so precariously.

Sabine's brow furrowed. "It's going to fall."

Vestior inclined his head. "That will be up to you."

"Me?" Sabine darted another look at Vestior. At his neutral expression, she cradled the partially fallen world, feeling a tingle of magic on her skin where she touched it. Unlike with the other worlds, the filament traveled in and out of the same hole, threatening to expunge it from the rest of the group. She looked on the opposite side of the sphere, but the hole where the string should have been was sealed.

"We need to push it through somehow," Sabine said, looking on the opposite side of the sphere at where the hole had been sealed. "If you have something that can bore a hole, you should be able to run the entire string through it again."

A small smile played upon Vestior's lips. "Perhaps you will find something in your travels to aid you with such an undertaking. It will take far more magic than you currently possess to reconnect your world with the ether. Only then will your sphere be woven back onto the tapestry the way it was meant."

Sabine met his gaze. "Did you bring me here to warn me?"

Vestior didn't answer right away. "Your world is dying. It is no longer a question of *if*, but a matter of *when*. Those of us who still remain are no longer interested in sustaining a world that does not offer anything in return."

"How is that possible?"

Vestior flicked his wrist, summoning what appeared to be a will-o'-the-wisp in his palm. Unlike normal glowing wisps, this one was as clear as a crystal. Sabine took a step closer, seeing an image forming within it. Trees, villages, and even cities, populated with a variety of different people, were revealed as though they were flying over the ground at breathtaking speed.

"Magic is the foundation of our existence. Some call it science or have other names for it. Essentially, we are all connected to the ether. When you dream at night or recall your memories, you slip into the in-between and experience that shared consciousness. Some possess the ability to traverse their dreams or visions even while conscious, but it's simply a glimpse behind the veil."

Sabine stared into the globe, recognizing some of the cities, either from her travels or through descriptions. "I've heard something similar from the Elders. That's how memorywalkers and dreamweavers visit other places."

"Indeed," Vestior said, waving his hand over the will-o'-the-wisp to make it appear like a larger version of the world spheres in the cabinet. "Each world has at least two distinct locations where magic flows in and out, transporting power throughout the universe. Should one of those locations become sealed, the magic bottlenecks, limiting the flow of power to and from the ether. That imbalance is why the fae are slowly dying, why fewer children are being born each year, and why even normal magic is easily corrupted."

Sabine stared at him, her eyes widening as realization slammed into her. "You're talking about the Dragon Portal. That's what causing the imbalance in our world?"

Vestior inclined his head. "We have made efforts to provide your world with enough magic to sustain you, but it has been a temporary measure. The portal seals are failing. Once they fail, your world will have an opportunity to rejoin the ether. Or you may choose to keep the portal closed."

"If we reopen the portal, the gods will pull us into rejoining the war that nearly decimated our world. Millions more will die." She rubbed her arms, not wanting to think about the battle still being waged between gods and dragons on the other side of the portal. "I gave my word to Malek that I would help him locate the artifacts and ensure the portal remains sealed."

"Is that what he told you? That he wishes it to remain closed to *everyone*?"

Sabine bristled at the insinuation that Malek had lied. "Malek has given me no reason to doubt him."

Vestior arched his brow. "Hasn't he?"

Sabine bit back the reply that was on the tip of her tongue. Malek had deceived her when they'd first met, hiding his true identity and masquerading as a human ship captain. While she understood his reasoning, there might be some truth to Vestior's words. There were things he was keeping from her, just as she hadn't shared everything with him. But still, she knew Malek's heart. He would never intentionally cause her harm.

Vestior dismissed the will-o'-the-wisp and closed the cabinet. "The Well of Dreams is drying up as magic becomes scarce. Soon, it will not be enough to sustain even the humans who live among you. Before that happens, you will need to make a choice: Reconnect with the ether or die."

Sabine lowered her head, trying to wrap her head around everything the Huntsman was saying. Part of her wanted to reject it outright and dismiss his outlandish claims. Unfortunately, his words held the bitter taste of a harsh truth.

Taking a steadying breath, she lifted her head to meet his gaze. "Our world barely managed to survive the battle with the dragons last time. If we open the portal and the war spills out into our world again, we won't survive it."

"Perhaps not."

"There has to be another way."

"We are weakening, child," Vestior said with a sigh and sat in one of the chairs. "We may be labeled as gods, but we are not omnipotent. We bicker and war among ourselves as easily as we do with others. Your world is a drain on us, and many of us are reluctant to expend our magic on a lost cause. We have other concerns and battles to fight."

"What are you saying?"

"Where does the magic of Faerie come from?"

Sabine blinked at the sudden shift in topics. Talking to Vestior was like talking to the Faerie Elders and their convoluted paths to enlightenment.

Still, he wouldn't have asked if the reason wasn't important. Most of the time, Faerie seemed sentient, wanting to learn and understand those who put their own magic into it. Every time Sabine had communed with the land—

She stared at him in shock. "The land's magic is *your* magic. Faerie is the essence of the gods."

He steepled his hands together. "You asked me earlier whether the magic of Faerie brought you here. In a sense, yes. It is the focused strength and will of those you call gods. In reality, we are the Tuatha Dé, the tribe of gods. We are the shapers of worlds, and Aeslion is ours."

Sabine sank into the chair across from him. Was it possible that everything she'd once believed was wrong? "How long do we have before the magic fails?"

"Time moves differently among the realms, but I do not expect it will take long before my brethren no longer have enough excess magic to save a dying world. Perhaps months by your standards. Once enough of us cease providing the necessary magic to keep the Well of Dreams open, Aeslion will die quickly."

Sabine stared unseeing at the wall covered with priceless books. Opening the portal went against everything she'd believed, but she didn't see an alternative. There was no guarantee they'd survive another war, but there was no chance if the magic died. Sabine ran her fingers along Lachlina's marks, recalling her promise to help the goddess protect their world and seal the portal. And Malek had spent years searching for the artifacts needed to keep the portal closed. She'd given him her word that she'd do everything within her power to prevent another war from happening.

Vestior cocked his head. "Our time is nearly up. The dragon searches the Hall for you. Azran has intercepted him, but he is determined."

"I should go." Sabine stood, knowing boundaries wouldn't stop Malek from finding her. Even now, she could feel his worry and fear through their bond. He'd tear the Hall apart if he thought she were in danger.

Vestior rose and then slanted his gaze in her direction. "Do you know why the fae do not lie, child?"

"Words have power," she said, repeating the mantra

drilled into her by countless tutors. "Magic is in the air we breathe and in the words we speak. Lies fracture the truth, confusing the reality of our world and upsetting the balance."

"The fae are tied to this world, and their primary purpose is to act as its caretakers. The purpose of the Tuatha Dé is to maintain the balance in *all* worlds. We refused to allow the fae to speak untruths since they do not have the ability to sense slight variations in the balance beyond Aeslion. Should the balance be willfully broken, the ripples extend beyond the boundary of any one world."

"That's why Lachlina was imprisoned," Sabine murmured and then frowned. She wasn't certain whether Lachlina was truly a villain in this scenario. The renegade goddess may have upset the balance, but she'd saved millions of lives in the process. Her efforts had bought them some time to figure out a solution or to ensure the war ended naturally. Then again, Sabine didn't know what had happened to the other worlds that had been affected by her decision.

Vestior led her back to the wall she'd stepped through when she'd arrived.

"How can we stop the war?" Sabine asked, turning to face him. "If we open the portal and reconnect our world with the ether, there must be a way to protect the millions of people on Aeslion. We can't survive if the Tuatha Dé continue to draw upon our power."

"It was our power before it ever belonged to Aeslion, child."

Before she could respond, a thundering boom shook the room. Sabine staggered backward. Books fell from their shelves, priceless tomes toppling onto the ground in crumpled heaps.

"Your dragon is trying to tear a hole through the ether!" the Huntsman shouted, flinging out a hand and opening a portal in the wall.

Sabine gasped, watching as the air around them began to shimmer, as though the place was fading.

"Go!" He sent Sabine sprawling toward the portal with a blast of power. It slammed into her chest, stealing her breath. She fell backward, into the portal and back into the Well of Dreams.

Chapter Eighteen

The water was so cold, it was nearly ice.

It was even worse this time. Sabine's lungs burned with the need to take a breath. Her wet nightclothes tangled around her legs as she tried to kick herself upward, desperately trying to reach the surface. The Huntsman must have buffered the worst of the effects the first time she'd plunged into the Well's depths.

A loud rumbling noise sent aftershocks through the water. A leathery tail wrapped around her waist and yanked her upward. Malek! She burst out of the well, gasping for air when she broke through the surface. A blinding light engulfed her, and a moment later, Malek's arms encircled her, as he'd shifted back into human form.

He lowered them to the ground, holding her tightly. "Shh, it's okay. I've got you. Just breathe, love."

She coughed, her teeth chattering from the cool air hitting her icy skin. She pressed even closer to Malek, desperately needing his natural warmth. Malek rubbed her back and blew out gently, sending a heated burst of air over her, drying her clothing and hair. Only a slight dampness still permeated her clothing, but it was much more manageable, especially with Malek holding her.

"Oh, gods," she murmured. "You're better than a firepit."

He chuckled and buried his face into her hair, his arms tightening around her. "I almost didn't reach you in time. A few more minutes, and I could have lost you."

Sabine shook her head. "I'm not planning on leaving you any time soon."

"And I'm glad to hear that." He leaned back, his gaze roaming her features. "It was the Huntsman, wasn't it?"

Sabine opened her mouth to tell him about Vestior's true identity, but a skeletal form appeared on the far side of the well. Malek lifted his head, narrowing his eyes on the Huntsman.

Malek leaped to his feet and took a threatening step toward the god who had brought them there. The barely restrained fury in his expression promised retribution.

"Malek, wait!" Sabine called, scrambling to her feet to stop him.

For the first time since she'd emerged from the water, Sabine caught sight of the destruction to the chamber. She gasped in horror. Statues and pillars had toppled from his earlier shift. She wasn't sure how he'd managed to nearly rip a hole in reality, but it had to be tied to the Well of Dreams being an anchor point like Vestior had described.

"You!" Malek shouted, his skin glowing as he prepared to shift again. "You dare try to hurt her? Steal her from me? She nearly faded!"

With a wave of the Huntsman's hand, tentacles burst through the floor and wrapped around Malek's arms and legs. A loud howling echoed from somewhere deep within the Hall.

"No! Stop, Malek! I'm not hurt!" Sabine shouted, trying to avoid the tentacles and reach him. "Huntsman, you have to release him!"

"I'll burn this chamber to the ground!" Malek roared, fighting his restraints. Everywhere they touched his skin, the glow dimmed, hampering his attempts to shift. His hands shifted into something like claws, and he sliced through the tentacles. A sharp, acrid stench filled the air. With each one he cut down, two new ones grew in its place. It wouldn't slow him for long. Sabine sensed Malek's fury and building power. Once he shifted, he'd destroy everything in the chamber.

Sabine dove under the tentacles to reach the man she loved. She stood, pressing her hands against Malek's chest, and felt the furious pounding of his heart under her fingertips. "Don't shift, Malek. I need you in human form right now."

When he didn't respond, she infused her touch with a trace of magic and spoke softly, "I'm not hurt, Malek. I crossed through the veil. That's why you thought I was fading. Look at me and see for yourself. I've returned to you, whole and unharmed."

Her words and touch broke through Malek's fury. With his gaze fixed on her, he began to calm, but she could see the wild ferocity still thrumming through his body. It wouldn't take much to set him off again.

"You were drowning, fading," he said, his voice taking on a rougher tone from the magic swirling around them. "I won't allow anyone to take you from me."

Sabine managed a small smile. "You didn't. You rescued me. Allow me to do the same for you."

She darted a glance at the Huntsman across the chamber. "Release him. He merely seeks to protect me from harm."

"Your bond with the dragon shall either be your undoing or your greatest strength."

"I choose strength," Sabine said, bringing her magic to the surface. "Release him or imprison us both. Or has the hospitality of the Hall been rescinded without warning?"

The skeletal figure studied her for a long time. The tentacles slowly withdrew, disappearing back into the cracks and crevices in the granite flooring.

She moved closer to Malek, looking up into his darkened eyes. "The magic in this place is fragile. When you tried to reach me, the power began to fracture. I had to return abruptly to stop you from destroying the chamber. I was shoved back through the veil without taking the proper precautions."

When the last of the tentacles disappeared, Malek swept Sabine into his arms. He turned his body, angling himself between her and the Huntsman. Looking over his shoulder at Vestior, he said, "Name your price, Huntsman. Whatever her family offered for her death, I'll pay it three-fold for assurances you'll leave Sabine alone and unharmed."

Sabine slid her arm around Malek's waist and pressed against his side. "You can't barter with him, Malek. He's not who—"

Sabine's mouth clamped shut, her lips tingling from a touch of magic. Something was preventing her from speaking. She lashed outward, trying to find a way to break its hold. It tightened its grip around her, forcing her to unnatural silence.

In a soft voice meant for her ears alone, the Huntsman said, *"A geas upon you, daughter. Your companions are bold, and the balance is fragile. In accordance with the pact forged with the Tuatha Dé more than a millennia ago, I have given up my identity until the world is once again reunited with the ether. While on this side of the veil, I may only be referred to as Huntsman."*

Sabine stiffened, mentally lashing outward. *"I see the arrogance of the gods hasn't diminished. You dare much for one who is seeking favors from me. Consider carefully your future treatment because it will determine whether I'm inclined to aid your purpose."*

The Huntsman's eyes began to glow. Goose bumps pebbled Sabine's skin, but she refused to back down.

"He's not who?" Malek asked, drawing her attention back to him.

With no small amount of irritation, she chose her words carefully. "I doubt even the gods could barter with one such as him."

The Huntsman held her gaze for a moment. *"Very well, child. You have made your point."*

A staff appeared in the Huntsman's skeletal hand. A pulsing, deep-red crystal swirled at the top. He lifted the staff and brought the end of it down onto the marble floor with an audible thud. Thin red threads of power moved outward like a wave and filled the room. Malek tensed, his entire body bracing as though preparing to ward off a strike. Sabine pressed her hand against his chest, urging him to calm.

"In exchange for your silence, I offer you a gift of knowledge," the Huntsman said.

Magic poured into her. Her bond with Malek flared to life, and with it came a strange awareness in the recesses of her mind. Along with Malek's, she felt Vestior's presence. His fingers were icy in her thoughts, quickly sifting through her memories. She started to pull away, but he held her still. After a moment, something shifted. It was as though a doorway had been created, similar to the portal that had brought them there.

"You may now use mind-touch to call your dragon, even while he is in his true form. Be warned that this gift cannot extend beyond this chamber unless you both accept this path. If it is rejected by either before you leave this place, this offer shall not be

made again. Choose wisely, daughter. Once bound, it cannot be undone."

Sabine stared at the Huntsman in shock. Pressing her fingers to her lips, she lifted her head to regard Malek. His dark hair was still tied back with a leather strap, his piercing blue eyes glaring at the Huntsman with wild ferocity. No matter how fearsome he might be to some, Sabine knew he would never pose a threat to her.

Perhaps love had blinded her to potential dangers, but she and Malek were stronger together. She'd be a fool to turn away from this gift.

"*Malek?*" she asked silently, reaching for him through their mental connection. It was similar to the pathways used to communicate with some of the beastpeople. Sabine had never been overly skilled with this form of communication, but her connection with Malek felt more familiar. It some ways, it was easier.

He whipped his gaze toward her. "*Sabine? How is this possible? Only other dragons have ever been able to touch my thoughts.*"

"It's…" Sabine glanced at Vestior. "A gift. From the Huntsman."

"Impossible," Malek said, turning back toward the Huntsman. "Not even the gods of this world could breach our mental defenses. What trickery is this?"

Sabine pressed her hand against Malek's cheek. "We're bound together, Malek, by something far more powerful than even the magic of the gods. If we both accept, the Huntsman simply offers the knowledge of how to deepen our existing bond."

Malek's brow furrowed. He glanced at the Huntsman with no small measure of suspicion. "My grandfather would have said something to me if this was possible. He and my grandmother were mated for centuries."

"Perhaps they weren't offered this gift," she murmured. "I trust him in this, Malek. The choice to keep this connection belongs to us, and only to us."

Before Malek could respond, the Huntsman said, "*You have violated the sanctity of the Well of Dreams, dragon. You are hereby banished from this place at dawn's first light. If you are still within the Hall at that time, you will be turned to dust.*"

Malek's arms tightened around her, his eyes narrowing. Recognizing he would defend his ardent will, Sabine leaned into him and urged, "Accept this edict as another gift, Malek. Bane already told us what happened the last time the chamber was breached. We've violated the rules of hospitality already. This punishment is generous, especially considering the circumstances."

"Very well. We'll be away by dawn."

The Huntsman turned his glowing gaze on Sabine. "*King Cadan'ellesar of the Seelie is not your only enemy among the fae. Many wish to see you dead, not for your actions, but for what you portend. They fear and covet what they cannot understand.*"

A cold chill wrapped around Sabine, creeping up the back of her neck like icy fingers. She rubbed her throat, recalling the way her father had tried to strangle her with magic she hadn't realized was possible. "I'll heed your warning, Huntsman."

The Huntsman's eyes glowed brighter, while the rest of him began to fade from sight. "*Find the remaining artifacts and quickly, daughter. The portal will call to you once you have embraced their power.*"

"Wait," Sabine called to him before he could disappear. "We believe the demons have one of the artifacts, but where is the other?"

"*Seek your answer from those who are gone.*"

"Who? The gods?" Sabine asked.

"*Look to the dragons,*" the Huntsman said, his mental voice softer as his physical form vanished from view. A moment later, there was no sign he had ever been there, other than the fallen columns from Malek's destruction.

"The dragons?" Sabine murmured in disbelief.

"If my people had knowledge about the location of the artifacts, I'd be further ahead in my search." Malek frowned. "If I can get word to Levin or some of my associates in the Sky Cities, we can begin our search anew. It may be that one of the older clans might know something."

Sabine made a noncommittal noise, replaying everything she'd learned tonight. Unfortunately, Vestior had left her with more questions than answers. The idea that she needed to make a decision that potentially doomed millions of people weighed heavily in her mind. But nothing could be decided until they located the rest of the portal artifacts. She needed to find the demon king and find a way to convince him to hand over theirs.

Malek turned back to Sabine, his gaze roaming her features. "You're truly all right? When I couldn't feel you through our bond, I thought—"

Sabine shook her head. "I don't believe the Huntsman intended any harm to come to any of us. He simply wanted to speak with me."

Malek's expression darkened. "So he put the rest of us into an enchanted sleep and lured you here when you weren't willing? What did he say to you?"

"He… spoke of the history of our world." Sabine paused, weighing her words and testing the boundaries of the geas. Interesting. It seemed as though only discussing Vestior's identity was warded against.

Focusing again on Malek, she continued. "Lachlina broke the balance when she gave us the artifacts used to seal the portal. The Huntsman wants it open again."

She rubbed the goddess marks on her wrist, unable to sense Lachlina's presence. She didn't know if the goddess could hear her, but Sabine doubted she'd view the conversation with Vestior favorably.

Sabine paused, wondering why Vestior was so tolerant of Malek. It didn't make sense, unless… She frowned as a thought struck her. Could Vestior be hoping she'd use Malek and the dragons' resources to reconnect their world to the ether? Was that why he was encouraging her to look toward the dragons for answers?

"Did the Huntsman say what would happen if the balance wasn't restored?"

"All the magical races will eventually die."

"Do you believe him?"

Sabine hesitated. "I'm inclined to believe him, but I don't know his motivations. Without knowing that, I can't say for sure."

Malek stared at the Well of Dreams. "Many will die if the war resumes."

"If he's telling us the truth, many will die either way," Sabine said quietly, lifting her gaze to meet Malek's eyes. "You told me that you want the portal to remain closed to prevent another war. But the Huntsman led me to believe you have other ambitions."

Malek's jaw hardened, and he glanced at where the Huntsman had been standing.

She placed her hand on his chest, feeling his warmth beneath the thin material of his shirt. "What do you truly intend to do with the portal, Malek? Is there any truth to his claim?"

Malek muttered a curse, looking pained. "I could strangle him for his interference."

Sabine stiffened and pulled away from him. "Have you been deceiving me?"

"No," Malek said, scrubbing his hands against his face. "I never lied to you, but I didn't tell you the full truth either. Timing was a large part of it. Since almost the moment we met, we've been running from one dangerous situation to another. In many ways, we've had very little time to get to know one another. Trust is a fragile thing, and I'd already fractured yours by waiting to tell you I was a dragon. I wasn't willing to push you over that line. I would never do anything to hurt you intentionally, Sabine."

She lowered her head, trying to sort through her feelings. His lack of forthrightness stung, but he was right about the rest. Their fates might be intertwined, but in many ways, she and Malek were still learning about one another.

If he'd withheld some piece of information, he must have valid reasons. Besides, she was doing the same thing with Vestior's identity. As much as it pained her, she couldn't— and wouldn't—demand his secrets.

Trust was a precious gift. Like magic, it wasn't something that could be demanded or taken by force. It was a gift from the heart, as pure and priceless as the rarest dwarven crystal. If she forced Malek to reveal his secrets before he was ready, she could potentially destroy the tender emotions that were growing between them.

Lifting her head, Sabine met his gaze and said, "I do trust you, Malek. Implicitly. I told you once before that I won't demand your secrets. I know who you are, and that's all I need to know. The rest will come in time."

"You humble me, Sabine," Malek murmured, taking her hand in his. His much larger hand seemed to dwarf hers in comparison. "I know it's a fae trait to not pry, but it still staggers me. If you were a dragon, you'd be demanding answers."

Sabine's mouth curved slightly. "My people are no less curious. We simply prefer eliciting answers in other, more subtle ways."

"I've noticed. Your methods are very effective," Malek admitted, surveying the columns that had fallen. "This wasn't how I envisioned having this conversation, but I doubt there will ever be a good time. You deserve the truth. All of it." He turned back toward her. "If you're willing to hear it, I'll tell you everything you want to know. I don't want anything to come between us."

Looking up into eyes that were the shadowed blue of a twilight sky, Sabine squeezed his hand and said, "All right. I'm listening."

MALEK WASN'T sure how the Huntsman had known, but part of him was relieved to have an opportunity to tell Sabine the truth. She might not completely understand everything until she visited the Sky Cities, but this was a start.

She pulled her robe around her tighter, but he caught the slight tremble that went through her slender form. He wanted to pull her into his arms again to warm her, but he didn't trust himself while his emotions were this close to the surface. He was too close to the mating frenzy to keep himself in check if she reacted badly. He would never hurt her, but the same couldn't be said for the chamber if she walked away from him.

Sabine lifted her head, her lavender eyes watching him expectantly. There wasn't any easy way to tell her the truth.

"My people are dying."

Sabine blinked. "What?"

"When we met, you told me how the fae are slow to reproduce. The same is happening to my people. It wasn't always like this, but over the past several generations, all of the dragons have been growing weaker."

Sabine was quiet for a long time. "It must be the imbalance. The Huntsman indicated there wasn't enough magic left in our world with the portal being closed. I thought it was only the first races who were affected, but it must be slowly killing all of us."

Malek frowned. "I hadn't realized it could be connected. Our physical forms are dependent upon our magic. When our females enter their cycle of kavenshin and find their mate, their magic is fractured so they might share it with their future child. If there isn't enough magic to share, the mother and baby both die."

Horror filled her eyes. "Both?"

Malek nodded sadly. "Our females no longer have enough magic to give birth to true dragons, those children who learn their dragon form first. Without their ability to encapsulate the dragonlings in eggs to mature their power, the mothers have begun trying to carry their children to term in human form."

"It's not working?"

"Dragons cannot exist in human form for prolonged periods. We *must* shift, or it will happen at the slightest provocation, like a powder keg waiting to explode. Dragons don't have the physiology to handle a human pregnancy."

Sabine tilted her head, a lock of her silvery hair falling across her cheek. "If the dragons are dying, wouldn't your people want to return to their home world? Why would you want to keep the portal closed?"

"This *is* our home, Sabine," Malek said, reaching up to tuck her hair behind her ear. "Some dragons would welcome the opportunity to once again roam the skies beyond this world, but many of us have never known anything else. I don't want the war to resume and lose what we have here."

She lowered her gaze. "If the Huntsman is right, it may be inevitable."

"It was my hope that we could find a way to allow enough magic to enter Aeslion. I've spent the past several years trying to research and understand the mechanics of how the portal works."

Sabine jerked her head upward, her eyes wide in shock. "You want to try to control it?"

"If it's possible," Malek said with a frown. "If not, I'm prepared to leave this world to seek out a possible remedy for my people."

Sabine paled. "What?"

A sharp pain stabbed through his chest at the thought of leaving her. He hoped things wouldn't come to that. It would destroy something inside him to walk away from the woman he loved. "Only if there's no other way. I can't let my people die, Sabine."

Sabine looked away, her gaze drifting back to the shimmering water of the Well of Dreams. "If the Huntsman was being forthright, I don't believe it can be controlled like a valve. It can either be open or closed, but there isn't a way to control the flow of magic."

Malek pressed his mouth into a thin line. "Given what I read in the dwarven archives, I fear you're correct."

She shook her head. "I wish I had known all of this earlier."

"Would it have changed anything?"

Sabine lifted her gaze to meet his eyes. "I don't know. At the very least, I could have helped you search for answers instead of wasting time on Faerie politics."

"This isn't your burden, Sabine." Malek closed the distance between them and took her hand. "Before Levin and Esme left with the ship, I told him I would tell you the truth before we met up with them again. He was going to tell Esmelle while they were sailing north. After you were hurt, I wanted to give you a bit more time to recover before putting more weight on your shoulders. You've taken on a lot over the past several weeks. This past week was the first time I've seen you simply relax in a long time."

Sabine's eyes softened. "This is what you were going to tell me back on the ship and then again when we were in Razadon."

Malek threaded their fingers together, needing to touch her. "Yes. I was hoping to convince you to travel to the Sky Cities with me. I thought you might understand more if you met my sister, Kaia. Before I left, she'd met a young drake and was talking about mating him."

"You're worried about her," Sabine said quietly.

Malek blew out a breath and nodded. Poor Kaia. She'd gone to him the morning before he left with tears in her eyes. His normally headstrong, willful sister had been terrified once she realized her volatile emotions around Thom were the first signs of mating.

"I can't make you any promises, Malek," Sabine said. "But you've shown me there's more to the dragons than I once believed. I'll do what I can to help your people."

An overwhelming rush of relief rolled through him. He pressed his forehead against hers, breathing in the soft scent of night-blooming roses.

She might not be able to turn the tide to save his people, but she was one of the few fae in history who were willing to consider them as something more than the enemy. Perhaps there was hope between their people after all.

Sabine pressed her hands against his chest, her touch sending a frisson of awareness through him. It was almost as though they were connected on a deeper level. It shouldn't have been possible between a dragon and a fae, but they'd already broken normal conventions. But even that wasn't enough. His love for her was already larger than anything he'd ever experienced, and yet… he wanted more. He wanted everything with her.

"Will you tell me what you know about this new ability? To speak to me with your mind?"

Sabine's brow furrowed. "When I speak with one of the beastpeople, a door opens in my mind, which allows me to communicate. When we're children, our parents forge new doorways for us by burning through our mental barriers. My people lose more of the ability with each new generation. I've never been skilled at it. Balkin is the only one I've ever spoken with in regularity."

"Then it's not something that's natural?"

Sabine shook her head. "No. Among the fae, only the sidhe have the ability and only because we're direct descendants of the gods. They were the ones who showed us how to communicate with the creatures of the forest. When the fae created the beastpeople to help protect Faerie, we used those same methods to speak with them. Not all of them are capable of human speech. Balkin was one of the few exceptions, which is why he's become something of a leader among his people."

"Interesting," he murmured, rubbing his chin. "My people use inherited neural pathways to communicate. It's part of the magic of our people, our ability to harness those connections between clans before we're even born. The most powerful of the dragons possess the most magic, enabling us to speak to every clan."

Sabine jerked back. "You can speak to the other dragons at any time?"

"No. Distance is a factor, and it's easier to speak with those we're more familiar with."

Sabine nodded. "That's similar to our mental speech. The Huntsman showed me how to access a shared mental connection with you, but we both need to walk through the door together to allow it."

Being tied to her in that way, able to communicate while he was in dragon form, was something Malek had never considered possible. He was more than intrigued by the possibility, provided it didn't cause her any harm.

"I don't like the idea of you burning through your mental barriers."

"All magic requires a sacrifice."

"It doesn't have to be yours."

Sabine tilted her head in acknowledgement. "No. It would be ours."

She turned away from him and walked to the edge of the pool. He had the impression she needed time to gather her thoughts before committing to this path. For himself, he wanted it, but he also recognized it could cause problems among his people. Many of them didn't trust the fae and still viewed them as enemies or worse. If they ever learned fae could have the potential to listen in on their mental speech, they would try to destroy such a vulnerability.

Unmindful of the direction of his thoughts, Sabine stared into the water and said, "When a fae infant is born to the royal line, one of the beastpeople is chosen to become their primary guardian. The child is put into their arms, and a ritual is performed to complete the blood bond."

"This was done to you? To tie you to Balkin?"

She nodded but didn't turn to look at him. "For the child, it's a forced and somewhat painful merging. Balkin often suspected our bond never formed properly because I resisted it and him. He believes my difficulties with mind speech is related."

She turned toward him, humor dancing in her eyes. "He often said I was too hardheaded and stubborn to do anything in proper fae fashion, including accepting a guardian."

Malek smiled, recalling the proud lionesque warrior who had treated Sabine as a treasured daughter. "I can picture him saying that."

Sabine turned away and stared at the water. "Forging this new ability between us wouldn't be the same as what occurred between Balkin and me."

Malek took a step toward her. "How is it different?"

She turned to face him again, the light from the torches on the wall behind her causing a golden nimbus to surround her. "It would be our choice, not something forced upon us by fate or circumstance. If we take this step, it would be because we both want it. Because *we* desire it—and each other."

"Is this what you want, Sabine?"

"It's not my decision alone, Malek," Sabine said, clasping her hands together. "We would both have to surrender ourselves to one another, opening our minds completely to the other. It's more than the bond we already share. It's seeing the best and worst of each other and still having the courage to move forward."

Malek flexed his fingers, wanting to touch her but recognizing her need for space. No matter how much he might want her, he wasn't willing to influence her if this wasn't what she truly desired.

"You haven't answered the question. Do you want to accept this gift?"

The love that shone in her eyes was staggering. "I never thought I would want anyone to touch my thoughts, until I met you. But you've managed to get past my defenses almost from the first moment we met. The thought no longer frightens me."

"I don't have any doubts about you, Sabine. Just as you claim to know who I am, I also know who you are."

Like Sabine was an oasis in the desert, Malek took another step toward her, needing the salvation she offered.

"I saw the real you the first time we met: a strong and capable woman who cut down her attackers yet still had the compassion to offer a street kid a chance for a future. I saw you when you risked everything to protect Rika and her city from those who would destroy it. I saw you again when you nearly sacrificed yourself to protect the merfolk and the dwarves from the imbalance plaguing the land. I see *you*, Sabine. I've always seen you. And I thank your gods for the gift of you every single day."

"Malek," she whispered, her eyes shining with unshed tears.

"I love you, Sabine. For me, there will never be anyone else. There never could be. From the moment you stepped into my life, you became my entire world."

A tear streaked down her cheek. "You undo me."

Cupping her face, he wiped her tears away and said, "I want you in every way, Sabine. You're already in my heart. I would be honored to have you in my thoughts as well."

She smiled, the expression making her even more radiant. "I feel the same way."

He leaned down and pressed a soft kiss against her lips. "I don't want any joining between us to cause you any harm. You deserve a life of happiness and pleasure, not one with pain, no matter how small."

"No pain is too great for the gift of having you in my life," she said, taking his hand in hers. "But this can also be a gift of equal pleasure. Since our bond was forged in love, we can use that same emotion to temper pain when we step through the doorway together."

"Then I'm yours," Malek said, lifting her hand and kissing it softly. Sabine smiled up at him and then closed her eyes.

A gentle breeze blew through the chamber, caressing

Sabine's hair and causing the water in the well to ripple. Her skin glowed, the silver-and-gold marks of power etched on her skin taking on a soft luminescence. They were different somehow, almost richer with more nuances. A few seemed to have shifted slightly, their patterns forming stronger and surer lines.

Malek's magic rose to the surface, responding to Sabine's unspoken demand. Even if he'd wanted to, he wouldn't have been able to resist her. She was pure, primal power, and her magic called to his in a way that no one else's ever had. In so many ways, she was everything he'd ever wanted and more.

Something stirred inside him, a tentative touch of magic that was impossibly fragile. It was as elusive as smoke and as alluring as a perfectly potent perfume. A spark shifted inside him, a burning ember that sought her out to bind her to him —forever.

She gasped and started to pull away, but Malek's hand tightened around hers. Tamping down on the embers that responded to her as well as the relentless demand of the mating frenzy, he forced himself to wait until she was ready.

Sweat beaded at his temple as need and desire warred within him. Patience, he reminded himself. This was new to her, and she needed to find her way without his interference. Even if he never had this additional connection with her, it wouldn't diminish what was growing between them. She was more than precious to him, a treasure that rivaled the greatest riches in the world.

After a moment, he felt her push past her instinctive fear and continue to reach for him. He opened his mind completely to her, cradling her essence in his thoughts. He held his breath, waiting for her to take the next step.

She opened her eyes, and wonder filled them. Her voice was as quiet as a whisper in his thoughts. "*Malek?*"

Elation soared within him. "*I'm here, my love.*"

Intertwining her fingers with his, she said, *"I feel you, in my head, in my heart. You're everywhere."*

He leaned down and kissed her lightly. *"I'll always be here whenever you need me."*

Her gaze softened. *"I'll begin the binding, if you're ready."*

Not trusting himself to speak, he nodded.

"By blood and magic, and by my rights to both, I share my power and my destiny—both to be shaped by our wills."

A touch of power accompanied her words, and with it, Malek's dragonfire seared a path between them. Her fingers trembled, but he held her steady, willing her to stay the course.

Locking her gaze with his, she continued. *"We accept this gift, freely offered and freely given, that we might merge our futures as one until the last of the magic fades from this world."*

Magic surrounded them, enveloping them in a shimmering cocoon. Her skin glowed even more brilliantly, and Malek's power surged like a tidal wave, matching her light with his. Flames erupted around them, dancing in colors of reds, oranges, and at the center, a vibrant blue-and-green light that pulsed with Sabine's essence.

Together, they were both light and dark. Fire and ice. Need and desire, blended together. His magic was blinding in its potency, chasing away the darkest shadows of her mind. And within him, he felt her smooth the jagged edges of his soul and quench the worst of his dragonfire with her love.

Their combined power engulfed them, sending both their passions alight with quicksilver heat and need. Her lips parted as her magic soared to meet his desperate desire with hers.

They came together as one, equal in both hearts and minds. Her skin was impossibly soft, like the finest of silks. He slipped her robe off her shoulders and the thin straps of her nightclothes, and she moved forward, allowing them to fall to the ground. They pooled at her feet, and he inhaled sharply at the sight of her standing in front of him.

She tossed back her silvery hair, gazing at him with luminous eyes. Her skin glowed with the vestiges of power, and his breath caught as he gazed at her. She was a goddess incarnate, a deity of desire and passion, and he was her most loyal of subjects.

Needing to taste her, he trailed kisses down her neck to her shoulders. The smell of night-blooming roses filled his nose, their heady scent as intoxicating as a drug. Thrusting his hands through her hair, he captured her lips again. She opened to him, and he swept in with undeniable hunger, wanting everything she offered and more.

He started to ease her to the ground but hesitated at the sight of the bed of moss that sprung from the marble floor. "Did you do that?"

She laughed, the sound resonating in his mind and warming his heart. She didn't laugh nearly enough.

"Marble is cold, even if I have a dragon to keep me warm," she teased, lifting his shirt until he pulled it over his head. *"Now kiss me before I freeze."*

She didn't have to ask him twice. Pulling her closer, he kissed her deeply, their tongues mating in a dance as old as time. Her magic teased his skin, beguiling him with unspoken promises.

"I love you, Malek," she whispered, her voice as soft as a caress.

His heart soared. It was only the second time she'd said those words to him, and it was as precious as the first. If he lived a thousand years, he would never grow tired of hearing her say it. *"I'll love you until the last of the magic fades from this world. My heart belongs to you, Sabin'theoria, now and forever."*

The sound of a bell rang in his mind, locking their

connection in place. Elation filled him, and he wanted to shout in victory. The magic between them was still building, promising even more wonders as it continued to grow.

The Well of Dreams shimmered, the water rippling and sending light dancing across the ceiling. Sabine's skin glowed softly beneath him, her marks of power flickering in time with the ripples. Malek's power flared higher, his possessive instincts rising sharply to the surface. He traced each of her marks with his lips, worshipping her body as he followed their path to discover her innermost secrets. She cried out, holding him tighter against her as he sent her spiraling with need.

"*Now, Malek,*" she urged, unfastening his pants with a flick of her wrist. "*I need you now.*"

He was helpless to refuse her plea. He didn't know if it was the magic in this place, her, or possibly both. It didn't matter. She was his, just as he belonged to her.

Driven by their combined needs, he released his inhibitions and unleashed his power. She gasped and arched her back, responding to his touch and demanding more. And by gods, he would give her more—as much as she could take. Everything he was, everything he could be, he surrendered to her. And in return, he felt her become pliant, opening to him fully.

They rolled together on the bed of moss, lost in waves of sensations and intimate touches. It was both humbling and riveting, that this woman had the power to tame a dragon's heart. When he finally slid inside her, the walls between them shattered. She threw her head back and cried out as he thrust deeply, her nails clutching him even tighter and urging him on.

The power between them continued to grow, a fiery volcano ready to explode. The floor beneath them trembled, but he was too lost in her to stop. She cried out again, her mental pleas spurring him to new heights. She was every-thing to him, his entire purpose for being, and he could feel himself the same in hers.

He gave himself over to the moment and to her. And when he finally poured his heat into her, she shattered beneath him. Together, they collapsed on the moss-covered floor, a dragon and his fae lover. Two once-sworn enemies, now forever bonded in love.

Chapter Nineteen

*W*ith her skin still flushed from their lovemaking, Sabine tied her robe closed. She darted a small smile at Malek, pleased she could still feel him at the edge of her thoughts. Only time would tell whether it was a foolish decision, but her heart had taken her down this path, and she intended to see it through.

Malek captured her hand in his and brought it to his lips, then placed a kiss against each of her fingers. "There's something to be said about using sex as a ritual rather than cutting your beautiful skin. I find I much prefer this method."

She laughed and kissed him lightly on his lips before dissipating the moss bed she'd summoned. "While I'm incredibly tempted to stay here and see if we can top that last 'ritual,' we should probably get back to our friends. We've been gone far longer than I expected. Dawn will be approaching soon."

Malek stood and helped her to her feet. She looked around, but there was nothing left for them in the Well of Dreams. The Huntsman had long since gone, and the water was once again calm. She wondered if the Huntsman had brought them there for more reasons than simply to discuss the portal. Between the power of this place and sex with Malek, her magic had been replenished. She was feeling stronger than she had in weeks.

"Your hair has traces of gold in it."

Sabine turned to look up at him. "It does?"

He picked up a lock of her hair and ran it through his fingers. "Mmhmm. It's pretty, but different. Do you think it could be the effects from the well?"

"Perhaps," Sabine said, studying the tips of her hair. The gold dusting on her skin and even her marks were more pronounced. They glimmered and shone in the light even without tapping into her magic.

Malek picked up the leather tie she'd tugged free and quickly bound his dark hair before taking her hand in his. With a pleased smile, Sabine walked hand-in-hand with him out of the room. The chamber doors closed behind them, sealing the Well of Dreams from view.

Testing their newly formed ability, she asked, "*Malek? Can you still hear me?*"

He darted a glance at her. "Your voice is very quiet. I wouldn't be able to hear you unless I was listening for it."

"I suppose we'll need to be patient and wait for the magic to evolve. Hopefully we won't need to rely on the ability anytime soon."

"If it's the same as dragon-to-dragon speech, it may take a few months. Before a dragon is born, we learn to communicate first with our parents and then our clan. By the time we reach puberty, our mental speech abilities are fully developed, with the capability to speak both privately and publicly over long distances."

"I hadn't realized you could do both."

"It's handy for clan meetings."

Sabine slowed her steps at the sight of several heaping piles of claylike dust littering the floor. A column had toppled, landing partially in one of the dust piles.

"What in the world? Our magic shouldn't have caused damage here."

"Golems."

Sabine jerked her head upward to look at Malek. "What? You think golems caused this?"

He made a noncommittal noise and absently ran his thumb over her hand. Sabine looked at the piles again and then back at the dragon at her side. Was he actually *blushing*?

No. He didn't. Wait. Did he?

Sabine's lips twitched as she surveyed the empty areas where the stone guardians had once resided. She counted at least half a dozen piles of dirt.

Schooling her expression, she arched her brow and asked, "Exactly how many golems did you destroy trying to find me?"

Malek rubbed the back of his neck, appearing decidedly uncomfortable. "Ah, well. Let's just say golems don't have much resistance to dragonfire."

Sabine bit back a grin. "And the column?"

He cleared his throat. "It, ah, got in the way of my tail."

A laugh bubbled out of her. Hooking her arm with Malek's, she teased him. "If we encounter any more golems, I'll be sure to stand well away from your tail and dragon breath. It's no wonder our invitation was rescinded. I'm not sure the Hall of the Gods would survive a longer stay."

Malek harrumphed, but his lips curved slightly. "Blossom's going to be disappointed she slept through the excitement."

Sabine's humor faded. "Yes, but I have a feeling she'll have more than enough before we escape the underworld. We still need to secure an alliance with the demon king."

"Any idea how we're going to do that?"

Her mother had been tightlipped about her experiences in the underworld. Queen Malia had been a force of nature, someone who was both feared and revered among the Unseelie, yet Sabine had the distinct impression that the demon king had unnerved her. It was the reason she'd rarely traveled to the demon homeland. Sabine herself had never stepped foot into Harfanel, but the stories had always unsettled her.

"The ritual acknowledging me as queen should give me some standing. The alliance will be another matter."

"Bane hasn't said much about the ritual."

"Did you see him when you were looking for me?"

"*The demon has left the Hall.*"

Sabine turned at the sound of Azran's mental voice. The hellhound trotted toward them, swishing his fiery tale.

"Where is he?"

"*We do not look beyond the Hall, except to discourage intruders. I can take you and your companions to the exit he used. The crystals will show you the way.*"

"He wouldn't have been foolish enough to try removing the curse without help, would he?"

"If he thought it would protect me, yes," Sabine admitted, with a muttered oath about the foolishness of arrogant, overprotective demons. "With his access to my magic being blocked, I'm not sure he trusts himself right now."

"Can you track him?"

Sabine hesitated. "When I tried to get a sense of him earlier, something wasn't quite right."

"What do you mean?"

"It almost felt as though he were both less and more. I'm not sure if it's because he's back in the underworld or if it's the curse, but he feels as though he's everywhere and nowhere at the same time."

"I don't understand how that's possible." Malek's gaze lifted upward to the carved ceiling. "Before Bane left, Rika said she'd sensed a change in his magic. But it may very well be this place. There's an energy even in the walls. It could be interfering with your senses."

"I will escort you to your quarters."

They followed Azran down the hall, in the direction of their beds. Sabine yawned, trying to stave off the mental and physical exhaustion. Her magic might have been replenished by the Well of Dreams, but her more mundane concerns still needed to be addressed.

Malek glanced at her. "You haven't slept at all, have you?"

"Only a few hours."

"We'll find a place once we locate Bane. I can keep watch while you both get some rest."

Sabine nodded, too tired to argue the point. They trudged into the room, and Sabine went straight toward her bed. While Malek woke both Rika and Blossom, Sabine picked up their bag and selected some clothing for herself and Rika. Most of what had been provided to her was court attire, which made sense if she was going to be visiting the demon king. She simply wished there had also been some practical travel clothing too. Although, Vestior probably had his own ideas about suitable attire for a Faerie queen. She'd have to check the bag in Bane's possession once she found him.

When she was done, Malek took the bag from her and said, "No luck waking up Blossom. She swatted at me and told me 'five more minutes' before she started snoring again. We might just have to pick up the plant and let her sleep it off. I'll get dressed in the bathing room while you two finish up in here."

Sabine nodded while Malek disappeared into the bathing room.

"Blossom doesn't do as well at night," Rika said, yawning widely. The girl's hair was astray, her eyes red-rimmed and glossy. From the appearance of her bed, she'd spent the past few hours tossing and turning restlessly.

"No," Sabine said in agreement, glancing at Blossom's potted plant. "The hours before dawn are the hardest for pixies to stay awake."

Rika rubbed her eyes. "Did something happen? It can't be morning yet."

"We had another visit from the Huntsman while you were asleep," Sabine said, handing Rika her clothing. "He's withdrawn his offer of hospitality. Bane left the Hall already. We need to head out after him and then then make our way to Harfanel."

"Is Bane okay?"

Sabine squeezed Rika's hand and stood. "I'm worried about him too, but he's resourceful."

Rika nodded. If she'd noticed Sabine hadn't answered the question, she didn't comment. She was either learning to be more circumspect or had accepted Sabine's response as being typical for the fae.

"Sheesh. I nearly strangled myself." Rika untangled herself from the blankets. "I'm glad we're leaving. I can't remember the last time I had such terrible nightmares."

"Oh?" Sabine arched her brow, pulling off her wrinkled robe. Malek might have dried it, but her dip in the Well of Dreams hadn't done it any favors.

"Yeah. It didn't make much sense." Rika folded the blanket into a neat square and placed it on the bed. "You looked different, sort of golden. You shouted something in a strange language and then threw bolts of magic at Malek that looked like knives. I've never seen you so angry. I kept yelling at you to stop, that you were going to kill him, but you…" Her eyes took on a faraway cast. "You said it was too late. You couldn't hear Malek's voice anymore. It didn't make sense."

Sabine froze, her skin prickling in warning. "What?"

Rika shuddered. "I'm glad we're leaving. I don't want to have another dream like that again. I know you wouldn't ever try to kill Malek, but it just felt so *real*."

Sabine swallowed, her mouth going dry at the thought of something happening to Malek. An icy spike of fear went straight through her stomach. "No," she managed to say in a hoarse whisper, her hands clenching around the silken fabric in her hand. "No, I can't imagine a time I would ever want to see him gone from this world, either by my hand or anyone else's."

Gods. She couldn't imagine losing him, much less wanting harm to come to him. Even when Vestior had alluded to Malek's deceit, she hadn't been angry with him. Hurt, yes. But not angry. She didn't think she'd ever given Rika cause to have those kinds of nightmares.

She paused, wondering if Rika's dream might mean something else. The golden glow she'd described was a little too close to what Sabine had seen in the mirror. "Rika, is this the first time you've had a dream like that? Could it have been something more?"

"You think it was a *vision*?" Rika asked, ended the question with a squeak.

Sabine sat on the edge of Rika's bed again. She placed her hand atop Rika's and said, "Among the fae, my people give weight to dreams as well as prophecy. I won't discount the possibility either. You've been using your abilities more actively lately. Dreams and prophecy go hand-in-hand. Can you tell me anything else you remember?"

Rika frowned. "Not much. Only flashes. I remember you

shouting something that sounded like 'shee leen vare-some-thing something.'"

Sabine inhaled sharply. "*Shelein varesein printemp?*"

Rika nodded, her expression growing alarmed. "That means something?"

"It's an archaic saying," Sabine said quietly. "There's no exact translation, but the closest would be 'a thousand cuts for the death of my heart.'"

"Malek wouldn't betray you, Sabine."

Sabine didn't answer right away. Not wanting to believe it either, she reached over and squeezed Rika's hand. "We need to hurry and get dressed. We'll talk to Malek about this later. If you have any more dreams like this or remember anything else, like a location or landmarks, let me know. If there's a way to avoid your vision coming to pass, we need to find the opportunity to change it."

Rika nodded. "Yeah. Okay. I'll try."

Sabine stood and dressed quickly in a dark-blue diaphanous gown that had a small dusting of silver and gold around the hem. The design spiraled upward in a starburst pattern, giving the illusion of movement. The lightweight material was better suited for the warmer climate in the underworld, compared to the mountainous region of the dwarven city.

Sabine checked on Blossom, who was curled up around the plant stalk and snoring softly. Sending a light trickle of magic over Blossom, Sabine said, "We have to leave. If you want to eat something before we go, I believe there are a few honeycakes left."

Blossom blinked open her eyes and sat up. "I told Malek you'd be okay. Was the Huntsman mad at him?"

"Perhaps a bit, but I don't believe there will be any lasting repercussions."

"Good. We have to stay on his good side to get into the

garden." She rubbed her eyes. "Did you say something about honeycakes? We have more?"

Sabine smiled. "Yes. And we have more adventures to go on, so you might want to hurry."

"I'll be right back!" Blossom launched herself into the air and darted into the next room where the food was laid out.

Chapter Twenty

*A*zran led them to the doorway that marked the boundary to the Hall of the Gods. He stopped abruptly before they crossed and nudged Sabine's hand. Sabine immediately placed her hand on his large head, ruffling his fur absently.

Four tunnel entrances gaped like open mouths, each appearing the same as the others. She could make out the gleam of small crystals jutting out of the walls beside each entrance, but there weren't any identifying marks. She had no idea which way to travel to find Bane or the demon city.

"In this, I may aid you," Azran said, looking up at her.

"How?"

"To reach the demon city, you must travel down the left corridor until you reach the first crossroads. Upon your arrival, press your hand against the crystal and keep your destination in your thoughts. Walk only upon the paths illuminated by the red crystals, and you will be led in the correct direction. Someone will intercept you long before you reach the boundary of Harfanel."

Sabine tilted her head in acknowledgment of his words. "Be well, Azran."

"Same to you, little goddess. Know that you carry the wisdom of the Hall with you, always."

Malek touched her arm and said, "We should go."

She nodded and allowed Malek to lead her down the corridor. Rika walked beside her, with her weapon at the ready, while Blossom sat on Rika's shoulder. Sabine heard the door sealing shut behind them but didn't look back.

"How are we going to find Bane?" Rika asked.

"I'm hoping he'll locate us."

Malek frowned. "Bane's able to track you with his abilities, isn't he?"

"Normally, yes," Sabine said, trying to sense him through their blood bond. "I can't quite get a read on him. I think the curse may be interfering, or we're still too close to the wards protecting the Hall."

As they moved toward the tunnel, Sabine's skin began to burn. She inhaled sharply, gripping her wrist where Lachlina's markings decorated her skin.

Malek stopped abruptly. "What is it? What's wrong?"

Blossom's wings fluttered, their tips turning red in agitation. "It's the goddess! She's really angry, Sabine. She couldn't reach you when we were inside the Hall."

Sabine gasped, the pain shooting up her arm like a branding iron. She stumbled, trying to stay upright and breathe through the pain. Gritting her teeth, she tried to find a calm oasis in her mind, but it was as though a tidal wave was pummeling against her natural defenses.

"She's so angry!" Blossom shrieked, clamping her hands over her ears. "I can't do it! I can't!"

Malek wrapped his arm around Sabine's waist, keeping her upright. He whipped his head toward Blossom and snapped, "I don't give a damn if she's angry! If she doesn't stop trying to control Sabine, I'll spend the rest of my days working to destroy her. On that, she has my most solemn oath."

"Don't threaten her!" Blossom shrieked, her wings fluttering wildly. "It'll make it worse!"

Sabine cried out, doubling over from the pain lancing through her. The marks on her wrist burned, while icy pinpricks stabbed into her thoughts, piercing them with a relentlessness that threatened to leave her mindless.

She fumbled for her knives and withdrew one from its sheath. She pressed the metal against her skin, drawing blood. With shaking hands, she cut into her skin, watching as her blood welled to the surface and dripped down her hand. If she had to cut the damn marks off her skin to avoid being a puppet, so be it.

An eerie howl sounded from somewhere in the distance. A moment later, another howl joined the chorus.

"No!" Malek grabbed Sabine's wrist, halting her efforts to flay the marks from her wrist. "Bane said the creatures are drawn to your blood. You can't cut."

"Burn them off!" she managed to say through gritted teeth. "Now, Malek! I can't handle much more."

Malek whipped his head toward Blossom. "Tell Lachlina what will transpire if she doesn't stop. She'll lose any ties to Sabine if she doesn't cease this tantrum."

Blossom clenched her fists and squeezed her eyes shut. Her wings fluttered furiously as she spoke with the goddess.

"Malek," Sabine cried, tears streaking down her cheeks. "Please!"

Malek muttered a curse. Lifting her wrist, he blew softly over her marks. Fire danced along her skin, its colors brilliant in their reds, oranges, and even blue at the center. The marks flared golden but remained wholly untouched.

"It's not working," Rika said, peering at Sabine's wrist. "Why isn't it working?"

"It's our bond. Sabine's immune to my dragonfire."

"What do we do?"

Sabine shook her head and pushed the knife toward Malek. She'd rather not have her left arm than deal with Lachlina's stubborn outcry for another moment. "Cut them off. You and Rika can leave me if those creatures come."

"Never," Malek said in a growl.

"I'm getting help," Rika said, running back to the Hall of the Gods. She shouted and pounded her fists against the stone door, but it remained shut.

Another eerie howl sounded in the distance, closer than the last one.

"Malek," Sabine whispered.

"I won't cut you, Sabine. We'll be overrun. The tunnels are too narrow for me to shift without bringing the ceiling down on our heads." Malek held Sabine's gaze and said, "Breathe through it. Feed the burn to me through our bond. I'm better able to withstand it."

She hesitated.

"Do it, Sabine!" he ordered, his tone nearly as sharp and biting as Lachlina's onslaught.

She nodded, knowing it was the only possibility. Reaching through the pain, she touched their bond and used it to anchor her. Malek swayed slightly as the shared onslaught hit him, his arm tightening around her. His magic swirled around her, softening the sharpest edges of the burning pain.

"She packs a punch, doesn't she?" Malek muttered.

Sabine winced and nodded.

"Here," Rika said, thrusting a small flask toward Malek. "This might help."

Malek cradled Sabine's wrist and gently poured the water onto it. Sabine slumped with relief as the cool water eased some of the pain.

"That does help," Sabine said, watching as the water bubbled against her heated skin. She wasn't sure if removing the mark would sever her ties to the goddess, but it might limit Lachlina's control. "It's not as bad now. I think she's finished for the time being, but her hold on me is growing stronger."

Blossom sniffled. "I'm sorry, Sabine. I told her I couldn't order you around because I'm just a pixie, but she threatened to burn me up from the inside. She said the pain you feel is just a taste of what she'll do to me if you ever return to the Hall of the Gods."

"I'm going to destroy her," Malek promised in a low voice. "I don't care what agreement you made with her. I won't allow anyone to harm you, Sabine."

"She's forsworn," Sabine said, turning toward Blossom. "Lachlina has violated her oath to do me no harm or my companions."

Blossom squeaked. She landed on Rika's shoulder and hid under the seer's dark hair. "Messenger! I'm just the messenger! Don't be mad! She says you violated the oath first by trying to banish her."

Sabine shook her head in confusion. Lachlina had offered to aid her in entering the Hall of the Gods, but now she was threatening her if she returned? None of this made sense. The only reason Sabine could think of was Vestior's involvement. He must have done something to temporarily suppress Sabine's ties to the goddess so they could speak privately. She couldn't help but wonder if he might have other ideas for a more permanent way of severing ties.

Sabine took a steadying breath, making an effort to gentle her tone. "I'm not angry with *you*, Blossom, nor did I try to cut off her markings until she attacked me. What does Lachlina want so badly that she would dare threaten one of my friends? Has she forgotten what happened last time?"

Blossom poked her head out, blinking at Sabine. "It wasn't because you tried to remove the marks. It was from before—when we went into the Hall of the Gods. The goddess is demanding to know what *he* said to you." Blossom scrunched her nose. "I think she means the Huntsman. When I asked, she got really mad and said, 'That's none of your concern.'"

"Arrogant and presumptuous, isn't she?" Malek muttered.

Sabine made a noise of agreement. It was interesting that not even Lachlina would identify the Huntsman as Vestior. Sabine wasn't sure why they were keeping his identity secret. It must have something to do with why he'd taken over the Huntsman's duties. At the earliest opportunity, she needed to research the lore regarding the Wild Hunt.

"We spoke of the Dragon Portal," Sabine said, settling on a partial truth to answer Blossom. "The Huntsman knows we're searching for the artifacts. He wanted to know our intent. I simply told him we wanted to ensure the war didn't resume again. Malek interrupted before we finished the conversation, and he banished us from the Hall."

Blossom's wings fluttered. "Okay. I think… I think she's satisfied."

Sabine bit back a harsh retort. It wouldn't do any good to rile Lachlina again. Not here, and not now. But once they were in relative safety, she'd make removing the markings a priority.

She frowned at the golden marks on her wrist. They still throbbed, like the aftereffect from a burn. The thought of keeping them on her for a minute longer chafed, but Malek had been right to stop her; it was too dangerous to cut them off here.

"Using the water flask was quick thinking," Malek said and capped the container before handing it back to Rika. He turned back toward Sabine, his expression grim. "We can't allow Lachlina to keep affecting you like this."

"I know." Sabine sighed and rubbed her wrist again. She wasn't even sure cutting off the marks would help. The magic in the artifacts had infused itself with her very essence. "I'd hoped we would have found some answers in the dwarven archives. The head archivist is still looking, but she hasn't found anything yet. The demons might know something."

"My people have made a study of your gods," Malek said, pulling out a bandage from the traveler's pack and binding her wrist.

Sabine arched her brow. "An enemy studying another for potential weaknesses?"

Malek grimaced. "Yes, but in this case, it may be to our benefit. Like the Unseelie, my people don't believe the rhetoric. If we don't find answers among Bane's people, the dragons might know something that can help us."

Sabine turned back toward Blossom. "Did Lachlina say anything else?"

Blossom shook her head. "I think she's distracted."

"What do you mean?"

"She's talking to someone, but I can't hear what they're saying. Lots of angry voices. But I think she'll leave you alone for now unless you summon her."

Sabine frowned. That didn't bode well. "Let's hope she stays distracted."

"On that, I think we can all agree," Malek said, motioning toward the ground. "Sit down and rest for a few minutes. I'll keep watch."

"I will too," Rika said.

Sabine was tempted to argue, but she knew they were right. They'd be in more danger once they traveled farther away from the Hall of the Gods. She sat and leaned against the rocky wall. "Wake me in a bit?"

"Of course." Malek sat beside her and put his arm around her shoulders. When she leaned against him, he kissed her hair and said, "Bane should have felt your pain. If I've learned anything about that demon over the past few months, he'll find us soon enough."

～

SABINE WOKE SUDDENLY. Malek still had his arm around her, and she'd curled into him while they slept. He made a fantastic pillow. Rika and Blossom were playing some sort of game they'd invented with pieces of rock they'd collected from the ground.

She rubbed her eyes and asked, "How long was I asleep?"

"A little over an hour," Malek said, climbing to his feet. He stretched and then held out his hand to her.

"No sign of Bane?"

"Nothing. It's been quiet."

Sabine frowned, growing more concerned. "We should go. We don't have much time to find Dax before they try to execute him."

He nodded and gestured for Blossom and Rika to abandon their game. Once they set off, they moved at a fairly good clip through the tunnel. The path sloped downward, making Sabine wonder how deep underground they were traveling. With one small earthquake or tremor, they could easily find themselves buried alive. It was a wonder her people had survived living underground for centuries without a glimpse of the sky or forests.

After about an hour of walking, and with no sign of Bane anywhere, they reached a large chamber. It was becoming increasingly hotter the farther they traveled. Her clothing was lightweight, but it still stuck to her skin. Rika didn't seem to be faring much better, but Malek was mostly unfazed. Blossom, on the other hand, was panting heavily, and her wings were drooping.

Blossom flew to Sabine and sprawled across her shoulder. "It's hotter here than the desert near Karga. I think I'm wilting."

Rika wiped the sweat from her brow. "I don't feel very well."

"Keep drinking," Malek suggested, handing her his flask.

Blossom panted. "Hotter than a firefly's butt in summer."

"We're getting closer to the heart of the volcano," Malek said, pressing his hand against the wall made of volcanic rock. "I believe there's a lava spring somewhere nearby. I can feel the heat emanating from the rock."

Rika finished the water in the flask. "I can't remember ever being so hot. Do you know a lot about this place, Sabine?"

"It'll be cooler when we get closer to the city," Sabine said, rubbing the grit from her eyes. "The fae gifted the demons with magic enough to temper the worst of the heat, making the city itself much more comfortable. I can't cool the tunnel without using a significant amount of magic, but I should be able to make all of you more comfortable until we reach Harfanel."

She lifted her hand and send a wave of magic over Blossom. The pixie trilled softly, color coming back into her cheeks as Sabine's power flowed through her.

Blossom's wings gently fluttered, the motion cooling the tiny pixie even more. "Wheeeee! Gimme more."

"In a bit. You already had a significant power boost earlier. I'm not sure the underworld can withstand a power-drunk pixie causing trouble. We still haven't found your missing goat."

"Aww," Blossom grumbled. "Poor Lucky. I wonder if he became a demon snack."

"Will you hand me your bag?" Sabine asked, gesturing toward the pouch fastened on Malek's belt. He handed it to her and she searched through it. Faerie wouldn't have sent them into the underworld without adequate protection from the elements.

Malek glanced at Sabine. "Do you need to stop and rest?"

"Not yet. I'd like to either find Bane or get to the cross-roads first. I didn't think to ask Azran how far it was to the landmark he mentioned. I'm hoping Bane will find us if we're in a more central location. In the meantime, I need to find something to help cool Rika off."

"Snow? Ice?" Rika asked, fanning her sticky face with her hands. "I'm not picky. I never thought I'd miss being back on Malek's ship."

Sabine grinned at her and continued searching the bag. She set aside a small crystal designed to locate water. It would come in handy soon enough, but it wouldn't help anyone cool off. All the springs down here were heated, and it would use too much magic to cool them.

"You still can't sense Bane?"

She shook her head at Malek's question. "No. He's alive, but that's all I know. I can't tell which direction he's in or anything else. It must be the curse."

She pulled a cloak out of the bag and shook it out. The rich, dark-blue material was lightweight but finely crafted with silver threading at the decorative hem. She infused a trace of her magic into the crystal disc embedded in the collar, watching as it flared brightly with power.

She handed the cloak to Rika and said, "Put that on. It'll keep you cool."

Rika eyed it skeptically but put it over her shoulders.

"Wow! I thought it would be even hotter. It's like a constant breeze over my skin. How does it work?"

"Magic," Sabine said, and fastened the cloak for Rika. "Do you need anything, Malek? There are enough cloaks for each of us."

"Dragon, remember?" Malek tapped his chest. "I'll be fine. Conserve your strength."

Sabine nodded and closed the bag. Their bond must be offering her some protection. She'd be fine for a while yet.

The tunnel widened enough that a score of people could walk side-by-side without touching. The walls had lost their polished gleam, with the dips and jags of the volcanic rock jutting out in places. Sabine wiped sweat away from her brow as the heat continued to build. When Blossom wilted again, Sabine sent a wave of cooling magic over the entire party.

Rika stared upward at the earthen ceiling. "I can't imagine living here. No wonder Bane enjoys living above ground. How do you know if it's day or night?"

"It's close to midafternoon," Blossom said and began plaiting Sabine's hair, siphoning off trace amounts of magic.

"What? How do you know?"

Sabine glanced at Rika. "Just like I can track the phases of the moon, Blossom can sense the sun's position, even when she can't see it. Their magic is strongest under the sun, just like demons are more powerful underground."

Blossom blew a raspberry. "Demons are kind of like ants."

Rika blinked. "Ants?"

"Yep. Ants." Blossom gently tugged on Sabine's hair, likely weaving it into a complicated design. "They live under-ground, they make tunnels, and people wouldn't mind if they got stepped on."

Sabine made a pained noise.

Malek choked on a laugh. "You might not want to repeat those comments when we run into Bane."

Blossom grinned. "You think?"

"I'm assuming you like having your wings attached to your body?"

The pixie wrinkled her nose. "Good point. But I still think I'm on to something."

The tunnel opened to a large chamber with its ceiling towering over them. The heat was nearly unbearable. Sabine's eyes watered from the stench of sulfur that rose from somewhere nearby. Rika coughed and gagged, while Blossom squeaked and moved closer to Sabine's neck.

"Cover your faces!" Sabine ordered, reaching for her flask.

Somewhere in the distance, a warning howl sounded, reverberating through the tunnel. The sound of scraping claws along the walls sent a chill down Sabine's spine. Malek went on alert, sweeping his gaze over the area while his hand rested on his sword.

"We may have more trouble incoming," Malek warned. "Try to hurry."

Sabine poured a splash of water into her hand. Using the knowledge the merfolk had gifted to her, she wove the water into a protective bubble and encased Blossom. It should be enough of a barrier to keep her safe from the toxic fumes. The shimmering bubble floated upward, fueled by Blossom's beating wings.

The pixie grinned widely and said, "I didn't know you could do that! I can breathe!"

"Rika needs help!" Malek called, reaching for the girl who had fallen to her knees. She was gasping and wheezing, her eyes bulging as the fumes stole her breath.

Sabine quickly wound the next splash of water around Rika's head, using her magic to infuse a burst of clean air into the bubble. Rika took several deep breaths, her eyes still watering.

Sabine took Rika's arm to help steady her. "Are you all right?"

Rika nodded and coughed again. "That was close. It was like my throat closed up suddenly. You're not affected by it?"

Sabine shook her head. "Not to the extent you are. It's not pleasant, but I can manage. My people spent centuries here building their immunity, and I think Malek gives me additional resistance."

"There are crevices along the wall," Malek said, gesturing at the side of the chamber. "There must be a vent where the lava flows. The fumes are toxic to humans, and apparently pixies."

Sabine lifted her hands and sent another blast of cooling air over them. "Then we need to keep moving. The water magic won't last long."

Taking the only tunnel out of the chamber, they moved as one. Malek helped Rika when she stumbled, while Sabine continuously refreshed the magic protecting Rika and Blossom. It wasn't high magic, but the unfamiliar power of the merfolk was clunky and awkward to wield.

After about an hour, the tunnel ended and the heat lessened. An enormous chamber that was easily several stories in height loomed in front of them. The entire room was situated on some sort of large ledge, with several more tunnels branching out in various directions. Sabine could feel a trace of cooling fae magic swirling around her, a sign they were approaching Harfanel. She dissolved the bubbles protecting Rika and Blossom, reclaiming the magic to fortify her strength.

A deep chasm ran along the entirety of one side of the chamber. Sabine peered over the edge and saw a fast-moving lava river flowing below them. This place might be protected from whatever creatures lurked beyond it, but there were dangers enough to urge caution.

"This is the crossroads, isn't it?" Malek asked.

Sabine nodded. "Apparently."

Painted murals covered the walls, each depicting fierce battles where the demons had claimed victory over their enemies. Large statues of fallen demonic kings graced the various entrances, each more terrible than the last. Multiple tunnels branched out, extending into darkness, but it was the large statue in the center that caught and held Sabine's focus.

One of the largest crystals she'd ever seen jutted from a pedestal. The base appeared to be made from hundreds of skulls stacked in a pyramid and then fused together with magic and metal. Smoke swirled within the crystal, beckoning them closer, while the remains of the dead warned them away.

Blossom gripped Sabine's braids. "I really don't like this place."

Rika audibly gulped. "Skulls? That can't be good."

"It's a warning to any who aren't aligned with the Unseelie," Sabine said. "But at least we've made it to the crossroads. There should be protections in place that prevent any of those spiders or wraiths from causing harm here. You can explore the chamber, but don't enter any tunnels. And stay away from the center crystal."

"Be careful," Malek warned. "Watch yourself around the ledge. The ground's a little uneven."

Blossom flew to Rika's shoulder. They explored the murals and statues, making a point to avoid the center crystal and the grinning skulls.

Sabine wiped her damp palms on the thin material of her dress. The crystal was dwarven made, but it had been infused with fae magic to create a waypoint for travelers. She studied the pedestal, hoping Azran hadn't let them astray.

A small path led up to it. As Sabine approached, the skull-lined base shimmered and shifted, forming a staircase that appeared to be made from bone. Ignoring the dead at her feet, she moved up the stairs until she was standing in front of the large crystal.

Gray smoke swirled within it, flowing in random patterns. Sabine took a deep breath and pressed her hand against the crystal. It glowed, first with a silver-and-blue light and then flared to gold. After clearing her thoughts, she recalled the stories from her childhood about the demonic city and their fearsome king.

"Show me the way," she ordered.

The smoke within the crystal turned red, illuminating the entire chamber with an eerie light. Smaller crystals, embedded in the walls outside one of the tunnel openings, glowed, their reddish gleam an echo of the one in front of her.

Sabine swallowed and removed her hand. "It looks like we have our direction."

Rika and Blossom wandered to the tunnel entrance to investigate the glowing gems. Malek turned toward her, waiting at a distance while she descended the stairs to rejoin him. He held out his hand toward her, and she took it. Pulling her closer, he leaned down and pressed his forehead against hers.

"You look worried. Is it Bane?"

She leaned against him for a moment. "Have I become that transparent?"

"Only to me," he said, leaning back to study her. "This chamber is large enough that I can shift and guard you three if you want to rest and wait for him. Once we arrive in the demon city, you'll need your full strength. Bane's part of that."

She nodded. "I'd rather not enter Harfanel without him. I don't like that he's been gone this long."

Malek opened his mouth to say something and then closed it.

She frowned up at him. "What is it?"

"There's a chance he may not find us, Sabine. He warned me that once he came down here, he'd no longer be completely under your aegis. Until you're proclaimed by King Kal'thorz as rightful queen of the Unseelie, all demons will follow their liege's orders before yours. That includes Bane."

"I suspected as much."

"No. It's worse than Bane led you to believe."

"How so?"

Malek blew out a breath. "You know how the gods used the demons to fight against my people?"

When she nodded, he continued. "The demons were better able to withstand the effects of the dragonfire than the fae or merfolk. We fought against them more often than not. Since they were such powerful foes, we made a study into them, searching for weaknesses."

Sabine nodded. "They were able to help push back the dragons from the edge of Faerie."

"Yes, but it shouldn't have been possible. They aren't as strong above ground, but they had an advantage the fae and merfolk didn't. Somehow, they could relay orders to different squads in the blink of an eye. My people have long suspected there's some magic in the underworld that gives them their tremendous strength and allows their king to communicate orders to them remotely."

Her brow furrowed. "Mind speech?"

"Or mind control. I believe Bane, along with all the other demons, are tied to Kal'thorz in ways beyond our understanding. He was reticent to say too much and couldn't break any oaths, but he made it clear that we couldn't trust him once he stepped foot into the underworld."

Sabine fell silent and gathered her thoughts, watching as Rika and Blossom investigated the various crystals jutting from the walls.

She'd never been able to communicate that way with Bane and had never heard of any demon with the ability, but it couldn't be discounted. Vestior had been one of the gods who'd once governed the underworld, and he'd opened the doorway for her to communicate with Malek. Perhaps he'd been trying to show her it wasn't outside the realm of possibility.

Turning back toward Malek, she said, "If you're right, that's why Bane wanted you to remain close to me. He knew I couldn't trust him."

Malek nodded. "He may have left so you couldn't depend upon him. No matter the issues I have with Bane, he cares for you in his own way. He'll do whatever is necessary to protect you, even removing himself from your presence."

Sabine rubbed her temples. "There's nothing to be done about it. We'll get some rest here and then make our way to Harfanel with or without Bane. Dax's life is still in danger, and I'll need all my strength to deal with this upstart king and put him in his place. I'll worry about severing Bane's ties to him then."

"All right." Malek removed the bag from his belt loop. "There's some travel food in there. I suggest you try to eat a little something and then get what sleep you—"

A noise caught their attention. Sabine whirled, her knife in her hand and her magic flaring to the surface. A goat raced into the chamber from a tunnel, running like a pack of hell-hounds was after him. He staggered to a halt at the sight of them.

"Lucky!" Blossom shrieked, holding out her hands toward him. "You found us!"

An ear-piercing howl filled the air. A hunched figure waving a lit candle loped out of the tunnel and headed directly for the goat. Flames seemed to dance over his skin as he bounded into the chamber.

"Mine!" the kobold shouted in a gravelly voice. He blew over the candle, causing a stream of fire to shoot outward.

Blossom dove sideways to avoid it, shrieking curses at the creature. Rika pulled out her weapon, brandishing it bravely.

"Stay back!" Sabine reached for the moisture in the air, wove it together, and shot it toward the creature in a stream of water. The candle extinguished, and the kobold's reddish skin became mottled and gray.

He shrieked in fury. "You no touch! Mine! Mine! Mine!"

Malek jumped forward, sword at the ready and prepared to strike. The kobold howled at Malek and shook the candle. Flames leaped to its wick again, shooting up over the kobold's skin and then outward toward Malek. Malek easily deflected the attack, swiping out at the creature and slicing off the top part of the candle. Malek stomped on it, extinguishing the flame again.

"Run, Lucky! Run!" Blossom shouted.

The goat let out a panicked bleat and, with eyes a little wild, darted toward the tunnel with the glowing red crystals. The kobold howled again and jumped over Malek. With a chortle, he shoved Rika and then raced down the tunnel in pursuit of his quarry.

Rika stumbled, her foot slipping on the uneven ground. With arms flailing, she screamed as she fell backward over the side of the ledge.

"Rika!" Blossom shrieked. "Sabine, she fell!"

Malek was already moving. Sabine was a half step behind him, racing toward the other side of the chamber. Peering over the edge, she caught sight of Rika on a small outcropping, crumpled in a heap. Her arm was twisted at an unnatural angle, and a pool of blood was steadily growing larger beneath her.

"Rika!" Sabine shouted, leaning over the side. But Rika didn't stir. "Dammit. She's too far down. Blossom, see if she's conscious. Make sure she doesn't move."

"On it!" Blossom said with a salute and darted over the side.

Malek jerked open his bag and pulled out a coil of rope. "Tie it against the crystal. I'll climb down for her."

"The crystal will burn the rope before we have a chance to use it." She studied the distance. "Lower me down. If she's hurt, she won't be able to make it back up on her own."

"You can't carry her by yourself."

"No, but the dwarven magic I claimed should allow me to move the earth. I can raise the ground and bring her to us. I need to be with her to ensure she remains steady."

"No!" a voice roared from behind them.

Sabine turned to see Bane racing toward them. A wave of relief rushed through her at the sight of her demon protector. She realized suddenly that she could feel him again, whereas before he'd been a dim awareness at the edge of her thoughts. "Bane? What in the world?"

"Do not use more foreign magic here, Sabine. Your use of the merfolk's power has already created ripples throughout the underworld. All who reside here know you have arrived. From this point on, you must rely upon your innate gifts and nothing more. There are eyes and enemies everywhere."

"We don't have time to worry about showing our hand. Rika's injured, possibly dying down there."

"You won't have a hand to show if you don't listen to me," Bane snapped. "I have no desire to see the young seer suffer, but if anything happens to you, she will lose the protection you've offered."

Blossom landed on Sabine's shoulder, panting heavily. Tears streaked down her cheeks. "She won't wake up, Sabine. I can't wake her up! She's really close to the edge. If she rolls over, she'll die!"

Thinking quickly, Sabine turned toward Malek and said, "Stay here. When we give the word, you'll need to pull Rika up. Blossom, you'll run communication between us. Bane, you're with me. Let's get her out of there."

Blossom saluted Sabine, while Malek gave her a curt nod. At her signal, Bane swept Sabine into his arms and leaped over the side.

They landed on the ledge below with a thud. The moment Bane lowered Sabine, she crouched to assess Rika's condition. Her arm was bent at an impossible angle while her dark hair was splayed out against the rocky ground, matted with blood. Her skin was impossibly pale, nearly translucent. The head injury worried Sabine the most.

Blossom's wings fluttered wildly. "How do we get her out?"

"Ask Malek to look through his bag for one of your plants. Bring me a piece, but make sure it's not just a leaf. I need part of the stem too."

"Got it!" Blossom said and flew upward.

Bane kneeled beside her and placed his hands over Rika's head. A blue light coated his skin as he tapped into his power. Rika's sword was still dangling from her hand. Sabine picked it up and sheathed it. Even with a broken arm, the young seer had held on to her weapon.

Bane slowly moved his hands over Rika's body and said, "Broken arm, a few cracked ribs, the head wound, and an assortment of minor cuts and bruises."

"How serious is the head injury?"

"She's stable enough for now, but we need to get her to a healer soon. We're not far from the city."

Sabine squeezed her eyes shut and nodded. "Give me a moment to send her deeper into sleep. I don't want the movement to awaken her when we lift her out of here. We can at least spare her that pain."

Pressing her hands against Rika's temples, Sabine reached for the girl's consciousness. She whispered soothing words in the musical language of Faerie, teasing favored memories from Rika's thoughts and offering her pleasant dreams. She spun them together on soothing waves of magic and fixed them into the young seer's thoughts with a gentle touch.

Sabine opened her eyes and urged, "Sleep, Rika. No further harm will come to you."

Rika sighed in her sleep, a trace of a smile on her face. Bane ripped off a large piece from the bottom of his shirt and handed it to Sabine. She cut it into strips, handing each one to Bane so he could bind Rika's wounds.

When she finished, Sabine looked upward but didn't see any sign of Blossom. She sat back on her heels and studied Bane. There was a small amount of dried blood on his pants, but she didn't see any wounds. He looked stronger.

"You've broken the curse?"

He gave her a curt nod. "The sorceress, Brexia, has been dealt with."

She gestured toward his pants. "Were you injured?"

Bane glanced down. "The blood isn't mine. Kal'thorz had guards lying in wait for me when I reached her home."

"You knew that was a possibility?"

Bane grunted an affirmative, tearing off a strip from Rika's clothing to bind another cut on her leg.

Sabine studied him. "Can I still trust you, Bane?"

He tied off the last strip and said, "As much as you ever could, but less once we reach the city. You will need to stand on your own and assert your dominance until you claim your place among my people. My ability to aid you will be limited, but I'll do what I can."

"We'll fix this," she said quietly. "I'll do what's necessary, but I will not lose you or Dax." Her gaze lowered to Rika. "Or her."

He started to say something else but fell silent. Sabine placed her hand on his arm and squeezed. No matter what was going on with him, she was going to resolve it. There was no other option.

He cocked his head. "There's something different about you."

She blinked at him. "What?"

He studied her, his expression puzzled. "There's gold and silver in your hair." Narrowing his eyes, he leaned closer and inhaled deeply.

With a snarl, he grabbed her arm and said, "Glamour it. Get rid of the gold. Now."

Sabine frowned but did as he'd asked. Before she could question him, Blossom returned. Bane shot Sabine a warning look and shook his head to indicate the need for silence.

Blossom held up a small sprig. "Will this work?"

"It should," Sabine said, placing the plant on Rika's stomach. Lifting her hands, she sent a strong pulse of magic over the flowering vine.

The plant shimmered and shifted, the stem growing longer and branches emerging from the original plant. Sabine moved her hands over Rika's body, crafting a vined cage around her. Bane grabbed the end of the rope Malek had lowered, and the demon motioned for Sabine to continue.

Waggling her fingers, she extended several vines and looped them over the top of the makeshift carrier. Bane threaded the rope through, securing it tightly.

Sabine started to reach for Malek with her thoughts but paused. If Bane was concerned about eyes and ears on them, it might be prudent not to share that they'd acquired such an ability. No one else knew about the gift Vestior had bestowed upon them.

"Tell Malek he can start lifting her out of here," Sabine said to Blossom.

The pixie nodded and flew away to relay the message.

A few moments later, the rope grew taut, and Rika was lifted. Sabine watched the slow progress for a moment and then turned toward Bane. Without a word, he swept her back into his arms. Using his claws and even his horns, he scaled the wall.

Sabine used her magic to keep the makeshift stretcher stable, blossoming the vine with flowers to offer additional padding to soften the jolts.

When they reached the top, Bane pushed Sabine upward so she could climb over the edge. She brushed off her hands and then bent to help Bane pull Rika back to solid ground.

"Clever use of the plant," Malek said as he cut the rope off the cage. He coiled it and returned it to the bag.

"We need to get her to Harfanel right away," Sabine said. "Can we carry her like this?"

"I've already summoned the fire imps. They'll conduct her safely to Harfanel. You'll need to barter for a healer's services."

Sabine turned to look at Bane. "Do you have any idea what the healer will want in exchange?"

"No, but it will likely pale in comparison to the demands of King Kal'thorz, high ruler of Harfanel and guardian of the underworld. I suggest you make yourself ready. I have no idea what's in store for any of us once we arrive."

Chapter Twenty-One

*I*t took less than ten minutes for the summoned fire imps to arrive. They appeared much like the one Sabine had met before, with reddish skin and nubs on the top of their heads where horns should have been. The moment they caught sight of her and Bane, they threw themselves to the ground in front of them. Blossom flew to Sabine and hid under her hair.

Malek arched his brow. "Which one of you are they worshipping?"

Sabine shook her head. She had no idea.

Bane spoke to them harshly in the demonic tongue, and they scrambled to their feet and lifted Rika's carrier. They placed it atop their shoulders, then trotted down the pathway to the tunnel with the glowing red crystals.

"What did you say to them?" Sabine asked as they fell into step behind them.

"I told them to ensure no further harm came to her, or I'd cut out their tongues and use them as a rope to hang them over the closest lava pool."

"I wouldn't mind seeing that," Blossom whispered.

Malek frowned at the fire imps, his hand lingering on his weapon. "You might want to tell them to stop eating the flowers on Rika's stretcher."

Bane moved forward and snarled something Sabine couldn't understand. The offending fire imp hunched his shoulders, and the others followed suit to avoid jostling Rika. Bane remained close to them, monitoring their progress and injured charge.

"You don't speak demonic?" Malek asked Sabine quietly.

She shook her head. "Not very well. I can understand and speak a handful of words and phrases, but it's not a language taught to many fae. Bane and Dax had been instructing me before we left Akros."

"Is that going to be a problem?"

"I don't believe so. Most of the upper demons speak the common tongue. I believe fire imps are similar to the dwarven cave trolls. Their complementary magic ties them together, and the language they share reinforces that bond."

Malek glanced at Blossom. "Sort of like the pixies with the fae?"

Blossom peeked out of Sabine's hair and nodded. "The fae also have the beastpeople."

Up ahead, the tunnel ended. Sabine caught sight of elaborate columns curving upward into an arch. Like the pedestal with the crystal at the crossroads, this archway had been comprised of bones. They jutted out at odd angles, offering both a warning and a chilling expectation.

A long, narrow bridge stretched out beyond the archway. Beneath it, a dark river flowed. The water was thick and syrupy, so dark she couldn't see past the surface. Something about it caused the hairs on the back of her neck to stand up. She didn't want to get anywhere near it.

Beyond the bridge, there was nothing except a large field made entirely of volcanic rock. Her skin pebbled from a strange awareness, and she slowed her steps. Something wasn't right about the empty space. All her senses were screaming.

Unnerved, Sabine lifted her hand and sent another pulse of magic over Blossom. In a quiet voice, she said, "No matter what happens, stay hidden unless we're alone."

"No one will know I'm here," Blossom whispered, burrowing close to her neck. Sabine felt a tickle of glamour against her skin as Blossom masked her appearance.

"A ladybug," Malek murmured. "Clever."

Sabine cautiously stepped through the archway and approached the large field. The fire imps trotted in front of her, with Rika still on their shoulders. Bane tensed, lifting his fisted hand in an indication to hold. Malek unsheathed his sword, sweeping his gaze over the field. Sabine frowned, searching for any sign of what was causing her unease.

A shout pierced the air.

"Ambush!" Bane shouted, his eyes flashing to silver.

Dozens of silver-eyed demons poured out from the archway behind them, while others leaped from hidden alcoves in front of them. Their red skin flared with power, the light from the torches illuminating their sharpened claws and lethal blades.

As one, they attacked.

They were surrounded. Everywhere she looked, more demons appeared. Bane crouched, his claws and horns cutting down their assailants. Malek's sword sliced through the air, each swipe striking with deadly accuracy. The fire imps dropped Rika's carrier and fled.

Sabine quickly tapped into her power, calling upon the plant magic she'd used to create Rika's stretcher. She sent the tendrils shooting upward, affixed them to the high ceiling, and pulled Rika out of harm's way.

"Protect Rika!" she ordered Blossom. The ladybug darted upward, flying after the carrier.

Sabine turned, seeing the horde converging on Malek. She backhanded a dozen demons with her power, knocking them away from her dragon. More began swarming, quickly gaining ground.

Bane shouted something in his harsh, guttural language, but the battle cries surrounding them nearly drowned his voice out. A handful of the demons stopped fighting at the sight of him, but they were too few to make a difference.

One of the demons landed a strike against Malek. Sabine cried out, feeling the sharp pain in her arm through their bond as though she'd been cut. *Poison*, she realized with disgust.

"Malek! Shift!" she screamed, watching the golden glow surround him.

With a roar, he shifted forms. A tremendous dragon took his place, his scales shimmering like the midnight sky. He stretched out his wings, eclipsing her view of the field.

He shot streams of dragonfire across the field, causing demons to scramble away. Others took advantage of the commotion to try to flank him. He swiped outward with his sharp tail and knocked a few of them away before Sabine realized the problem. He was pinned, his ability to fight hampered while she and Rika remained on the field and in harm's way.

Even with Malek changing forms, the demons still held the advantage. It was clear he was their target. Malek was holding his own at the moment, but it wouldn't last. There were too many, and the surrounding area was too tight for him to navigate his large form.

Malek roared again, sending another stream of dragon-fire through the cavern. Screams filled the air, the stench of burnt skin and sulfur filling her nose. Still, the battle raged around them. Crystal-tipped lances flew through the air and struck Malek, embedding themselves in the cracks of his scales. They might not be enough to kill him, but the pain was evident, along with the uncharacteristic sluggishness plaguing him from the poison.

She wouldn't allow him to die. Not as long as she had breath.

Tapping into her magic, she disregarded Bane's earlier warning and reached for every fragment of power she possessed. She wove together both Seelie and Unseelie magic, binding them together with the collected strength of the dwarven and merfolk magic gifted to her. Even her bonds with Bane and Malek were used, their magic blending seamlessly with hers to strengthen and fortify.

It still wasn't enough.

More than a hundred demons spread across the field in front of them, their harsh battle cries piercing the air.

Her skin glowed more brilliantly than the sun and moon combined. Her hair lifted as an invisible wind whipped through the cavern. She spread her arms, calling the magic of the underworld to her. Dimly, she heard Azran's howl, followed by dozens of other hellhounds in the distance. She felt their strength flock to her, pounding against her psyche like a drum.

Azran spoke in her mind. "*Use the Well, little goddess.*"

Sabine didn't stop to question him. If Azran offered, so be it. Reaching for him in her mind, he pushed her toward the Well. She inhaled deeply, breathing in the power and letting it fill her. She was full, her magic nearly overflowing. Tears streamed down her cheeks, her legs threatening to buckle under the sheer force of power she held.

The ground trembled. The walls shook. Rocks fell. Flames surrounded her. She was one with the land and beyond it. *She was power.*

With a harsh scream, Sabine unleashed her might in a brutal, magical tsunami.

Demons went flying, the sharp whip of her destructive force slicing through them. Some who had tried to run collapsed, their lifeless bodies twitching from the onslaught.

She moved across the field like a general, ignoring the bodies and blood that coated the ground. A few demons stumbled across her field of vision, but Sabine flung them aside and out of her path.

"*Malek*," she called to the dragon, who was trying to pull a spear out of his thigh.

Malek abandoned his cause and turned his great head toward her. He staggered in her direction and collapsed with a thud. Smoke billowed from his nostrils. Either the mind-touch connection between them was still too new, or he was too weakened to respond.

Bane limped toward her, his arm hanging at an awkward angle. She reached out to him, embracing him with her power. He inhaled sharply, using her magic to heal his injuries.

Reassured he would live, she focused on the large dragon in front of her. Two of the spears had penetrated his scales, one in his thigh area and the other close to his belly. She couldn't see any blood, but it was impossible to tell if they'd caused him internal injuries. Her primary concern was the poison. It would kill him if she didn't find a way to help him.

"They targeted him specifically," she said, glancing at Bane. "We need to remove the poison."

The demon approached his hind quarters and said, "Brace yourself, lizard. The spears will continue to magnify the effects of the poison until we remove them."

Bane grabbed the spear and pulled with all of his strength. Once it was free, he tossed it aside and went to the other.

Sabine turned back toward Malek and pressed her hands against his snout. She closed her eyes, sensing the poison leeching his strength. Even with the spears enhancing the effects, he shouldn't be this weak. If he'd shifted the moment they'd attacked instead of remaining in human form to protect her, he wouldn't have been hurt so badly.

"*Azran,*" she cried, reaching for the hellhound once again. "*Help me!*"

The power of the Well once again filled her. Sabine glowed with the same golden light, her hair lifting as a strange wind kicked up and moved across the field.

Sabine took a deep breath and then exhaled, pushing the magic outward. Her golden light encompassed Malek, burning away the poison that filled his veins. When it was gone, she slid to the ground in exhaustion. Azran reached for her again, filling her magical reserves with the power of the Well.

"*Take care, little goddess. Calling upon the Well's magic will be ineffective once you enter Harfanel. Such is the pact that was made eons ago.*"

"*I'll heed your warning.*"

She felt the faintest of embraces from Azran before he slipped from her thoughts.

Malek's image shimmered. A moment later, he was back in human form. He wrapped his arms around her, holding her close. She curled into him, breathing in the smell of charred demon. She couldn't find it in herself to care overly much.

He ran his hand along her hair. "They didn't hurt you?"

She shook her head, curling her hands into his shirt. "I wasn't the one they were trying to kill." She lifted her head. "You're all right?"

He cupped her face and kissed her. "I don't know how

you did that, but I owe you my life. The poison is gone, along with my wounds."

"Messy, but effective," Bane said, studying the tip of the crystal-tipped spear. "Unfortunately, you've shown Kal'thorz the full scope of your abilities. He will not underestimate your power again."

"The alternative wasn't an option," Sabine said.

Malek glanced over at Bane. "Should we anticipate any more ambush attacks?"

"We're demons," Bane said with a shrug. He shattered the crystal affixed to the end of the spear and tossed it aside.

Malek rose and helped Sabine to her feet. Bane studied her with a critical eye and said, "Do not hide our victory behind your glamour."

She jerked her head upward. "What?"

He gestured at the blood staining the hem of her gown. "When you walk through the streets of Harfanel, all will know you defeated those who stood against you."

Sabine pursed her lips but nodded. They'd need every advantage, but as she looked at the dead lying in the field, she concluded the cost was too great.

Lifting her hands, Sabine gently lowered Rika's stretcher from the ceiling. Blossom, still in the guise of a ladybug, floated down with it and then leaped onto Sabine's shoulder.

She darted into Sabine's hair and said, "Hot bee crap on a flower petal! I thought we were toast!"

"You did well, protecting Rika," Sabine said, checking over the unconscious girl. Fortunately, Rika hadn't been harmed in the battle.

Bane scowled. "Damn fire imps. The second there's trouble, they disappear. We'll need to carry her until we reach the first gate."

Sabine coaxed the vined cage to shift a little more, creating handholds. "You should be able to carry her more easily now. I don't want to jostle her any more than necessary."

Bane and Malek each grabbed one of the handles and lifted Rika. Sabine led the way, stepping over the remains of fallen demons. Some groaned as she passed, an indication they'd merely been struck unconscious, but she hardened her heart and ignored them. Whatever game Kal'thorz was playing, she was determined to eradicate him from the playing field—even if she had to destroy his pieces to do it.

Chapter Twenty-Two

wo demon guards, a male and a female, stopped them at the first gate. They were both wearing some sort of dwarven-crafted armor that protected their vulnerable points yet also allowed ease of movement. Their exposed skin was darker than Bane's, but they had spidery, glowing red veins that pulsed with magical intent. They were smaller than Bane, but unlike him and Dax, these demons both had long tails that ended with sharp, pointed tips.

They watched her approach with a measure of wariness. The one on the left stepped forward, her spear-like weapon striking the ground in front of them.

"Bane'umbra Versed," the demon hissed, appearing reluctant to address Sabine directly. "Do you claim this human as your possession?"

"I claim the human on behalf of Queen Sabin'theoria of the Unseelie, daughter of former Queen Mali'theoria and descendant of Vestior, Harbinger of Nightmares and Lord of the Underworld."

The demon's eyes flickered toward Sabine. "Do you claim this human as yours, fae?"

Sabine straightened and took a step forward.

She. Was. Done.

With a sharp lash of power, she forced both demon guards to their knees. The arched gate over their heads trembled, causing a few of the bones to fall to the ground.

"I do not answer to underlings," she snapped, infusing her voice with power. "I am here at your king's invitation, and this *welcome* is an affront to the rules of hospitality."

The female demon glared at her, struggling against Sabine's magical grip. The man, at least, had surrendered to her power with little difficulty. Perhaps there was some hope for them after all.

Sabine lifted her hand, clenching her fist as she tightened her hold on the woman. The woman settled, but her tail continued to twitch in agitation.

"If you wish to avoid any further *unpleasantness*, you will immediately notify your king that I have arrived as per his invitation," Sabine demanded and then gestured toward Rika. "You will also arrange for an immediate escort to your most skilled healer. If I even think you're dragging your feet, I'll level this city to the ground!"

The demon paled, trembling in Sabine's magical grasp. With a muttered curse, Sabine released both demons. The female guard threw herself prostrate in front of Sabine, mirroring her more sensible companion.

"Fetch the fire imps and return to your post, Figin." A woman's musical voice filled the air. She moved into sight, a stunning, dark-haired fae woman of indeterminate age wearing an exquisite gown that shimmered with silver, black, and red accents as she moved. A small silver tiara embedded with tiny lava stones held back her nearly waist-length hair, while a matching gorget was fastened around her neck. Compared to the woman's rich appearance, Sabine felt drab and plain in her travel clothing.

She was beyond lovely, with a heart-shaped face, full lips, sculpted cheekbones, and an aura of power that surrounded her like a cloak. Her marks of power were some of the most extensive Sabine had ever seen, rivaling even those of some Faerie Elders.

The woman lowered herself into a graceful curtsy and bowed her head, her dark hair momentarily obscuring her features. "Greetings, Your Highness," the fae woman said, her pale-blue eyes peering upward at Sabine. Her gaze drifted briefly to Malek before returning to Sabine. "King Kal'thorz had sent an escort to Razadon's gate to await your arrival. We should have anticipated that the newest ruler of the Unseelie fae would make her own arrangements. Had we received word of your arrival through traditional means, I'm sure a different sort of welcome would have been arranged."

Sabine narrowed her eyes at the woman. That was a little too close to a lie, and they both knew it. Still, Sabine knew how the game was played. She might not have as much experience as Kal'thorz, but she was a fast learner.

Sabine motioned for the woman to rise. "Your name?"

"I am called Leena, Your Highness," Leena said, omitting her family name. "King Kal'thorz has entrusted me to be your guide while you are in Harfanel. It was suggested that you might be more at ease with another fae attending you."

"Well met, Leena," Sabine said, attempting to keep frustration out of her voice. No matter how much the senseless display on the field revolted and infuriated her, she couldn't let it govern her actions.

It had been a long time since she'd spent any significant time with one of her own kind. The woman's substantial magic called to her own, making Sabine wonder what such a powerful fae was doing in the underworld. Her skin markings identified her as Seelie, but she didn't appear to be a captive or under any sort of duress. Sabine had heard of some fae who had turned away from their origins, but she didn't know of any who had volunteered to reside in the underworld.

Four fire imps scampered toward them. Leena spoke softly and directed them to Rika's makeshift stretcher. Sabine wasn't sure if they were the same ones that had carried her earlier.

"I know she's fae, but her magic smells funny," Blossom whispered near Sabine's ear.

The fire imps lifted Rika's carrier and settled it on their shoulders.

Leena gestured toward the gate. "With your permission, I will escort you into the city and arrange for you to meet with a healer who can attend your injured human. Afterward, it would be my honor to introduce you to King Kal'thorz."

Sabine glanced at Bane, but he was focused on the woman standing before them. There was slight tension in his posture as he gazed upon Leena. *Well then*, Sabine mused. Perhaps there was some history there. She knew Bane well enough to tell he didn't care overly much for the woman.

Recognizing the need for both caution and diplomacy, she inclined her head and motioned for Leena to lead the way. Bane spoke sharply to the fire imps, and they trotted ahead with Rika's carrier, taking care to not disturb her.

Sabine stepped onto a bridge crossing another dark river. Bones and other body parts drifted in the current before they disappeared beneath the black flowing liquid. She couldn't help but wonder whether any of the bodies from earlier would end up in the same place.

"*Malek?*" she called in her thoughts.

He caught her eye, his voice a faint echo in her mind. "*Tread carefully, Sabine. They addressed Rika as being human, but they didn't challenge my presence beyond what happened in that field. They likely have safeguards to ward against my kind.*"

Sabine gave him a barely discernible nod.

"Are there many fae living in Harfanel?" Sabine asked Leena.

"Not as many as there were when Queen Mali'theoria ruled the Unseelie. Most who remain are permanent 'guests' confined to the prison district."

It was tempting to ask more questions, particularly about why Leena was living in the underworld, but it was considered rude and unfaelike to make personal inquiries. Once she got Bane alone, she could see if he had any information about the woman.

As the first gate disappeared behind them, she noticed an even larger one looming ahead. Between the two waypoints were several lava pools. Fire imps used large black spears to stir and stab at the molten lava. Demons patrolled between the pools, calling out insults and slashing the fire imps with their whips when they didn't move fast enough. They eyed Sabine and her companions warily but didn't challenge their progress.

"We use the fields to harvest lava stones, Your Highness," Leena said, noticing her interest.

"I thought lava stones were found deeper in the underworld."

"Normally, yes," Leena said, her voice taking on a singsong quality, designed to set them at ease. "The rarest and most precious are found in the wild, but smaller ones can be harvested by creating suitable conditions."

Sabine warded herself and Malek against the magical effects of Leena's voice. Bane didn't appear affected. Leena dipped her head in acknowledgement of the ward and continued speaking as though she hadn't been trying to beguile them.

"While the stones harvested in this field are lovely, they lack the clarity and richness of the wild lava stones chosen for your enticement gift. King Kal'thorz personally oversaw the selection of those and had one of the most skilled dwarven artists design the finished set."

Sabine inclined her head, recalling the exquisite workmanship in the gorget and bracelets Kal'thorz had sent to her. "They were lovely."

Leena smiled and touched her own gorget. "King Kal'thorz will be pleased to hear that. Perhaps you will decide to wear it while you are here."

Bane tensed slightly, but it was enough that Sabine took his warning to heart. She wouldn't dare put it on while they were in the underworld.

They approached the larger gate, made from some sort of volcanic-rock-and-crushed-crystal combination. Another river ran in front of this one, the thick, flowing liquid reminiscent of blood. Four more demon guards protected this entrance and stepped aside at the sight of Leena. The large black door blocking their path swung open.

"Welcome to Harfanel, Your Highness."

A trail of magic flitted over her skin. She felt a flare of heat as her Unseelie magic sharpened within her. Odd... but it didn't feel harmful, more like a warding effect. Dismissing it as a side effect of being in an Unseelie city, she assessed her surroundings.

Her first impression of the demonic city was lackluster. The dwarven influence was undeniable, with paved streets and buildings reminiscent of those found in Razadon. It should have been beautiful, with glittering crystal windows and lamps that twinkled brightly. But there was an oppressive stillness, as though the city was anxiously holding its breath.

The streets were virtually empty, but Sabine could feel the weight of eyes upon them. Blossom shivered against her neck. There was a chill in the air that wasn't simply from the fae magic cooling the city. Trash floated down the street, carried by unseen fingers. It was eerily quiet.

The metal gate slammed shut behind them. Malek whirled around, his hand reaching for his weapon as two of the demon guards fell into step behind them. Sabine tensed, bringing her magic to the surface.

"What is this?" she demanded. "Haven't enough of Kal'thorz's people died today?"

Leena held up her hands in a peaceable gesture. *"Bakis, Shel'lavein.* Be at ease, Your Highness. This is one of our lesser-used entrances to the city. It is to be kept sealed on orders from King Kal'thorz."

Sabine arched her brow. "And if I ordered the gate reopened to depart?"

Leena's expression remained annoyingly neutral. It reminded Sabine of being back in the Faerie courts, where smiles often hid nefarious plots and hidden daggers were part of the status quo.

"King Kal'thorz has expressed his desire that your stay in this city be a pleasant one. The underworld can be a harsh place, with many undesirable elements lurking beyond this gate." Leena darted a pitying glance at Rika. "These walls do much to protect those who cannot protect themselves, as your human has apparently learned."

Sabine was fae enough to read between the lines. Her question about leaving remained unanswered. If she forced the point now, she might lose the healer's aid in helping Rika. She'd never survive the trip to the surface in time to find another healer. Not to mention, Sabine didn't have enough magic readily available for a repeat of her last performance. She was now cut off from the Well.

Rika thrashed and mumbled something in her sleep. Sabine moved forward and waved her hand over Rika's body, pushing her into a deeper sleep. The girl stilled, but Sabine kept her hand hovering over her for another minute to ensure she wouldn't awaken.

Bane scowled. "Your song and dance is entertaining as always, Leena, but we have more pressing business."

Leena's mouth curved, her eyes glittering with unnamed emotion. "I follow my king's instructions, Bane'umbra, as do all who enter his realm. He has ordered me to see to Sabin'theoria's needs and assure her comfort, a duty I intend to fulfill."

"*Queen* Sabin'theoria," Bane said sharply. "I doubt King Kal'thorz will be pleased if Queen Sabin'theoria's lady-in-waiting dies in the streets because you were wasting time. The human's heartbeat grows weaker while you natter on."

Leena bowed low to Sabine. "Until you are acknowledged as queen here, I dare not address you as such, Your Highness. However, if you will follow me, I will escort you to the healer with all due haste."

Sabine gave her a curt nod and gestured for her to lead the way. Leena did as promised, moving quickly through the streets. The city was larger than Sabine had expected, full of twisting and turning roads. Part of her suspected Leena wasn't taking them on the most direct route. Every time they turned down a different street, Sabine glimpsed movement out of the corner of her eye, but she never saw another living soul.

"Where is everyone?" Sabine asked.

"The lower part of the city is not open to the public. To protect your fae sensitivities, King Kal'thorz has ordered most of the residents to remain in their homes until you reach the palace." She offered Sabine a knowing smile. "Many who grow up in Faerie are often uneasy when dealing with demons and their ilk."

Sabine gave her a wry look. "While I may not have visited

Harfanel in the past, the Unseelie court has always embraced their darker brethren."

"There is a difference between high demons and the general populace, Your Highness. Many consider the lesser demons to be both terrible and fearsome in appearance and deed. Those are not typically tolerated in any of Faerie's courts."

Sabine tilted her head in acknowledgment. Some creatures of nightmare had been known to affect humans with merely a single look. It was probably for the best that Rika wasn't conscious.

Leena stopped at a large stone building that towered nearly three stories in height. She rapped briskly on the door, waited for a moment, and pushed it open. The smell of pungent herbs and foul concoctions wafted out the door, nearly knocking Sabine over with their stench.

Leena stood at the entrance and called, "The new ruler of the Unseelie fae wishes to barter for your services, alchemist." Turning toward Sabine, she said, "I will wait outside with the guards while you conduct your business."

Sabine nodded and stepped inside, resisting the urge to cover her nose. The floor was littered with refuse. Unfamiliar herbs and other components hung overhead in drying racks. Dark liquid, which bore a disturbing similarity to the consistency and smell of blood, dribbled down one of the walls. Sabine felt her stomach churn at the realization some of the bottles on the shelves were filled with body parts from a variety of creatures.

A blood troll hunched over a large cauldron, stirring the bubbling green liquid with a large spoon. Tiny wisps of hair floated on top of his otherwise bald head. His gray skin was gnarled and wrinkled, and he had a hooked nose that was nearly as large as his head. Two large tusks jutted out of his mouth, somehow helping to balance the size of his remarkable nose.

He cut off the tip of his thumb with a dagger and tossed it in the pot. Before he finished one stirring rotation, his thumb had grown back. He clucked his tongue in approval before lifting his head. His beady black eyes peered at Sabine and her companions over the edge of his oversized snout.

Blossom gasped against Sabine's neck. In a shaky voice, she whispered, "It's the underworld alchemist. Be careful, Sabine. He's evil! He eats baby pixies for breakfast!"

At Bane's signal, the fire imps carted Rika inside and placed her on the floor of the main room. There was a small shriek and a group of furry black creatures the size of hamsters made a mad dash for the door.

"Rinexes," Bane muttered, his lip curling in disgust.

"Close the bloody door!" the troll shouted. "Ye'll be lettin' all the tasty bits out."

"Stay!" Bane ordered the rinexes with a growl.

The furry creatures stopped short and piled together, trembling and squeaking in dismay. Bane growled at them again, and they quieted.

"Myco, yer dinner is crawling away!" the troll yelled and gestured at the rinexes.

A creature bearing an uncanny resemblance to a mushroom emerged from a cupboard under the stairs, leaving a trail of slime behind him. He scooted to the small furry critters and simply sat on top of them. When he returned to the cupboard, there were no signs of the rinexes, except for a few tufts of black fur sticking out from the slime.

Blossom gagged.

"Your familiar has eaten, Anje," Bane said sharply, crossing his arms over his chest.

"Aye, so he has." The troll rubbed his hands together and

approached Rika. "Now then. What's the king's bit of fluff bringing to my door this time? More tasty bits?"

"Queen Sabin'theoria of the Unseelie wishes to barter with you. You will treat her and the injured human with respect, or I'll see how many body parts I can cut off from you before you stop regenerating."

"Heh." Anje chuckled, his gaze calculating. "A faerie queen, a dragon in hiding, a wee little bite, a battered human, and the bastard demon king's spawn. Mmm. I can think of a few tasty treats for my coffers."

Blossom squeaked. "He can see me!"

Sabine frowned. He shouldn't have been able to sense Blossom's presence, unless he possessed some sort of talisman that allowed him to see through glamour. Such devices were extremely rare and highly coveted. She swept her gaze over the room, but nothing called to her. He must have the item hidden somewhere on his person and masked by something else. He could likely see the gold in her hair, but there was little she could do about it now.

Setting her worry aside, Sabine took a step forward. "My human companion needs healing. I wish to barter for your services, alchemist."

The troll sniffed the plant cage containing Rika's still form. "Might be better just to cook her up. Someone already tenderized her."

Malek crossed his arms over his chest. "Try it and you'll be the one in your pot."

The fire imps giggled and shuffled their feet. Bane swept them up in his arms and shoved them out the door, kicking it closed behind them.

Sabine straightened. "Your price, alchemist. What do you wish in exchange for healing the human?"

The troll shuffled toward her, sniffing along the way. "Tasty, tasty. High magic, eh? More than a mere Faerie queen, it seems. How about a lick? Just a taste to show me yer wares? You can't expect me to trade if I don't take a sample." He waggled his eyebrows.

Malek drew his knife and angled it under the tip of the troll's nose. "That's close enough."

Anje rubbed his hands together. "How about a dragon scale? Or perhaps a tooth? Aye, I could make lots of tasties with those."

Sabine narrowed her eyes. "You barter with me, alchemist. Not with my companions."

"A shame, a shame," he muttered with a sniff. "How about a kiss from the delicious Faerie princess?"

"Don't do it," Blossom whispered, tugging on Sabine's hair. "Blood trolls turn to stone in the sunlight. Your Seelie magic will release him from his prison. A kiss from you will remove the curse."

Even without Blossom's warning, Sabine had no intention of doing any such thing. She would give much to heal Rika, but not at the expense of potentially thousands of innocents. Unleashing him aboveground to wreak havoc upon the world would be devastating. Blood trolls were nearly impossible to kill.

She shook her head. "A fair trade, or our business is done."

The alchemist huffed. He angled his snout in Bane's direction before dismissing the demon out of hand. "Fair trade, fair trade."

"What is it you wish in exchange for healing Rika, alchemist?"

He sniffed. "Tonight, before the moon reaches its zenith, ye'll bathe and leave the water to cool. I'll be taking it when yer done with it."

Sabine blinked. "What?"

"My price," the troll said, shuffling back to Rika. He

picked up a piece of her dark hair and sniffed at it. He licked it and made a noise of pleasure.

Bane darted forward and cut off the tip of Anje's nose with his claw. "Touch her again without an agreement, and I dice off more body parts."

Anje cackled, his nose growing back in front of them. He turned toward Sabine and pointed at her. "You wish the tasty human to keep fattening up, you leave yer bathwater for me to collect."

Blossom gagged. "Ew. That's nasty."

"You dare much, troll," Malek said.

Bane leaned close and murmured, "While somewhat distasteful, it's a fair trade, Sabine. He won't be able to cause too much harm from it. You'll need to leave Rika in his care overnight. He's skilled, but his methods take time."

Distasteful was an understatement. Not wanting to think too hard about what the alchemist intended, Sabine said, "Done. You will heal this human's ailments in exchange for my discarded bathwater. No further harm will come to her at your hands or any others while she remains in your care. She will be returned to me or my companions well and whole by dawn tomorrow."

"Agreed."

"Witnessed," Bane said.

She gave Anje a curt nod. "The deal is struck."

The troll grinned widely around his tusks. Waving his hands, he shooed them away. "Go! Go! Must work now! Send the messenger when yer bath is done."

He shuffled to a shelf and grabbed a few bottles, whistling a merry tune. Sabine shuddered.

"I don't like it," Malek said quietly, sheathing his blade.

"Nor I," Sabine admitted, concerned about leaving Rika alone. Kal'thorz had already attacked them once.

"Wait!" Blossom said, tugging on Sabine's hair. "We're

leaving Rika here? With the evil troll that drinks bathwater? He sniffed her!"

Bane took Sabine's arm and said, "It's the best bargain you could have made under the circumstances. Once you finish bathing, I'll make the arrangements. Rika will remain safe. On that, you have my word."

Sabine relaxed. Even Blossom ceased her objections. Sabine approached Rika one last time and placed her hands on the girl's head. Reaching for Rika's consciousness, she pushed it even further downward to ensure the seer would sleep peacefully until morning. At least she wouldn't wake up terrified and alone.

Feeling more confident about the situation, Sabine turned and left the laboratory, with Malek and Bane falling into step behind her.

Leena was standing a short distance away with the two guards. She was speaking quietly over a small, glowing crystal in her outstretched hand. At the sight of Sabine, she straightened and placed the crystal in her pocket.

"The pact has been made?"

"It has."

Leena bowed her head. "Then, with your permission, I'll show your other companions to their quarters before taking you for an audience with King Kal'thorz."

"My companions remain with me."

Leena flicked her gaze briefly in Malek's direction before returning it to her. "Very well, but King Kal'thorz has only decreed that the rules of hospitality be extended to you, not your companions."

"I'm not leaving Sabine," Malek said, his tone brooking no argument.

Magic pulsed softly around them, almost as though it were testing the veracity of Malek's words and the connection Sabine shared with him. Sabine didn't miss the surprise that flashed across Leena's exquisite face before she hid it behind a carefully composed court mask. Sabine frowned, wondering if Leena could read emotions and intentions.

"It is not my place to challenge your wishes," Leena said, dipping her head. She turned and walked down the cobbled road.

Sabine and Malek exchanged a look before falling into step behind her. If Sabine had to guess, she'd say Leena had been speaking directly to King Kal'thorz. She wasn't sure what instructions the fae woman had received, but Sabine doubted it was anything good.

Chapter
Twenty-Three

*S*abine followed Leena down the street, while Bane
and Malek kept pace on opposite sides of her. The
two demon guards accompanying them fell into step behind
the group. Malek didn't appear pleased at having potential
enemies at his back. His hand never strayed far from his
weapon. Sabine continued to occasionally see movement out
of the corner of her eye, but the watchers disappeared before
she could catch sight of them.

From a distance, Sabine made out the distinct clanging
sounds of battle. Above it, a symphony of chilling screams
filled the air while cries of pain played an accompaniment.

"What is that?"

"The prison," Bane said, a warning in his eyes. "The sparring fields and prison stand between the lower and upper
districts. We'll pass by them on the way to the palace."

Sabine nodded her understanding. No matter what she
witnessed, she couldn't show revulsion or weakness. Not for
the first time, she missed the ease of simply being Sabine, a
"human" in Akros. Despite the hardships they'd faced, the

easy acceptance her friends offered her was more rewarding than anything she could have imagined.

Another set of demon guards stood watch at the base of a hill. Leena stepped aside, providing Sabine with an unobstructed view. They were closer in appearance to Bane, although their horns weren't nearly as large as his. They were both bare-chested with long, curved swords strapped at their sides. Several scars covered them, a testament to the number of battles they'd fought and won. Their reddish skin had been oiled, making it glisten in the light.

"King Kal'thorz offers you a gift," Leena said, gesturing at the two guards. "Quiron and Xenith have fought and won the right to be first among the volunteers to act as your personal honor guard."

Sabine narrowed her eyes. After what she'd just experienced at the hands of other demons on that field, she wasn't letting another near her or her friends.

Blossom snorted softly and whispered, "Ew, demons as a present? I guess he's never heard of giving someone flowers and honeycakes instead?"

Sabine bit back a smile at Blossom's comment. The two demons thumped a fist against their chests and kneeled in front of Sabine.

The one on the left lifted his head and said, "I am Quiron, Your Highness, and this is my blade-brother, Xenith. Word of your victory outside of Harfanel has already spread among our brethren. It would honor us to protect and serve you."

From the way his gaze roamed her body and the emphasis on the word 'serve,' Sabine suspected their offer was more than simply fetching her drinks. Malek narrowed his eyes on the two demons, but he remained silent. At least he was content to let her handle this.

"You both appear to be fierce and skilled warriors,"

Sabine said, choosing her words carefully. "However, I must decline your offer of protection. I already have an honor guard to see to my needs."

Xenith bowed his horned head, but neither demon appeared surprised by her refusal. Their eyes lit in challenge. "We shall escort you to the palace and endeavor to change your mind, Your Highness."

At a discreet signal from Leena, both Quiron and Xenith rose and stepped aside. The fae woman lifted the hem of her dress and headed up the winding hill.

In a quiet voice, Bane said, "They will not gracefully accept your rejection, nor will they be the last to volunteer. To prevent more bloodshed, it would be wise to select at least one group to help guard your person while you're in the city."

"I'm not surrounding myself with anyone I don't trust implicitly."

"I suggest you reconsider. While I may be able to remain by your side, Malek's presence will not be tolerated in some areas. If any of these volunteers believe him to be an obstacle in securing your favor, they'll work doubly hard on removing him."

Sabine muttered a curse.

Malek kept his voice low. "I can handle myself, even if I have to take out the whole damn street to shift. I won't trust anyone else with your safety."

"You'll both need to sleep at some point," Sabine said, glancing back at the two demons who had fallen into step behind them. The heat in Quiron's eyes was nearly scorching. Good gods. What had she gotten herself into? They needed to locate Dax, fetch Rika, and get the hell out of this place.

"Are there any demons you're willing to vouch for?"

"Not these two." Bane aimed a derisive sneer in Quiron's

direction. "They'll be too busy trying to fuck you to stop the person trying to slit your throat."

"Lovely," Sabine muttered.

At the top of the hill, the path divided a large clearing. Hundreds of demons, both male and female, were engaged in mock battle on one side. From all appearances, some weren't quite pretending. They fought with weapons, claws, horns, teeth, and tails. The graceful ferocity and speed with which they fought were shocking, even to her. Sabine wished Rika were there to witness it.

The sparring wasn't confined to only demons either. Sabine counted numerous ogres, trolls, and a handful of giants, among others. Each appeared to be lethal in their own way. Some fought with magic, while others used more traditional weaponry. Blood spilled freely like wine, yet they showed no signs of slowing down.

On the opposite side of the path, Sabine caught sight of a looming black building that was comparable in size to her family's winter palace in Faerie. An oppressive heaviness hung in the air, broken only by the screams carried on the wind.

In front of the prison, men and women were strung up and chained to large posts. Sabine spotted several fae, along with trolls, ogres, humans, and even a few of the beastpeople who had been taken captive. Some were being whipped, their desperate pleas falling on deaf ears. Others were being tortured by lava-dipped pokers searing their flesh, the sharp and acrid stench wafting in the air. Goblins darted in and out of the rows of prisoners, lapping up blood and other bodily waste.

Sabine slowed her steps as she caught sight of a fae being systematically beaten. His wrists and ankles were bound to a post with what appeared to be obsidian bands adorned with glowing dwarven crystals. She'd observed such shackles when she'd visited the prison in Razadon. They were designed to cut off ties to magic.

The blond man was vaguely familiar. She couldn't place him, but she recognized his marks of power. They identified him as Seelie royalty. In some distant past, they shared a common ancestor. Her heart pounded in her chest, wondering if her father's side of the family knew one of their relatives was imprisoned in the underworld.

"Who is that man?" Sabine asked, gesturing at the captive.

Leena turned, her lips forming a thin line. "That would be Prince Síolas'ellesar of the Seelie."

Sabine stared in shock. This was her father's brother? She'd thought he'd died during the Dragon War. Could he have been here, imprisoned and tortured, for centuries? This must be part of the reason her father hated the Unseelie. Perhaps there was a way to free him without ruining her chances to secure an alliance with the demons.

Bane shot her a warning look. "Sabine."

She held up her hand to stop him. "I would speak with him a moment."

Bane muttered a curse and stepped off the path with her and Malek. At their approach, Síolas lifted his head. His pale-blue eyes seared her with undisguised hatred and loathing. It was enough to stop her in her tracks.

"Unseelie whore," he snarled and spat in her direction. "Just like your bitch of a mother. Off to spread your legs for the demon king? Your father should have drowned you when you were born."

Sabine reared back in shock.

Bane barked out a harsh word. The demon torturer withdrew his dagger, grabbed the man's head, and sliced off his lips. Blood dribbled down the man's chest while the demon beat the fae with renewed vigor. The captive laughed, the maniacal sound sending chills through her.

"I'll get out of here and kill you! I'll slice you to pieces and fuck your corpse!"

Bane withdrew his dagger and murmured in a voice too low to be overheard, "You have an audience. Make it look good."

Sabine took the dagger from him. Her hand tightened on the hilt of the blade. How much darkness would she have to embrace to prove herself to these people?

She started to refuse, but Bane's silvered gaze stopped her. A group of demons had gathered around them. She swallowed, realizing she no longer had a choice. She had to do this. For Rika. For Dax. For everyone she'd ever cared about. If she didn't, they'd all be ground to dust. Even if the demons didn't kill them, her father—this man's *brother*—would make sure of it.

Stepping up to the captive Seelie prince, she held his gaze and shoved the blade in his gut. "It's good to see you too, *Uncle*."

The demons escorting her hooted and hollered, elbowing one another in approval. Her uncle laughed, the sound like an ice pick stabbing at her brain. Something inside her broke. A cold fury wrapped around her, leeching the warmth from her body and inviting in darkness. Blossom whimpered and scooted closer to her neck, the small pixie trembling in fear.

Wrenching her wrist, Sabine twisted the knife in his belly. She yanked it out and stabbed him again, ignoring his high-pitched laughter. She shoved the blade in a third time and then pulled it back out, halting only when her uncle's body went slack and his head dropped to his chest.

"Is he dead?" she asked, her tone deceptively mild compared to the tumultuous emotions threatening to shatter her to pieces. She could still hear his maniacal laughter in her head.

The demon torturer checked to make sure Síolas was still breathing and then removed him from the rack. "Nice cutting, Your Highness. He's got a bit of life in him yet. I'll take him to the fixer so he'll be ready again for tomorrow's entertainment."

Unsure whether that was worse than death, she inclined her head and handed the bloody blade back to Bane. He shouted something and held up the dagger for the nearby demons to witness. A resounding cheer filled the air.

Shaken to her core, Sabine forced herself to turn away and head back toward the main road. She had to get herself under control and stop her hands from trembling before someone saw through her mask.

She'd known there were fae prisoners in Harfanel, but the reality was worse than she'd imagined. She knew her uncle, like her father, would kill her if he ever got free, and for what? Because she'd been born able to wield Unseelie magic?

Malek reached out, his fingers discreetly brushing hers. He didn't say a word, but the compassion and understanding in his gaze helped center her. She took a deep breath and squared her shoulders. She could do this. She *would* do this. Not all the Seelie wanted her dead. She had to trust there was something to be salvaged between their people. But gods, she wasn't sure she'd ever forget the way his blood had spilled over her hands. Even if they made it out of there alive, she wasn't sure her soul would remain intact.

At the top of the hill, the view of the city changed dramatically. The road was relatively free of refuse, but that could be attributed to the goblins darting through the streets. Shops and homes lined the streets, bearing an eerie resemblance to Razadon's market district. Trolls, ogres, demons, and even a few Unseelie fae went about their tasks with a briskness that spoke of some urgency. At the sight of Sabine, many of them paused, and a few curiosity seekers moved in their direction. Sabine's guards unsheathed their weapons, making it clear they weren't welcome to approach.

The palace loomed ahead, its imposing dark walls glittering with crushed crystals. A gong sounded somewhere in the distance. She felt the ground beneath her feet tremble slightly. Blackened rock formations she'd assumed were merely decorative erupted, spilling lava over themselves like wax from a lit candle.

Several demon children darted in their direction, dipping their clawed fingertips or tails into the lava and licking it off like candy. One of them got too close, catching his tail on fire. A nearby adult grabbed him and flung him in a nearby pile of ash. The child shook himself off, grinned, and scampered off to taste the next lava spire.

"What was that sound?" she asked Bane.

"It has formally announced our presence," Bane said in a dry voice. "We'll have an audience when we reach the palace."

Another pair of demons, a male and a female, stepped in front of them and thumped their fists on their chests.

Their armor was more substantial than any Sabine had seen thus far. Like most other demons, they both had horns and tails, although the woman's tail was considerably longer, with several sharp-looking discs attached to it. They kneeled in front of Sabine and withdrew their curved swords, placing them on the ground in front of them.

The female demon lifted her head to meet Sabine's gaze and said, "I am called Rakva, first of the Reeva Clan. My blade-brother, Rothir, and I would swear to your service. Your honor would be ours, and we shall strive to serve you in darkness and in blood."

Sabine's eye twitched. She was exhausted, hungry, dirty, covered in blood, and completely out of patience. If one more pair of demons tried to swear fealty to her, she wasn't sure they could hold her responsible for her actions. She was ready to strangle someone.

Battling back her frustration, she took a steadying breath. She glanced at Bane, who gave her a barely perceptible nod. Fine. At least he approved of one group. If the best way to get them to stop throwing themselves at her feet was to select a pair to act as an escort, so be it.

Sabine inclined her head. "You honor me, Rakva and Rothir. While I currently have a primary honor guard to protect and serve me, your blades would be welcome. You may escort us to the palace and defer to Bane regarding any assigned duties."

Both demons sheathed their blades and stood. Rakva reached forward and clasped wrists with Bane before doing the same to Malek, murmuring a warrior's greeting Dax had taught Sabine years ago. Malek appeared bemused at first but went along with it. Sabine tilted her head, surprised and suspicious of the demon's easy acceptance to being around a dragon.

Blossom tugged on her hair. "I'm confused. Are we making friends now?"

"We're going to try," Sabine murmured quietly.

Feeling a little like a bedraggled mother duck leading her demonic ducklings behind her, Sabine approached the palace gates. They had positioned more guards outside the building, these wearing strange harnesses with dozens of small sheathed daggers in their straps. Despite herself, Sabine slowed her steps to get a better look. Bane and Dax had told her stories about these terrifying warriors, known as the morthal. After she'd developed an affinity for using daggers, they had modeled many of their training sessions after the morthals' tactics.

As one, they stepped aside to allow her to pass. The heel of Leena's boots clicked against the polished volcanic floor. It was as though they'd embedded the night sky into the floor, with crystal stars scattered carelessly across it.

A large throne room loomed ahead, filled with hundreds of demons. At the front of the room was a large throne that appeared to be made entirely of bone and sharpened, glowing red crystals. Seated on the throne in his position of power was King Kal'thorz Versed, ruler of the underworld.

"That's Bane and Dax's big, bad, demon daddy?" Blossom whispered with a squeak.

"Yes, and we're going to make him regret raising his hand against us," Sabine said with grim determination before entering the room.

"Oh, good. I thought this trip was going to be boring."

Chapter
Twenty-Four

"Your Majesty," Leena said, infusing her voice with enough power to project it throughout the room. "Allow me to introduce you to Sabin'theoria of the Unseelie, daughter of Queen Mali'theoria, descendant of Lachlina, Bringer of Shadows, and Vestior, Harbinger of Nightmares…"

Sabine tuned out the list of familial ties and instead focused on the horned demon sitting on the throne. Like Bane, his skin was a deep red color, surging with the same power that flowed through the city like rivers of lava. It was lifeblood magic, the heart of the underworld, and it pulsed within the demon king like the heartbeat of the world. It filled the room, calling to her and enticing her to respond.

She allowed her magic to flare, the silver markings on her skin shimmering brightly. Her luminescence matched the intensity of the red crystals embedded on his throne, and the resulting light show filled the room with a brilliance few had ever seen. Many of the demons in the audience gasped or averted their eyes. Hushed and uneasy whispers flitted through the crowd, their gazes darting between Sabine and their king.

Kal'thorz stared at Sabine with a look that could only be described as insatiable hunger. He held up his hand, the gesture causing Leena and the rest of their audience to immediately fall silent. The fae woman lowered herself to the ground in a position of obeisance. The others did the same.

Blossom squeaked and slipped under the collar of Sabine's dress. "Please don't see me. Please don't see me."

Without tearing his eyes away from Sabine, Kal'thorz stood. His movements were both graceful and predatory as he descended the dais. The more curious or daring onlookers lifted their heads to watch as he passed, but he ignored them. His sole focus was Sabine, and she felt his gaze as intimately as a caress. He exuded charisma and power, an intoxicating mixture that captured and held Sabine's attention.

It was too bad he needed to be brought to heel.

"Tread carefully," Bane warned quietly.

Sabine tensed and then forced her body to relax. No matter how furious she was over the needless slaughter on the field, she needed an alliance with the demons.

Whatever Kal'thorz's purpose had been in bringing them here, he'd show his hand faster if she played him correctly. Bane had said Kal'thorz expected an untried yet powerful princess of Faerie. She'd give him what he wanted, while keeping her true intentions in sight.

"Sabin'theoria," Kal'thorz purred as he drew closer. The velvet in his voice possessed its own form of power, reminiscent of her people's ability to sway with their speech. "Or may I call you Sabine?"

When she inclined her head, his mouth curved in a way that reminded her of Dax. The similarities between father and son were stronger than she'd realized.

"I have long awaited the day when you would grace the underworld with your presence."

"Kal'thorz," she murmured in greeting as he captured her hand. His touch sent shock waves through her, causing her Unseelie magic to flare in response to his nearness. Gods. No wonder her mother had been reluctant to visit the underworld. The demon packed a serious punch.

"You must call me Kal." He kissed her hand, his lips lingering on her skin. "Rumors of your beauty do not do it justice."

Before she could respond, he tucked her arm against his side. She barely resisted the urge to pull away and slap him down. Bane caught her eye and gave her a barely discernible nod of approval.

Kal'thorz ignored Bane's presence and instead turned toward Malek. He assessed the dragon shapeshifter with the same interest as a farmer shopping for livestock. "And this is your tamed dragon? How intriguing. Perhaps we'll see a display of his abilities later."

"The one you just witnessed wasn't enough?" Malek asked, narrowing his eyes at Kal'thorz. "We can take a walk on the field if you need a refresher."

The demon king bristled at the venom in Malek's tone. His hand tightened around Sabine's possessively, his eyes flashing to silver. Bane tensed, his expression demanding she do something.

Sabine sent a distracting trickle of complementary magic over Kal'thorz. His predatory gaze immediately flew to her. The hungry look was enough to steal her breath and make her heart pound.

Projecting a playful mien, she tilted her head and offered Kal'thorz a disarming smile. "I trust our unconventional arrival hasn't inconvenienced you, Kal. In truth, I'd hoped to arrive sooner, but there were some unpleasant matters that needed my attention in Razadon."

"Ah, yes," Kal'thorz murmured, idly caressing her hand, still tucked against him. "I'd heard about that. Rumors claim the would-be assassins were eliminated in a most entertaining fashion."

"It definitely caused a stir."

His lips curved in a calculating smile. "And how exactly did you manage to slip through the escort I'd prepared for you at the gateway to Razadon?"

She fluttered her lashes at him. "Why, Kal, you can't expect me to reveal all my secrets before we've had a chance to get to know one another. What fun would that be?"

He threw his head back and laughed. Several of the demons around them let out a forced chuckle.

Kal'thorz purred. "You are a delight."

She peered up at him flirtatiously. "I'm pleased there are no hard feelings about that little mess I left at your back door. Apparently, some of your subjects didn't get the message about my invitation to visit."

"If they were unfortunate enough to have been bested by you, my dear, then I had no more use for them." He leaned in close and breathed in her scent, the flames of his power trailing over her skin.

Malek stiffened. Sabine kept her body relaxed, inwardly urging Malek to hold. His jaw clenched, but he remained where he stood. She knew it was costing him dearly to allow the demon king such liberties.

Kal'thorz leaned back, his expression smug as he glanced at Malek. "Fascinating. I look forward to getting to know you better, Sabin'theoria."

She gave him a demure smile.

"Come, my dear," he said, leading her toward the exit. "I'm

sure you're eager to get settled in, and I have a few things to take care of before you take your place here."

She cocked her head. "You're referring to the ritual?"

He chuckled and absently patted her hand. "No need to concern yourself with trivialities. After you've refreshed yourself, I'd love to hear more about your adventures. Dax has told me marvelous tales about your time in Akros."

Sabine straightened at his mention of Dax. "Your messenger indicated Dax was going to be executed."

Kal'thorz's lips curved in a smirk. "Ah, yes. My son has been very naughty." He glanced at Bane. "Both of my sons have proven to be something of a disappointment."

Sabine tensed, her gaze automatically going to Bane. Whatever Kal'thorz saw in her expression made his smile deepen.

Kal'thorz snapped his fingers at the dark-haired fae woman still kneeling. "Leena, show Sabine and her companions to the quarters we've prepared in the west wing. You may prepare her for the rite of passage once she's ready to accept her place among us."

Leena rose and said, "Of course, Your Majesty."

Kal'thorz kissed Sabine's hand and said, "I eagerly await the minutes until we meet again. Leena will be at your disposal if there's anything you need."

"Your hospitality is generous," she murmured.

Leena pasted on a courtly smile and led the way out of the throne room. While the woman chattered politely about the construction of the palace, Sabine tried to untangle the knots in her stomach. Kal'thorz had always been described as a brute of sorts, but the scene in the throne room had been orchestrated to make him and the rest of the demons appear more polished and cultured.

Sabine didn't buy the shift for a minute. Living among

both Dax and Bane had shown her enough about the true nature of demons to not fall into that trap.

Bane had always been skilled at subverting his true nature until he attained his goals. Perhaps Bane had more in common with Kal'thorz than Sabine had guessed. She just wasn't sure if he was more volatile like Dax or more calculating like Bane. If he were both, she was in serious trouble.

"The entirety of the west wing is yours to use," Leena said, leading them up a wide staircase. "There are several suites that have been prepared in anticipation of your visit. No one who is not authorized is permitted entry."

"Yeah, but who *is* authorized?" Blossom grumbled. "I bet it's more stinky demons."

Sabine made a noise of agreement. She had no doubt that the entire west wing would be monitored and every detail of their interactions relayed to Kal'thorz.

Leena opened a door to reveal a large courtyard. The floor was made from the same polished volcanic tile as the throne room, but large pots overflowing with colorful volcanic flowers helped soften the severity of their surroundings. Several fountains with pale-purple water gurgled and splashed, creating a soothing gardenscape. Four sets of doors led out from the courtyard, likely leading to individual quarters. Each doorway was affixed with dormant crystals, while a larger crystal hung from the ceiling and provided the room with light.

Sabine swept her gaze over the area. "It's lovely."

Malek moved into the room, opening doors and inspecting their surroundings. Bane remained at Sabine's side with his arms across his chest. Rakva and Rothir entered silently, standing at the threshold like twin bookends.

Leena gestured toward the door where they'd entered. "King Kal'thorz has entrusted additional guards to be stationed at the entrance to the wing. To prevent any further unpleasantness, King Kal'thorz requests the dragon remain confined to these quarters when not in your presence."

Sabine pursed her lips. "I will consider his request."

Leena hesitated. "Of course, Your Highness. The goblins are preparing a small repast for you and your companions. I'll have it brought to you shortly. If you wish to bathe and refresh yourself, you may do so and then I will escort you to the quiet."

Malek turned toward her. "What is the quiet?"

Leena darted a quick glance at Malek before turning back toward Sabine. "I was under the impression you had already performed a ritual in Razadon proclaiming you queen, Your Highness. To accept you as ruler of all Unseelie residing within the underworld, you will be required to embrace your true self. The quiet will offer you the solace and opportunity to do so."

Sabine frowned. "Can you tell me anything about the ritual?"

"Such discussions are forbidden."

"I see."

Bane straightened and gestured toward the door. "That will be all, Leena. I'll handle things from here and escort Sabine to the quiet myself."

Leena paused for a moment and then inclined her head. "I'll relay your intention to King Kal'thorz. She is expected in the quiet before midnight." Turning back toward Sabine, she said, "If you require assistance, simply place your palm against the crystal panel on the wall, and it shall summon me."

Sabine nodded at the woman, waiting until she'd withdrawn. Bane spoke quietly to the two demon guards Sabine had accepted, and he directed them to remain on guard outside.

Once everyone was gone, Blossom darted out from under

Sabine's hair. Sabine pressed her finger against her lips and made a gesture to circle the area. Blossom saluted her and then flew off to search for spying devices.

Malek scanned the courtyard again. He leaned down and whispered in her ear, "I found some observation crystals hidden around some fountains. There may be more in the bedrooms. Would you like me to deactivate them?"

She shook her head and spoke in her mental voice. *"Blossom will handle it."*

He nodded and skimmed a hand down her back. "Are you all right?"

"I've had better days," Sabine admitted, relaxing against him when he wrapped his arms around her. His magic enveloped her, warming her like a fire on a cold day. For a few moments, she allowed her tension to melt away and embraced the comfort he offered.

Bane crossed his arms over his chest and frowned at them. He made a gesture, indicating the need for privacy.

Pulling away from Malek, Sabine created an obfuscation bubble that would give them a few minutes to speak with no one overhearing them. She just hoped her efforts at circumventing Kal'thorz's surveillance didn't endanger Bane or Dax. "Blossom is deactivating the observation crystals. I'm assuming Kal'thorz has the entire palace monitored."

Bane nodded. "A fair assumption. It won't be limited to spying crystals either. Even the walls have eyes and ears, with passages nestled between for spies and would-be assassins."

Sabine lowered herself to a nearby bench and rubbed her temples. "All right. I can create wards to notify us if anyone tries to enter."

Malek frowned. "We'll need to sleep in shifts."

"What can you tell me about the quiet or the ritual involved in claiming my place here?"

Bane hesitated, his expression conflicted. "Like Leena, I'm

bound from saying too much. What I can tell you is that you'll need to go into the quiet alone. If you have the strength to leave, you shall. If you do not, you will remain there."

Malek placed his hand on Sabine's shoulder. "She's not going alone. We agreed she'd remain by my side while we're in the underworld."

Sabine placed her hand over Malek's in a show of solidarity. "There's no reason Malek can't accompany me."

Bane shook his head. "You must relinquish your ties to the light and fully tap into your Unseelie magic." Turning toward Malek, he explained, "Your presence brings her Seelie magic to the forefront. That cannot happen. A moment ago, when you embraced her with your power, you shifted her alignment to become more Seelie."

"I hadn't realized it was that noticeable," Sabine said, releasing Malek's hand and folding hers in her lap. "I don't like the idea of being separated, but it's likely similar to the ritual I performed in Razadon. You couldn't help me then either."

"You were permitted to have someone remain with you," Malek said. "I may not have been able to step inside the circle with you, but another person there may be the difference between success and failure. I don't trust Kal'thorz."

"I don't either, but our situation is more dire than it was back in Razadon. If I can't embrace my Unseelie side, I'll lose any chance of having an alliance with the demons. Without them, I'll never be safe from my father, and neither will my people. Hiding in the Sky Cities with you isn't an option, Malek."

Malek ran his hand though his hair. "How are we supposed to protect you if Bane has to follow Kal'thorz's orders and I'm forced to keep my distance from you?"

Sabine lowered her gaze to stare at the floor. She was

more concerned about them than herself. Malek had been the target on that field, not her. Kal'thorz viewed her as a potential pawn. He wouldn't hurt her, not as long as he thought he could use her.

Bane kneeled in front of Sabine. "You must look within yourself to find your strength. You are the only one who can break the chains binding you in the quiet."

Something in his eyes made her pause. It was almost as though he was trying to tell her something beyond his uttered words.

Reaching for him, she drew him down to the bench beside her. "What *can* you tell me, Bane?"

He paused and then said quietly, "Do not trust anyone you have not cultivated a relationship with outside the underworld. I may be limited in how far I can aid you, but you have my word that I will do everything within my power to protect your life."

Sabine kissed his cheek. "I've never doubted you."

Bane squeezed his eyes closed and nodded.

Sensing the privacy bubble weakening, Sabine stood and said, "It sounds like we all need to keep our guard up. The sooner we can get out of here, the better. In the meantime, I desperately need to get some rest. If I'm going to go into this 'quiet,' I'll need whatever strength I can find."

"You should eat something too." Malek reached out to her and then dropped his hand with a muttered curse. "This distance thing is going to be challenging."

She managed a smile and kissed him lightly. "Yes, but it's only temporary."

Bane scowled at them. "Your time in this suite is limited. You should bathe while you have the opportunity—alone. Once you've finished with your bath, I'll send a messenger to the alchemist."

Sabine wrinkled her nose but nodded in agreement.

Malek chuckled. "If it makes you feel better, I'll monitor Rika once she returns."

Bane nodded. "The alchemist will stay true to his word. Rika should be brought here shortly after dawn. If Sabine does not return by then, the young one will be entrusted to your care for safekeeping."

Sabine took a steadying breath. "At least we have a plan."

Chapter Twenty-Five

*M*alek waited until Sabine had closed herself off in one of the bedrooms before turning back toward Bane. The demon was prowling around the courtyard like a caged nafghar. The giant spotted cats were notoriously ill-tempered and vicious.

"What aren't you telling us?"

Bane lifted his head. "Many things, dragon. My loyalty is to her, not to you."

Malek crossed his arms over his chest and waited. They'd both come too far to play this sort of game when Sabine was in danger. Bane would eventually talk. Malek just had to wait the stubborn demon out. If that didn't work, he had enough pent-up frustration and anger to beat it out of him.

Blossom landed on Malek's shoulder and said, "This is a terrible place."

"I know."

Blossom shook her multi-colored hair and said, "Almost everyone down here is stinky. It's like they all share the same magic."

"What do you mean?"

Blossom cocked her head. "It's kinda like watered-down pollen. The pollen is always strongest when it's fresh on the flower. Once the rain hits it or the bees take it away, it loses something or changes. But it still has the same smell."

Malek frowned. "The source being Kal'thorz?"

Blossom nodded. "Sabine doesn't like him, but she is curious about him. I think he reminds her of Bane and Dax. She's not scared of them, but she *should* be afraid of B.B.B.D.D."

"B.B.B.D.D.?"

"Bane's Big, Bad, Demon Daddy."

Malek's mouth twitched in a smile. It faded a moment later when he considered the implications of Blossom's words.

Bane growled and continued pacing. "Sabine should not have come here."

"No shit," Malek snapped and pushed away from the wall where he'd been leaning. So much for patience. "You may be oathbound not to reveal certain things, but not all. If there's anything we need to know to help protect her, start talking."

Bane paused for a moment and then frustratedly said, "How did Rika get injured?"

Malek frowned, replaying the events with the kobold in his mind. "Are you suggesting Kal'thorz somehow orchestrated her fall?"

Bane didn't respond.

Blossom's eyes widened, her wings fluttering rapidly. "Someone hurt Rika on purpose?" the pixie shrieked.

Malek clenched his jaw. If Rika had been standing a little farther away, she would have missed that ledge entirely and they would have lost her. "What reason would anyone have to harm a human girl?"

"We have to go get her!" Blossom said, her wings tinged with red.

When Bane didn't answer, Malek blocked his path and demanded, "Are you sure Rika will be safe with the alchemist? If there's a chance they'll hurt her or worse, I'll fly everyone out of here right now."

Bane grunted and resumed his pacing. "For now, she is safe. The pact with the alchemist was made with Sabine and witnessed. Whether she remains that way once she arrives here is another matter."

Rika wasn't any sort of threat. They'd only begun Rika's weapon training, and even if she were proficient, she wouldn't stand a chance against a demon. Her seer abilities could be part of the reason, but they were too erratic to be much of a concern. Still, if Malek could help Rika tap into her foresight, the young seer might provide them with advance warning if Sabine were in danger.

"Sabine handled herself well at the prison."

Malek's gaze sharpened on the demon. Bane rarely handed out compliments or engaged in meaningless chitchat.

"She did what was necessary," Malek said carefully.

"She shouldn't have done it," Blossom said with a sniff. "Her magic smelled funny after she stabbed her uncle. It smelled funny after she killed all the demons too. I don't think she should stay here."

"How did her magic smell funny?"

Blossom cocked her head and then shrugged. "It was peppery. I think it was because she doesn't like hurting people. When we lived in Akros, Bane and Dax used to take the darkness from her when she would do stuff like that." Her wings fluttered as she glared accusingly at Bane. "Why didn't you take it from her?"

"The curse may have been lifted, but I am still bound to the rules governing all underworld denizens. I may not interfere with Sabine's magic without Kal'thorz's leave."

Malek narrowed his eyes. "He's trying to bring her over to the dark side."

"She is already Unseelie, dragon," Bane said to remind him. "Having a fae queen with ties to the light is of little use to him."

"Dammit," Malek muttered, scrubbing his hands against his face. He needed to get her out of here, and soon. If Kal'thorz had his way, he'd try to install Sabine as his queen and use her magic to unleash hell on the world. He hadn't missed the flare of intrigue in Sabine's eyes or the way she'd flirted with the demon king. Malek knew she didn't have any overt interest in him, but her soft spot for Bane and Dax might make her believe she could handle Kal'thorz in the same way.

"Incoming!" Blossom said and darted into the foliage on the far side of the room. Her appearance shifted and took on the form of another volcanic flower.

The door to the courtyard opened and Leena entered the room, followed by a pair of goblins pushing a large cart with several covered trays. Leena gestured to the goblins on where to set it up.

"I trust everything is satisfactory with your rooms?" she asked in a soft voice, her diaphanous dress clinging to her body as she moved toward Malek.

He nodded and glanced at the goblins. One of them was uncovering the dishes, revealing a variety of meats, cheeses, and sliced fruits.

Leena approached Malek, her expression turning curious. Her striking eyes were the palest of blues, enhanced only by the dark contrast of her long lashes. Like many of the fae, she was extraordinarily beautiful, but there was something about her that made Malek wary.

"I saw a dragon from a distance a long time ago," she

admitted, her voice soft and alluring. "You're the first I've spoken to while in human form."

"Both forms have advantages," Malek said absently, wanting to monitor the goblins. Blossom might be hiding, but the green creatures had a penchant for sniffing out and eating the wings off pixies.

"Most of us assume all dragons hate the fae. It's strange to see a dragon accompanying a fae, a human, and a demon." Leena tilted her head and peered up at him, the disarming gesture reminding him of Sabine. "You don't have a problem with us?"

Malek frowned at her. "I'm not in the habit of judging an entire group by the actions of a few."

Bane growled at the goblin when he started sniffing at the nearby vines. Flushing a sickly green, he went back to preparing their meal. He hauled a miniature cask onto the table and tapped it before placing a few mugs close by.

One of the goblins uncorked a bottle of what appeared to be Faerie wine. Unlike some of the other bottles Malek had seen, this one had a black label. He knew the gold indicated boosted magic, and the red-labeled wine was a bit of an aphrodisiac. Malek tried to remember if Sabine had ever mentioned the black bottles.

He opened his mouth to ask about the wine, but Leena stepped closer to him and placed her hand on his arm. He jerked his gaze toward her and narrowed his eyes.

"I've always been fascinated by the way dragons can shift forms," Leena said, her lips curving in a small smile. Her magic was subtle, dancing along his skin with a light and teasing caress.

He started to pull away but thought better of it. There was an element to Leena's power that was different from Sabine's remarkable yet elegant magic. If Sabine was going to be around this woman for any length of time, he needed to know what was off about her.

"Many races can shift forms."

Undeterred by his lackluster response, she continued. "Some fae use illusions to give themselves different appearances, but they're a poor substitute to the realities your kind can create. Does it require much of your magic?"

He arched his brow, wondering if she was actually foolish enough to expect he'd answer. It was interesting that Sabine had never questioned him overly much about his abilities. He'd volunteered to share some information, but she'd never pried. His fae grandmother had been the same way. He'd always assumed it was a cultural thing, but now he couldn't help but wonder. Either that or Kal'thorz had ordered Leena to elicit information from him.

"Don't you have other things to do?" Bane asked Leena in a dry tone.

Leena's smile faded as she pulled her hand away from Malek. She swept her gaze over the table and nodded her satisfaction at the presentation. She clapped her hands, motioning for the goblins to depart. On her way to the door, she moved closer to Malek than necessary and sent him a flirtatious look.

"If there's anything else you desire, let me know."

Now *that* was similar to Sabine's ability to charm and seduce.

Malek gave her a curt nod. "Will do."

Bane muttered something under his breath and escorted Leena to the door. He didn't exactly slam it behind her, but he wasn't quiet about it either.

"That whole show almost put me off my dinner," Bane muttered, prowling to the table.

Blossom darted back out of the flowering vines and landed on his shoulder. "She was flirting with you!"

"Caught that, did you?" Malek asked, walking to the food and assessing it critically.

"Demons find poison to be tedious," Bane said. "We prefer looking into our target's eyes before we strike. The food is likely safe."

Good enough. Malek grabbed a plate and loaded it with some of the meat. He didn't want to think too hard about what or whom the demon king was serving them for dinner, but he was ravenous.

"I don't like her." Blossom landed on the table and sniffed the fruit.

Malek made a noise of agreement. He started to reach for the wine, but his gaze darted to the closed door where Sabine slept. It might be better to wait and share the wine with her. He'd stick to the ale stamped with a dwarven maker's mark until then.

Bane sat at the table and dug in. Malek claimed the chair across from him and studied his plate. The meat had been seared only on the outside, which was exactly the way he liked it.

He picked up a long, stringy piece of meat and sniffed it. He couldn't swear to it, but it looked and smelled like raftin steaks. The large grazing animals were usually found in plains areas. "Where did this food come from? Nothing smells like it was harvested from the underworld."

"Offerings, raids, or thefts," Bane said with a shrug and tore off a chunk from a bone. "The humans provide us with offerings to leave their settlements alone. If they don't, we take our due and a little extra for the inconvenience."

Blossom carried a leaf with small slivers of fruit to the table. She licked one piece and cocked her head. "Northern fruit. Decent soil. Human farmers. Could be better. Needs a pixie's touch."

Malek chewed thoughtfully. "I'm not sure the demons

care too much."

Blossom shrugged and shoved it into her mouth, her cheeks bulging like a tree rat.

"Any idea about Leena's intentions?" Malek asked the surly demon.

"Fuck her and find out."

Blossom choked on her fruit. With a finger, Malek tapped her back in between her wings.

Partially chewed fruit flew across the table as Blossom exclaimed, "He can't do that! Sabine and Malek love each other. He's her balance!"

Bane gave her a look of disgust. "Since when are fae monogamous?"

Blossom's wings drooped. "Pixies mate for life."

"Pixies only live a handful of years before they're on someone's plate." Bane nudged his plate toward her. "Is it your time yet?"

Blossom sputtered, her wings turning bright red. With an angry shriek, she flew off toward the flowering plants and shouted, "I hope you choke on the next pixie you eat!"

Bane smirked and pulled his plate back in front of him.

Malek knew fae weren't often monogamous, but dragons mated for life. Until recently, Sabine had been reluctant to admit her feelings for him. Now that she had, it was almost as though the floodgates had opened. Their connection had deepened, and being able to communicate with her mentally would only bring them closer. He wasn't in a hurry to push her further, especially when the future was so uncertain.

No matter what happened, he had no intention of giving up or walking away from her. He'd talk her around. After all, dragons never gave up their hoard, and she'd become more precious to him than all the treasures in the world.

With a grin, Malek took another bite of his food. All things considered, it was a damn good steak.

Chapter Twenty-Six

*S*abine nibbled on a piece of waskin fruit and wandered the courtyard, admiring the volcanic flowers that had grown in a riotous display of color. The blossoms were deep red, a vibrant purple, or a striking yellow. They created a small oasis in the bleak darkness of the underworld. They filled the air with their rich perfume, teasing her with a reminder of home. Her mother had always loved them and often had vases filled in the grand entryway. These flowers had helped her people get through the worst of their exile after they'd fled Faerie.

Blossom darted from flower to flower, sipping on nectar, while Malek reclined on a nearby bench with his feet propped up. His eyes were closed, but there was still a slight tension in his shoulders. She doubted he would truly sleep while they remained in Harfanel.

Bane had woken her a short time ago, suggesting she eat something before they had to depart. Her stomach was too tied in knots to eat more than a small amount.

Bane poured a glass of wine and handed it to her. She

glanced at the bottle, but the maker's mark and cap had already been discarded.

When she hesitated, Bane said, "It's safe for you to drink."

Sabine nodded and took a sip of the wine. The sharp and tantalizing taste, of sweetened fruit harvested under a full moon, danced upon her tongue. Power flowed through her, calling upon the darker magic sleeping within her.

Her magic shifted, changing and aligning to complement the potency of the wine. Interesting. She hadn't tasted a blend like this one since she and her friend, Alveria, had broken into her mother's wine cellar. She drank deeply and closed her eyes, smiling at the memories the wine evoked.

"The bottle had a black cap," Malek said from the bench. "I don't think you mentioned that one the last time we shared wine."

She opened her eyes to meet Malek's gaze. "It's rare. I've only had it once before. It's specially crafted for those possessing Unseelie magic. I only know of two vintners capable of making this blend." She frowned at her cup. "Most of the Seelie have severe reactions to it. You should probably avoid it just in case."

"It should give you a power boost before you enter the quiet," Bane said, topping off her glass. "It would have been better if you had been able to get more rest, or if you hadn't cleared a field of demons."

Sabine shrugged. She'd managed an hour of sleep after her bath, but she'd been too disconcerted by everything happening to fully relax. Not for the first time, she wished her mother had conveyed more about the expectations surrounding the ritual.

"I think I like the purple flowers better," Blossom said and darted to another vine. "They're kinda tangy, with a peppery aftertaste. I bet it's the fertilizer they use."

Sabine took another sip of her wine. "I doubt the underworld gardeners ever thought they'd be judged by a pixie's discerning tastes."

Blossom grinned at her and landed on a vine. "I'm just glad they had flowers here. I thought I'd have to eat stale pollen for days."

Sabine laughed. Bane headed back over to Malek, and the two talked quietly, trying to give her time to collect her thoughts. In truth, she wanted to delay this ritual as long as possible. She felt ill-equipped to perform whatever tasks were going to be expected of her. As soon as she finished this glass of wine, she'd ask Bane to take her. She needed to get it over with so she could turn her attention to saving Dax.

She took another sip of wine and wandered through the courtyard. Colorful murals lined some of the walls in the fashion of dwarven artistry, but they had altered many of these from their original forms. She stopped in front of an image of Lachlina that had shocked her when she'd first seen it. The goddess was completely nude, except for a silver filigree necklace with a large blue stone resting on her bosom. She was lounging suggestively on a pile of pillows with her finger crooked and a come-hither expression on her face. That was disconcerting enough, but the size of her overly large breasts was almost horrifying.

"Ahh. A favorite of many young demons, but I've always preferred your breasts."

Sabine spun around, dropping her goblet at the sight of the demon who had once been both her protector and lover.

"Dax!" she cried, running across the courtyard to him.

He swept her up, his arms around her tight and unyielding. His familiar smoky smell filled her nose, reminding her of their shared times. She buried her face against his neck, blinking back the tears that threatened. He'd been her home, her safety net, and an impossible frustration for over a decade.

If it weren't for him and Bane, she never would have survived living among the humans for so many years. Their ways had been so strange to her, but she'd always respected their strength. They were predictable in their ferocity, something she'd come to depend upon.

Wrapping her arms around his neck, she held on to him. He pressed his body against hers, making it clear every inch of him was equally pleased to see her. Her mouth curved into a smile, her face still buried at his throat. She hoped he never changed.

She leaned back and drank in his image, running her hands down his bare chest. Dax's body had once been as intimately familiar as her own. Dozens of new scars crisscrossed over his skin as though he'd lived a lifetime of agony over the few months they'd been separated. Her breath hitched at the sight. When her gaze flew back up to meet his, his expression was hard.

She swallowed and placed her hand atop a long scar that had barely healed. Demons typically couldn't heal themselves aboveground, but he should have been able to down here. Sending a strong surge of magic over him, she felt the wound finish knitting together beneath her fingers. Burying her concern, she gave him a brilliant smile and pressed a light kiss against his lips. "I've missed you, you pain-in-the-ass demon."

"Fuck that for a greeting," Dax retorted and thrust his hands into her hair. He yanked her close and claimed her mouth with his. His tongue swept into her mouth in a brutal and punishing kiss.

He drank in her magic like a man desperate for salvation. She sent her power outward, embracing him with everything she was. It wasn't enough. He demanded more, and she gave what she could, her mind reeling from the onslaught. What had depleted so much of his strength? Her head swam, and her vision started becoming blurry.

Malek yanked Sabine away from Dax a second later, his sword aimed in Dax's direction. "Try it, and you'll die."

Dax roared his fury at being denied, his eyes silvered and deadly. Malek readied himself to attack, but Bane leaped into the air and tackled his brother.

With a shout, the two demons fell upon each other, swiping with claws and jabbing with punches. They rolled across the floor and slammed into a bench, where they continued fighting.

Malek pressed his hand against Sabine's midsection, gently nudging her safely behind him. "At least I don't have to worry about making you angry when I kill him. It looks like Bane's going to do it for me."

Blossom landed on Sabine's shoulder and said, "Who's taking bets? Should I start a pool?"

"That won't be necessary." With a wave of her hand, Sabine sent the two demon brothers flying across the courtyard.

Bane leaped to his feet, his silvered eyes glaring at his brother. Dax simply continued to sprawl on the ground, staring at Sabine with a smirk.

He dipped his finger into the spilled wine on the ground near him. He slowly licked it off, keeping his eyes on her the entire time. Her face warmed, remembering the time he'd poured Faerie wine on her naked body and then licked it off.

He grinned at her. "Did you come to the underworld because you raised your standards? Or are you still fucking the dragon?"

"Watch it," Malek warned.

Sabine narrowed her eyes at Dax. She squeezed Malek's arm before pulling away and stalking toward the demon. "If you weren't already at my feet, I'd send you there."

Dax chuckled and rose to his full height, towering over her. Malek moved toward her, but she held up her hand to stop him. With a sly grin, Dax grabbed her hand and pulled her close, nuzzling her neck.

"If I'd known I'd get such a welcome from you, I would have tried harder to leave this shithole."

"You're still as impossible as ever," she said in exasperation.

Blossom huffed and flew over to Malek, grumbling something about icky demons.

"Give me an hour alone, and we can have a real reunion," Dax said, his voice husky and demanding.

Malek's sharp and biting emotions pulsed against their bond like a loud roar. She paused and glanced at him in surprise. It wasn't possessiveness—or at least not entirely; he truly believed Dax was a potential threat. It was taking everything he had not to tear her away from him. The thought was both unsettling and worrisome.

Sabine carefully extricated herself from Dax's grip and walked back to Malek and Blossom. Malek immediately wrapped his arms around her. The second he touched her, the strain affecting their bond eased. They'd need to talk about this, but now wasn't the time.

She'd wondered how Malek and Dax would handle seeing each other again. It was both better and worse than she'd expected. At least everyone was still alive. That had to count for something.

"You're a fool," Bane said to Dax. "Why don't you demand the rest of her magic while you're at it? There are more important things at stake than your comfort."

Dax's eyes flashed silver. "Careful, *brother*. I've held up my end. We all do what we must."

Malek studied them both. "What is that supposed to mean?"

The demon brothers exchanged a meaningful look between them but didn't answer.

Blossom leaned over and whispered, "Dax doesn't look very good."

Malek sharpened his gaze. "No. He doesn't."

Sabine frowned, comparing the demon brothers. Blossom was right; Dax looked exhausted. There was a weariness in him Sabine had never seen before. It was almost as though his soul was starving. What had Kal'thorz done to him?

Bane snatched up the goblet and refilled her wine. He handed it to Sabine and ordered, "Drink."

She scowled at him over the rim of her glass but drank it down. Dax had taken quite a bit from her, but he hadn't depleted her magic, not anywhere close. It made her wonder how much her dip in the Well had amped up her power, not to mention all the artifacts she'd been absorbing. If Dax had done that when they had been back in Akros, she probably would have passed out.

"Is it true she took out a squad of demons at the back gate?"

Bane nodded, a trace of amusement on his face. "She did."

Dax chuckled. "Kal'thorz must have shattered at least a dozen scrying crystals when he flew into his rage. They'll be talking about it for the next century."

Bane's expression sobered. "She's expected in the quiet in less than an hour."

Dax's jaw clenched, his nostrils flaring. "You're taking her?"

Bane gave him a curt nod.

Dax slid his gaze to Malek. "The dragon is staying here?"

"For now."

"The dragon can speak for himself," Malek said, crossing his arms over his chest.

Dax chuckled. "He's gotten feisty now that he's no longer playing human."

Sabine finished her wine and placed the goblet on the table with a little more force than necessary. If she had to sit there and listen to their cryptic conversation for another ten minutes, she was going to throw the rest of the bottle at them.

Turning back around, she asked, "What are you doing here, Dax?"

"Looking to get rid of me already, beautiful?" Dax walked to the table and used his sharpened claw to slice off a piece of meat. He popped it into his mouth and chewed.

She frowned at him. "You seem fairly cheerful for someone about to be executed."

Dax captured her wrist and pulled her into his arms. "Should I assume you're here to grant a dying demon's last request? I can think of a few things I'd been meaning to try back in Akros."

Malek straightened and looked like he was about to interfere, but Bane grabbed his arm and asked, "What do you think of the ale, Malek?"

Sabine paused, surprised by Bane's tone. He rarely addressed Malek by name, preferring to refer to him as "dragon" or equally dismissive forms of address.

Malek hesitated.

Sabine caught his eye and sent a trace amount of reassuring magic through their bond. *I need to talk to Dax privately. No matter what, you cannot interfere. If you do, he'll focus on taunting you instead of telling me about Kal'thorz.*

Malek frowned. After a moment, he turned back toward the food and asked Bane about trade between the dwarves. While they kept a running commentary in the background, Sabine created a small privacy bubble.

"We don't have long," she said once it had been set into place.

Dax's arms tightened around her. In a voice that was barely more than a whisper, he said, "I was ordered to drain as much of your magic as possible from the moment I entered."

"So I gathered, but you didn't seem to suffer overly much."

"Only with the case of blue balls I'm going to have from being this close to you."

"Dax…"

Dax chuckled, his breath tickling her ear. "Just listen, and try to look like you're about to tear the rest of my clothing off. We need to give the spies something interesting to report."

She grabbed his waistband and yanked him closer. Lifting her head, she whispered in his ear, "Start talking, or I'll bring out my knives. Then the spies can try to decide whether your screams are from pain or pleasure."

"Fuck, I've missed you." Dax squeezed her ass and then his voice became all business. "I can circumvent most of Kal'thorz's demands, but ones that are personally issued are a bit more challenging to resist. Bane also has his ways of avoiding following orders, but we're both going to be limited with how much we can aid you."

"All right. Tell me what I need to know."

"Once you enter the quiet, you'll be cut off from everyone. Neither Bane nor I can help you once you cross the threshold. Even your dragon and pixie will be out of reach. If you value the pixie's life, keep her away."

"Can you tell me what I'm supposed to do?"

"Survive," Dax said coldly. "Kal'thorz has spent the past several months using his preferred sorceress to tap into my memories of you. Bane assassinated the bitch last night. She may no longer be able to trap you in memories, but make no mistake: Kal'thorz will use everything he's learned about you to get past your defenses."

Sabine's entire body went rigid. "To what end?"

"He wants you either as his queen or under his thumb. If he has control of you, he can break free of the shackles binding him to the underworld. He believes you'll be powerful enough to bring all the demons into the light. After that, you're expendable."

She started to deny it, but Dax's gaze hardened.

"Since the moment you stepped foot in the underworld, Kal'thorz has been watching you. He knows the hellhounds acknowledged you and you entered the Hall of the Gods at their invitation. He may not know exactly what transpired while you were inside, but we have a damn good idea." He ran a lock of her hair between his fingers. "The gods have touched you, Sabine. Kal'thorz suspected it, but now it's confirmed."

Her eyes widened. "What?"

"My fucking brother didn't tell you to glamour yourself soon enough. While he was off slaughtering Brexia and her guards, you were taking a damn swim in the Well and having a heart-to-heart with a goddess in the middle of the fucking underworld." Dax paused, his arms tightening around her again while his eyes shone silver. "Bane will join me soon on the chopping block. The fool. He should never have left your side. I would have handled the sorceress bitch."

Sabine pressed her hands against Dax's bare chest. "What will Kal'thorz do to you? To Bane?"

Dax chuckled, but it was a harsh and bitter sound. "Whatever the fuck he wants, unless one of us kills him."

"Then we'll kill him and be done with it."

"So bloodthirsty," Dax said, a gleam of approval in his eyes. "It's not that simple, beautiful. Only Bane and I have the right to challenge his throne. I've been kept too busy fighting off would-be assassins to issue a challenge, and Kal'thorz is currently too powerful. When I die, Bane will be the only other option for uprooting Kal'thorz from his throne. We need him distracted or weakened first. Both would be better."

Sabine shook her head. If she didn't convince Dax to leave the underworld with her, she would lose him forever. Balkin might have negotiated a life debt with Dax to her benefit, but it held no bearing on what had developed between them in the following years.

Maybe she'd been a fool to resist binding him to herself for so long. Dax could be volatile and terrifying when he challenged her authority, but he'd always kept her safe.

The past few months had changed her more than she'd realized. The thought of binding him to herself no longer scared her. Finding a new balance between them wouldn't be pleasant, but it would be far less painful than losing him forever.

"Ask me to anchor you, Dax," Sabine said urgently, needing him to say the words aloud to initiate the binding. "I know we danced around it for years, but I'm not willing to lose you. Not like this. Balkin arranged for you to be released into his custody once before. There's no reason I can't do the same. We can leave together and work on a plan to eventually remove Kal'thorz."

Dax's gaze sharpened on her. "Fuck. You're serious."

Sabine brushed her lips against his, feeling his body respond to her touch. Cupping his face, she whispered in the language of her birth, "Swear your oath to me, Dax'than Versed, and all I am will be yours. By blood and by magic, you'll feel both the sun and the moon on your skin until the last of the magic fades from this world."

She sent a strong pulse of power over him, enticing him

to accept her offer. His clawed hands dug into her hips. There was a wild hunger in his gaze as he stared at her.

"Dammit, Sabine," Dax whispered, his voice strained. "You're a beautiful little fool. You don't even realize the ramifications of what you're offering."

She tossed her hair back in challenge. "What do you wish of me, Dax'than Versed?"

He squeezed his eyes shut and muttered a curse. When he opened them again, his expression was pained. "Break the privacy ward, beautiful. You need to conserve your remaining magic."

She froze, her heart falling into her stomach. Blinking back the tears that threatened, she said, "Dax, you can't—"

"Don't fucking start, Sabine. I'll do as I damn well please, just as I always have." He smirked. "And when the bastard on the throne is finally dead, I fully intend to celebrate by licking another bottle of wine off every inch of your delectable body."

Sabine pressed her forehead against his chest and managed a halfhearted laugh, but it hurt. He was doing it again. He was willing to sacrifice himself if it would protect her. "Make sure you survive, and I just might let you."

He grinned. Darting a smug look at Malek, he lowered his head and claimed her lips again. Sabine leaned into the kiss. She wrapped her arms around him, sending a rush of power over him. There was no way she'd send him off to suffer Kal'thorz's wrath without first helping to bolster his strength.

They were still locked in their magical embrace when the ward fell around them. Sabine broke their kiss, her heart thundering in her chest. It wasn't too late. She could still find a way to convince him to leave. Maybe once she completed the ritual, she could negotiate directly with Kal'thorz.

Dax blinked back the silver in his eyes and growled.

"Fuck, you're potent. More than you used to be, and that's saying something."

"Are you two finished yet?" Bane asked, sounding almost bored.

"For the time being." Dax drawled, squeezing her ass again. "Think I'll check out the wine cellars a bit later. I'm sure we've got another bottle of Faerie wine around here somewhere."

Sabine shook her head in exasperation as Dax pulled away. He wandered back to the table and cut off another slice of meat.

Malek didn't look happy by the easy affection between her and Dax, but the overwhelming emotion she felt from him was concern and worry. She instinctively reached out to him, caressing him with her power. Malek's eyes held hers, warming with undeniable heat as he gazed at her. She was attracted to Dax and the challenge he offered, but it paled in comparison to the fiery and passionate inferno Malek evoked. Gods. The dragon consistently stole her breath whenever their eyes met.

"Say your good-byes, Sabine," Bane said quietly. "We need to leave."

Sabine went to Malek. He wrapped his arms around her, caging her against his large body. Her hands curled into his shirt, and she breathed in the familiar aroma of burnt leaves that always surrounded him. Something inside her eased.

If she were honest with herself, she was scared. But a larger part of her was angry. For years, she'd been nothing but a pawn with the threat of assassination shadowing every corner. It seemed nothing had changed. No matter how vast her powers grew or what she accomplished, someone was still trying to use her for their own purposes or to destroy her.

For a long time, Malek simply held her. It was almost as though he could sense she needed time to collect herself.

When she relaxed against him, Malek ran his hand along her hair and said, "Sabine, if you need me while you're there—"

She pressed her fingers against his lips to silence him. Their mind-touch ability wasn't reliable, but it seemed to work better when she was touching him.

Reaching out to him with her mental voice, she explained, *"Kal'thorz has been spying on us since we arrived. He doesn't know what transpired between us in the Hall of the Gods or that we can communicate this way. Don't tell anyone, not even Bane or Dax. They're still on our side, but I'm afraid of what Kal'thorz will do to them if he believes they're withholding information. I don't think either of them expects to live through—"*

Sabine broke off and looked away, unable to continue. Malek's arms tightened around her. He nuzzled her neck and spoke softly in her thoughts.

"Be careful, Sabine. I don't have a good feeling about letting you go off alone. Kal'thorz has been trying to manipulate you since we were back in Razadon. Bane's already warned that you can't trust him while we're here."

Sabine squeezed her eyes shut. *"I realize this might be a trap. But even if it is, I don't believe Kal'thorz wants to harm me. I'm more concerned about leaving you here with no allies other than Blossom."*

"Sabine, I'm a dragon. Demons are formidable, but dragons are more so. Your gods gave demons an affinity for fire because they hoped it would provide them with some resistance to dragonfire. If I held back on that field earlier, it was only because I wasn't willing to harm you or Rika."

Her fingers curled into the soft material of his shirt. *"Promise me if they come after you that you'll fight them with everything you have. Don't hold back, Malek. Not for anything."*

"I'll do what's necessary to protect myself—and Rika too," Malek said with promise. *"Focus only on completing the ritual and coming back to me. If you don't, I'll destroy this city to find you."*

She let out the breath she'd been holding and relaxed her grip. He was right. Malek could hold his own if necessary, or at least buy himself enough time to get him, Rika, and Blossom away safely.

Sabine said, "Blossom, I need you to stay here and help protect Malek and Rika."

"You don't want backup?" Blossom asked with a frown.

Sabine smiled and held out her hand for Blossom to land on. "You'd help far more by remaining here and protecting Malek and Rika. I can't bring any ties to the Seelie with me. It would be too dangerous for you."

Blossom wrinkled her nose at Dax and Bane. "I don't have to protect them, do I?"

Dax crossed his arms over his chest. "How did she not end up in some demon's belly before now?"

When Blossom's wings turned bright red in anger, Sabine sent a strong wave of magic over the pixie. Blossom fell on her butt and hiccupped.

"Wheee! There are two of you, Sabine!" Blossom slurred her words, her gaze a little unfocused. She pointed at Bane and Dax, her finger moving back and forth. "Thatsa whole lotta demons."

Sabine transferred Blossom to Malek's hand and said, "She'll fall asleep in a minute. I've given her enough magic to remain comfortable in the underworld for at least a day. Keeping her near the flowers will help." Pointing at Dax, she said, "Your word that you won't eat her."

With a huff, Dax nodded his agreement. "One pixie isn't much of a meal anyway."

Blossom tried to stand but fell over, her wings twitching.

She yawned and rolled over, grabbing hold of Malek's finger. A minute later, Blossom was snoring in Malek's outstretched palm.

Malek's lips twitched. "I'll keep an eye on her."

Sabine turned back toward Malek and said, "Keep an eye on my dragon too. I've grown rather fond of him."

Dax made a noise of disgust and went back to the table.

"*You're my heart, Sabine.*" Malek tipped her head back and kissed her softly. "*No matter what magic flows through your veins, you're mine to protect.*"

Love, strong and vibrant, soared within her. For a moment, she allowed herself to fantasize about running away with him. She could simply be Sabine and leave all of this behind—her throne, the alliance, the life-and-death politics, everything. She'd found more happiness in the past few months with a dragon than she'd experienced in her lifetime.

But it was simply that, a beautiful dream. If she ran away without seeing this through, they'd be running forever. At some point, her father or the Wild Hunt would find her. Everyone close to her would be equally at risk. She couldn't allow it to happen.

Sabine wound her arms around his neck, her magic flaring to the surface. All of her fears, her hopes, and her desires blended together as she returned his embrace. She opened her thoughts, allowing him to see the depth of her feelings for him. He inhaled sharply, pulling her closer as he deepened their kiss. His heated magic surrounded her for a moment and then faltered at Bane's warning growl.

With a muttered curse, he broke their kiss and pressed his forehead against hers. "You make it far too easy to forget myself around you."

She smiled. "I wouldn't have it any other way."

"Remember, Sabine," he said quietly. "Whatever needs to be done."

She nodded. Sweeping her gaze over the three men who had changed her life for the better, she realized it was true. Somehow, they'd become a strange sort of family. She loved each of them in their own way and would do whatever was necessary to protect them.

In Bane, she'd found a fierce protector and friend. He was more than an advisor. He had a way of cutting through noise to get to the heart of the matter. The harsh truth he often showed her could be painful, but she valued him all the more for it.

Dax had shown her what it meant to be truly independent, challenging her at every turn until she had no choice but to stand on her own or risk being overrun. He'd taught her how to laugh in the face of despair and to thrive when the world was intent on destroying everything she held dear. He'd been her first real lover, teaching her to harness and control her magic far beyond all expectations.

But it was with Malek that she'd learned to trust and love beyond all reason. He'd shown her in words and deeds that long-held beliefs and ideas could, and should, be challenged. He'd shown her endless possibilities and given her hope for a future she'd never had the courage to imagine. And in him, she'd found the answer to a question she had been asking her entire life.

He'd shown her she was worthy of love.

They all had.

Sabine straightened, marveling at each of these three powerful men who had touched her life. She didn't know what would happen when she went into the quiet, but she couldn't regret a moment of what had brought them here.

She prayed she had the strength to meet them on the other side.

"All right. Let's do this."

Chapter Twenty-Seven

*B*ane was silent as he led her through the palace hallways. The two demon guards, Rakva and Rothir, remained a handful of steps behind them, their eyes alert for potential danger. No one troubled them. The demons and creatures averted their eyes as they passed. A few lesser demons scampered in the opposite direction at the sight of Sabine and Bane.

On the ground level, Bane walked past the throne room and toward the rear of the palace. The air was cooler there, with a hint of moisture that hadn't been present anywhere else in the city.

Bane stopped at a large wooden door. He placed his hand on the door and lowered his head for a moment. His skin glowed a deeper and more brilliant shade of red that reminded her of the lava fields they'd passed. Sabine felt something change in the air, causing her skin to prickle. Withdrawing a large skeleton key from his pocket, Bane unlocked the door and pushed it open.

Sabine's wrist began to burn. She winced, clamping a hand over the marks Lachlina had etched into her skin.

Rakva and Rothir snapped to attention, their suspicious gazes searching for potential threats. Bane's eyes sharpened on her. She shrugged and gestured toward her marks. After what Dax had told her, she couldn't risk confirming her connection to the goddess around other demons.

"Rakva and Rothir, you will need to remain here," Bane said, gesturing for her to go ahead. "No one is permitted to enter this wing without Kal'thorz's leave."

Sabine stepped inside, feeling a slight tingle across her skin, but the pain eased. Bane followed her, then closed and locked the door behind them. Sabine took the opportunity to rub some feeling back into her wrist.

A long, narrow tunnel stretched out before them. The blackened walls had flecks of reddish, glowing crystals embedded in them, which gave off a soft luminescence. A buzzing noise caught her attention. She lifted her gaze and saw several of the insectoid creatures known as the tarjin helping to circulate air through the tunnel. She hadn't seen many of them in the other parts of the underworld, but most of the other passages had been much larger.

Bane pressed his hand against her back, guiding her down the hallway. There were no other doors or tunnels. Even the air carried a weight to it, as though no one had trespassed in years. Something about this place felt very wrong. Sabine looked over her shoulder, but the tunnel had sloped downward enough that she could no longer see the exit.

Trying to bury her unease, she asked, "Is anyone else down here?"

"No."

She darted a quick look at Bane, but his expression was inscrutable. Her thoughts drifted back to what Dax had told her about them being in danger. Once Kal'thorz recognized her as queen of all the Unseelie, not just the dwarves and fae, she could intervene on Bane's and Dax's behalf. And if that failed, well, she'd find another way to smuggle them out of the underworld.

After nearly ten minutes of walking, Sabine caught sight of a doorway at the end of the tunnel. It appeared to be made from the same type of stone as the walls. Colorful crystals had been embedded into the stonework, creating an artist's rendition of a Silver tree with gracefully sloping branches. Above it was a glowing silver disc that appeared to represent the moon shining brightly overhead.

Bane stopped her at the door and said, "Sabine, it's not—"

He muttered a curse and slammed his fist against the nearby wall. Sabine started. Even the nearby tarjin ceased beating his wings for a moment.

"Bane?" she asked, taking a step closer to him. "What is it?"

He closed his eyes and rubbed the center of his forehead. After a moment, he cleared his throat and focused on her. "Once you cross the threshold, you will not be able to leave the quiet until you've fully embraced the darkness." He paused, his gaze lingering on the door. "Use whatever skills and magic are at your disposal to find your way back."

Sabine placed her hand on Bane's arm. "If this is what's needed to secure an alliance with Kal'thorz, I'm prepared to see it through."

He yanked her close and kissed her. Shocked by his uncharacteristic show of emotion, she stiffened for a moment before tentatively returning his embrace. She sent a light trickle of reassuring magic over him. After a moment, he broke their kiss and pressed his forehead against hers.

There was a slight growl in his voice as he whispered, "It's not too late to leave, Sabine. I'm still bound to you. Order me to take you away from here, and I'll return you to the dragon."

It wasn't bravado. She was truly terrified of what was to

come, but it changed nothing. "You know I have to do this, Bane."

His jaw clenched, and he gave her a curt nod. Using the skeleton key, he unlocked the door and swung it open. Sabine squeezed his forearm gently and then stepped inside the room.

Her brow furrowed as she studied her surroundings. The crystal lights overhead glittered brilliantly, bathing the entire room in a warm glow. At first glance, it appeared to be a sort of bedroom suite, but it was unlike anything she'd expected to find in the underworld.

The furniture had been made from a combination of wood and crystal, similar to what they had in the Unseelie palace back in Faerie. Delicate vases were filled with night-blooming flowers she'd never seen outside the Silver Forest. A comfortable sunken seating nook took up one side of the room, with several bookcases overflowing with books.

There was a small dining table for two situated just beyond the seating area. A steaming kettle sat on the table with an empty cup placed beside it. A decorative cabinet filled with crystal dishes and glasses took up a portion of the nearby wall while several floor vases overflowing with flowers offered a splash of color.

There was a bedroom on the opposite side of the suite. The bed had been crafted from what appeared to be a living tree. Branches curved upward and around the sleeping area, offering a soothing canopy of leaves overhead. Flowering vines curled around the branches, filling the air with their sweetened perfume. A large wardrobe and carved wooden dresser took up most of the nearby wall. Mounted above the dresser was some sort of large crystal, which doubled as a mirror.

Everywhere she looked, she saw more reminders of her

home. It was almost as though the entire room had been plucked out of Faerie.

Curious, she walked to an archway leading to another room. Dense foliage had created a makeshift wall, offering a modicum of privacy to the small grotto serving as a bathing room.

A small waterfall cascaded, ending at the large, heated spring. Steam rose from the water's surface, making the air thick with moisture. They had carved out a smaller area to act as a sink and also a privy. On a nearby ledge was a collection of perfume bottles.

She frowned, wondering what she was supposed to do. It was a lovely suite and much nicer than their current quarters, but she didn't see any sign of a ritual. In Razadon, there had been a large crystal set up in the center of the room that she'd had to activate. She saw no such signs anywhere in this suite.

Before she could ask Bane for direction, the door slammed shut behind her. Sabine whirled around, but it was too late. He was already gone.

More irritated than anything, she headed back to the entrance. There was no handle on the door. Instead, a duplicate of the crystal tree design was also embedded on this side. She ran her fingers along it, searching for some sort of hidden puzzle to unlock the door.

"Bane?" she called, but there was no answer.

Tamping down the tendrils of fear creeping up her spine, Sabine tapped her nail against each of the crystals. They flared briefly with a burst of color but otherwise appeared to be nothing more than pretty decorations. She didn't want to think about the possibility that Bane had been trying to warn her, even as he was setting her up.

"Bane, if this is some idea of a joke, I'm going to hurt you."

Sabine pressed on the crystal moon. Its silver color pulsed brightly when she made contact, but nothing else happened. It looked similar to the crystal panels installed in most rooms to activate various features. With her luck, she might have just summoned Kal'thorz himself. She pursed her lips. If so, she had a few choice words for him.

"Not good," Sabine muttered, giving up on the door for the time being. "Think. Bane brought me here for a reason. There's got to be something else here."

Her gaze landed on the dining area and the steaming kettle sitting on the table. A small heat-infused crystal stand was keeping the pot warm. Curious, she poured herself a cup of the pale-green liquid and sniffed it.

The light herbal aroma was a familiar blend that many Unseelie fae enjoyed, but she hadn't had it in years. Most of these herbs were grown close to the Silver Forest. She took a small sip but detected nothing unusual about it. At least no one was trying to poison her.

Leaving the cup on the table, Sabine walked to the two bookcases in the seating area. When she'd lived in Akros with Dax and Bane, they'd never shown much interest in the books she'd "borrowed" from various personal libraries. She knew there were some ancient archives in the underworld, but she'd never seen them.

She trailed her fingers along the spines of the books, reading the titles. They were mostly stories or fanciful collections. There were a few history books, but most were strictly for entertainment value. She recognized several titles that had been in her mother's library back in Faerie and had been personal favorites. Odd.

Abandoning the small library, Sabine headed back into the sleeping area. Standing on one of the low-slung tables near the bed was a small crystal portrait. Curious, Sabine picked it up, her grip tightening on the image. Shaken to her core, she lowered herself onto the edge of the bed.

"How can this be?" she whispered, tracing her fingers along the image of Queen Mali'theoria.

Her mother had often been cold and calculating, but the woman in this image was softer and more approachable somehow. Her long silvery hair was pinned up, held in place by a crown adorned with both silver and blue stones. A small and mysterious smile touched her face, suggesting she was on the verge of laughter or amused by some secret. Sabine shook her head, unable to recall ever seeing her mother like that.

When Sabine had left Faerie, there hadn't been time to take anything with her. She'd left in her nightclothes, fleeing for her life. The last time she'd seen her mother was when she'd been murdered, left brutalized and bleeding on the forest floor. Seeing her like this, alive and even happy, brought Sabine's pain back to the forefront. Unsettled, she swallowed and placed the portrait back on the table beside a small, decorative box.

Desperate for a distraction, she lifted the lid of the box and found a stunning and strangely familiar necklace resting atop a satin cushion. A large, blue twilight diamond was encased in the center of delicate silver filigree. The priceless gem shimmered in the light, appearing almost otherworldly as the colors deepened and shifted to reveal darker and bolder hues.

She looked at the portrait and then back at the necklace. It was the same one her mother had been wearing. She frowned, taking a closer look. It bore a striking resemblance to the one Lachlina had also been wearing in the mural. Odd.

Her mother had rarely spoken about her time visiting the underworld. She'd made it clear she loathed Kal'thorz and had eventually planned to have him removed from his throne. Nothing had ever come of it, but these sorts of plots sometimes took centuries to come to fruition. What if Queen Malia's hatred for him stemmed from circumstances similar to Sabine's? Could she have been a prisoner here?

Sabine stood and paced, trying to think it through.

Balkin had been the one who had often visited the underworld at Queen Mali'theoria's behest. That was how he'd met Dax and Bane. Given everything Bane had shared in the Hall of the Gods, Sabine couldn't help but wonder if Balkin had been ordered to foster a relationship with the two demon brothers. If they were the only ones who could kill Kal'thorz, it made sense she would seek an alliance with them.

Balkin had negotiated to have Dax released into his custody after he'd been slated for execution years ago. Sabine wasn't sure what had been promised for that exchange. All she knew was Balkin had used that life debt to ensure Dax protected her from harm while she was hiding from the fae.

"Dammit, Balkin," Sabine said, rubbing her temples. "Why didn't you warn me? Or did my mother not tell you because she didn't want to admit her weakness?"

Sabine surveyed her surroundings, recalling the way this room was situated apart from the rest of the underworld. Bane had used a significant amount of magic to deactivate the ward when they'd entered. Such security measures were usually only found in the strongest of prisons.

A prickle of magic caused Sabine to lift her head. The large, mirrored crystal over the dresser shimmered before an image of Kal'thorz appeared. He looked to be in some sort of study. Bane was standing off to the side, his expression blank.

"My dear Sabine," Kal'thorz said, his smug smile chilling her. "I trust you're making yourself at home?"

Sabine stood, her hands curling into fists. "What's the meaning of this?"

He tsk-tsked at her. "I would have thought it was obvious. We have no need for trappings and rituals such as the one concocted by the dwarves. Acknowledging your place among us is a simple matter."

"Is that so?"

"Of course," Kal'thorz said, gesturing toward Bane. "I understand you desire an alliance between our people. Is this true?"

She inclined her head.

Kal'thorz steepled his clawed hands. "Very well. I see much potential in a union between us. With an Unseelie fae queen at my side, we would have the power to shape the world as we see fit."

Sabine narrowed her eyes. "I'm interested in an alliance, not a union."

Kal'thorz's lips curved upward. "Accept me as king to your queen, my dear Sabine, and I shall deliver your father's and brother's heads as a wedding gift. Refuse, and you shall remain where you are indefinitely."

Sabine stepped toward the mirror, allowing her power to rise inside her. She cast aside her glamour, her skin and hair glowing with silver-and-gold light. Kal'thorz's gaze sharpened on her, the covetous look in his eyes making it clear he would do anything to claim her for himself. She wanted to gouge his eyes out with her nails.

"Is that all you're willing to offer me, Kal? Bane and Dax both offered me their heads months ago. Even my dragon lover promised to burn the Silver Forest to the ground if I wished it. Perhaps I'm not as much of a prize to the ruler of the underworld as I thought."

"On the contrary, my dear," he said, leaning forward. "Name your price and you shall have it."

She tilted her head as though considering it. "Anything I want?"

"Whatever you wish, my dear. Would you prefer riches? Jewels or costly clothing from the far reaches of the world? Or perhaps something a little more interesting? Name your enemy, and I will have their head delivered to you."

She tossed her hair back and straightened, her voice cold as she said, "The only head I want at my feet is yours, Kal'thorz."

With a sharp lash of power, she fractured the crystal mirror and split it down the center. She slammed her magic against it again. Kal'thorz shouts and curses filled the room before his image winked out. Pieces of sharp and jagged crystal fell to the ground in a pile of dust.

Turning on her heel, she stepped over the shattered remains and walked back to the entrance.

"Queen to his king," Sabine said in disgust, slamming her power against the door.

It held fast.

"Think you can cage me like one of your demons until I agree?"

She hit it with a stronger blast of power, but it didn't even tremble. Her fury ratcheted up. She pressed both hands against the door. Taking a deep breath, she allowed her magic to explode from her fingertips.

Nothing.

With a muttered curse about using Kal'thorz's balls in a slingshot, she ran her fingers along the edge. Sharp pain pierced her fingertips each time she tried to pierce the door's protections, but the wards held fast.

"Come on, come on," she muttered, closing her eyes to better focus on reading the energy signature.

Layer after layer of complex magic had been used to create this prison. The ward was only on the door itself, but it had been somehow fused and tied into the crystals embedded in the walls. It would take months or possibly even years to wear away even the weakest portion at the edges. That was assuming the walls were made of lesser materials than the prison in Razadon. She doubted Kal'thorz would have tried to keep her here without using the strongest resources at his disposal.

Sabine leaned against the door and bit out a harsh laugh. "I walked into the trap like a fool. Both Bane and Dax warned me I'd be cut off from them once I crossed the threshold. Bane even tried to talk me into running away. I didn't listen. Stupid. So stupid."

She slammed her fist against the door in frustration. "That's why Dax was ordered to steal what magic he could when he came to see me. I would have felt the wards embedded into the walls before I entered if I had been at full strength. Even Lachlina tried to warn me. Dammit!"

Sabine swept her gaze over the room, determined to find a way out. Even if she was temporarily cut off from her allies, she wasn't alone. If Dax or Bane weren't able to help, Malek would come looking for her.

"Unless Kal'thorz tries to kill him," she whispered, her face paling. "Oh, gods. He will. If his hold on Bane or Dax is strong enough, he could force them to wield the knife. Malek would be blindsided."

Sabine mentally reached for Malek. A dull pounding sensation took up residence right behind her eyes. She winced and rubbed her temples. The blasted wards wouldn't even allow her to draw upon their bond while she was trapped inside the suite.

With renewed determination, she pushed away from the door. She needed to protect Malek. But first, she had to find a way out of the room. The walls might be infused with the same materials used in the prisons, but it didn't prevent her from using magic inside the room. There were plenty of items that could be used as tools or weapons.

"Quiet indeed," she muttered, walking back to the dresser. She yanked open drawers and found beautiful and costly clothing folded neatly inside. She pulled everything out, searching each individual piece before tossing it aside. When the drawers were empty, she ran her fingers along the bottom and sides, searching for hidden compartments. Nothing.

With a pulse of her power, she pushed the dresser away from the wall and checked behind it. A round and flat opaque crystal disc had been embedded into the wall. It was situated almost at waist height, forcing Sabine to bend down for a closer look.

She traced the edge with her finger and sent an experimental pulse of power against it. The crystal flared gold for a moment and then faded. The marks on Sabine's wrist warmed, almost as though the crystal was resonating with her magic. She frowned, uncertain that was a good thing.

She continued to check the walls and found a total of six crystal discs. Each one behaved the same way when she sent her magic into it.

"Void crystals," she said with disgust.

For a fae, using magic was a necessity. The longer they went without using it, the more their power built until it would finally explode out of them in an uncontrolled burst. Back in Faerie, children were taught to use void crystals to expel their excess power until they learned proper control. They were often found in the walls of nurseries, where they could drain their power before it reached that pinnacle.

It explained how food and drink would be delivered. They would try to drain her magic before someone would enter. She'd be too weakened to stand, much less fight her way free.

Sabine returned to the table beside the bed. She fastened the necklace around her neck and picked up the box, checking its weight. With grim determination, she slammed the edge of the box against the void crystal. Nothing happened. Using her magic to heighten the power of her swing, she brought it down hard a second time. An eerie shriek filled the room, and the crystal turned a dull gray.

Sending an experimental pulse of magic outward, she saw the crystal stutter as it tried to glow. But all it managed was a sickly yellow. Good enough. Any little bit could help give her an advantage.

Sabine smirked. "Let's see how you like that, Kal."

She repeated the gesture against two more crystals, but the box broke before she could destroy the others. She dug around the cabinets, looking for something else she could use, before settling on the kettle. She dumped out the contents, unmindful of the mess she was causing.

Once the rest of the crystals were broken, she dropped the kettle on the ground and wiped off her hands.

Systematically, she began going through each book in the large bookcase, thumbing through the pages and shaking them out one by one. Nestled behind one of the books on the history of the gods was a small, thin volume of poetry. From the broken binding and frayed edges, it appeared to be well read. Sabine pulled it out and frowned. Her mother had never been a fan of reading poetry, preferring to only listen when it was recited by a performer.

Curious, Sabine opened the volume and glanced at the handwritten words on the page. She flipped the cover back over to find the name of the author and stared in shock. Theoria, Lachlina and Vestior's daughter, had written it—apparently a furious and bitter Theoria if the scathing words were any sign. Interesting.

Thumbing through the pages, Sabine discovered that the handwriting changed toward the back of the book. Instead of the heavier block-style lettering, the writing transitioned to a familiar, lighter script.

Sabine's heart pounded at the sight of her mother's words. She lowered herself onto a nearby chair, reading her mother's thoughts.

"Time has become an endless loop, with each day the same as the last. I can't say for certain how long it's been since Kal'thorz lured me here. For the first month, I attempted to record the days of my captivity, but with each passing day, my hopes dim. Perhaps it's better to not think of such things.

Kal'thorz appears at least once a day in the wall glass. His moods are mercurial. Often, he seems content to simply converse with me. Other times, he flies into his rages, and I fear for my continued safety. His patience thins the longer I remain his unwilling captive.

If I cede to his demands and allow him to become king to my queen, I'll lose my throne under the force of his will. Yet, I'm not strong enough to stand against him on my own. We remain at a stalemate."

"Why didn't you tell me?" Sabine whispered, her heart breaking at the words. "Was the need to appear strong so great that you wouldn't warn me to expect such treachery?"

Or maybe she had. Sabine might have been too young to hear the details, but she had left this book here for a reason… perhaps in the event circumstances repeated themselves.

Sabine turned the page and continued reading her mother's words documenting the days of her imprisonment. By the time Sabine reached the last few pages, her hands shook with barely restrained fury.

"I've come to realize this prison is one of the oldest within the underworld. During one of our daily visits, Kal'thorz let it slip that it once housed the goddess Lachlina. After she betrayed the other gods to seal the portal, they sentenced her to remain here for all eternity.

"She somehow escaped, which gives me hope that within my blood lies the knowledge of how to do the same. The necklace I discovered, and had thought was another gift from Kal'thorz to sway me, had once belonged to her. I believe I may be able to use the pendant as a touchstone to search the darkest places in my memories. While the path to reach Lachlina's essence may be dangerous, I've nearly given up hope that I'll feel the moonlight on my skin again."

Sabine closed the book, her knuckles turning white from how hard she was gripping it. So Kal'thorz had imprisoned her in the same jail originally created to hold Lachlina. Her eyes lowered to the goddess's marks glowing faintly with power.

For the first time since stepping foot in this room, a real smile crossed her face. Magic couldn't escape from the room, but her ties to Lachlina were through her blood. And that, fortunately, was right where it belonged.

"All right, Lachlina. Let's have a little talk."

Chapter Twenty-Eight

alek paced the length of the courtyard. It was approaching dawn, and he still hadn't seen any sign of Sabine, Bane, or Rika. The goblins had come and gone, clearing the table and bringing more refreshments. But that had been hours ago. Since then, Malek had been going out of his mind waiting for word about the woman he loved. Every time he tried to reach her through their bond, he could only detect a faint glimmer of her presence. It was almost as though something were blocking him.

Dax was still lingering in the suite, his feet propped up on the table while he drank his umpteenth mug of ale. The demon hadn't said more than a handful of words to him since Sabine had left. They'd given each other a few dark looks, but they lacked much heat. Dax almost seemed to be a different demon from the one Malek had met in Akros. The demon was still brash, but there was a cold and calculating gleam in his eyes that reminded Malek more of Bane.

A rustling in the flowering vines caught Malek's attention. Blossom had awakened about an hour after Sabine had left, hyped up from the power boost she'd received from

Sabine. She'd been pleased with the additional magic but nervous about Sabine being out of reach. Malek had caught sight of her swinging in a makeshift hammock a few minutes earlier, but she was now burrowed deeper in the foliage.

A small, rounded twig flew through the air and bounced off Dax's head. The demon slammed his mug onto the table and stood.

"Again?" Dax shook the bushes violently and snarled. "I may have agreed not to eat you, but no one said anything about tearing off your wings."

Blossom poked her head out and blew a raspberry at him. Dax dove for her, but she squeaked and disappeared into the plants. Malek shook his head and wondered, not for the first time, how Sabine had handled both of them for so many years. As though sensing his thoughts, Blossom peered out from another leaf and shot him a grin before darting back into the bushes.

"Do it again, bug, and I'll burn the bush with you in it." Dax flicked the leaves with his hand and stalked to his chair.

"She's worried about Sabine," Malek said, walking to the table to grab an ale.

Dax grabbed his mug and took a long drink, eyeing the flowers with annoyance. "Sabine can take care of herself."

Malek took a sip, but the ale had grown warm since the goblins had last delivered it. With a sigh, he put the mug down and asked, "What can you tell me about this ritual?"

"There is no ritual."

"Excuse me?"

Dax eyed him carefully. "You should worry less about Sabine and more about yourself. Sabine has something Kal'thorz wants, which will ensure her safety. You, on the other hand, are surrounded by enemies who would gladly skin you alive."

Blossom flew over to land on Malek's shoulder. She put

her hands on her hips and said, "You shouldn't threaten Malek. He's bigger and can squish you. Besides, I saw him eat a dwarf once. I bet he could eat a demon too."

Malek's mouth twitched. "Demon horns get stuck in my teeth."

Blossom's eyes rounded. "Ohhh."

Dax snorted and took a drink. "Our blood is poison, bug. We took out quite a few dragons before they caught on."

Blossom patted Malek's neck. "You'll just have to step on them."

"Suppose so."

At the sound of the door opening, Malek turned and then relaxed. It was only Leena. Blossom made a gagging noise and slipped under the back of Malek's shirt.

The dark-haired fae swept into the room, wearing a different gauzy dress. It left even less to the imagination than the previous one. Like earlier, she was wearing a small gorget around her neck that reminded him of the one Kal'thorz had gifted Sabine.

Ignoring Dax, Leena gave Malek a brilliant smile and said, "You're still awake. I'd wondered if you kept to Unseelie hours or if you were a creature of the daylight."

He shrugged. "Dragons can be both."

She approached him, the sheer material of her dress clinging to her curves in a way that was more than a little distracting. A strange warmth surrounded him, relaxing his muscles and making it difficult to focus.

"If you'd like to stretch your legs a bit, I'd be happy to take you on a tour of the palace. There are some lovely gardens tended by the Unseelie fae in the southern courtyard."

Malek hesitated, wondering if Blossom might get some benefit from visiting a garden. Besides, it would be a once-in-a-lifetime opportunity to reconnoiter the heart of the underworld. No other dragon had been able to breech their defenses.

Leena smiled at him, a few loose tendrils of her dark hair curled softly around her face. She was a beautiful woman, with delicate features and aura of power that surrounded her. If he'd never met Sabine, she might have caught his eye. But comparing the two was like contrasting the brightness of the moon with the sun. One was simply a pale reflection of the other. His thoughts drifted to the woman he loved, and he frowned. If he could at least feel her through their bond, he'd be slightly less concerned.

Leena placed her hand on his chest, peering up at him flirtatiously. He nearly jerked back at her unwelcome touch. It could be his mating instinct, but he didn't think so. Something about Leena was off. He shook his head, wondering where that thought had come from.

"The gardens aren't far," she said, her melodious voice strangely soothing. It reminded him of a song he'd heard once before, during simpler times. "I'd be happy to leave word with the guards in case they need to find us."

It wouldn't hurt. She was harmless. He could sneak away for a short time. Wait. He frowned. That wasn't right. He was waiting for Sabine. He'd never leave her.

Taking a deep breath, he allowed his dragonfire to surge through his blood. His thoughts cleared, and he narrowed his eyes on her. If she thought to weave her enchantments over him, she had another think coming. He wouldn't be taken unaware again.

He took a step back, forcing Leena's hand to fall away. She hesitated for a moment and then pretended as though nothing had happened.

Dax leaned back and said in a bored tone, "Doesn't look like dragons give a shit about gardens. Didn't you guys burn their forests to the ground?"

Malek crossed his arms over his chest. "That was a bit before my time, but yes, we did."

Dax chuckled. "Instead of offering to go look at flowers, why don't you take off the dress and offer to fuck him right there on the floor? It would save time on the whole seduction thing."

Leena glared at Dax. "I'm assuming the messengers failed to deliver King Kal'thorz's summons to you. He has requested your presence in his observatory. There are a few matters he would like to address with you."

Dax leaned forward and said, "Go. Fuck. Yourself."

Leena's entire body went rigid, her fingers curling into fists. Dax smirked, leaned back in his chair, and propped his feet on the table.

"Why don't you make yourself useful and summon the goblins?" Dax said lazily, his eyes at half-mast. "My ale's gone warm."

Shooting Dax a scathing look, Leena nearly spat out her words. "Of course, Your Highness. I live to serve the Versed family."

Dax scowled at her. Tossing her hair back, Leena walked to the crystal panel by the door and placed her hand on it. After a moment, she said, "The goblins will be here momentarily with a meal and refreshments."

Turning a more pleasant expression on Malek, she said, "Bane'umbra has gone to fetch your human and will return shortly. I've arranged for some items to be included that are better suited for human consumption."

"That's considerate of you," Malek said, narrowly skirting the edge of thanking her. The last thing he needed was for her to claim a debt against him.

She inclined her head. "We've had very few human guests in the underworld. Is there anything else she will need?"

Before he could respond, Dax rolled his eyes and said,

"Get lost, Leena. Run along and play the whore with someone else. You can tell my father your efforts at seducing the dragon didn't go as planned."

Her face flushing, Leena whirled on Dax and said something sharp in their harsh, guttural language. He chuckled and put aside his mug. When he stood and prowled toward her, Leena paled and scrambled backward.

Dax's hand shot out and wrapped around her throat, halting her escape. "Speak that way to me again, and I'll toss you into the barracks. Perhaps an evening as entertainment will make you more biddable."

Despite his irritation with her, Malek wasn't about to let Leena be brutalized. He stepped forward to intervene, but Dax glared at him with amber eyes. Recognizing the demon was still fully in control, Malek nodded at him to continue. Both Dax and Bane appeared to have an issue with Leena. He was beginning to understand why.

"You can't touch me," Leena whispered, her voice cutting off when Dax squeezed.

Dax scoffed. "Haven't you learned that laws in Harfanel only apply if you're strong enough to enforce them? How about it, little fae? Can you stop me?"

"The king will kill you," Leena said, her face paling even more.

"Eventually," Dax replied with a grin. "But my coin says you'll go first. Say the word and I can end it now for you."

She made a high-pitched noise like a squeal. Dax studied her like a bug, his grip tightening slightly. When her eyes bulged, he leaned forward and said, "Just a little more pressure..."

"Dax," Malek said sharply. "That's enough. Let her go."

With a chuckle, Dax shoved Leena backward. The woman stumbled.

Malek caught her arm and steadied her. "Are you all right?"

Leena rubbed her throat and nodded. She angled close to him, as though seeking his protection. He started to say something, but a sharp pain in his back made him wince. Did Blossom just bite him?

The same three goblins from earlier pushed open the door and wheeled in another cart of food and drink. They were careful to avoid eye contact with Dax, scrambling to set everything up as quickly as possible. When they were finished, they darted out of the room like hellhounds were after them.

Dax glared at Leena. "You've fulfilled your obligations. Now get out."

Without a word, Leena fled the room.

"What the hell, Blossom?" Malek asked, shaking his shirt. "Did you bite me or dust me?"

Blossom crawled out of his shirt and took flight. "I bit you! If I dusted you, you'd feel it for days. What were you thinking talking to the stinky magic lady? I never thought I'd agree with Dax, but she needed to go."

Malek frowned at Dax. "Do you make it a habit of terrorizing women?"

Dax refilled his ale and sat in his chair. "The pixie's right. You're a fool."

"Excuse me?"

"She's a viper," Dax spat in disgust. "That woman will give you a doe-eyed look one second and try to cut your throat the next. Fucking fae and their machinations."

"You seem to like Sabine well enough."

"She doesn't play games like most fae, nor does she hold back. She'll cut out your eyes if you offend her, and her loyalty can't be bought."

Malek studied Dax in surprise. It sounded as though the

demon actually respected Sabine. Before he could comment, Dax smirked and said, "Besides, she's a firebrand in bed, especially when she gets riled up."

Malek narrowed his eyes at Dax, wondering how angry Sabine would be if the demon's head were removed from his body. "Enjoy the memories, because that's all you'll have."

Dax chuckled, the look in his eyes making it clear he intended to change that. Malek scowled and tried to tell himself that Sabine wouldn't take too kindly to finding Dax's body in pieces. But it was a beautiful image.

Blossom flew to the table to inspect the food and said, "I don't like that fae woman either. She tried to magic you, Malek. She's up to something."

Malek didn't respond, having already figured that out. He couldn't help but wonder why such a powerful fae was living in the underworld. It could be something as simple as enjoying a position of power, but he couldn't imagine anyone enjoying Kal'thorz's volatile temperament.

Dax snorted and took a drink. "Why the hell do you think I'm sitting here drinking the night away with a fucking dragon?"

"I've been wondering the same thing."

Dax gestured toward the door. "Bane warned me you might be stupid enough to potentially fall for that one's wiles. Pisses me off when he's right."

Malek's lips twitched. "Gee. Never thought I'd have a demon protecting me from a wee little fae."

"Fuck off," Dax muttered and took another drink.

Malek threw his head back and laughed. He didn't much care for Dax, but he had tried to intervene in Leena's efforts at circumventing Malek's will.

Blossom perked up and looked at the door. "Rika's back!"

A moment later, the door swung open to admit Bane and Rika. Other than wearing torn and dirty clothing, the young seer looked surprisingly refreshed and healthy. Malek couldn't see any obvious injuries.

"Yay!" Blossom dove toward Rika, talking rapidly. "You missed all the excitement! First, Malek turned into a dragon and squished a bunch of demons. Then Sabine stabbed a prisoner and blood went everywhere! Then we got to meet the scary demon king. I rate that experience two out of ten— don't recommend. Then Sabine gave me a bunch of magic and went off to do the underworld ritual. Now Dax and Malek are giving each other dirty looks, and I'm trying to play ring toss with Dax's horns."

Dax scowled at her. "That's what you were doing with the sticks?"

Blossom grinned and gave him a thumbs-up sign. "I'm trying to beat my cousin's high score. You're good practice."

Rika stared at her. "I didn't think I was asleep *that* long."

Blossom giggled and landed on Rika's shoulder. While the two chatted and got caught up, Malek turned toward Bane and asked, "Have you heard anything about Sabine?"

"Not within the past hour. She shattered the communication and void crystals."

Dax chuckled and took a drink. "Good girl."

Malek exhaled, relieved Sabine was at least alive. "What are communication and void crystals?"

Bane hesitated and then shrugged. "Kal'thorz wanted to keep tabs on Sabine. She objected."

"She's not hurt?" Malek asked.

"Not when I last saw her," Bane said, crossing his arms over his chest. "She's as angry and pissed off as a fury, but otherwise unharmed."

Dax drummed his claws on the table. "Kal'thorz will act soon, especially now that she's openly defied him."

Malek frowned. "I know you're oathbound not to discuss certain things with outsiders, but Sabine is my priority. Is there anything you can tell me? Or anything I can do to help her?"

"Your time will come, dragon," Dax said, leaning back in his chair. "What happens then will be up to you—and her. None of us can help her currently, but neither can anyone harm her."

Rika carried Blossom to the flowering vines. The pixie hopped onto a leaf and yawned.

Bane glanced at Rika and frowned. "I need to return to Kal'thorz. Make sure the human stays clear of Leena and any demons. Sabine has a soft spot for her, and the girl's a trusting sort."

"The fae bitch left a few minutes ago," Dax said, taking another drink. "Looks like I owe you a hundred gold."

Bane gave Malek a look of disgust. "Seriously?"

Malek held up his hands in protest. "I sloughed off her influence quick enough. It simply took a minute to figure out what she was doing."

Dax snorted and settled back in his chair. "I thought Sabine had higher standards."

Rika walked back toward them and said, "Blossom's going to take a nap until we hear from Sabine. She wants us to keep an eye out for any dangerous bugs while she's sleeping."

Bane gently guided Rika in the table's direction. "You can stand guard and eat at the same time. The alchemist's remedies require a great deal of energy. After you've eaten, you can use the bedroom to wash and clean up. Sabine left clean clothing for you."

Rika's eyes landed on the food, and her stomach let out an eager rumble. She blushed and pressed her hand against her belly. "I guess I am hungry."

"I'll check back when I can," Bane said. "Stay out of trouble."

Before Bane could leave, Malek stopped him and said, "If you hear anything—"

Bane shook his head. "No. Sabine is safe. That's all we can share with you. Beyond that, we must allow events to play out as they will. Otherwise, it will break her."

It went against everything in him to allow Bane to leave without further challenging him, but he had to remember that Sabine trusted the demon. Dax's voice interrupted Malek's thoughts.

"So Sabine dragged one of her street kids all the way from Akros?"

Rika stiffened. "I'm from Karga."

"As if that's any better," Dax said with a sneer.

"Enough," Malek said, glaring at Dax. "Rika, you were going to get something to eat. I'm not sure the meat will be to your tastes, but there's some fruit and cheese."

Rika stopped in front of the table, casting a wary look at Dax. "You're Bane's brother, right?"

Dax didn't respond. He merely continued to drink his ale. Malek leaned against the wall and crossed his arms over his chest, watching as Rika continued to dart surreptitious glances at Dax.

It hadn't taken long for her to wrap Bane around her little finger. Dax was a different matter. If he hurt the girl's feelings, Malek would string him up by his horns.

Rika bit her lip. "I don't know if he told you, but Bane just started teaching me how to fight. I'm not very good yet. Sabine told me you were the one who taught her."

Dax eyed her over his mug but didn't comment.

Rika grabbed a plate, continuing to chatter as she selected several pieces of fruit and cheese. "Sabine's talked about you a lot. She told me you were one of the most skilled warriors she's ever met. She said she's never seen you lose a fight."

Dax grunted and finished his ale, but his eyes never left Rika.

"I've only known Sabine for a couple months," Rika said, reaching to collect Dax's empty mug. "She's been talking about coming here to find you since we met. When she found out Kal'thorz was going to have you executed, she wanted to leave right away, even though she was hurt. You're pretty important to her."

Dax drummed his fingers on the table.

She refilled his ale and placed it in front of him before continuing to fix her plate. "Bane's the only other demon I've met. Sabine seems to be careful about choosing her friends. I figure you must not be a bad sort since she thinks so highly of you."

After a moment, Dax picked up his mug and took a sip.

Rika popped a piece of cheese into her mouth. "I think one of my favorite stories was when you took on a dozen guards in Akros. She said you stripped them of their clothing and left them tied up and naked on a councilor's portico."

Dax chuckled and put his mug back on the table. Gesturing toward a small bowl of red fruit on the side of the table, he said, "I've heard humans enjoy those."

"Yeah?" Rika perked up and grabbed the fruit. She brought her plate to the chair next to Dax and sat down.

He smirked and took another drink. "I think they taste like shit, but that's just me."

Rika grinned and took a bite. "I've had worse, but then again, I grew up in a sandpile."

Dax barked out a laugh. "All right, little human. What else did Sabine tell you?"

Rika straightened and launched into a story about how Dax broke into the temple and destroyed their bell because it kept waking him up. He added a few comments to clarify the circumstances, but he appeared riveted by Rika's animated descriptions.

Malek stared in astonishment at the teenager, who had somehow charmed not one but two of the most vicious demons he'd ever met. Out of everything he'd seen so far in his travels, this had to be the most bizarre.

Chapter Twenty-Nine

*D*warves created memory stones as a way to preserve recorded events, just like the fae crafted magical wines to delve into the past. The principle in using Lachlina's necklace to reach Sabine's memories should be the same. Unfortunately, Sabine had never performed such magic without the aid of a ritual to guide her. Even when she'd scried for the Seelie murderers, she'd followed the formulaic steps taught to her by Faerie Elders.

Still, it was possible, but only once had she seen an Elder delve into memories using a touchstone. It was far more dangerous, similar to plunging into a fast-moving river without a tether. If her situation weren't so desperate, she wouldn't consider it.

"Let's hope I don't drown," she murmured, unsheathing the dagger strapped to her thigh.

Sabine pricked the tip of her finger. She allowed a drop of her blood to fall onto the stone. It disappeared almost immediately, as though eagerly accepting her offering.

Sabine picked up and cradled the blue diamond pendant in her hands. It was the color of the night's sky at twilight and nearly the same shade as Malek's eyes. As she gazed into its blue depths, she could see a flicker of what almost appeared to be stars swirling within the stone.

Infusing her breath with the power of her ancestors, she blew over the stone. Light surrounded the necklace in a golden nimbus of power. Magic radiated up her arms, both beguiling and irresistible in its potency. She inhaled deeply and closed her eyes, willing her blood to lead her to the source of her most ancient memories.

She was lost, dizzy and tumbling through space and time. She couldn't breathe, couldn't see anything. It was both light and dark, icy cold and fiery hot all at once. Every part of her was ripped apart. She wordlessly screamed, her mind tearing itself apart, searching for a handhold. The marks on her wrist flared to life, and she reached for them, clinging to them like a beacon in a storm.

Suddenly, everything was quiet. The world righted itself somehow, and Sabine blinked open her eyes and found herself in the middle of a strangely familiar garden. Her head ached, but at least she was no longer adrift in that darkened abyss. Unfortunately, she had no idea where to go from there.

It was nighttime. The surrounding plants pulsed with magic, glowing softly in shades of vibrant blues and greens. Several trees cascaded upward in graceful lines, their boughs overhead shimmering with silver leaves. Their canopy was broken only by the dancing blue wisps that cast a soothing light over the garden. Flowers and plants she'd only seen within the boundaries of Faerie filled the air with their sweet perfumes. It was a small glimpse of paradise, an Unseelie night garden that had been lovingly tended for centuries.

She turned slowly, trying to understand the strange displacement coursing through her. She could have sworn she'd never been there, but it was strangely familiar. Something about it called to her on an elemental level.

Reaching out to brush her fingers against one of the night-blooming roses, she gasped. Her hands glowed with a brilliant gold instead of their normal silver. Her clothing was also different. Instead of the lightweight material better suited for the heat of the underworld, she was in a heavy brocade gown that would have been the envy of all the courts in Faerie. She ran her hands along the fabric, unable to tell whether it was real or an illusion.

Wisps floated down from the trees, illuminating a winding crystal pathway. More curious than concerned, Sabine moved deeper into the garden, allowing the wisps to guide her steps through the exquisite gardenscape. Other than the soft gurgling sounds from nearby fountains, the garden was otherwise silent.

The dense canopy cleared, and Sabine found an endless shroud of darkness looming overhead. There was no sign of the sky, just a black oblivion that chilled her to the bone. Was it a reminder that this place wasn't real? Even when using the memory stones, she'd still been able to see the sky.

Disconcerted, Sabine averted her eyes and instead focused on the garden. It was lovely beyond measure, but even here, there was something a little cold about it. It took Sabine a minute to realize what had been bothering her; there were no signs of birds, pixies, or any other sort of creature. Even the plants didn't seem to possess the familiar life energy she felt when she walked the land.

The pathway ended at a small clearing. A hauntingly beautiful woman sat on a bench, staring into a reflective pool with a faraway expression. Something about the woman's heartbreaking beauty called to her on an instinctive level, promising unspeakable power if Sabine was willing to ease her burden. She wanted to go to the woman immediately but resisted the impulse. Even within memory, brashness could have disastrous results.

Sabine took a moment to better study the woman. Her skin and hair glowed with a golden light far more brilliant than Sabine's luminescence. It deepened the surrounding shadows, making it difficult to see her features clearly. Whoever she was, she was finely attired in a similar dress to the one Sabine currently wore. However, instead of the blues and silvers Sabine preferred, hers was a deep forest-green gown, trimmed with shimmering golden orbs of light.

When the woman didn't seem to notice her presence, Sabine continued her approach and then stopped abruptly when recognition slammed into her.

This wasn't a memory.

She was staring at the living embodiment of Lachlina, the renegade goddess who had begun her family line and had betrayed the gods. This was her penance—an eternity in a prison and trapped between worlds.

Sabine lifted her head to stare again at the black abyss overhead. It was truly a void, a gaping maw she could easily disappear into. This garden existed in a place between realms, a place Blossom had recently described. It was beautiful and lovely but empty of all life, except for one. Sabine took a shaky breath. She'd somehow moved from one prison to another.

Standing in front of the goddess who had once held the power of life and death had Sabine breaking out in a cold sweat. Only her fear for Malek's life kept her rooted to the spot instead of backing away. She had to convince Lachlina to help her escape. The longer she remained Kal'thorz's captive, the more likely Malek would die.

As though sensing her silent observation, Lachlina lifted her head. Sabine couldn't quite muffle her gasp. The woman in front of her wasn't fae and could never be confused as such.

Her eyes were a hypnotic purple with startling silver flecks that swirled in their depths. Her hair was long and unbound, cascading in shining waves down her back. Sabine had no words to adequately describe the color. It was as though each strand had been made from the finest of crystal. Sabine's chest ached from the woman's sheer, otherworldly beauty.

Other than possessing similar height and coloring, Sabine found it hard to believe Lachlina shared her blood. Compared to the radiance of Lachlina, Sabine felt drab and plain beside the goddess. She briefly thought back to the murals she'd seen of Lachlina in Harfanel. Poor Dax. He was going to be incredibly disappointed that Lachlina's real breast size wasn't anywhere close to what the creative artist had envisioned.

As though sensing her thoughts, the goddess laughed. It was a light and merry bell-like sound that filled Sabine with unbridled joy. It was full of hope, cheer, and pleasure—the sound of every wish being fulfilled. Sabine nearly wept from the intensity of the emotions surging through her. Lachlina's laughter had no comparison, and Sabine was struck by the fear that disappointing the goddess would result in never hearing such a wondrous sound again.

She quickly spun a warding around her thoughts. Lachlina's radiance lessened, but she was no less potent.

Lachlina stood, her bearing more than regal. The sudden urge to kneel before her was nearly overwhelming. Subtle waves of charismatic magic surrounded Lachlina, seeming to intensify as she focused on Sabine.

Sabine took a shaky breath, her legs trembling from the strain to remain standing. She curled her hands into fists, her nails biting into her palms with enough force to draw blood.

The pain cut through the strongest of Lachlina's glamour. Sabine wasn't sure how much longer she could resist the goddess's influence.

Lachlina walked toward her, the shimmering gold orbs on her dress dancing as she moved. The flowers growing near her turned in Lachlina's direction, as though desperate for her light to continue shining on them.

"Daughter," Lachlina said, holding out her hands toward Sabine. "I have long since dreamed of this moment."

"Lachlina," Sabine said, unsure of the proper protocol for greeting a goddess. She took Lachlina's outstretched hands and gasped. The wards protecting her mind fractured, her blood humming from the sudden rush of power.

Sabine cried out as wild magic surged through her, blazing a path through her memories. She once again relived her mother's death, her desperate flight from Faerie, meeting Dax and Bane, and barely surviving the Wild Hunt. The marks on her wrist flared with power, searing her again as her past came to life. Desperate to stop the agony, she tried to pull away from Lachlina. The goddess tightened her grip.

"Breathe and open yourself to me, my darling," Lachlina said, her voice echoing in Sabine's thoughts. "The pain will last but another few moments."

"Enough," a man shouted, causing the ground to shake beneath them.

Several of the wisps winked out, and the flowers closed up as though hiding. Sabine blinked rapidly, her thoughts clearing when Lachlina released her. She crumpled to the ground, shaking and trembling from whatever Lachlina had done to her. It was almost as though she'd flayed her mind, exposing her innermost psyche and leaving her raw.

Blinking through unshed tears, Sabine watched the striking image of Vestior stalk through the garden in a long black coat. It surrounded him like a shroud, and she realized dimly that he'd cloaked himself in shadows. He was the god of night, darkness to Lachlina's light. She might be the Bringer of Shadows, but he was the Harbinger of Nightmares.

His expression was thunderous, a terrifying visage so unlike the deity who had addressed her in the Hall of the Gods. At that moment, she wasn't sure which one frightened her more.

He stopped a short distance from them. "You will not beguile our blood in my domain."

Lachlina glared at him, the fury in her eyes making her even more striking. "She sought me out, *husband*. You will not deny me such when it is her magic that has brought her here."

He crossed his arms over his chest and said, "Very well, but I will remain to ensure there is no treachery, *wife*. Despite your marks, she is not yours to command, nor are her memories yours to behold."

Lachlina tossed her hair back and turned a cold gaze on Sabine. "It would seem you have a champion of sorts for the moment. Make your request, and I shall decide if you are worthy."

Sabine looked back and forth between Lachlina and Vestior, bemused by what appeared to be some sort of long-standing domestic dispute. She still wasn't sure what Lachlina had been searching for in her memories, but her emotions were wrung out and raw.

Swallowing back the hysterical laughter that threatened, Sabine managed to say, "I seek the knowledge of how to escape from the prison used to hold you in the underworld."

Lachlina plucked one of the nearby roses from its bush and held it to her nose. After a moment, she returned it to the plant, where it blended seamlessly as though it had never been removed. "What do you offer in exchange for your freedom?"

Sabine paused, weighing possible responses. She was fairly desperate, and Lachlina knew it. There had to be a way to negotiate without becoming more in debt to the goddess. She glanced at Vestior, but his expression was shuttered.

She climbed to her feet and said, "I'm of no use to you while I'm being held captive."

"You've proven to not be of much use when you're free of my prison either."

Sabine squeezed her eyes shut. Lachlina was worse than a petulant toddler. Apparently, she was going to punish Sabine for threatening to remove the marks. "What do you want?"

Lachlina's smile became cruel. "Many things. But for now, I will simply give you a gift."

Vestior tensed, the darkness around him growing ominously. It was almost as though the void above them reached for his embrace.

Suddenly wary, Sabine asked, "What gift?"

Lachlina sat on the bench again and smoothed out her gown. "It's nothing too distasteful. I suspect you may even enjoy it."

"I'm listening."

"Despite your dip in the Well, I'm afraid you're still too mortal to fully comprehend the enormity of the power required to break the wards caging you. However, there is another way."

"And that is?"

"If you surrender control of your physical form to me, I will remove you from the prison."

She reared back in shock. "No. Absolutely not."

Lachlina lifted a shoulder in a half-hearted shrug. "Very well. Return to your prison and leave me to my contemplations."

Sabine frowned, her thoughts turning to the journal she'd read. Lachlina had to be the reason her mother was able to escape. Was it possible that Malia had made such a pact with the goddess? Some of the dwarves had insisted that Queen Malia's personality had changed after visiting the under-world. The thought of allowing Lachlina such control had Sabine breaking out in a cold sweat.

Frustrated and growing increasingly desperate, Sabine turned toward Vestior. "Do you know how to escape Lachlina's prison in the underworld?"

"Now, now, child," Lachlina said, wagging her finger in Sabine's direction. "You may not bargain with him until ours is concluded. As long as you remain in my garden, you may only barter with me."

Her eyelids lowered slightly, and a smirk crossed her lips. "You would think your parents never taught you any manners."

"She speaks the truth," Vestior said, his voice brusque. "When you used Lachlina's touchstone to reach this garden, you surrendered yourself to her power. Lachlina's magic holds your physical form in stasis while your consciousness remains here. Should I enter an agreement with you now, it would only be with that part of yourself. You cannot carry that knowledge back with you."

Recognizing she was sorely out of her element bartering with two gods, she asked, "If Lachlina returns my conscious-ness to the underworld, would you be willing to barter with me?"

Vestior's jaw clenched. "It is forbidden. The pact prevents me from entering Harfanel in my true form, just as I am unable to enter Razadon. The Huntsman may pass where he will, but he cannot aid you."

Lachlina laughed. "What I offer is hardly distasteful, child.

I am giving you the chance to act as a true goddess with untold power at your fingertips."

"Perhaps, but it wouldn't be me."

Lachlina pursed her lips. "I would be willing to sweeten the deal."

Sabine frowned, unsure whether she could trust anything Lachlina offered. "How?"

Lachlina stood again and smiled, the expression making her radiant. "Surrender yourself to me *temporarily*. I will escort you out of the prison and put this upstart demon in his place. Afterward, you may take control over your body. It will be similar to what occurred when you encountered the treeheart in Atlantia."

Sabine's thoughts drifted back to Rika's premonition about Malek. Shaking her head, she said, "I will not do anything that puts Malek or the rest of my companions in danger."

Lachlina considered her for a moment. "Very well. You have my word that I will not harm your precious dragon, the odd little human, the pixie, or your bonded demon while I'm in possession of your physical form unless they attack me first. Will that be sufficient?"

Sabine frowned. If there were any other option, she wouldn't even consider this.

"And what would you want in exchange?"

Lachlina waved her hand absently. "You will cease this nonsense about cutting the marks off your body. I mean, really. Who continues to threaten bodily defacement when they're out of sorts?"

Sabine tried to rein in her temper but failed. "Excuse me? You're the one who's been throwing tantrums when I ignore you or don't behave exactly the way you want."

Lachlina's gaze turned furious. Somewhere overhead, Sabine heard the distinct sound of thunder. "You are a willful and disobedient *child*. If I choose to reprimand your unfortunate behavior, I am well within my rights to do so. You only draw breath because *I* will it."

"Lachlina," Vestior said, his tone dark and biting.

Lachlina held his gaze for a long time and then inclined her head. "You have heard my terms. Accept the agreement or not, but there shall be no further discussions."

Suddenly weary, Sabine rubbed her temples. She knew she couldn't trust Lachlina, but her options were limited. Either way, she was trapped.

"With your leave, I will negotiate on your behalf."

The thought slipped into her head like a thief's nimble fingers. Sabine jerked her head toward Vestior, but his countenance was hidden behind an expressionless mask. She wasn't sure she trusted him completely either, but he'd been more forthcoming than Lachlina.

Turning toward Vestior, she asked, "Am I within my rights to ask you to negotiate with Lachlina for me?"

Lachlina's head whipped toward Vestior, her gaze both furious and suspicious. "You dare?"

Vestior gave her a bland look. "Are you accusing me of something, wife?"

Lachlina's jaw clenched, and she waved her hand toward them. "By all means."

Vestior approached Sabine and held out his hand toward her. The moment she slipped her fingers into his hand, a strong shroud of power enveloped her. Lachlina approached and did the same, placing her hand in Vestior's outstretched one.

His voice took on a strange, echoing quality as he spoke. "Sabin'theoria shall temporarily surrender possession of her corporeal form to you, Lachlina. The term of possession shall end before Aeslion's sun touches its horizon on the following day.

"During that time, you will ensure no undue harm or distress comes to Sabin'theoria's corporeal or incorporeal forms, or the terms of this agreement shall be broken immediately. Sabin'theoria will further retain full awareness of all events, and she shall be the adjudicator in severing the possession."

Sabine swallowed. "I agree."

Lachlina inclined her head. "Done."

Vestior placed Sabine's hand in Lachlina's and said, "The pact is sealed."

Power slammed into Sabine, and she gasped as the binding settled over her.

Vestior turned toward her and said, "Once Lachlina has departed, simply gaze into the reflective pool to look through her eyes. You will see what she sees, but you will not be able to interact with the world around you."

Vestior's thoughts merged with hers for a moment. *"Should you need to break her hold, you must be resolute and steadfast in your desires."*

Despite her misgivings, Sabine nodded her understanding. Resolute and steadfast. She could do this.

Lachlina smiled and said, "Now, my child, open your mind to me, so we might deal with these pesky demons."

Sabine took a steadying breath and said, "All right. I'm ready."

Chapter Thirty

*A*n explosion rocked the underworld.

Malek tackled Rika, pushing her out of harm's way when a large stone dislodged from the ceiling. He pushed Rika under the large table, which offered a modicum of protection. Dust and debris fell from above, obscuring his vision. Dax darted into a nearby doorway, bracing himself while the walls shook.

The ground beneath them trembled, causing more stones to fall. Rika crouched low to the ground and said, "There's a lot of magic building."

Blossom dove toward him and clung to his neck like a barnacle. "The volcano is going to erupt! We have to get out of here!"

"Stay down," Malek ordered, covering Rika with his body to protect her from the worst of it.

"The wards are under attack!" Dax shouted from the doorway. "We need to get to the Great Hall. This wing isn't safe without a fae to anchor it."

When the shaking subsided, Malek leaped to his feet and

reached for his sword. Dax was already in motion, his eyes silvered as he darted for the door.

Malek pulled Rika to her feet. "Stay close to me. The demons here aren't like Bane and Dax. They'll kill you without thinking twice."

With a look of grim determination, Rika unsheathed her short sword. "I'm ready. I'll do what I have to do."

"Hold tight to that resolve and follow me," Malek said, running down the stairs after Dax with Rika right on his heels. They weren't the only ones who were trying to flee this wing of the palace. Demons, goblins, fire imps, and even a troll were rushing down the stairs trying to escape the madness.

"Incoming!" Blossom shouted.

The walls shook again. A terrible groaning noise filled the air, and with a loud crash, a beam fell to the ground behind them. Rika jumped clear of it just in time. He heard several screams behind them from those who had been trapped under the rubble. Malek had to get them out of here before the entire place fell apart.

"Ick," Blossom said, wrinkling her nose. "That's going to leave a mark."

"Dax!" Malek called to the demon over the commotion. "We need to find Sabine!"

Dax tried to push a large fallen stone out of the way. "Follow the destruction."

Malek grabbed the other end of the stone and helped Dax move it. "What are you talking about?"

Dax scowled. "What the hell kind of power boost did she get in the Hall of the Gods? She'll bring the whole damn city down on our heads."

"Sabine is causing this? You're sure?"

Dax gave him a dry look over his shoulder, pushing aside fleeing demons and fire imps. "No demon has this sort of magic at their fingertips." With a sly grin, he said, "Should be interesting next time I get her into bed."

"You have a death wish, don't you?" Malek growled.

Another beam fell, blocking their path. Dax turned on his heel and rushed down an adjacent hall to a different stairwell. Trying to make any sort of headway was growing increasingly difficult. Without Dax guiding them, they'd be well and truly lost.

Rika dodged another falling rock and said, "It's getting hotter in here. I think Blossom's right about the volcano erupting. The magic is still building too."

"I don't want to be right," Blossom said, hugging tightly to Malek's neck. "I'm too cute to die!"

"None of us are going to die if I have anything to say about it," Malek said, grabbing Rika's wrist and pulling her out of the way of a fire imp. The creature was eyeing Rika like she was a tasty treat to nibble on.

At the bottom of the stairs, chaos ensued. Many underworld denizens were screaming and fleeing the commotion. Dax grabbed a goblin by the scruff of his leathery neck and yanked him into the air.

"Stral," Dax said with a growl. "Report."

"Th-th-the Faerie queen's broken free of the prison, master," the goblin said, his purple eyes bulging. "King Kal'thorz has ordered his remaining sorcerers to contain her. Barring that, the morthal will try to subdue her."

"Prison?" Malek demanded, narrowing his eyes at Dax. "That's where Sabine was taken?"

Blossom's eyes rounded. "No wonder she's angry. I see lots of demon squishing in the future."

"You don't have to be a seer to foresee that," Rika said dryly.

The goblin nodded, his pale skin flickering between grassy and pea green. "Very angry. She leaves great bounty for my clan, but we cannot feast while the walls shake. Those who tried have died."

Blossom nodded sagely. "It's always better to keep your distance until the walls stop shaking."

With a barely contained growl, Dax shook the goblin again. His eyeballs rolled around in his head before finally settling on Dax.

"Enough of this. Where is the Faerie queen now, Stral?"

"I-I-I can't say, master. We fled the Great Hall when the roof collapsed. The wards are failing."

Another explosion rocked the palace. Malek heard more screaming from somewhere in the distance. He tried to reach for Sabine through their bond, but he couldn't sense her. It was as though his tie to her had been severed.

"Dax, we need to keep moving."

"Summon the Ordinand to deal with the volcano," Dax said, dropping the goblin on the ground, where he landed with a thud. "You're authorized to begin evacuations for all non-magical lesser demons to Midorul. Any half-breeds with a trace of magic need to report to the northern point and help anchor the wards."

"Right away, master." The goblin turned and fled back the way he'd come.

Dax led them deeper into the palace. The structural damage was worse the closer they came to the Great Hall. It looked like the throne room had been partially destroyed.

The injuries were numerous. Malek counted at least a dozen demons who were either stunned, bleeding, or trying to bind their wounds. Several were unconscious, lying on the ground in a heap, while a few of the more industrious fire imps were helping themselves to the demons' belongings. A handful of goblins were darting around, lapping up blood with their long forked tongues as they made their way toward the exit.

"What's the Ordinand?" Rika asked, moving out of the way of a frenzied troll rushing past her. "And what does it have to do with the volcano?"

Dax glanced at her. "They're demonic priests who can quell the lava storms. Their preferred method is human sacrifice."

Rika paled. "I think I'll avoid them for the time being."

"Good plan."

Malek kicked aside a fire imp taking advantage of the commotion to take a swipe at Rika.

Blossom shrieked, her wings turning gray as she dived toward the fire imp. "Take that, you evil little imp!"

He yelped and fell to the ground, twitching uncontrollably.

Another darted forward, his claws extended toward Rika. Rika thrust her sword in the fire imp's direction. Before she made contact, Dax reached down and ripped the imp's head off. He grabbed Rika and hauled her out of the way as the imp's body exploded in flames.

Rika's eyes widened. "Wow. That's one crispy critter. Do they all do that?"

"They're handy when we're away from any settlements." Dax broke off one of its burning fingers. He snuffed out the flames and offered it to Rika. "Hungry? They taste like chicken if they're not overcooked."

She wrinkled her nose. "Um, think I'll pass."

Dax chuckled and tossed the finger aside. A goblin leaped at it and gobbled it up before racing away. Three demons launched a sneak attack, their eyes silvered and claws flashing. Instead of Rika being their target, they were focusing on Dax.

"Behind you!" Rika shouted, pointing out a fourth demon. She darted forward, plunging her blade into its midsection. Its tail whipped around, intent on striking her. She gasped and leaped backward. With a roar, Dax slashed outward with his claws and eviscerated the demon.

Malek pushed Rika behind him, fielding the other two attackers, while Dax fought the last one. "Friends of yours?"

"Fucking assassins," Dax said with a grin, clearly enjoying himself. "Timing could be better, but they have to take the opportunities as they come."

"Charming." Malek thrust his sword into his last attacker, watching dispassionately as it collapsed.

A heavily armed demon ran by, but Dax reached out and snagged his tail, then whipped him back around. Malek readied his sword, but Dax merely bit out several words in his harsh, guttural language. The other demon spoke quickly, using gestures to point at a side door. Malek could only make out Kal'thorz's name.

Blossom sidled up to Malek's neck again and whispered, "I can't feel Sabine. I can usually track her magic, but she's gone. Malek, I think she's in trouble."

Malek didn't respond. The dragon within him roared in fury, demanding to be set free of the confines of his human skin. The only thing holding him back was the damage he might cause to Rika or Blossom. But if anything had happened to Sabine, he would destroy every single one of these demons and grind Harfanel to dust.

"I tried to ask the goddess what's going on, but she's not talking to me either. Something terrible is happening, Malek. We have to find her soon."

"We're going after Kal'thorz," Dax said, motioning for them to follow.

"He's not my priority," Malek bit out, barely keeping hold of his instincts that demanded he protect his mate. "I'm only interested in finding Sabine. Kal'thorz can go fuck himself."

Dax chuckled. "We're in agreement. However, I suspect

our little firebrand of a fae is hunting him. I can track him easier than I can Sabine."

Malek gave a curt nod. "Fine. Where is he?"

"Outside the palace walls. When the wards broke, he went to gather his sorcerers and organize an assault. He's been planning this for too long. He won't allow Sabine to escape him."

Malek pushed forward, intent on their destination. Another tremor rocked the palace, and he staggered from the magical force. Several of the demons near them also stumbled, with some collapsing to the ground.

"There's too much magic." Rika fell to her knees, clamping her hands over her ears as a high-pitched wail filled the air.

"There's fighting up ahead," Dax said, handing Malek a lethal-looking dagger that glinted red, as though it were infused with power. "Avoid the sorcerers and give that to the girl once she recovers. Its magic will help her strike her mark. If you see Bane, tell him I'm going to run interference with Kal'thorz. If he captures Sabine, it's over."

Without waiting for a response, he rushed forward. Malek grabbed Rika's arm and pulled her upright. Whatever was happening must be affecting her seer senses. She seemed to be worse off than anyone else.

Dammit. He couldn't remember the last time he'd been so ineffective. Now more than ever, he needed Sabine. None of his abilities would help Rika, except shifting and destroying whatever was causing the magical backlash.

Another wave of power hit them. Rika cried out, her eyes watering from the pain. Her legs buckled, but Malek kept her upright. "Blossom, do you have any ideas?"

"I've got this!" Blossom said, landing on top of Rika's head. Her wings turned a brilliant gold, and she fluttered them rapidly, sending pixie dust onto the seer.

Rika's shoulders slumped in relief. Lowering her hands, she said, "I don't know what you just did, but it helped. A lot."

Blossom patted her hair. "It's kind of like a ward, courtesy of Sabine's magic. It won't last long though. Even with Sabine's boost, I don't have enough magic to protect big people for long. Pixie magic works better with pixies."

"We have to keep moving," Malek said and handed Rika the dagger Dax had left with him. Bane had been looking into having a weapon crafted specifically for her, but he was still assessing her skills. This one was better suited for her smaller stature.

Demons weren't altruistic, which made Malek wonder if Dax had some other purpose in giving such a priceless magical weapon to a human.

Rika fell into step beside him, brandishing her dagger at anyone who approached. A few of them looked like they might test their luck, but one hard look from Malek had them moving away.

The corridor ended abruptly, revealing a large balcony overlooking a training field similar to the one they'd seen near the prison. Thousands of demons and other under-world creatures filled the clearing. The roar was deafening. A few were shouting orders, while others fell into ranks behind them.

Despite the circumstances, Malek couldn't help but admire their fearsome display. Demons had been created and bred for one purpose—to fight. There were no tougher adversaries in the world, and this was the largest army he'd ever seen. While they were only a shadow of the power they'd once been, it was no wonder they'd pushed back the dragons' advance during the last war. Should the gods ever return and empower the demons again, he didn't want to think what would happen to his people.

Beyond the field was a shimmering effect that curved

upward, like some sort of wall. It must be the ward protecting the city from the volcano's fury. He hadn't realized they were so close to the heart. Even during the war, his people had never penetrated the magical barriers protecting the city. If those wards failed, there was no doubt the entire city would be destroyed.

Malek caught sight of Dax hastening down the ramp and charging into the action. With his claws extended, he sliced and cut down any would-be challengers as he made his way toward his destination. Malek had expected to see the demons fighting an adversary, but it looked like a free-for-all. Demons fought other demons with no clear lines dividing them, except for one.

In the center of the field stood a sole woman, her arms extended and her face lifted upward as though calling down the moon's blessing. The source of the remarkable power was emanating from her. Golden light surrounded her, the sheer force of her brilliance almost painful to behold. At her feet were countless bodies, and she stepped over them as though they were nothing more than fallen leaves in the forest.

Some demons had already tossed aside their weapons and were kneeling before her. Others had picked up arms and turned on their brethren, fighting alongside her. Malek watched in amazement as she briefly placed her hand on the shoulders of those who were kneeling. They shuddered under her touch and then picked up their weapons to continue the fight.

Several demons broke through the line and tried to rush her, but she stopped them with a wave of her hand. The one closest to her froze in midair, writhing and struggling to free himself from her magical hold. With a flick of her wrist, Sabine sliced off one of his horns with her magic. It flew into her hand, and she plunged the horn into the center of his chest. The demon fell to the ground. Sabine simply gathered her skirt and stepped over his still-twitching body.

"I didn't know she could do that," Blossom said, a trace of amazement in her voice. "Hey, how hard would it be to get a piece of a demon horn? Do you know how cool that would look over my mantle?"

"You don't have a mantle," Rika replied. "We're vagabonds, remember?"

"Details, details," Blossom groused. "I'll have a garden again one day, and you'd better believe I'm going to have a demon horn sitting in the middle of it."

"*Sabine!*" Malek shouted, reaching for their mind-touch connection. There was no answer. He wasn't sure if she simply didn't hear him or if their ability was still too new. He couldn't sense her at all.

"It doesn't feel like Sabine," Rika said, angling closer to him. "I don't know what's happening, but there's something wrong with her magic. Every time she kills someone, her aura darkens."

Malek didn't respond, unable to tear his gaze away from the woman on the field. Wave after wave of power crashed over the field like a tsunami, all of it emanating from her. Every time another wave hit, more demons surrendered to her awesome power. Rika was right; he might not see auras, but the magic Sabine wielded was different somehow.

Calling upon his heightened dragon senses, he focused more on the details. It was Sabine, but it also wasn't. Her features had shifted slightly, becoming harsher and more alien. Even her movements were slightly awkward, as though she were unaccustomed to her body. The last time he'd seen her like that had been when Lachlina had taken over to free her from the treeheart.

Blossom gasped. "It's the goddess."

Malek muttered a curse. He didn't know if Sabine had

allowed Lachlina to control her or if the goddess had simply pushed to the surface again. This was worse than he'd thought. "We need to bring her back to herself."

Rika frowned. "What is she trying to do? Punish them for putting her in prison? I thought Sabine wanted the demons as allies."

"She's trying to force them to submit to her," Malek said as Sabine used her magic to rend a troll's limbs from its body. Her dress and hair were splattered with enough blood and viscera to make her features barely recognizable.

The more she killed, the more it would hurt the real Sabine when she finally came back to herself. If they didn't stop her, Malek wasn't sure she'd be able to live with the consequences. Despite her remarkable power and determination, Sabine had one of the gentlest hearts he'd ever known.

Blossom landed on his shoulder. "This is bad, Malek. Really bad. How do we get Sabine back?"

Another fire imp darted toward them. Malek kicked it aside before it could make contact. It squealed with dismay and then leaped for them again. Rika stabbed it with her dagger and then yanked the blade clear. With a growl, Malek cut off its head with his weapon, watching as it caught on fire.

"I'll never get used to that," Rika said with a grimace.

Malek made a noise of agreement, focusing again on the field. They needed a plan. Even once he cut through the demons surrounding Sabine, he had no idea how to force Lachlina into relinquishing control.

Malek scanned the field, locating both the demon king and Leena on the far side of it. Kal'thorz was standing beneath a command tent, overseeing his troops like a general surveying the action. Sabine was slowly moving in his direction, but Malek couldn't be sure whether she'd seen Kal'thorz yet. Judging by his body language and the smug satisfaction on his face, Kal'thorz didn't seem bothered by the fact that he was taking heavy losses. If anything, he seemed pleased. That didn't bode well.

A group of hooded individuals was carefully approaching Sabine, attempting to form a circle around her while keeping their distance. It looked like they were using other demons as fodder, allowing them to distract her while they worked their magic.

"The sorcerers are converging on her," Malek said, sweeping his gaze over the field to find a safe place for Rika. He needed to get down there and help Sabine. "Blossom, can you get down there and warn her? We won't make it in time."

"On it!" she shouted, her image flickering before she changed to a moth.

"I'm a liability," Rika said, frowning at him. "You would be down there helping Sabine if it weren't for me."

"You're simply a tactical consideration, but yes, we need to reach her. Once I shift, I can protect you from my dragon-fire, but only if you remain in physical contact with me. Unfortunately, I suspect Sabine's magic is going to get stronger the closer we get to her. I don't know how long Blossom's protection will last. Can you handle it?"

Rika turned a little green, her hand tightening on the hilt of her weapon. "I'll be fine. Yep. No problem riding a dragon. We have to save Sabine, right?"

Malek grinned. "Then come with me. We need more room if I'm going to shift."

He pushed forward, growling at anyone who approached. Most darted out of their way, but a few required a bit more force. He needed to clear enough space from the building so he didn't bring down more of the walls. His skin began to glow from his impending shift as it hardened to form scales.

"Wait, Malek," Rika said, grabbing his arm. "I see Bane. I think he's hurt."

As Bane raced up the stairway toward them, Malek clamped down on his magic. Someone had gouged deep claw marks into Bane's side, and a slight hitch in his steps indicated other more serious injuries. The demon was spattered with blood and gore, his eyes still silvered from the vestiges of the battle.

"If you want Sabine to live, you must not shift yet," Bane said, clamping a hand over his wound. His skin shone with power as he knit the injury back together.

"Explain."

"Not here. Follow."

He led them off to the side of the balcony and away from anyone who might be listening. Even so, he was careful to keep his voice lowered when he spoke.

"Kal'thorz knows she's goddess-ridden," Bane said, his eyes reverting to their normal amber color. "I was ordered to escort her to the prison under the guise of a ritual."

"You tricked her."

Bane inclined his head. "Not by choice. While we are in the underworld, I must follow my liege's orders. The only exception is if his orders countermand my sworn oath to protect Sabine's life. Since the prison was only designed to hold her, she was in no physical danger. I could not refuse nor warn her."

Malek scowled. "What does this have to do with me shifting? Those sorcerers are going to entrap her if we don't stop them."

"I'm aware," Bane snapped, his eyes flashing silver. "Listen carefully. We have little time. Kal'thorz is distracted by the battle, which is the only reason I'm able to share this information with you. His spies are focused on her."

"We're listening," Rika said, taking a step closer to him.

"The prison was originally designed to hold Lachlina, Bringer of Shadows, after she betrayed the gods. Viz'gamoth, the son and slayer of our first king, offered Lachlina the knowledge of how to escape her shackles. In exchange, she agreed to gift him with no small measure of power. When Sabine allowed the goddess to ascend, Lachlina used that same knowledge to release Sabine from the prison."

Malek narrowed his eyes. "Kal'thorz *wanted* Sabine to escape?"

"She now holds the power of a goddess," Bane said, his tone indicating he thought it should be obvious. "The prison was merely a means to force Sabine into tapping into her hereditary magic. The pact between Lachlina and Viz'g-amoth was bound with blood."

Rika frowned. "I don't understand. What difference does that make?"

"Sabine was the one who benefited from the arrangement and now carries the weight of the blood debt. As a descendant of Lachlina's bloodline, Sabine is now indebted to the current demon king."

Rika's eyes rounded. "Uh-oh. That really doesn't sound good."

"What does Kal'thorz want?" Malek demanded.

"Power," Bane explained. "Kal'thorz believes Sabine may be able to break the shackles binding us to the underworld. With her ability to call down the moon—and the goddess strengthening her magic—Sabine has the potential to bind the world in darkness. We will no longer simply be wardens of the underworld but will be restored to our former glory. But first, Kal'thorz must destroy all her ties to the light."

Malek's jaw clenched. "I need to get to her."

"Hold a moment," Bane ordered sharply. "Sabine currently straddles the edge of light and dark magic. If you shift and go to her without something to dampen your light, you will put her in more danger. Those who are fighting below have been trained to extinguish the light at any cost. They have prepared their entire lives for this battle."

Malek frowned, looking at the bloody field below them. Sabine was still holding her own, but she wasn't making much progress against the endless rush of demons. If he didn't help her soon, she'd exhaust her magic and fall. Unless that was Kal'thorz's plan.

Malek frowned, recalling the last time he'd seen Sabine lapse into unconsciousness after she'd expended too much magic. It would be a simple matter for the demon king to take her captive. Hell, it was how his own grandfather had captured his fae step-grandmother. But then what? Even once she regained consciousness, Sabine was too headstrong to meekly succumb to Kal'thorz's demands. There was something he was missing.

"You know she won't surrender to Kal'thorz," Malek said, the urgency to protect his mate becoming overwhelming. "She'll keep fighting or die in the attempt."

Bane grunted in agreement. "They've been ordered to capture and to not harm, which is why Kal'thorz is taking such heavy losses. But make no mistake, Kal'thorz *will* eventually break her spirit. Once he does, she will have no choice but to surrender."

Rika looked down at the field. "Malek, I think he's right. They're mainly fighting the demons who are flocking to her side. She's killing the ones who are getting in her way or who get too close to her."

"With every death, her light is extinguished more," Bane explained and turned toward Malek. "You and the flying bug call to the light within her. Once you step onto that field, both of you will be targeted. Once they exterminate you, Sabine will fall shortly after. She will spend too much of her magic focusing on retribution or protecting those she cares about."

Rika swallowed. "Blossom already flew down to warn Sabine about the sorcerers."

"Then we are already running out of time," Bane said and motioned for them to follow him. "There is a way for you to approach her without many of my brethren realizing who you are. If you can convince the goddess to relinquish control at the right moment, we have a chance to save her. The timing is going to be critical."

Bane led them toward an obscure archway hidden behind a stone sculpture of a demonic warrior. He pressed his hand against a rune carved into the archway. He spoke a few words in the demonic tongue. It flared with a red symbol and then disappeared. Bane motioned for them to follow.

Once they were inside, Bane said, "This tunnel is off limits to all but Kal'thorz's closest advisors. We'll avoid most of the fighting traveling this way. But we need to hurry."

"Wait." Rika interrupted him. "Dax wanted us to tell you that he's going to intervene with Kal'thorz."

Bane nodded and moved quickly down the winding stone stairs. "Dax will issue a challenge for Kal'thorz's throne the moment Sabine returns to herself. If Dax falls, I will issue a second challenge. We must remove Kal'thorz from power before he claims his boon from Sabine. This is our one chance to remove him forever."

Understanding slammed into Malek. He glared at Bane. "How long have you been planning this?"

"Since before we ever laid eyes on Sabine," Bane said dryly. "Every step Dax and I have taken for over a century has been to remove Kal'thorz from power and to create a stronger alliance with the ruler of the Unseelie fae. Sabine was the reason we both agreed to go into exile and why Dax bound himself to Sabine's beastman, Balkin. It was imperative that we foster a closer relationship with her."

"You've both been using her the entire time," Malek murmured as they stepped onto a landing. From the sounds of battle that could be heard dimly overhead, Malek suspected this twisting stairway was more of a tunnel leading underneath the battlefield.

"Does Sabine know all of this?" Rika asked.

"No," Bane admitted, leading them up another staircase. "She may suspect some of it. Dax and I agreed to keep our silence in the event she wasn't strong enough to withstand Kal'thorz's influence. Once Sabine accepted her birthright, our timeline had to be moved up. It would have been better if she had time to fully develop her magic, but we no longer have such a luxury. It's my hope that your presence, dragon, will give her enough strength to withstand Kal'thorz. Your connection to her is strong enough that you should be able to recall her back to herself."

"I thought you cared about her," Rika said quietly. "About all of us."

Bane stared straight ahead and didn't reply. From the rigidity in his shoulders, Rika had hit a nerve. Bane might not want to admit it, but he did care for Sabine and even Rika. Malek suspected things didn't start out that way.

"You swore an oath to serve and protect Sabine from harm," Malek said. "That wasn't part of your original plan, was it?"

Bane's jaw clenched. "No."

"But it's why you and Dax were at odds, wasn't it?"

"In part." Bane hesitated. "Before we met Sabine, Dax was under a death sentence for attempting a coup. Balkin was the one who'd negotiated his release and proposed a plan to remove Kal'thorz with Sabine's help. I was expected to claim Kal'thorz's throne while Dax would remain by Sabine's side."

"But that changed?" Rika asked.

Bane nodded, his expression turning pensive. "Sabine was… different from what either of us expected of an Unseelie princess. When she made the offer to act as a permanent anchor for me to remain on the surface, I realized I had no desire to leave her side and return to the underworld. I relinquished first claim to Kal'thorz's throne and agreed to become her blood-bonded protector. Dax was not pleased, especially since she did not make the same offer to him."

"He thought Sabine should have been his," Malek guessed aloud, the pieces of what he'd suspected falling into place.

Bane gave him a curt nod. "Yes, especially given their relationship up until that point. He'd been her lover and primary protector, yet in his mind, I'd stolen her from him. The truth was that I simply did not wish to lose her."

Rika's eyes widened. "And now Dax has to assume the throne or die?"

"Without a blood bond tying him to Sabine, yes," Bane said. "If Dax fails, Sabine will have to release me from my oath before I can challenge Kal'thorz."

Malek fell silent. Sabine had been right, he realized. Both demon brothers cared about her more than he'd thought. Bane had not only given up his birthright to remain by her side but he'd also placed Sabine's wellbeing above his brother's life. He doubted she knew the truth of the situation, or she would never have accepted Bane's oath. She would have hated the idea of dividing the brothers.

"Why are you telling us this now?"

Bane slowed his steps as they approached another archway. "None of us may live through the next few hours. In the event you survive and I fall, Sabine will want to know the truth. It was not my desire to keep all of this from her, but we could not risk Kal'thorz learning of our plans before it was time. Sabine, powerful as she may be, lacks experience. She has never encountered someone like Kal'thorz."

"And what exactly is your plan?" Malek asked, stopping beside him. The fighting sounded as though it was right outside the heavy stone door.

Bane pulled something out of his pocket. He opened his palm to reveal a small medallion dangling from a leather strap. It was made from some sort of silver metal and had a pulsing red stone in the center. Strange runes had been etched into the metal around the stone.

"This bloodstone pendant was forged in the deepest part of the underworld. It will suppress your power enough that Sabine's light won't be called to it. Simply put it around your neck and none of the demons who are allied with Kal'thorz will attack you. The only caveat is that it will not work while you're in dragon form."

Malek eyed the medallion for a moment and then picked it up. It was cool to the touch and heavier than he'd expected. After everything Bane had told them, Malek decided to trust him. No matter what he thought of the demon, Bane truly loved Sabine. If he thought Malek was the best way to keep her safe, that was good enough for him.

He tied the leather strap around his neck, making sure the metal touched bare skin. The tingle that cast over him was peculiar and a little stifling, but not unpleasant. It felt similar to the warding medallion that damped his power so he could pass as a human, but this one felt dormant. He suspected he could still shift while wearing it, even if it negated the effects.

"There's blood on it," Rika said, pointing at a stain on one of the leather straps.

Bane grunted. "The sorcerer who once wore it no longer has any use for such items."

"Huh." Rika cocked her head and squinted at it. "I don't sense much magic from it. You sure it works?"

"The pendant does not possess any harmful magic. It simply acts as a beacon of sorts. The bloodstone is tied directly to the Heartstone, the source of all life in the underworld. Even with the medallion masking your light, it is not glamour. Kal'thorz has offered to richly reward any who achieve your death. Any demons who recognize you from earlier will still attack you. You must move quickly to intercept Sabine."

Malek made a noise of agreement. Whether or not they attacked him, they would die if they interfered in his efforts to reach Sabine. "That won't be a problem, provided you keep Rika out of harm's way."

"Done," Bane said in agreement. "We need the goddess to relinquish control of Sabine before she exhausts the last of her magic. Once Sabine returns to herself, you may discard the medallion and embrace your true form. Do whatever's necessary to keep Kal'thorz from approaching Sabine and demanding repayment of her debt. Dax will attempt to issue his challenge before he reaches her. When he does, you must not interfere in their fight."

"Understood."

Bane looked down at Rika. "You will need to remain with me, little seer. I've been ordered to escort you to the command tent, where Kal'thorz is waiting. While he has ordered Malek's death, he believes you may be a useful pawn in the event we need more leverage against Sabine. Whatever you do, you must pretend to be wholly human and not reveal your true nature. I will do what I can to ensure no harm comes to you."

Rika swallowed but nodded her agreement. "Got it." She turned toward Malek. "Please keep an eye out for Blossom. She might have found a way to reach Sabine."

When Malek nodded, Bane pressed his hand against the doorway. The warding fell away, and he pushed it open.

"Good luck, dragon. Keep her safe."

Malek's muscles tightened with readiness, his hand gripping the hilt of his sword. Without another word, he left the tunnel and dove straight into the heart of the battle.

Chapter Thirty-One

*S*abine jerked back in revulsion, watching as Lachlina flayed the skin off a demon before dropping him to the ground. She didn't know how it was possible, but she could smell the sharp metallic scent of the blood that coated the field. She'd lost count of how many the goddess had murdered. Every time Lachlina slaughtered another demon, something inside Sabine died a little more.

"She's playing with them," Sabine said, her hands curling into fists. Although her hands were clean, they felt sticky, as though her palms were coated with blood.

"So it would appear," Vestior said, his shadowy cloak billowing around him as he gazed into the reflection pool to watch the carnage. If the needless slaughter bothered him, she couldn't tell. The Harbinger of Nightmares continued to wear an expressionless mask, his mostly silent presence somewhat disconcerting.

Her scope of view was limited to Lachlina's field of vision. The view through the water was slightly distorted, similar to how witches used a scrying bowl to survey their surroundings.

Lachlina turned at another assailant's approach, and Sabine straightened. Beyond the attacking demon, Sabine caught sight of a familiar dragon shapeshifter—whole and unharmed. A wave of profound relief and unbridled love soared through her.

"Malek," she murmured, drinking in his image. Even through the ripples of the pool, he was captivating to behold. With his dark hair accentuating his strong jaw and fierce eyes, he looked like one of the heroes from legend. All of her concerns faded into the background, as though even the universe held its breath at the sight of Malek.

He moved away from a large stone archway, determination in every step as he stalked in her direction. Although he was surrounded by enemies, Malek moved with a predatory grace that left no doubt he was a force to be reckoned with. The surrounding demons stepped out of his path or turned aside at his approach. No one was challenging him.

Sabine searched through the surrounding faces, but she didn't see any sign of Dax, Bane, or Rika. Concern for the young seer had been in the back of her mind since she'd left her with the alchemist. If Anje hadn't honored their agreement or had allowed anything to happen to Rika, Sabine would make sure he didn't live to see the dawn.

Sabine spotted a familiar dark-haired woman a short distance away. Leena was standing near a tent holding some sort of rounded object that pulsed like a heartbeat. The stunning woman was staring across the field, her expression sending a cold chill through Sabine. Her skin glowed softly, like moonlight had touched it, her marks of power visible for the first time. Even her hair had lifted, floating on a mystical wind only she could feel.

Sabine inhaled sharply. Leena was performing some kind of major magic. Most fae who weren't of the royal line couldn't control that much power. It would sputter and flicker or have other disastrous consequences. She'd sensed Leena was skilled, but harnessing magic like this should have been beyond her capabilities. Sabine frowned and leaned closer, wondering if the device in Leena's hands was responsible.

It was smaller than a melon and appeared to be comprised of some sort of silver webbing. Inside the metal cage, a large reddish stone pulsed at regular intervals. She'd heard about such things from the dwarven tinkerers but had never seen one before. It must be one of the power amplification devices they'd been working on. They were supposedly extraordinarily difficult to create since they required multiple forms of magic and components only found in the deepest parts of the underworld.

Several of the robed demons carried similar devices. If Sabine was right about their purpose, the cost of creating so many was astronomical. It was hard to tell through the reflection pool, but they seemed to pulse in time with one another, like they were interconnected. Well, almost. The device Leena was holding was pulsing faster and more brilliantly than the others. She appeared to be the one directing the robed figures—and they were carefully circling Lachlina, almost like a dance. The goddess might be able to hold her own against them, but Malek was vulnerable in his human form.

Sabine's eyes flew back to where Malek had been, worried he might get caught in whatever they were planning. Before she could spot him, another demon raced toward Lachlina, distracting the goddess. She lifted him into the air with a flick of her wrist, impaling him on a nearby stalagmite. Sabine inhaled sharply, the weight of his death settling over her like a shroud.

It made little sense. They were throwing themselves at Lachlina piecemeal rather than in a concentrated attack. Did they want to die? She didn't know enough about demonic culture to know if this was some sort of bizarre rite of passage. It was obvious they were being fairly careful not to harm Lachlina, but to what end and why?

"Yoo-hoo! Calling Sabine," a tiny voice shouted from somewhere nearby. "Can. You. Hear. Me?"

Sabine reared back. "Blossom? Is that you?"

A tiny moth darted in front of Lachlina and then off to the side. The goddess was ignoring the moth, focusing instead on one of the hooded demons carrying one of those odd devices. Before Lachlina could focus on the robed figure, another demon darted forward and attacked. Lachlina quickly grabbed hold of him, forcing him to disembowel himself with his own claws.

Sabine winced, unsure how much longer she could stomach watching this. It wouldn't be so bad if Lachlina didn't seem to derive such pleasure from it.

"I've been trying to get your attention," Blossom said, hovering near Lachlina's shoulder. "Oh… um. Hmm. Give me a minute."

Her dark wings fluttered wildly. She glowed and then disappeared. With a pop of air, Blossom appeared in front of her with a wide grin on her face.

"There you are! Hi! Guess that power boost you gave me had a bit of a kick."

Sabine stared at Blossom in shock, automatically lifting her hand for the pixie to land.

"I don't think you're supposed to be here," Sabine said softly, darting a quick glance at Vestior. The Harbinger of Nightmares focused his dispassionate gaze on Blossom for a moment before turning back to the battle.

"Ohhh," Blossom whispered, her eyes widening as she looked around. "We're in the garden, aren't we? Look at all those pretty, pretty flowers. I think I like the blue ones the best. No, wait. There's a purple one! I bet those petals would make an amazing dress. What do you think?"

Sabine snapped her fingers to get Blossom's attention. "Focus, Blossom. Flowers later. What are you doing here? And how did you get here?"

She blinked at Sabine and shrugged. "I tried to give the goddess my message, but she's ignoring me. I think she's having too much fun killing demons. I knew you'd listen though. I think your magic made it easier for me to move between realms."

Lachlina momentarily distracted Sabine by ripping the heart out of a robed demon's chest. The goddess lifted the heart into the air and shouted something, then tossed it to the ground. She brought her foot down hard, crushing it beneath her boot.

"Are you okay, Sabine?" Blossom whispered. "You don't look so good."

Sabine made a noncommittal noise. "Tell me your message."

"Malek wanted me to warn you about the sorcerers. Dax said they're going to try some magical whammy to capture you. Malek was pretty angry about them trying to hurt you, especially after Rika said your magic was changing. Every time the goddess kills someone, your aura darkens."

Sabine took a deep breath. So that was what she'd been feeling. Even though Lachlina was the one causing the harm, Sabine was the one who carried the weight. It was too bad she couldn't consider these deaths undue stress. But she'd agreed to allow Lachlina some measure of vengeance against the ones who had imprisoned her. At least she'd managed to elicit Lachlina's agreement not to harm her friends.

Sabine had never been fond of killing. When she was living in Akros, Dax and Bane had taken that darkness from her, savoring it like a fine wine. That wasn't an option this time. Offering them even a taste of her darkness after slaughtering hundreds, if not more, would leave an imbalance that would forever change them. Without knowing how it would affect them, it was too dangerous to risk such a move. No. She had to resolve this debt on her own.

The second Lachlina violated their agreement, Sabine would be within her rights to step in. Until then, she had to allow the goddess to continue wreaking death and destruction in her name. She just hoped her magic wasn't forever changed as a result.

Pushing those thoughts aside, Sabine turned back to watch the events unfold on the battlefield. "You mentioned Rika. I'm assuming she made it back safely?"

Blossom started to nod and then shook her head. "The alchemist fixed her, but she's having a bad time with all the magic being thrown around. Whatever the goddess is doing is affecting the wards around the volcano. I tried to put a dampener around Rika, but I don't have enough magic for it to work for long."

Sabine frowned. "Anything else?"

Blossom cocked her head and thought about it for a minute. "There's a point when a fire imp bursts into flames that the meat is perfectly cooked. If you extinguish it fast enough, they taste like chicken."

Ew. That would go into the column of things she didn't need to know. "I'll take your word for it."

Blossom grinned. "You ready to get out of here? Malek's really worried about you. I think he's going to start stepping on demons soon."

Shaking her head, Sabine said, "I can't leave yet. Lachlina and I agreed to temporarily switch places in exchange for freeing me from the prison."

A look of horror crossed Blossom's face. "What? You're

letting her steer the dragonfly? But the volcano. Your magic. Sabine, you have to come back!"

"The garden requires an anchor to remain part of the in-between," Vestior said, his rich baritone wrapping around her like a blanket. "Unless Lachlina violates the terms of the agreement or Sabin'theoria suffers from any undue harm or distress, she is required to remain here until one full day has passed. The pact is binding."

Blossom cocked her head and rubbed her hands together. "Aha. We've got a loophole. Maybe I should go see what sort of mayhem I can cause. That always distresses you."

Sabine smiled, but it faded a moment later when she caught sight of Malek again. Lachlina was busy crushing someone with a boulder and not paying attention to what was happening a short distance away. Four demons had circled Malek, falling into a formation Sabine recognized from her training days with Dax and Bane.

She straightened in alarm. "Why hasn't he shifted? He's too vulnerable in human form."

"I don't know," Blossom whispered, her breath hitching as she stared at the pool.

Malek swung his blade, decapitating one of his attackers with a single stroke. The one behind him darted forward, his claws slicing down Malek's back and ripping away something from around his neck. Sabine cried out in alarm. Malek spun around, grabbed the demon by the horns, and tossed him onto the other before attacking the last.

The fight had captured the attention of other nearby demons. Each of Malek's movements was one of grace and power, but he was no match for the number of demons who were converging on him.

When Lachlina turned and shifted her view away from Malek's fight, Sabine leaped to her feet and shouted, "Turn back! Malek's in trouble!"

Lachlina didn't react to Sabine's warning, except to send a strong wave of magic over the field. Dozens of demons toppled over, including a few who'd been targeting Malek. She lifted her hand again and send another blast of power in Malek's direction. Most of the demons didn't get back up, but she hadn't felt the weight of their deaths.

"What was that? What did she do to them?" Sabine demanded.

Blossom shook her head. "I don't know. Do blue sparkles heal demon poison?"

Before she could respond, one of the robed demons threw something in Lachlina's direction. The goddess sent up a ward, but the resounding backlash was like a kick in the stomach.

Sabine doubled over, struggling to take a full breath. She coughed and lifted her gaze. The robed demon was already dead. Lachlina had decided to not draw out that one's torment.

"Uh-oh. It's the demon king," Blossom said when Lachlina turned her sights on a nearby demon.

With his horns and eyes glowing with a silvery red light, Kal'thorz was even more formidable than when she'd last seen him. Black leather straps affixed with glowing red crystals crisscrossed his otherwise bare chest. The number of scars on his body was staggering, each a testament to his ferocity. He was less armored than many other demons, but he obviously didn't need to bother with such protection. They moved out of his way, almost by some unseen command.

Kal'thorz shouted something at one of the robed figures. When the priest shook his head and pointed at the center of the field, Kal'thorz quickly snapped his neck and dropped him to the ground. He picked up the device that had been dropped and handed it to another robed figure.

"What is he doing? Is he going after Lachlina or Malek?"

Blossom gazed downward, her wings beating wildly. She pointed at the edge of the pool. "There's Malek! Uh-oh. The demon king sees him."

Sabine took a step closer to the pool. Malek was bleeding from a deep claw mark, but it was the sight of the blackened spidery veins creeping along his skin that had her worried. While he was still holding his own, his movements were already becoming sluggish and awkward.

"Shift, Malek," she whispered. It wouldn't fix the poison, but it would give him some immunity until someone healed him. If Vestior could pull him into the in-between, she could pull the poison out.

She glanced at where the Huntsman had been standing, but he was gone. Panic rushed through her. When had he left and why? If the poison didn't kill Malek, the demon king would.

"Lachlina!" she shouted, but the goddess didn't respond.

Clamping a hand over her wrist, Sabine sent her power into Lachlina's marks. They glowed brightly for a moment and then faded. Lachlina was ignoring her. She tried reaching for Malek through their bond, but he was gone. She couldn't feel him at all.

Muttering a curse, Sabine paced the edge of the pool. She'd never felt so helpless. Why wasn't Malek shifting? Why wasn't Lachlina intervening? Where the hell was Dax or Bane? She kicked the edge of the stone enclosure surrounding the pool. She needed to get out of there. With Vestior disappearing, she wasn't sure how to return to her body. If this wasn't undue stress, she didn't know what was.

A brilliant red light blinded Sabine for a moment, forcing her to avert her gaze. She blinked rapidly, still seeing spots. "What was that? Did Malek shift?"

"No," Blossom said, shaking her head. "I think the priests

did something. It was some kind of magic, but it seemed to come from everywhere at once."

"Those devices," Sabine guessed aloud, trying to focus on what was happening. "It was the same color as the stone. I thought it was some sort of power amplification device."

"What did they do with it?"

"No idea."

The light had dazed everyone. Lachlina rebounded fairly quickly, shoving both Malek and Kal'thorz away from her with a blast of power. A nearby demon picked up a fallen sword. In the next second, he thrust the blade through Malek's chest.

"NO!" Sabine shouted, diving toward the water. She plunged into its icy depths, the cold a shock to her system. Desperate to reach Malek, she kicked her legs and swam downward, sliding into darkness. Vestior had told her to be resolute. She *would* make it through, no matter what.

For a moment, she hovered in nothingness. It was similar to what she experienced when she stepped into a portal. Inky blackness surrounded her. Focusing on Malek, she reached for him with their bond. There. A faint flicker. She moved in that direction, hearing the sounds of battle grow louder until she slammed into an invisible wall.

Sabine pushed her magic against the barrier, trying to break through and return to her body. Her power slid away from it like water flowing over a stone. She had to reach Malek. She slammed against the barrier again and again, each time being thrown backward with equal force. It felt like she was being torn in two. Her physical form was still on that field, but her mind was trapped here.

A high-pitched voice spoke from somewhere nearby and said, "The Huntsman told me to show you how to move through the in-between."

Sabine turned and saw a wisp of light glimmering in the darkness. "Blossom?"

The wisp giggled. "It has to stay a secret, okay?"

"All right," Sabine replied, watching as the light danced toward her.

"Look down."

Sabine did, but she didn't see her body. Instead, she was simply a glowing figure with no true form. Against the inky-black surroundings, she looked like a star sparkling in the night's sky.

"What in the world?" Sabine asked, lifting her hand and marveling at the way the rays of silver-and-gold light penetrated the darkness.

The wisp twirled in the air, shining as brilliantly as the sun. "It's still you, Sabine. Well, it's you without any illusions or weaknesses. While you were in her prison, the goddess used your magic to create the illusion of your mortal body. Once you left her domain, you returned to your true state."

Sabine frowned—or would have if light could make such a gesture. "I don't understand. Where are we?"

"We're still in the in-between, a crossroads between realms. There's no pain, no decay, and no death in this place. Time moves differently here too. Days could pass, but it would only be seconds on the battlefield."

Sabine recalled the last time she'd been in the in-between. The Huntsman had told her she could live forever in this place. Was that what he had meant?

Particles of dust or something similar floated through her beams of light. She shivered at the strange sensation. It wasn't painful, just peculiar.

Turning back toward the invisible wall, she asked, "How do I move through the barrier?"

"It's easy," Blossom said. "You just have to change your light."

"What do you mean?"

"Each doorway reacts to your light's frequency," Blossom explained. "You have to alter your light to match the doorway's resonance. Only then can you pass through. It's sort of like how you use your illusions to change your appearance. Use your magic to change your light the same way."

Sabine stared at the glowing wisp in shock. Could it be that simple? "This is portal magic, isn't it?"

Blossom's light bounced up and down like she was nodding. "Yes, but not everyone can do it. Most fae don't have strong enough glamour to alter their inner light. Since pixies are so small compared to the fae, it doesn't require as much magic for us. It's just hard to find the old doorways without help."

"My people still use some of the doorways. We used one of them back in Atlantia."

"The gods anchored some doorways to the Well. It drains a bit of its magic whenever someone passes through. This one isn't anchored. You can only pass through it with your own magic. I don't think very many people have the power or knowledge to move through barriers like this one anymore."

Understanding filled Sabine. When she'd been in the Hall of the Gods, Vestior had expressed regret that the existing doorways were still active. If they were draining the remaining magic from the Well of Dreams, it was likely speeding up the rate at which their world was dying every time someone used them.

A thought struck her. Lachlina had infused most of her power into creating the artifacts to seal the Dragon Portal. If she no longer had enough of her own magic to alter her inner light, she wouldn't be able to use any of the doorways without help. Keeping her in the in-between was the perfect prison, especially if she'd already escaped from one made of mortar and stone.

"Clever," Sabine mused. "This must be how the gods finally imprisoned Lachlina. She used my magic to pull me through to the garden. She escaped the same way."

With the amount of Sabine's magic that Lachlina was using, it was a wonder she was still standing. The goddess must have some way of quickly regenerating power. It was doubtful Lachlina would ever share that particular secret.

Sabine studied the barrier, listening to the slow and muffled sounds of the battle in the distance. She turned to ask Blossom another question but froze at the sight of a large flash of blue light in the distance. It shone brightly for a moment before the darkness swallowed it.

Blossom's voice lowered until it was barely audible. "Even though time moves differently here, it's not a good idea to stay too long. Your light is a lot brighter than mine. Lots of scary stuff passes through the in-between, including some of the old gods. I'm not sure we want to draw their attention."

Sabine nodded and turned back to focus on the barrier. Gathering her magic, she began weaving an illusion to match the barrier. Her image vibrated, a low thrumming pulsing through her as she pinned the mask in place. It was surprisingly easy, simpler than the human form she'd adopted when she had gone into hiding. Satisfied she'd matched the barrier as closely as possible, she stepped through the invisible wall as though it didn't exist. On the opposite side, she paused, unsure what to do from there.

"Blossom? Now what?"

"Recreate your body," Blossom's voice shouted from a distance, sounding like she were underwater. "Hurry! We've got trouble!"

The pixie had already slipped back into reality. Sabine hadn't even seen her do it.

"Recreate my…" Sabine bit out a curse and removed her glamour. Once again in the form of a shining light, Sabine focused on the details of her body—the shape of her hands, the weight and color of her hair, the marks of power on her skin. Once the illusion had been crafted as close as possible to the reality, she pinned it in place and willed it to be true.

A sharp burning sensation slashed against her wrist. Sabine cried out, collapsing to the ground as the battle raged around her. Her hands bit into the hard volcanic rock while the sharp smell of sweat, blood, and death choked her senses.

Blossom darted in front of her and clapped. "You did it! Now get up, up, up! No time for congratulations. The goddess is mad, the demon king is right over there, Malek is in trouble, and you're low on magic and surrounded by enemies."

"Is that all?" Sabine asked and stood, trying to clear her head. She was back in her body and wearing the same clothing from earlier, even if it was covered with things she didn't want to think too hard about. Dozens of demons surrounded her, angling their sharp claws or weapons in her direction.

"Find Bane and Rika," Sabine ordered Blossom, trusting the pixie to obey her command.

Taking a page from Lachlina's book, Sabine blasted her power outward and sent the demons flying. It cleared enough for her to make out the crumpled form of Malek bleeding out on the ground. The sword was still embedded in his chest, his body limp and unmoving.

"Malek!" she screamed, racing toward him. Magic shot from her palms as she flung away anyone who crossed her path or dared to try to stop her. She dropped to her knees beside him, desperate to find a pulse.

"Please, no," she whispered, tears streaming down her

face. She couldn't sense him through their bond, except the smallest flicker of life. He felt so far away. She leaned down and kissed him, mentally willing him to use her power to give himself strength. His blue eyes fluttered open for a moment, his gaze unfocused.

"Stay with me, my love," she urged, rising to her feet. Her hands were slippery on the hilt of the sword. It took her several tries to get a good enough grip on it. She yanked the sword free and dropped it to the ground, pressing her hand against his injury. She squeezed her eyes shut and whispered a fervent prayer to any gods who might still listen through the in-between.

"Sabine!" Kal'thorz shouted on a roar.

She lifted her head and saw the demon king running toward her. She narrowed her eyes and flung her hand outward, sending him flying away from her. He regrouped quickly, barely impacted by her magic, and moved in her direction once more.

"Shift, damn you. Shift!" she pleaded, gripping Malek's shoulders tightly. She sent a strong surge of magic into him, trying to burn away the poison. His back arched, his entire body spasming. Then with a final, strangled gasp, he went lax in her arms.

"NO!" she screamed, her heart shattering. He couldn't be gone. She wouldn't allow it.

Blinded with rage and intense fury, she reached for the sword she'd tossed aside. She sliced her hand down the edge of the blade and slapped her hand over his wound, allowing her blood to intermingle with his. Pressing down on his chest, she flooded him with her power.

"Stop her!" someone shouted.

"My life to yours, Malek Rish'dan," she whispered, holding the man she loved in her thoughts. "In darkness and in light. In death as well as life. Until the last of the magic fades from this world."

Sabine gasped as his wound knitted together. He didn't open his eyes, but he lived. His breath was shallow, his skin clammy, but his heart beat weakly under her fingertips. She'd never possessed the gift for healing, unless this was some remnant of the goddess's power. If that was the case, Sabine intended to use it—and a lot more—to punish the demon responsible.

Infusing her voice with power, she said, "By blood and magic, and by my rights to both, I command the elements to attend to me."

A sharp wind blew through the cavern. Clouds that should have never been seen in the underworld formed overhead. The volcanic rock trembled beneath her feet. Lightning struck the ground near her, and rain began to fall.

Sabine lifted her head, the rain blending with her tears and falling to the ground. Dimly, she heard screams and shouts in the distance. She ignored all of it. There was only one person who held her focus now. With her last breath, she'd see Kal'thorz's dead and broken body lying at her feet for hurting the man she loved.

She reached for the elements, calling them to herself like a lover's caress. The ground rumbled again, the rocks beneath her feet responding to her power. As the heady earth magic filled her, her resolve and will strengthened. Rain continued to fall, coating her skin with its silky embrace. She tilted her head upward, accepting the gift of clarity and fluidity.

From the nearby lava, she absorbed heat, blending it together with the ferocity and strength of the wind to create a fearsome fire whirl within her. She rose from the ground, more than a mere echo of the goddess who had previously inhabited her body. She was power incarnate, and justice would be hers.

The storm raging around her was but a shadow of the hurricane churning within her. Lifting her hands toward the sky, she spread her fingers, readying her power to take flight.

"Sabine, stop," Kal'thorz demanded, his voice coming closer. "You'll destroy the wards if you unleash that much power."

She turned, the wind whipping her silvery hair away from her face. She stared at the demon king, allowing him to see a glimpse of the fury that raged within her. Most of the surrounding demons had already fallen to their knees.

"You dare ask for favors after what you've done? I'll see you broken and ground to dust for the suffering you've caused. *Shelein varesein printemp!*"

Kal'thorz staggered to a halt, staring at her in shock. "Sabine?"

"My name is Sabin'theoria, Queen of the Unseelie," she said, magic shooting out of her with the force of a thousand knives.

Chapter Thirty-Two

A *thousand cuts for the death of her heart?*

Sabine's power sliced through Malek with the force of a hurricane. He flew backward, lightning striking the ground dangerously close to him while freezing rain and hail pelted his skin. With a roar, he summoned his magic and embraced his true form. He landed on the ground with a thud, all leathery wings and diamond-hard scales. If he hadn't been bound to Sabine, her strike would have killed him.

"Sabine! Stop, dammit!" he shouted, using his tail to whip away nearby demons. They'd taken the opportunity to leap into the fray. He blew a steady stream of dragonfire over his would-be attackers, sending them scattering for the moment.

He needed to get Sabine to stop fighting him without hurting her in the process. At least, he thought it was her, especially after she'd somehow revived Dax after he'd taken a sword to the chest. The power she'd wielded had been beyond potent, but the goddess wouldn't have shed tears over a fallen demon.

"Ignalis!" Sabine shouted, fire erupting from her fingertips

in a burning whirl. A fire tornado? Interesting. He hadn't realized she could summon one.

Malek inhaled deeply, breathing in the fire and absorbing her tornado with his magic. If he weren't a dragon, that would have hurt a lot more. It was as though she didn't recognize him. Malek caught sight of Kal'thorz standing smugly on the far side of the field. The demon king looked entirely too pleased with himself.

Sabine lifted her hands again. He slammed his tail down hard, shaking the ground near them. Sabine stumbled, her magical attack misfiring.

"*I'm not your enemy,*" he said, reaching for her again over their mental connection. "*I don't want to hurt you.*"

Dozens of demons attacked anew, their sharpened claws tearing into his scales. With a roar, he turned and knocked them aside, stretching his leathery wings to send them flying. He blew dragonfire at them, charring them to bits.

Sabine flung out her hand, ripping stalagmites off the ground and hurling them toward him. He lifted his tail, knocking aside their trajectory and sending them flying in the direction of the command tent. He heard several loud crashes and screams from behind him. Sadly, Kal'thorz had moved out of the way.

One of Sabine's weaponized stalagmites hit its mark, its angle striking the edge of Malek's scales and embedding in his thigh. With a hiss, he grabbed it with his teeth and yanked it free. He dropped it on the ground and stepped on it, grinding it into dust.

"*Dammit, Sabine,*" Malek said, wrapping his tail around her and lifting her into the air. "*Knock it off. That one hurt.*"

Her eyes widened for a second and then she slipped out of his grasp, leaving a cold wind where she'd been. She backed away, a trace of fear in her eyes as she sent several sharp lances of power in his direction.

They slammed into his side, forcing his dragonfire out in a *whoosh*. The smell of charred hair and skin filled the air. Quite a few demons hadn't gotten out of the line of fire in time. Malek narrowed his eyes at Sabine. Something was very wrong.

"It's an illusion, Malek! She thinks you're Kal'thorz!" Rika yelled, running onto the field toward Dax. A tiny pixie chased after her, trailing glittering dust behind her. Bane kept pace with Rika, knocking aside demons when they tried to stop the seer from reaching the injured demon.

"Destroy the amplification devices!" Bane shouted, fighting off several attackers. Rika spun and dove under Bane's arm, using Dax's blade to help keep them at bay.

Amplification devices? Illusion? Malek whipped his head around, noting almost a dozen robed figures holding silver balls that gleamed with a reddish light.

He inhaled deeply, then let out a stream of dragonfire at a group containing at least three robed figures. Two of them tried to create wards, but it was no use. They turned to ash, the silver balls falling to the ground still intact.

Malek lifted his foot and brought it down hard on one of the devices. It shattered beneath his claws, leaving a tingle of magic behind. He shook himself off, the peculiar magic sliding away like sheets of water. Strange that the devices had an immunity to dragonfire. He quickly destroyed the other two before glancing back at Sabine.

Sabine's long silvery hair whipped away from her face, revealing a trace of puzzlement and confusion in her eyes. She was still glowing softly with power, her silvery marks disappearing under her blood-spattered clothing. From the way her light had dimmed and her erratic breathing, she must quickly be exhausting her magic. He needed to end this fast.

Turning away from Sabine, he went after another group

of three robed figures. They proved to be more of a challenge —or rather, their guards did. Once they were dead, he stepped on the rest of the devices and ground them into dust. Rika and Blossom took advantage of the distraction he was causing, cutting across the field to reach Dax.

"You will not touch him!" Sabine shouted, power exploding from her fingertips in a shocking blast.

Rika screamed and dropped to the ground, throwing her hands over her head.

Malek brought his tail down hard in between them, blocking the onslaught of Sabine's power from hitting Rika and Blossom. Malek roared as Sabine's magic flayed some scales from his tail. Sabine cried out and staggered, holding her arm at an awkward angle. His gaze sharpened on her, noting the way her eyes shimmered from unshed tears. Was she feeling what he did?

"I'm trying to help him, Sabine!" Rika shouted, brushing angry tears from her eyes. "It's me, Rika! I'm not your enemy!"

Sabine lowered her head, her silvery hair hiding her features from view. He couldn't see what she was doing, but his scales tingled from a sudden gathering of power. Dammit. She was stubborn. He likely only had seconds until she launched her next attack.

Blossom flew to Malek. "Leena's the one making the illusions and using the priests to help her. Sabine doesn't recognize any of us. Rika tried to break the illusion, but it's too strong. It shouldn't be possible for a normal fae to fool Sabine like this."

Malek turned his head, trying to locate Leena. He'd put a stop to it right now.

"Lizard!" Bane shouted over his shoulder, fighting off another set of demons. "We need you to break the devices to weaken the glamour. Leave the bitch for later. She's already cast the illusion."

Malek growled, a low rumble in his throat. He spun around, located another of the robed figures, and set them on fire. Another tried to run, but Malek simply lifted his foot and pinned him to the ground, using his teeth to rip the demon in half. Two more devices destroyed. He scanned the demons around him quickly, counting at least four more devices in the sorcerer's hands. His efforts were paying off. They were slowly backing away from him.

Rika had made it to Dax and was kneeling beside him. She helped him get to his feet while Bane kept the other demons from approaching. Sabine clapped her hands together, breaking off a group of stalactites from the ceiling and throttling them in Rika's direction. Malek lifted his wing and covered her, gritting his teeth as the sharp rocks tore into his wing. That would leave a mark.

Sabine cried out, dropping to her knees and wrapping her arms around herself. Even through her glimmering tears, the hatred in her eyes was staggering. She pushed up from the ground and took a step toward him. Despite the harm she'd caused, he had to admire her perseverance and determination. As long as she believed them to be in danger, she would continue fighting.

Even if it killed her.

He'd had enough. Pushing up from the ground, Malek shifted forms with a flash of light. He used the momentum to tackle Sabine. He spun at the last second, taking the brunt of the force, and cradled her against his chest.

She struggled in his arms, lashing him with her magic. He muttered a curse and tried to hold her tighter, but she fought like a crazed hellcat. He jerked as the wind lashed against his back with the force of a whip. Her nails scored his skin, drawing blood. He grabbed her wrists, yanked them over her head, and pinned her with his body. He'd never wanted to assert his will over her, but he'd be damned if he was going to lose her.

Angling his head down, he pressed his lips against hers and breathed his dragonfire into her. Surrounding her with his heated power, he reached out to her with his thoughts.

"Trust in this, Sabine, and feel the truth. You're mine, just as I'm yours, until the last of this world's magic fades. I love you, now and always."

She stopped fighting abruptly. He loosened his hold on her, and she scrambled out of his grasp. Her lavender eyes were stricken, her gaze darting between him and Dax.

"What trickery is this?" she whispered, pressing her fingers to her lips. "How did you steal his power?"

Keeping his movements slow, he held out his hand toward her and said, "I'm not Kal'thorz. Trust what you feel, not what you see. The priests have helped Leena create an illusion."

She eyed his hand warily but made no move to touch him. "She's doesn't have the ability to create such strong glamour, and no demon has the power."

"I can help," Rika said, stumbling to a halt when Sabine's glow brightened threateningly. Blossom squeaked and dove under Rika's hair.

Malek quickly stepped between them and said, "It's Rika and Blossom. Even if you don't trust we are who we say, I'm asking you not to hurt them."

Rika peered around him and said, "I know I look like a demon, but I'm really a squishy human. Please don't shoot lightning bolts at me. Malek is trying to protect me, just like you asked him."

"I was with you in the garden a few minutes ago, Sabine," Blossom called from her perch on Rika's shoulder. "Leena didn't know about me, so she didn't include me in the illusion. But I think she put an obfuscation spell over me. I knew I didn't like that stinky magic lady."

Sabine frowned, staring at the spot where Blossom was sitting. "I don't sense any active glamour."

Rika held up her hands in a peaceable gesture and took a step toward Sabine. "I'm a seer. I was living in Karga with my grandmother when you found me. I knew you were fae when we met, even though you pretended to be human. You've been helping me see through glamour."

Sabine shook her head. "Kal'thorz has sorcerers who can steal memories."

"Seriously?" Blossom asked, crossing her arms over her chest. "That's just rude."

Several demons broke through the ranks. Malek whirled around, cutting them down. Sabine lifted her hand, flinging the others away from him. Malek glanced at her in surprise. She lowered her head, studying him thoughtfully. At least she wasn't attacking him and Rika anymore.

"Hurry it up over there," Bane shouted, still trying to fight off the demons who were targeting Dax. "I need her to break my oath. Dax isn't in any condition to offer a challenge."

"Working on it," Malek retorted, thrusting his blade through another attacker. "Rika, if you can break the illusion, do it. Quickly."

"If you take my hand, I can show you the truth," Rika said, reaching toward Sabine. "No demon has that power. If I'm lying, you can always kill me afterward."

After the slightest hesitation, Sabine slid her hand into Rika's outstretched one. The air in the cavern became crisper and slightly tangy, filling the air with the scent of apples and honeysuckle.

Sabine released Rika's hand, staring at them in shock. She grabbed Rika and hugged her tightly before sending a wave of magic over Blossom.

The pixie's wings twitched, and she threw her arms into the air. "Sabine's back!"

Rika grinned, looking extraordinarily pleased with herself. Sabine turned toward Malek, his heart soaring at the overwhelming love and happiness that coursed through their bond.

With tears filling her eyes, she threw herself into Malek's arms. He pulled her close, burying his face against her hair and breathing her in. Something eased inside him at her touch. Her inner light was a shining beacon, soothing the ragged tears in his soul that he hadn't realized existed until he'd met her.

"You're alive," she whispered, clinging to him tightly. "Malek, I thought you were—Oh, gods! I hurt you!" She jerked back and ran her hands along his chest as though searching for injuries. "How bad is it? You're still bleeding!"

"Shh," he murmured, pulling her back into his arms. "I'll be fine. It was just a few love taps. No permanent harm."

"Too close to a lie," she chided gently, her words not packing much heat. She cupped his face and kissed him, using her power to nullify the effects of the poison he'd absorbed.

"Sabine," Dax whispered, his voice little more than a croak.

Sabine pulled away from Malek and gasped. Dax was leaning heavily against his brother, unable to remain standing without aid. She went to him and pressed her hand against Dax's chest. Her skin glowed softly, the barest flush of power.

"Take what you need to heal yourself," she murmured. "I have little magic left, but what I have is yours."

Malek frowned and barely resisted the urge to pull her away. Sabine was far too pale and growing increasingly unsteady. She was almost to the point of exhaustion.

Malek eyed Dax and said, "Better, but you still look like a wet kitten could topple you."

Dax snorted. "Feel about the same too. Fuckers nearly got me."

"Sabine, I need you to release me from my oath," Bane said, his voice and tone urgent. "Quickly, before Kal'thorz approaches."

Sabine reared back in shock. "What?"

Before Bane could explain, Kal'thorz broke through the crowd. The surrounding demons stepped aside, allowing their king to pass.

Kal'thorz did a slow clap, prowling toward them with a smirk. "Well done, my dear. I hadn't realized you'd conscripted a young seer. How clever of you."

With a muttered curse, Bane straightened. He tried to catch Sabine's eye, but she was focused on Kal'thorz. He jerked his head toward Sabine.

Malek reached for Sabine's hand and urged her. *"Sabine, you need to release Bane from his oath. He can't challenge Kal'thorz for the throne until you do."*

She met his gaze and then looked at Bane. She opened her mouth to say something, but Kal'thorz beat her to it.

"Now then, my dear, let's discuss the debt you—"

"I challenge you, Kal'thorz Versed, in a test of will and might." Dax interrupted, his voice resonating through the clearing. "By rights of birth and blood, I claim the Heartstone as my due." He sliced his wrist with his claw, allowing his blood to spill to the rocky ground.

Kal'thorz hissed, his eyes silvering. The surrounding demons stomped their feet, causing the ground to rumble beneath them.

A thick black vine grew up and out of Dax's offering. It rose into the air, reaching and stretching into what appeared to be a doorway. The air in the center shimmered for a moment and then became smoky.

A robed skeletal figure stepped out from the center of the newly formed portal, carrying a large walking staff tipped with a crystal skull. The glowing red eyes of the Huntsman swept over the clearing. All the demons fell silent, immediately lowering their horned heads in obeisance.

He lifted his staff and brought it down hard, the resounding thunderclap reverberating throughout the underworld.

"A challenge has been issued," the Huntsman intoned, his voice echoing through everyone's minds. *"Through claws or blades, the victor claims the right to lead their people. From now until the last of the magic fades from this world, the pact is sealed. You have a quarter bell to prepare yourselves."*

Chapter Thirty-Three

*T*he Huntsman remained in the center of the field while Kal'thorz headed back to the partially-destroyed command tent, where Leena and a group of demonic priests were waiting.

The moment Kal'thorz was out of earshot, Sabine whirled on Dax. He could barely stand, much less fight. "This is madness. Why are you doing this?"

"Worried about me?" Dax asked with a smirk, but the exhaustion on his face belied his nonchalance.

When he didn't elaborate, Bane took her arm and murmured, "Only a blood descendant may challenge Kal'thorz. I'm still bound to you, leaving Dax the only viable option. The challenge had to be issued before our king demanded repayment of the debt you owe him."

Sabine's brow furrowed. "What?"

"A blood pact was forged centuries ago between Lachlina and one of my ancestors. Viz'gamoth shared the secrets of the prison, providing Lachlina with the means and ability to escape. By tapping into your ancestral magic, you received the benefit of such knowledge. The debt is now yours to repay."

Sabine squeezed her eyes shut and bit out a curse. Of course that was how Lachlina had escaped, through manipulation and deceit. And when Sabine allowed her to take possession and use that knowledge... She shook her head. It was no wonder her mother hadn't warned her in the book. She likely hadn't learned about the consequences until after she'd escaped.

"You need to tell her the rest," Malek said, crossing his arms over his chest.

"Dax and I are the last of Kal'thorz's bloodline," Bane said quietly. "He's ensured none of his other children survived to adulthood. Once Kal'thorz collects his boon and his strength increases, he'll become too powerful for us to kill. This is our one chance to stop him. If we fail, our people will suffer the consequences."

Fury had her snapping her eyes open, her skin glowing once again. Kal'thorz was truly a monster. How many of Bane and Dax's siblings had been murdered before they had a chance to live?

She curled her hands into fists and said, "What can we do to bolster Dax's position?"

"I can dust Kal'thorz before the fight begins," Blossom said. "He'll be too busy itching and squirming to fight very well."

Dax arched his brow. "Helping me, bug?"

"Better you as the demon king than him."

Dax chuckled. "I'll be damned if the winged nuisance isn't growing on me. It'll be a pity when she finally gets eaten."

Blossom blew a raspberry at him. Sabine looked across the field at where Kal'thorz was standing. Leena was facing him and they were touching palms, exchanging magic and power in an ancient dance. There were several other fae standing near him, and Sabine had no doubt they'd all be sharing their strength with their king.

"Malek, I need your knife."

When he unsheathed his weapon and handed it to her, Sabine cut off a small lock of her hair. She handed it to Blossom and said, "Hide yourself carefully and wait to strike moments before the challenge. If you think you've been spotted, do not approach him."

"Got it!" Blossom said, watching as the pixie quickly braided the hair around her wrist.

"How much more magic can you spare?" Bane asked Sabine. "We can't intervene once it begins, but you can bolster Dax's power before then."

When she hesitated, Malek said, "Her strength is all but gone."

"Malek's right," Sabine admitted grudgingly. "Blossom doesn't require more than a trifle. If we can negotiate for more time, I can replenish my magic once I step outside Harfanel. Barring that, I'm not sure what else to do."

"Not enough time," Bane said with a frown. "We only have a few minutes."

"Give Dax your darkness," Rika suggested.

Sabine's brow furrowed. "What?"

"Every time you killed someone, your aura turned darker," Rika explained. "When you healed Dax, I watched some of the darkness slough off and surround him. His aura is still thin, but yours is heavier than it should be. You're out of balance, but if you share your darkness with him, it'll even both of you out."

"No," Dax said with a growl. "Out of the question. I refuse."

"You think we would leave Sabine unprotected?" Bane demanded. "Don't be a fool. Kal'thorz is using the Heartstone to block your ability to heal yourself. He knew we would challenge him."

Dax scowled at him.

"I can decide for myself," Sabine snapped. She knew why Dax was hesitating, but it was ultimately her choice. Malek pressed his hand against her back, the contact helping to steady her.

"I don't understand," Rika said. "You did it before. Would it be so bad to do it again?"

Sabine turned toward Rika. They had little time, but she needed to explain and also warn Malek. "This information falls under the oath you swore to me when you agreed to keep my secrets and those of my allies."

When Rika nodded, Sabine continued. "What you're suggesting isn't a gift of magic. It's sharing your soul with another to strengthen them."

"I didn't know that was possible."

"After they forced the demons into the underworld, their souls became tied to the Heartstone. They cannot leave for any length of time without a strong enough magic user to anchor them. If they do, they eventually go mad and die."

Rika stared at her in stunned shock. "You anchor Bane, right? That's why he's okay?"

Sabine nodded. "I agreed to share the light of my soul with Bane, and in exchange, he's offered me his protection. He can travel beyond the confines of the underworld without consequences."

Her eyes widened. "Oh. That's why he has to remain close to you."

"Yes."

"Those pacts usually end badly for humans who try it," Malek warned her. "They don't have enough magic for a prolonged exchange."

Rika nodded her understanding.

"What are you not saying, Sabine?" Malek asked quietly. "Dax wouldn't be hesitating if this wasn't dangerous to you."

Dax snorted. "He's gotten to know her well, hasn't he?"

Bane made a noise of agreement.

Sabine sighed. "Dax is right to be concerned. Normally, sharing the light of someone's soul requires a blood bond. If Dax challenges Kal'thorz while he's in possession of my bond, it would transfer to the demon king upon his death."

Malek's jaw hardened. "And if you do this without a bond?"

"It'll deplete my remaining strength. If Kal'thorz wins, he'll not only have the boon he expects, but I won't be able to resist his influence. All the Unseelie fae will be in danger if I succumb to him."

"He'll enslave her," Dax said baldly.

Malek frowned, his arm tightening around her. "Absolutely not."

"I don't see another option," Sabine said. "If I don't do this, he'll kill Dax and then Bane will step in to challenge him. Dissolving my bond with Bane will weaken him. There's a good chance they'll both die, and for what? I'll still need to repay the debt, and I need an alliance with the demons."

"She's right," Bane said, crossing his arms over his chest. "I suspect part of the reason Kal'thorz ordered the fire imp to curse me was to break my ties to the Heartstone. Once Sabine terminates our bond, it will take time for me to regain my full strength—time we don't have."

"Cut your losses," Dax said. "Take Bane and leave the underworld. The dragon can get you out of here."

"Not going to happen," Sabine said and jabbed her finger against Dax's chest. "Back in Akros, you left me on Balkin's orders and nearly died trying to protect me. You will not run off again and sacrifice yourself for my sake. This is *my* decision."

When Dax opened his mouth to argue, Sabine stepped toward him and said quietly, "Please, Dax. After everything we've been through together, don't ask me to stand here and watch you die."

Dax muttered a curse and spun away from her. She knew it was playing dirty, but she couldn't stomach the idea of losing him again. He'd never been able to refuse her the scarce few times she'd asked for a favor. In fact, he'd always seemed to relish having her indebted to him.

Bane slipped into the demonic tongue, speaking harshly to his brother. Dax spun around, his eyes silvered and nostrils flaring. He bared his teeth at Bane and crouched as though he were about to attack. Rika gasped and stepped backward. Malek moved protectively in front of Rika.

Sabine swallowed. Dax was more terrifying in that moment than she'd ever seen him. It made her realize that the sparring between the brothers over the years had been little more than play fighting.

They argued for several minutes, nearly coming to blows before Bane turned back toward her. Dax still looked angry, but the worst of his fury had subsided.

"Dax will do it," Bane said, eyeing his brother in irritation. "In the event he falls, you must release me from my oath immediately. Kal'thorz cannot leave this field alive."

She looked at Malek, wanting his acceptance. This would put him in danger as well. They were bound together, so her decisions affected him.

Malek blew out a breath. "I don't like it, but I'll respect your decision, Sabine."

Sabine kissed Malek, knowing how difficult this was for him. With their deepened connection, she could feel how his instincts demand that he steal her away and keep her safe from all harm. That he loved her well enough to fight against his very nature spoke louder and more forcefully than mere words could describe. The next part would be harder still, yet she wouldn't do it unless he understood how much he meant to her.

She reached out to him across their bond and said, *"Kal'thorz never should have tried to kill Dax while he was glamoured as you. When I saw you dying on that field, I would have sacrificed everything and everyone to save your life. My love for you is the reason Dax still lives. You're mine, Malek, just as I'll remain yours. Always."*

His gaze softened as he reached up and brushed his hand across her cheek. *"You're my heart, Sabine. I would move the heavens for you if you wished it."*

Her heart broke at the thought of losing any of her friends, but Malek's death would have shattered her. Taking a steadying breath, she forced aside her emotions and faced Dax. Time was running out.

"There must be an equal trade to maintain the balance. Otherwise, there can be no pact between us."

"He can't swear an oath to serve you," Bane reminded her.

"I'm aware of that *now*," she said, irritated they'd kept all of this from her. If she'd known sooner, she could have taken steps to better protect them. Foolish demons. They always thought they knew better than anyone else.

"What are you suggesting?" Dax asked, his gaze sharpening on her.

Sabine straightened, having already considered it while they'd been arguing. "Since I arrived in the underworld, I have taken hundreds of demonic lives. For each death I share with you, you will commit an equal number of lives to my efforts in safeguarding my throne. Upon your death, you will return those souls to the Heartstone until the cycle begins anew."

For the first time since they arrived, a smile curved Bane's lips. "Clever girl."

Dax chuckled, his shoulders relaxing at her request. "Indeed. Even should our efforts fail, Kal'thorz won't be able to claim their strength for himself."

"Then we have an agreement?"

"We do." Dax held out his hand to her.

"Last chance to change your mind," Sabine said, placing her hand in his.

"There is no revoking the challenge once it's been issued," Dax said, wrapping his arm around her waist. She pressed her hand against his chest, feeling the steady beat of his heart beneath her fingertips.

Dax cupped her face, tracing the blunt edge of his claw along her cheek. "Would you walk away from your people and leave them to their fate?"

Sabine glanced at the demon king. Leena and two other fae were crumpled on the ground, their strength exhausted. Kal'thorz vibrated with power, his silvered eyes glaring daggers at Dax.

"No," she admitted. "He needs to be stopped."

Sabine took the dagger Bane offered and cut into her palm. Dax did the same before returning the weapon. Taking a deep breath, she reached for Dax and clasped his hand. Her power slammed into him, his back bowing from the sudden rush of it. His entire body glowed with a red so dark, it was nearly black.

He hauled her against himself, fisting her hair as he claimed her mouth. She returned the kiss, using his passion as a stepping-stone to push past Dax's defenses and delve into the innermost parts of his heart. Sabine relaxed against him and, for one perfect moment, allowed her aura to warm the chasm where Dax's soul had once been.

When the gods had stripped the demons of their power to

punish them, they'd sundered their souls and infused them into the Heartstone. The demon king was its designated caretaker, ordered by the gods to safeguard the Heartstone by infusing it into his body. Over time, through malicious deeds and violence, the darkness of those souls would slowly poison their appointed guardian.

Kal'thorz had been the Heartstone's guardian for a very long time.

Sabine reached for the lives she'd taken and offered them to Dax like a banquet feast. He deepened their kiss and drank them in, taking possession of their souls and binding them with his own power.

When she was empty and adrift, nearly limp in his arms, he broke their kiss. He was breathing heavily, his eyes still silvered as he gazed at her with a wild and insatiable hunger.

"We're out of time," Bane said quietly.

Rika sniffed and wiped away her tears. "I don't think I've ever seen anything that beautiful before."

Malek stepped forward and made a move to extricate Sabine, but Dax's grip on her tightened. He growled and clutched her close, his entire body pulsing with barely restrained power. She didn't have the strength to fight him, even if she'd wanted to.

Malek narrowed his eyes at Dax. "Release her."

"Dax," she murmured, reaching up to caress his face. He could be so fierce and headstrong, but she'd touched the place where his soul should have resided. There was a vulnerability there, just as it existed for all demons. No matter how much she wanted to soothe his hurt and share the warmth of her soul with him, it would be temporary. Bane had taught her that.

Dax's eyes flew back toward her, his expression tormented. He leaned into her touch, even though she knew it pained him. She was a reminder of everything his people had lost and what they still sought to regain. But as long as the gods remained absent from their world, that would never come to pass.

"Fuck Kal'thorz," Dax said on a groan. "Make me the offer again."

She smiled and cupped his face, kissing him lightly. "You're the fiercest of demons, and a warrior of renown. But we both know you'll never be mine."

"You're wrong."

She shook her head sadly. "No, I'm not. When I was lost and alone, you were the one who protected me and kept me safe. You taught me to be strong and how to fight for what I believe in. Without you, I wouldn't have survived these last ten years."

"Sabine," he whispered, his voice hoarse.

She pressed her fingers against his lips. "Your people need someone who can lead them with their whole heart, someone powerful yet also protective. That someone is you, Dax'than Versed. Don't allow them to continue to suffer at Kal'thorz's hands."

"Fuck," Dax said, his voice gruff and wrought with unspoken emotion. He lifted his head and pinned Malek with his gaze. "Should I fall, I want your word you'll get Sabine away from here as quickly as possible and protect her with your life. If you do this, any debts between us are resolved."

Malek gave the demon a curt nod. "It will be done."

Dax held her for another moment before finally releasing her. Malek wrapped his arms around her, cradling her against himself and surrounding her with his heated power. She leaned into his touch, breathing in the scent of burned leaves while tears streamed down her face.

"I don't envy you, brother," Dax said, still gazing at Sabine. "I only had a brief glimpse of all she is, and I'll feel the loss of her for the rest of my days. I'm not sure I'd survive the loss if I'd been tied to her for years."

"Nor I," Bane said quietly.

Rika walked up to Dax and offered him a dagger that pulsed with magic. "May it fight as well for you as it did for me."

Dax studied her for a moment and then took the weapon with a curt nod. Sabine watched with a heavy heart while her former protector marched across the field to where his destiny and the Huntsman awaited.

Chapter Thirty-Four

*O*nce Kal'thorz and Dax were facing each other in the center of the field, the Huntsman raised his staff. In a rich baritone that echoed through their minds, he said, *"The time of determining and challenge has come. In penance for the betrayal of that which you were sworn to protect, your souls have been sentenced to an eternity in the Heartstone."*

He brought the staff down sharply, causing the ground to rumble beneath them. *"Descendants of Tav'shesin, Trespasser of the Hall of Awakening and Betrayer of the Tuatha Dé, one among you has issued challenge for the right to possess the Heartstone and act as guardian. Step forward."*

Dax kneeled before Vestior and said, "I am Dax'than Versed, second-born son of Kal'thorz Versed, Guardian of the Underworld and Keeper of the Heartstone."

Vestior turned toward Kal'thorz. *"Do you recognize this challenger?"*

Kal'thorz inclined his head, his horns shimmering with power. "He is of my blood."

"Then rise, challenger, and face your opponent."

Dax stood, legs apart and shoulders squared. He stretched his neck and pinned Kal'thorz with his determined stare. Sabine felt the world take a breath and hold it, awaiting the outcome of the battle. The winner would determine not only the future of the demons in the underworld, but her own people were now irrevocably tied to Dax's fate.

Vestior swept his staff in a large circular pattern. A transparent beam of light sprang up from the ground, shimmering gold with a faint sheen of red at the edges. *"None may step over the barrier upon pain of death, their souls forever claimed."*

"He's created a pocket of the in-between," Sabine murmured, her eyes widening. She hadn't realized it was possible for him to merge realities in that fashion. But it explained why Bane had warned them they couldn't help Dax once the challenge began.

Rika cocked her head and squinted at the circle. "I don't think the Huntsman really looks like that. There's something about him—"

Sabine clamped a hand over the seer's mouth and whispered urgently, "Shh. Never speak of it."

Rika gaped at her and hastily nodded.

At some unspoken signal, the two demons attacked. Their claws were like blades, flashing so fast they were nearly a blur. The demons grappled together, each attempting to dominate the other with their respective powers and fighting prowess.

They each fought with a ruthless intensity that went beyond vicious. Sabine had spent years sparring and training with Dax, but it was clear he'd been holding back. Whether it was the boost she'd given him or simply natural skill, Dax's fierce skill and agility rivaled that of an apex predator.

Despite Dax's ferocity, Kal'thorz clearly held the advantage. He hadn't maintained his position as ruler of the demons through complacency. Each of his movements was carefully orchestrated and lethal, honed by centuries of experience. Sabine winced when his claws raked across Dax's chest, blood splattering on the ground.

Blossom landed on Sabine's shoulder, breathing heavily. "Whew. That was rough. I almost didn't make it out in time. The itching should commence any second."

"Well done," Sabine murmured, jerking in Malek's arms when Kal'thorz landed another strike. "Let's hope it gives Dax more of an advantage."

Malek's arm tightened around her. "We've got trouble."

Sabine turned to see at least a dozen warriors moving in their direction. She inhaled sharply, recognizing the terrifying warriors from the leather harnesses strapped across their chests. Her hand immediately went to the sheath strapped to her thigh. She gripped the hilt of one of her daggers, watching their approach.

"It's the morthal," Bane said, his eyes flashing silver. "They've been ordered to subdue Sabine and kill the rest of us. We need to buy Dax some time. If they can bring Sabine to Kal'thorz, he's still within his rights to demand repayment, even through the barrier. The debt was forged before the challenge was issued."

"Can you stand on your own?" Malek asked her. "I can't shift again so quickly. We're going to have to fight them."

Sabine nodded, not bothering to tell him she could do little more than remain upright. He likely sensed her exhaustion through their bond. He unsheathed his sword, readying himself.

"Try to keep out of their line of sight," Sabine said to Rika. "They're masters at daggers, both throwing and striking. You need to keep as far away from them as possible."

"Got it," Rika said, unsheathing her blade.

"We will fight at your side," a woman said from behind them.

Sabine turned at the sight of Rakva and Rothir, the two demons who had pledged to protect her while she was in Harfanel. Bane gave them a curt nod.

In the next second, the attackers were on them. Malek fought like a man possessed, each thrust and strike of his sword forcing the demons back. Bane switched to a dirtier and grittier style of fighting, better suited to the back alleys of Akros. He threw punches, kicked one of the demons in the balls, and grappled with warriors who were more accustomed to dancing with blades. It seemed to work; his modified backroom brawling was throwing off the well-orchestrated techniques of the morthal.

Sabine remained close to Rika, wanting to protect the more inexperienced seer. The morthal appeared to be focusing on who they believed to be the largest threats: Malek, Bane, and the two demon guards. Sabine didn't intend to squander that advantage.

"Blossom!" Sabine called, needing a distraction. "Thin the herd!"

"On it!" she shouted, diving over and under the attackers. She was a shimmering whirlwind, scattering pixie dust everywhere. A few of the demons sneezed, while others tried to grab the pixie.

One of them darted forward as though making a move to grab Sabine. She kicked out her leg and struck the demon hard, causing him to stagger. Unfortunately, Sabine wasn't quite steady on her feet. It had been too much exertion. Her vision darkened around the edges, and she struggled to take a deep breath.

Rika dove forward, thrusting her sword in his chest and finishing him off. She turned toward the next one, waiting until Bane had partially disabled him before stabbing with her sword. If they survived this, Bane was definitely going to need to work on Rika's technique. But her clean-up efforts were appreciated.

A demon grabbed Sabine, hauling her against himself. Her instinct was to fight, but she allowed her body to go completely limp. When he adjusted for her dead weight, she straightened quickly and rammed her head under his chin. He loosened his grip, and she spun around, slicing her dagger across his throat. Hot blood sprayed over her, and she had a brief thought to warn Rika about the dangers of demon blood.

The world spun. Sabine fell to her knees, her palms biting into the blood-soaked ground. The clash of weapons rang in her ears. There were too many to fight. She couldn't help them, not with her strength and magic fully exhausted. She stared down at the marks on her wrist. The goddess was silent within her, either angry at being evicted or equally drained.

Someone grabbed Sabine again and hauled her upright. She stared into the silvered eyes of an unfamiliar demon. He grinned in triumph.

Oh, hell no. Narrowing her eyes, she gathered her remaining strength and warned, "If you don't take your hands off me, you're going to find your horns shoved so far up your ass, they'll be caught in your throat."

He hesitated. She lifted her hand as though to use her magic, and he released her. She stumbled backward. Before she could count her bluff as a victory, another demon swooped in and grabbed her.

Sabine blew out a breath. This was absurd. She tried to push him away, but her efforts were pathetically weak. Furious at her own shortcomings, she reached for Malek and Bane through their bonds.

"Sabine!" Malek shouted, kicking aside an attacker to

reach her. He roared in fury as four more leaped at him, blocking his path. He had already been injured before the fight had begun, but there were more cuts along his side, and his left arm wasn't working right. Bane was equally over-whelmed.

"Let her go!" Blossom shrieked, dive-bombing the demon. He swatted the pixie away and hefted Sabine over his shoulder.

"Bad move," Sabine muttered, knowing Blossom would be pissed. She might be little, but Blossom could hold an ogre-sized grudge. The demon yelped, jiggling Sabine as he danced away from the pixie's attack.

"Get that damn bug away from me!"

Blossom shrieked, dive-bombing him again. "Not. A. Bug."

"Take that, sucker!" Rika shouted and slashed the demon's ankle. Sabine landed hard enough to knock the air out of her lungs. She tried to push herself up again, but her efforts were sluggish. It was like moving through molasses.

Blossom landed on the ground near her and said, "Get to the in-between! They can't touch you there!"

"I'm a little low on magic if you haven't noticed," she managed to say.

Blossom reared back and smacked Sabine in the middle of her forehead. "You don't need magic. You *are* magic. Do it! I'll push you through."

She didn't know if this would even work, but she was a liability the longer she remained here. Fumbling with her dagger, she sliced her hand. As the blood welled to the surface, she used the brief burst of power to force a hole through reality. She rolled on the ground and slid into the in between.

And rolled right back out into the center of the challenge circle.

Crap.

Dax and Kal'thorz were still fighting, oblivious to everything except each other. They were both wounded, but the savageness of their attack hadn't lessened. Dax had gouged out one of Kal'thorz's eyes and broken the tip of one of his horns, and Dax no longer had the use of one of his arms. They hadn't noticed her yet, but the same couldn't be said for the Huntsman.

He stared down at her with none of the civility he'd shown previously. The shadows comprising his dark cloak had deepened. His eyes glowed like red embers, scorching in their intensity. If she had the strength to stand, she'd be fleeing for her life.

He flicked his wrist, lifting her into the air and repositioning her so she was standing beside him. With strong air bindings wrapped around her, he kept her upright.

"Explain yourself," he demanded. *"It is within my rights to claim your soul. Why should I not do so?"*

Sabine winced. *"Technically, your instructions said no one could step over the barrier. I rolled through."*

He paused. *"You created a portal?"*

"I don't know. I was trying to get away from the demon trying to abduct me. The in-between seemed like a safer bet."

He didn't respond. Instead, he turned back toward Dax and Kal'thorz. Sabine tried to catch a glimpse of Malek and Bane, but there were too many demons obstructing the view. She had no idea if they were okay.

"Your companions still live."

Sabine squeezed her eyes shut and nodded in relief. They might live for the time being, but every second this challenge went on brought them closer to that edge. She needed to find some way to motivate Dax without doing anything that gave Kal'thorz the opportunity to demand repayment. Timing was going to be critical.

When they'd been living back in Akros, Dax had been instrumental in teaching her not to rely on her magic like most of the fae. It went against her nature, but it had proven to be effective in keeping her hidden.

She'd learned to maneuver carefully around the demon brothers. Dax, in particular, had always been more volatile. Certain actions or situations that evoked strong emotional responses within her always seemed to bring him to a frenzied state. If she could touch upon one of those triggers again, it might be enough to give him a temporary boost of power.

Passion? Or pain?

She darted a quick glance at the Huntsman, but he didn't acknowledge her. Still, she needed to ask. All of their lives depended on Dax winning this challenge.

"Would you be willing to release my restraints?"

The Huntsman turned toward her, his glowing eyes nearly searing her soul. *"There are consequences to interfering in a challenge."*

"I will not directly interfere with either combatant," Sabine said with promise. *"You have my word that I will not use any magic or mundane weapon to influence either Kal'thorz or Dax during the challenge."*

The Huntsman didn't reply. Sabine was about ready to abandon all hope when the bindings suddenly fell away. She fell to the ground with a thud. *Ouch.* She was going to be black and blue for days at this rate. Still, she couldn't fault the Huntsman. She hadn't asked him to nicely put her down, and he was likely still annoyed with her for entering the circle.

She hoped this worked.

Focusing on all the heartache and suffering she'd experienced in the past few months, she replayed every painful memory. She recalled seeing Malek hurt and nearly dying, and the desperation she'd felt when she thought she'd lost him. She remembered the way Dax had said good-bye to her back in Akros after taking her power and how Bane suffered torment in the dwarven jail. Each precious and heart-wrenching memory was resurrected, the pain as fresh and vibrant as when it had been new.

She'd lived a lifetime of pain, and she allowed it to cover her like a shroud. With tears streaming down her cheeks, she took a deep breath and let out a soul-shattering scream of anguish.

Dax froze, his head whipping toward her. "Sabine!" he shouted, his skin turning a brilliant red as he summoned the vestiges of his remaining power.

Kal'thorz leaped at Dax, his claws digging in and shredding Dax's left thigh.

She gasped. Oh, gods. She'd erred and badly. Kal'thorz was going to kill him. Before she could warn him, Dax roared and grabbed Kal'thorz by the horns. He flipped the demon king into the air and slammed him to the ground, snapping his horns off. Straddling him, he yanked him up and snapped his neck. Kal'thorz dropped to the ground.

Dax pulled out the dagger Rika had given him and cut off his father's head, ensuring he was well and truly dead. Tossing it aside, he raced to Sabine and gathered her in his arms. His gaze roamed over her, lingering on her cut hand and the bruises marring her skin.

"Who the fuck was it? Who touched you?" Dax snarled, his expression thunderous. "I'll kill them."

She swallowed and shook her head. He'd done it. He'd truly managed the impossible and was too far gone with bloodlust to realize the implications of his actions.

Pressing her hand against his blood-spattered cheek, she said, "I'll be fine, Dax. So will you."

He narrowed his eyes. "Explain."

"You've won, Dax'than Versed," she said, glancing at Kal'thorz's mutilated body. "The Heartstone is yours for the taking, including everything that goes along with it."

Dax went still. He stared at her for a long time before looking back at Kal'thorz. When he faced her again, his expression was blank.

"Dax?"

He didn't answer. Instead, he stood and limped to the former demon king. Using his claws, he sliced through Kal'thorz's chest harness to reveal the pulsing red stone that had been embedded into his skin.

Dax carefully carved the Heartstone out of his father's body. It fit in the palm of his hand, and the light contained within it was almost as bright as the sun. He cradled it in his hands, his expression filled with reverence as he gazed upon the ember containing the souls of his people.

Using his dagger, he made a nick in the center of his chest, just over his breastbone. He shoved the glowing ember inside.

His back bowed from the sudden rush of power. His body lifted into the air as bright red beams of light burst out of skin and filled the challenger's circle. Sabine gasped, watching as his injuries knit together and he accepted the Heartstone's strength.

"*You play a dangerous game, child,*" Vestior said. "*Meddling with the natural order of things often has unforeseen consequences.*"

"*Perhaps, but I don't regret my part in it.*"

The Huntsman gave her a curt nod. He lifted his staff, then brought it down with a resounding thud. The barrier fell away, merging the circle back into reality. At the sight of Dax, every demon in the field lowered their weapons and stopped fighting to kneel before their new king.

Dax ignored them and walked back to Sabine, holding out his hand to help her stand. He wrapped his arm around her waist and grinned at her. "Well, beautiful, looks like I'm the one you're indebted to now."

She pressed her head against his chest. "I'm too tired to go a round with you."

"I can do a little something about that," Dax murmured, tilting her chin up with one clawed finger. He pressed his lips against hers and devoured her mouth. Dax had never been a gentle lover, and his kiss was almost punishing. Seductive power flowed into her, its rich and heady taste over-whelming her senses.

Sabine broke the kiss to stare up into his silvered eyes in surprise. She pressed her fingers against her lips, the power boost helping to revive her. Dax had never possessed the ability to share magic with her before. Despite their circum-stances, she couldn't help but be intrigued. "New ability?"

His mouth curved upward. "Let's just say that when I finally get you back into bed, we'll have a very interesting night ahead of us."

She laughed. "I think you're going to have your hands full with other duties for a while."

"A pity that you're right," he murmured and winked at her. "It'll give you time to grow weary of your dragon. Meet me in the throne room after you've gathered your strength. There are a few things we need to discuss."

He released her and prowled toward the command tent, where Kal'thorz's former retinue awaited. Sabine watched him for a moment, wondering what sort of leader he would become. In Akros, he'd led his people through fear and an iron fist, but he also protected them. His followers had been fiercely loyal, and despite their claims that he was merciless when crossed, he'd had their respect.

Sabine turned, searching the crowd for any sign of Malek.

At the sight of him standing safely beside Rika and Bane, she let out the breath she'd been holding. Even covered in blood, wounded, his clothing torn to rags, and with exhaustion darkening his features, he was the most beautiful sight Sabine had ever seen.

With his sword still clutched in his hand, he pushed his way through the throng of kneeling demons to reach her. She stared at him, this fierce dragon whom she loved and trusted above all others. It hadn't been his fight, but he'd stood beside her and fought, willing to make the ultimate sacrifice to protect her.

Dropping his sword to the ground beside her, he gathered her in his arms. Sabine threw her arms around him and buried her face against his neck.

"Malek," she whispered, pouring all of her emotion into that one word. She loved him beyond reason and beyond all boundaries. For him, she would sacrifice anything—even the crown she held dear.

He pulled back and kissed her, flooding her senses with his magic. She fell into his touch, riding the flames of his dragonfire as he shared his power with her. Her lips parted on a gasp, and he deepened the kiss, his touch warming her soul and balancing the darkness Dax had left behind. His magic trailed over her skin in a heated embrace until the world around them fell away.

She clutched him tighter, wanting everything he offered. With each touch and caress, he awakened something within her. It no longer mattered to her that he was a dragon, the feared enemy of the fae. She knew, without a doubt, she would never give him up. She couldn't, without destroying herself in the process.

He broke their kiss and pressed his forehead against hers. In a ragged voice, he said, "When you disappeared, I thought I'd lost you."

"Never," she said, cupping his face and looking up into his dark-blue eyes. "I'm yours, just as you're mine, Malek Rish'-dan, from now until the last of the magic fades from this world."

He lifted the hand she'd cut and pressed a kiss against her palm. "Are you all right?"

She smiled up at him and kissed him lightly. "I will be, but we need to get those wounds of yours tended. I'll regain the rest of my strength soon enough. Dax wants to see us in the throne room after we've rested."

Rika walked toward them, her sword practically dragging on the ground. Her hair was disheveled, and dirt and blood covered her all the way down to her toes. Other than a gash on her arm that had already been treated with a light dusting of pixie dust, she didn't appear wounded. Blossom was sitting on her shoulder and flew to Sabine as they moved closer.

"You did it!" Blossom said with a grin. "I knew you could."

The Huntsman turned toward them and said, "*Pixie, you have violated the edict cast down on all lesser fae by manipulating a doorway without leave. How do you plead?*"

Blossom's eyes rounded. "Um… Could it have been a different pixie? There are a lot of us, you know."

The Huntsman continued to stare at her.

"Maybe the goat did it?"

He didn't respond.

"An accident?"

Sabine straightened and displayed her injured palm. "The doorway was created by blood and magic. Blossom was not responsible."

Blossom landed on Sabine's shoulder and whispered, "Actually… I might have had something to do with *where* you landed. I was worried you'd get lost again or end up in the garden. I think the goddess is a little grumpy."

Mentally cursing, Sabine squeezed her eyes shut. It took several breaths before she was calm enough to open her eyes and face the Huntsman. If Blossom hadn't acted in the manner she had, Dax wouldn't have won. Sabine could right now be Kal'thorz's captive and standing over the bodies of her friends.

Squaring her shoulders, Sabine said, "If Blossom has violated any edict, it was to keep me safe from harm and to protect the lives of others. I will accept whatever punishment you dictate on her behalf."

Malek tensed. "Sabine…"

She shook her head and continued to focus on the Huntsman.

He studied her for a long time and then turned to address Blossom. *"You have been found guilty of your crime, no matter the mitigating circumstances. While Sabin'theoria has been granted permission to travel freely through doorways, she lacks the knowledge or a suitable teacher."*

Blossom gulped and clung to Sabine's neck, pixie dust shedding everywhere. "Sorry, so sorry. I didn't want you to die, Sabine."

"The punishment is as follows," the Huntsman said. *"You are both hereby banned from manipulating any doorways to the in-between for one lunar cycle. During that time, the pixie will serve as an instructor to explain the principles and theories behind manipulating doorways. At the end of your sentence, your knowledge will be assessed."*

He brought his staff down on the ground with a thud and stepped back into the doorway behind him, disappearing from view. The vines that had been holding it in place withered and crumbled into dust.

Sabine swallowed. "I think we just got very, very lucky."

Blossom straightened. "No kidding! I thought he was going to ban me from the garden or something equally bad.

Now I get to be the teacher and you're the student! Our first task is to find a demon horn without an owner."

Sabine arched her brow. "A demon horn?"

She nodded. "Decorative inspiration. No, wait. A focusing object! Yeah. That's it."

Sabine turned toward Rika and asked, "Are you all right? You weren't hurt, were you?"

Rika shook her head and gestured at her arm. "Blossom said pixie dust could help counteract demon poison. She dusted me to make sure."

"Good," Sabine said and then looked at Bane. He was staring at Kal'thorz's body, a mixture of conflicted emotions on his face. She leaned in close to Malek and said, "I need a minute alone with him."

When Malek nodded in understanding, Sabine walked to Bane and wrapped her arms around his waist. He tensed for a moment and then pulled her closer. For a long time, they stayed like that until he finally broke the silence.

"I wanted him dead, Sabine. I envisioned seeing him like this for more than a century. We plotted and planned, carefully maneuvering our positions to achieve this result."

She curled into his side and said gently, "He was your father, Bane. No matter what he was or did, some ties hurt when they're broken or betrayed."

He flicked his gaze toward her. "You think I mourn him?"

She tilted her head. "Don't you?"

"You are too Seelie at times," he muttered.

She pressed her hand against his cheek, drawing his attention back to her. "Seelie or Unseelie, I understand loss. Do you think because you hated him that you won't mourn him? You and Dax may have been the ones who set this plan in motion, but you weren't alone in shouldering the responsibility."

He lowered his head. "Do you want the truth, Sabine?"

She nodded. "If you wish to share it."

"The Heartstone eventually corrupts its guardian," he bit out. "It takes centuries, but eventually, the weight of those souls twists something inside the owner. That is the other part of our curse, and why only one of Tav'shesin's descendants can hold the ember in their body."

Her gaze drifted to Dax, who was issuing orders. She'd suspected as much after learning everything about the Heartstone. When she'd felt the weight of those deaths and then the lightness after giving them to Dax, she'd wondered how and if it would change him.

"When I chose you over the Heartstone, it wasn't simply because of how I feel about you," Bane said quietly.

"You feel guilty because Dax took up the mantle?"

"Shouldn't I?" he asked, his tone sharp.

Sabine straightened and said, "No. You should see this as an opportunity. The two of us have a better chance of preventing the same fate from happening to Dax. What demon king has ever had a fae queen willing to do whatever's necessary to save his life?"

Bane studied her for a long time. "You would, wouldn't you?"

"You both saved my life," Sabine said, putting her hands on her hips. "Isn't it my turn to do the same? Fortunately, we have a few centuries to figure out how to stop him from turning into a demented despot."

Bane shook his head and chuckled. "You are a priceless treasure, Sabin'theoria. If I hadn't already sworn to serve you for the rest of my days, I would do so all over again."

"And I would accept without hesitation." Sabine took his clawed hand in hers, leading him away from his father's body. "We need to meet Dax in the throne room soon, and I'd like to get cleaned up and changed before then. It's been a very long night, and I suspect I'm going to need some liquid courage before Dax claims the boon I owe him."

"Shit," Bane muttered. "I forgot about that. The dragon is going to have some issues with this."

Sabine looked at Malek and sighed. "I suspect you're right."

Chapter Thirty-Five

Sabine entered the throne room for the second time since they'd arrived in the underworld. The room was packed with onlookers, while several fire imps and goblins worked to clear the rest of the rubble from Lachlina's explosive temper.

Malek, Bane, and Rika walked beside her, but Blossom had elected to remain perched on her shoulder and hidden from view. Masquerading as a moth, Blossom was convinced the demons would eat her simply on principle after she'd dusted so many of them during the battle. Sabine didn't argue. She wasn't willing to tempt fate either.

Dax was lounging on his new throne, one of his legs haphazardly thrown over the armrest. The skulls seemed to grin, their jeweled eyes sparkling as though they were privy to some dark secret. Sabine recognized a few of the demons standing close by, but it was Leena who caught and held her attention.

The dark-haired fae woman was standing beside the throne, wearing a thick silver collar around her neck that glowed with runic symbols. A heavy chain was looped through the collar and the shackles around her wrists. Dax held the end of the chained leash loosely in his hand, but he appeared to be ignoring Leena.

Sabine frowned, eyeing the fae woman. Leena may have been the one to cast the illusion during the battle, but the look of unbridled hatred on her face made Sabine wonder if she hadn't been acting strictly on Kal'thorz's orders.

At some unspoken signal, everyone in the audience fell silent and turned to watch Sabine's approach. She stopped a short distance away from the throne and waited. Dax had always enjoyed playing games, and Sabine suspected Leena was going to play a part in the next round. Sabine didn't mind entertaining him while he asserted his authority over his people, but there were limits to how much she would tolerate from him.

"I used to think Bane's ass would be the one sitting here," Dax mused aloud, absently swinging Leena's chain as he watched the fire imps repair a hole in the roof.

"Better you than me," Bane said drily. "That chair looks like it chafes."

Dax chuckled and turned his head toward them. Giving Sabine a lascivious wink, he patted his lap and asked, "Care to join me, beautiful?"

Sabine's mouth twitched. "I'm afraid there's another throne that has a prior claim over me."

"A pity," he said and rose to his feet.

Tugging on Leena's chain, he forced the fae woman to stumble after him as he descended the stairs. Sabine tensed, watching as the woman nearly tripped over her feet. Malek straightened as well, his hand lingering on the hilt of his sword.

"Kal'thorz was remiss in making the proper introductions when you arrived. Allow me to rectify that." Dax gestured toward Leena and said, "Sabine, I'd like you to meet Leen'ellesar of the Seelie, sister to King Cadan'ellesar."

Sabine couldn't hide her shocked horror. "You're my aunt? My father's sister?"

Leena sneered at her. "I claim no ties of blood with you, dragon whore. My brother should have tossed you to the hounds when you were born."

Dax yanked on the chain, sending her sprawling on the ground. He pressed his boot on her back, holding her there. "Now, now. I warned you about your temper. Besides, weren't you trying to fuck the dragon?"

"I wanted to kill him, you listegth," Leena spat, referring to the scaled bottom-feeders that wallowed in their own waste at the bottom of lava pools.

Dax grabbed her hair and yanked her head back. He slammed her head on the ground, knocking her unconscious. "Bitch never shuts up," Dax said with a growl.

Sabine startled at the sudden brutality, even as she understood the need for it. Dax needed to assert himself and couldn't permit a perceived challenge.

Malek pressed his hand against Sabine's back, his light touch offering comfort. She barely resisted the urge to curl into him. Gods. What had she done to these people to make them hate her so much?

It took all of her effort to adopt a court mien and keep her expression neutral. Refusing to look at her aunt, she asked, "How long has she been here?"

"A few centuries, but it only took a couple of decades to break her in," Dax said with a shrug. "Most of your people don't have the ability to withstand our brand of torture for long. Kal'thorz thought she might make herself useful in subduing you, provided she didn't try to kill you outright."

Sabine swallowed. "What do you intend to do with her?"

"That depends on you."

When she stared at him in puzzlement, Bane explained, "If you wish her dead, we'll end her life and send her head back to Faerie with your regards. However, you may wish to use her as leverage. It's unknown how much fondness Cadan'ellesar has for his sister."

Sabine took a deep breath, feeling the weight of another life settle on her shoulders. She didn't want to make this decision. There had been enough death in the past few days to last her several lifetimes.

Her first inclination was to order Leena's release, but it wasn't practical. Judging by the bitterness and hate on her face, Leena would do everything possible to kill Sabine. She couldn't risk allowing Leena to go free, but she didn't want to order her death either.

Sabine lifted her gaze to meet Dax's eyes and said, "If she's fared well enough here for the past several centuries, she might as well remain until she can be of some use to me."

The corner of Dax's mouth curved. He snapped his fingers, and a nearby guard stepped forward and took possession of Leena's chain. He threw her over his shoulder and carried her out of the throne room.

"With that being settled, there are a few other matters we need to discuss."

"I'm listening."

"The first involves the human," Dax said, his gaze landing on Rika.

"Dax, she's under my protection," Sabine warned, knowing his penchant for toying with humans.

"You'll get her back in the same condition," he said, motioning for Rika to step forward. The seer worried her lower lip, but she did as instructed.

Dax unhooked his dagger and sheath from his belt loop and handed it to her. "I believe this belongs to you."

Her mouth dropped open. "It's for me?"

"No, the other human who offered me her weapon before stepping into battle," Dax said with a growl. "Take the damn thing."

Rika beamed a smile at him. "Th—"

Bane cleared his throat before she could thank Dax. Rika flushed and said, "I mean, it's a great weapon. I love it."

She darted forward and kissed Dax's cheek. Sabine had to bite her cheek to keep from laughing at the bemused expression on Dax's face.

Bane snorted at his discomfort.

"Teach the human how to use it properly," Dax growled at Bane. Rika clutched the dagger against her chest, practically bouncing with enthusiasm.

Bane chuckled. "I'll see what I can do, My King."

Dax narrowed his eyes. "Fuck you."

Bane gave a mocking bow, earning a growl from Dax.

"And now for our last order of business," Dax said, his gaze sharpening on Sabine. "We need to discuss the matter of your debt."

Malek tensed at her side. Sabine reached for his arm, sending a trace of soothing power over him. This had the potential to go very badly. "What does the demon king seek in exchange for the knowledge used to leave the prison?"

Dax leaned forward and said, "As it happens, I'm thinking about holding it in reserve."

Sabine blinked at him. "What?"

He chuckled. "For ten years, I wanted you indebted to me. Now that it's happened, I find I rather enjoy it."

Sabine gaped at him. "You can't be serious."

Dax smirked at Malek. "Maybe I should have her wear my mark. I can think of a few interesting locations I could put it. Or better yet, maybe I'll get a little creative and have her work it off in bed."

"I'll kill you," Malek said, taking a threatening step

forward. "You fucking touch her, and I'll bring this entire place down on your head."

"Try it, worm," Dax challenged.

Sabine stepped between them, pressing her hands against their chests to keep them apart. "While this is rather entertaining, I'm not going to run around with such a sizeable debt hanging over my head. We need to resolve this, Dax. Now. And stop baiting Malek. We both know you prefer your bed partners willing, not simply fulfilling some twisted obligation."

Dax shrugged. "A pity. You'll tire of the dragon soon enough, I expect."

She sighed and lowered her hands. "What do you want from me?"

Dax motioned toward a guard standing nearby who was holding a black box. The guard stepped forward and opened the lid to reveal one of the most unusual weapons Sabine had ever seen.

It was slightly larger than a throwing dagger with a curved and deadly looking blade that gleamed with a faint reddish luminesce. The hilt of the weapon was peculiar, made from some sort of organic matter Sabine couldn't identify. Dark symbols that looked demonic in origin had been etched into the hilt.

"We call it Tav'shesin's Regret. The blade is a weapon of power, entrusted to us by the goddess Lachlina centuries ago. The hilt was made from the intestines of our first king, Tav'shesin, before the gods ordered a halt to his torture."

Sabine jerked her head upward to stare at him. "This is one of the artifacts used to seal the Dragon Portal."

"Yes. I understand you've been looking for it."

Her brow furrowed. She glanced at Bane, but he shook his head to indicate he hadn't discussed it with Dax.

"How?"

"Before he departed, the Huntsman informed me of the details involving your search," Dax said, his voice clipped and his features tightening. "The boon I ask is for you to take possession of this weapon's power."

"Um, Sabine?" Blossom whispered from under Sabine's hair. "The goddess is really mad that the Huntsman is involved. I have a bad feeling about this."

Sabine froze, staring at the weapon like it were a venomous snake. It appeared Vestior had decided to manipulate the situation, even after he'd warned her of doing the same. Now she was potentially caught between two incredibly powerful gods. Lachlina wanted the portal to remain closed, while Vestior had made it clear that it needed to remain open. Lovely.

Either way, she had to take possession of the artifact. What she chose to do with the power once she attained the final portal key was another matter.

She blew out a breath. This was going to be a disaster.

"Are you sure about this?" Malek murmured in a low voice.

She glanced at him sideways. "The Huntsman didn't give me much of a choice, did he?"

Blossom folded her wings tightly against her back. "She has to do it or be forsworn. Her magic will break, and she'll die."

Malek muttered a curse.

Bane motioned toward Dax. "You might want to clear the throne room. If this goes the way I expect, the backlash will be the equivalent of what happened earlier. Rika should go back to our suite. This won't be safe for her."

Sabine looked at Blossom. "You need to go with Rika. If this artifact was entrusted to the demons, it will be tied to their power. I don't know how it'll affect you."

"You'll be careful?" Blossom asked, flying to Rika's shoulder.

Sabine nodded. "You have my word."

Dax let out a sharp whistle, and the onlookers scattered. He grabbed one of the heavily armored demons and ordered him to escort Rika back to her suite and stand guard.

Once the room was clear of everyone except her, Dax, Bane, and Malek, Sabine took a deep breath and stepped forward. She reached into the box and curled her fingers around the hilt of the dagger.

Nothing happened at first.

She started to relax and then a slight chill wrapped around her hand. It swirled around her wrist, traveling up her arm like icy fingers. Her breath frosted and her teeth chattered as the room's temperature plummeted. Her hair froze, forming icicles at the ends while her clothing hardened into icy sheets.

"Sabine?" Malek asked, reaching for her before abruptly pulling back. "Dammit. I don't know if I can touch her without the artifact killing her. Something's not right."

"S-s-s-stay back," Sabine said through chattering teeth. Until she reached an accord with the power contained within the artifact, it was too dangerous for him to get close. Whatever was happening to her didn't seem to affect anyone else. She needed to keep it that way.

"What the hell is going on?" Dax demanded as snow formed at Sabine's feet. "We're in a fucking volcano, and she's making it snow?"

"I've touched that knife myself without an issue," Bane said with a frown. "This is different from the other artifacts. I would have expected fire, not ice."

Malek scowled. "I don't give a damn what it is. She's going to freeze to death if we don't stop it or get her warm."

Warmth sounded fantastic right about now. Her feet had

gone numb, and she couldn't feel her fingers. They'd frozen around the hilt of the knife. The power was still growing, its icy chill penetrating deep until it felt almost as though it had touched her soul.

It was more than simply cold. This was the absence of all warmth and life. It was the touch of death.

Drowsiness crept over her. It was getting harder to keep her eyes open. Malek's skin glowed, heat radiating from his skin. Gods. She wanted to wrap herself up in him and never let him go.

"If I can't touch you, I'll do what I can to keep you warm," Malek said, his glow becoming even brighter. Perspiration dripped down his face, and she knew it was costing him a great deal to use his dragonfire while in human form.

Unfortunately, it wasn't warming the ice that was freezing her internally. The power of the blade had penetrated beyond her defenses. If anything, Malek's efforts made her even more aware of the cold taking root inside her.

A familiar voice slipped into her thoughts like a shadow and whispered, *"He must not intervene, child. You must embrace death before you can understand it."*

She tried to open her mouth to tell Malek to stop, but her lips were already numb. Unable to form words, she tried to reach for him over their mental connection, but her efforts were awkward and clunky. She sent a desperate glance at Bane, mentally begging him to intervene.

"Stop!" Bane grabbed Malek's arm and yanked him away from her. Malek's light dimmed and then faded. "Look at her! I don't know what the hell is happening, but she doesn't want your help. If you kill yourself using dragonfire in your human form, she'll never forgive me."

"I will not let her die," Malek snapped. "Long-lived the fae might be, but they're not immortal. I will not lose her."

"Are all dragons this stupid when they decide to take a mate?"

"A mate? Are you fucking kidding me?" Dax demanded.

Malek went eerily still. Whatever he said to Bane and Dax was too low to be overheard.

Despite the whispered words she'd heard, Sabine fought against the power. She would accept it, but she wouldn't allow it to take her over. It was no use. The cold kept pushing her down, tightening its grip on her the more she struggled. Her vision blurred, her thoughts becoming fuzzy and confusing.

"*Death comes to us all, child,*" the voice whispered. "*Embrace yours.*"

She was so tired. It would be so easy to let go. Part of her wanted to keep fighting, but the cold chill of death was incredibly seductive. She startled at the thought. No. She'd never give in to death so easily. This wasn't right.

Or was it?

When she'd fought the power in the other artifacts, she'd nearly died. This one felt as though it was also trying to kill her, but what if there was something more to it? If Lachlina and Vestior had wanted her dead, she would be. There had been ample opportunities for them to have taken her life. No. They wanted something from her. It was a risk, but she had no choice.

Sabine released her inhibitions and surrendered to the magic. The chill surrounded her, cradling her like a death shroud. She fell into darkness, lost in the artifact's power.

The throne room had disappeared, her body no longer under her control. She didn't know if her eyes were open. She could feel the cold, but it no longer bothered her. Some dim part of her knew her heartbeat had slowed and she was hovering in the place between life and death.

"The place between life and death is the true in-between,"

Vestior explained, his voice coming from somewhere almost next to her. She couldn't see him, but she could feel his presence and hear his voice.

At a loss for what he meant, she said, "You told me I wasn't allowed to enter the in-between for a month."

"No, child. I only ordered you to not create a doorway for a month. Such things are dangerous without proper training," Vestior explained, but his tone carried a hint of urgency that made her uneasy. "We have limited time. Your mortal form will die if you linger, and I cannot hold you here indefinitely without draining the Well.

"You must travel with haste to the Sky Cities and locate the last remaining artifact. With your ties to the dragon, you alone are in a position to discover its final resting place. The Wild Hunt may not cross the border into the Sky Cities, making its location beyond my reach."

Sabine didn't want to think about what the dragons would do if they found out there was another god living this close to Aeslion. If they knew Vestior still existed, would the war begin again? She inwardly shuddered, not wanting to think about the possibility.

"Should you need to contact me, simply allow one drop of your blood to fall upon the blade. I will hear your call and answer but be careful. No one can learn my identity or the ties we share."

"Why are you helping me? I haven't agreed to open the portal."

He paused for a moment. "I have spent many years observing you, child. You carry the burden of responsibility for all who inhabit your world, not simply those who are able to grant you power. I have seen you safeguard those who cannot protect themselves and embrace those who should be your enemies. I believe, when the time comes, you will stay true to yourself and do whatever is necessary to protect them."

Sabine remained silent, refusing to make promises. The price of making the wrong decision was too high for her to make alone. She needed to consider it carefully and discuss her options with her friends.

"The weapon you hold was the final key Lachlina needed to seal the portal. It acts as the binding that connects this world to the in-between. Unlike the other artifacts, the power contained within the blade is mine alone. Lachlina connived to use our shared blood bond to steal my magic, but she lacks the ability to wield it without my consent. As you are the most powerful living descendant of my blood-line, she now seeks to use you for that purpose."

The reasons Vestior had been helping her made sense. If Sabine could harness the power of Lachlina's artifacts and Vestior's power, they didn't have many other options, except maybe her brother, Rhys. Too many of the fae had died during the war.

"That's why she gave the first races the knowledge of how to seal the portal instead of doing it herself, isn't it? Because she couldn't wield your magic?"

"Yes," Vestior said, a lifetime of regret in his one word.

"You're not responsible for her actions."

"Ah, child," Vestior said, his voice grim. "It is to my regret that I must shatter your naivete. We are all responsible for our choices, including whom we choose to trust."

A tight band of power wrapped around her, enfolding her in its embrace. It was neither hot nor cold, painful nor plea-surable. It was almost too complex for her to fully compre-hend the enormity of the magic. She breathed it in, feeling it settle in a dark corner of her soul like a thief waiting for the right moment to strike.

"This is my power to give, and I am entrusting it to you.

To wield this gift, you must fully accept and embrace death, because only then can you truly appreciate life. Death is the great equalizer. It eventually comes for us all."

Sabine felt him move beyond her reach, leaving her alone in the darkness. A strange peace filled her, an acknowledgment that this could be the end if she so chose. There was power in that, a quiet inner strength that she'd never quite realized before. This was what he wanted her to learn and to understand.

Bane had tried to explain it to her once. He'd compared his gift to that of weaving a tapestry, with the ability to cut threads or weave them together. Sabine had never seen it as such. With each life she'd prematurely cut from the fabric of the world, she'd felt the imbalance like a smudge of darkness on her soul. If she cut too many threads, her tapestry would unravel.

Demons were the ultimate fighters in that they never experienced the imbalance when taking a life. By infusing their essence into the Heartstone, the very punishment the gods had decreed safeguarded their souls. It was only the leader, the demon king who possessed the Heartstone, who would suffer the effects of the imbalance from each new death.

Sabine realized the only way to save Dax from the insidious corruption would be to release the demon's souls from the Heartstone. But as long as the gods were absent from their world, it wasn't possible to rescind their punishment. Vestior was counting on her affection for Dax to motivate her to shatter the portal seals.

It was a clever trap.

To protect the ones she loved, she would fight to keep them safe. She would fight against death to keep it from claiming her loved ones, even as she embraced it for her enemies. There weren't any lengths she wouldn't go to protect her friends and the innocents of her world.

She needed the power he offered if she had any hope of saving them. While she no longer feared her own death, she wasn't willing to go peacefully either.

"Death isn't something to be feared," she murmured, knowing Vestior could still hear her. "Fought and railed against, yes. But never feared."

"Then why do you fight against it?"

"Because while there's no pain here, there's also no joy. It's only through living that we can experience love, passion, happiness, and hope."

"Then fight, child," Vestior whispered in her ear. "Fight for all of them and live."

Sabine reached for the strongest of her ties to life, the burning ember of love she felt for Malek, for Bane and Dax, and for Rika, Blossom, and everyone who had touched her life. She embraced the love she felt for her friends, holding it close and allowing it to ward against the cold chill of death.

The slow and steady beat of a drum sounded in her ears, its rhythmic pounding growing louder. Magic blossomed within her, a warm golden glow that thawed the ice forming on her skin. The tempo of the drum grew louder and faster, mirroring the pounding of her heartbeat.

"I accept this gift," she murmured, gripping the blade tightly. "I accept the gift of life, knowing death eventually awaits."

Magic burst out of her in a shocking blast, both hot and cold, fire and ice. It wrapped around her, threatening to drown her in a tidal wave of power. She bowed her head, allowing it to crash over her with relentless fury.

It differed from what she'd experienced when she had first touched the knife. That had been Vestior's true power, control over life and death. Lachlina had tried to steal his magic, twisting it into the artifact for her own purposes. It was the goddess now who railed against Sabine, furious that Vestior had shared the secrets of his gift when Lachlina had had to acquire it through treachery and deceit.

Pain slashed across her wrist, biting into her skin with the force of a knife. Blood welled to the surface and ran down her hand. Sabine gritted her teeth, refusing to cry out in pain. After Sabine had seen the face of death and come out the other side, Lachlina's temper carried as much weight as a child's tantrum.

Sabine spread her blood onto the blade and said, "I claim you, by blood and magic. In tribute to the god Vestior and the last sacrifice of the goddess Lachlina, I swear by all I am and the last of this world's magic to uphold my family's oath in defense against those who would see this land destroyed."

The blade of the knife grew brighter and sharper until it became nearly blinding. It lifted into the air, hovering overhead. Two voices, a male and female, spoke as one.

As we will it, the pact is sealed.

For a brief moment, Sabine could feel both Lachlina and Vestior standing beside her. Light and magic exploded from the knife. Everyone was thrown back, away from the weapon, in a tremendous blast. The stone seating near them flew backward, slamming into the wall and breaking into pieces. The walls groaned, and the floor trembled.

Power shot out of the tip of the blade in the form a golden light. It seared into Sabine's skin, illuminating her skin etchings. Every moment of suffering she'd endured flared to life, forcing her to relive years of agony in the span of a few heartbeats.

A scream ripped from her throat as she dropped to her knees. Her luminescence brightened, the marks pulsing wildly in time with her racing heartbeat. So much pain. Everywhere. It was almost as though two warring powers were taking place inside her, threatening to tear her apart. Each marking Lachlina had given her surged to life once more, their power warring with Vestior's gift.

Death offered an oblivion, but she had to cling to life. For Malek. For Bane and Dax. For Blossom. Rika. Esme. Dagmar. She repeated their names like a mantra, using the thought of her friends as a lodestone to help her endure.

"I accept this!" she shouted, uncertain whether either god would hear her. "I accept this sacrifice!"

There was another brief surge of agony, as though a knife had pierced her wrist, and then it was gone. Sabine slumped to the ground, exhausted and spent. But very much alive.

Malek crawled toward her and pulled her into his arms, holding her tightly. Bane did the same, taking her still-bleeding hand in his. He ran his finger along her injured hand, knitting the skin back together. Through her still-falling tears, Sabine looked back and forth between them. They were her balance, light and dark, life and death.

They were hers to protect.

Just as she was theirs.

Chapter Thirty-Six

"We have to leave already?" Rika asked.

Sabine folded the last of her clothing and placed it in one of the traveler's packs. "The Huntsman said we're running out of time to find the final artifact. It's also a good idea to give Dax some space while he…" She paused, considering. "Let's say, 'handles any dissenters.' My presence may undermine his authority."

"He's going to kill any challengers, isn't he?"

Bane walked into the room, holding several weapons. "No one will challenge him for his throne, but they may try to circumvent his rule. He needs to strike fear into his subjects now, before they attempt to topple his regime."

"Politics stink," Rika muttered.

"Indeed, little seer," Bane replied and handed her a sheath for her dagger. "Try that one for your new blade. We'll have to adjust the fit for you, but it should work."

"Wow! This is really great, Bane," Rika said, sliding her dagger into its sheath before handing it to Bane for inspection.

"I can't wait to see the sky again," Blossom said wistfully, landing on the dresser near Rika. "Riding a dragon is going to be epic!"

"I'm a little scared but also excited," Rika said, watching as Bane fastened the dagger to her belt. "I hope we see Esme and Levin. Malek said they're probably on their way back to the Sky Cities."

Sabine pressed a hand against her stomach, trying to settle her nerves. While she was looking forward to seeing Esme, the thought of her feet leaving the ground wasn't appealing.

Blossom peered up at her and grinned. "Malek wants to talk to you before we leave. I think he's in the courtyard."

Bane picked up the traveler's pack. "I'll finish up in here. Dax should be ready for us in about fifteen minutes."

Sabine nodded and headed into the suite's courtyard. Malek was sitting on a bench, his elbows resting on his knees as he stared at the ground. He looked up when she entered, his expression warming. She felt her body respond to the heat in his gaze.

She smiled. "What are you doing out here?"

"Waiting for you," he said, holding out his hand. She took it and let him pull her into his lap. He wrapped his arms around her.

"Someone's going to walk in," she teased lightly.

He nuzzled her neck, caressing her with his heated power. "Not sure I care."

She laughed and cuddled against him. "Bane said you needed to speak with me. Are you all right?"

"It's not me," he murmured, kissing her neck and sending little tingles all the way to her toes. "I can feel your unease. Are you worried about going to the Sky Cities?"

"In part," Sabine said, tilting her head to give him better access.

"Tell me," he said, sending shivers through her body as he

kissed her neck. It was impossible to focus on the conversation when he was touching her.

"I'm also worried about—" Her voice cut off when he lightly nibbled on her ear. "Gods, Malek. I can't concentrate when you're touching me."

"That's the point," he said, kissing her softly. "You're not as worried now, are you?"

"No, but now I'm hot and bothered, and we're going to be interrupted any minute."

He chuckled and traced one of her skin etchings with his fingers. "You don't need to worry about anything once we're in the air. It'll probably take a week or two to reach the Sky Cities, but we'll take frequent breaks and make camp on the ground. If you start getting nervous, I'll land immediately."

She splayed her hand against his chest. "I'm more concerned about when we arrive. Your people don't think too highly of fae or demons."

She wasn't concerned about Blossom or Rika. Malek had told her about the family of pixies who had once lived in his fae grandmother's garden. As far as Rika was concerned, humans didn't pose much of a threat to dragons.

He hesitated and wrapped his arms around her tighter. "How much do you know about the Sky Cities?"

She shook her head. "Very little."

"We're going to be traveling directly to my clan's home. No one will harm you there."

She arched her brow. "What aren't you telling me?"

"He's not telling you that the fae are both feared and desired in the Sky Cities. Half will want to kill you, while the other half will want to claim you as part of their hoard," Bane said, entering the courtyard with Rika and Blossom. "Demons, on the other hand, are universally hated."

"So much for privacy," Malek muttered.

"We're not here!" Blossom said from her perch on Rika's

shoulder. She clamped her hands over her eyes, her fingers spread far enough that Sabine could see her eyes twinkling mischievously.

"Nope, not here." Rika giggled and walked to the far side of the courtyard, pretending to be fascinated by the potted volcanic flowers.

Bane snorted. "Lizard, if you want to talk to her privately, you shouldn't have parked yourself in the middle of the courtyard."

Sabine tensed. "Is what he said true? Are we walking into more danger?"

Malek grimaced. "Not exactly. Some of my people are wary of the fae. We may have been the aggressors during the war, but your people taught us to be cautious. More than anything, you'll intrigue them. That could present a problem."

Sabine frowned. "How big of a problem?"

"Your magic is extremely desirable, Sabine," Malek said. "I won't tell you that there won't be danger. You'll be safe in my clan home, but beyond it, things may be… uncomfortable. Especially for Bane."

Sabine glanced at the demon. "Bane, maybe you should—"

"No," Bane said, interrupting her. "Don't even finish the thought."

Sabine blew out a breath. "Fine. But we have no idea where the last artifact is. I highly doubt it's going to be tucked away safely in Malek's home."

"No," Malek replied. "But I have some ideas on where to start our search."

Bane crossed his arms over his chest. "If you truly want to prepare her, tell her about the other fae."

Malek glared daggers at Bane. "Keep it up, and I won't even get her in the air."

Bane shrugged. "I'm happy to keep her in the underworld. I suspect Dax will be too."

Sabine squeezed her eyes shut, her stomach sinking. "Your people are holding fae captives, aren't they?"

"Some," Malek said, running his thumb across her cheek. "But I swear to you, I will not allow anything to happen to you. Every dragon in my clan home will die to protect you. So would I."

Sabine looked into his eyes, his sincerity undeniable. "That's not exactly reassuring, Malek. I nearly decimated the underworld when I thought you were dead."

He grinned and kissed her. "I'll treasure the memory of my lost scales for the rest of my days."

She poked his belly. "Very funny."

The door to the suite opened, and Dax stepped inside. His lips curved in a smirk when he eyed her in Malek's lap. "Done slumming yet, Sabine?"

Malek wrapped his arms around her and pulled her against his chest. "Yes, which is why we're leaving."

Dax growled at him, his eyes flickering briefly.

"Behave," Sabine said to both of them and stood. "Were you able to find what I needed?"

Dax shrugged. "No idea why you wanted a bunch of silver sticks and the other junk, but it's done. It's waiting for you at the entrance to the surface."

"She's going to make a carrier big enough for all of us to fit inside," Rika explained. "It'll be easier for Malek to carry us instead of riding on his back."

Dax grunted. "Are you ready to go?"

Sabine surveyed the courtyard one last time and nodded. "I think we have everything."

"Let's go," Dax said, heading out of the suite.

Sabine fell into step behind him. As though sensing her unease again, Malek brushed his fingers against hers in a reassuring gesture. She smiled at him before descending the stairs to reach the main hall area.

Dax led the group out of the palace and through the city streets. This time, the streets were crowded with people going about their business. There were a few curiosity seekers, but they kept their distance. Dax's presence was enough to cause most everyone to give them a wide berth.

A demon ran toward them, his tail flicking in agitation. Unlike most of the demons who wore armor, this one was robed like the priests she'd encountered on the battlefield. She stiffened, suddenly wary.

He bowed low and said, "King Dax'than, I bring an urgent message."

Dax growled at him. "What is it, Kegon?"

"The sentries just sent us word that they've located one of Queen Sabin'theoria's missing companions."

Dax arched his brow at her. "Missing someone?"

Sabine frowned and shook her head. "Not that I'm aware."

"Could it be Esme or one of the dwarves?" Rika whispered.

Blossom perked up. "We should go check!"

Sabine doubted the part-dryad witch had found her way to the underworld. Still, they couldn't risk not investigating. It was more likely it was a wayward dwarf.

Sabine reached for Dax's arm and said, "We can spare a few minutes to check, can't we?"

Dax placed his hand over hers and said, "Lead the way to this missing companion, Kegon."

The demon bobbed his head and led them through several alleys. The moment they stepped beyond the boundaries of the city, Sabine could feel the Well's presence reach out to her.

Azran slipped into her thoughts and said, *"A parting gift, little goddess. Vestior wishes you safe travels."*

Sabine stopped in her tracks as the cool magic of the Well enveloped her. Power surged through her, strengthening and fortifying her. She could almost feel Vestior's presence at her side.

"She's glowing again," Dax said.

Bane made a noise of agreement. "She's been doing this quite a bit."

Blossom sniffed. "I smell magic. Lots and lots of yummy magic."

"Sabine?" Malek asked, his expression concerned.

She smiled at him. "It's fine. Azran was saying good-bye."

She felt Azran chuff with laughter. "*Be well, little goddess.*"

"*You as well, Azran,*" she called as he withdrew from her mind. She gave her friends a halfhearted shrug and explained, "He was offering a power boost."

Dax harrumphed and motioned for Kegon to continue walking. As they approached a large tunnel, Dax said, "This is the way to the surface. Where is this companion?"

"Just off the main branch, Your Majesty," Kegon said, ducking his head as though expecting Dax to strike him. When Dax simply shrugged and waved him on, Kegon's brow furrowed in puzzlement.

Sabine bit back a smile, wondering how the demons' lives would change now that Kal'thorz was gone.

Kegon stopped outside a smaller tunnel, clasping his hands together worriedly. He had to be one of the most passive demons Sabine had ever encountered.

"The fire imps have… detained your companion," Kegon explained, darting a worried glance at Sabine and then at Dax. "I admit, I wasn't sure how you wished us to handle this situation."

Dax's brow furrowed as he stepped into the small tunnel. He threw back his head and roared with laughter.

Sabine moved to stand beside him and gaped at the sight

of a goat sitting on top of a raised stone. A wreath of volcanic flowers was around his neck, while stone bowls of food and other offerings rested at his feet. Candles were spread around the small chamber, making it appear almost like a shrine.

Half a dozen fire imps surrounded him. Most of them were prostrating themselves on the rocky ground, worshipping their horned guest.

At the sight of them, the goat turned his wide-eyed gaze on them and bleated.

"Lucky!" Blossom exclaimed, her wings fluttering rapidly. "We found you!"

Rika clamped a hand over her mouth to hold back her laughter. "Oh my goodness. I can't even…"

Malek chuckled and shook his head. "Sorry, Sabine. You're on your own with this one."

Sabine stared in disbelief. "I don't even know where to begin."

Kegon floundered. "I-I-I apologize, Your Highness. Before her demise, the sorceress Brexia had detailed her observations about your companions. We found her partial report in her home when we went to collect her body. She had written about a goat in your embassy that appeared to hold some place of honor."

"Only with regard to dinner," Bane said dryly and then turned toward Sabine. "Brexia was the sorceress controlling the fire imp back at the dwarven embassy. Apparently, I missed her report in my haste to return to you."

"What in the world am I supposed to do with that?" Sabine asked, gesturing at the absurd scene in front of them.

Dax cocked his head. "Eat dinner?"

Bane pursed his lips. "If we kill one of the fire imps, we could roast him up."

"Someone has to clean the fur off first," Malek reminded them.

"You can't cook Lucky!" Blossom protested. "He's important! Look at him! They're worshipping him. It's all about the horns down here."

"Maybe someone wants a pet?" Rika asked, wiping away tears of laughter.

Dax chuckled. "He'd make a better dinner, but we'll keep him for a bit. The underworld could use a new mascot."

"Of course, King Dax'than. We'll issue an official proclamation at once." Kegon bobbed his head and hastened off.

Dax straightened. "What the fuck? Proclamation? Wait a damn minute."

Bane roared with laughter and slapped Dax on the back. "Well done, King Dax. For your next trick, would you like to create a national holiday in the goat's honor?"

"Don't you have a dragon to ride out of here?" Dax snapped, turning and stalking away. "Find your own way out."

Malek chuckled. "Well then. How do we get out of here?"

"This way," Bane said, leading them away from the goat and back toward the main tunnel.

Sabine stopped for a moment and turned in the direction Dax had disappeared, knowing he hadn't gone far. She found him almost immediately. He was leaning against a wall with his arms crossed over his chest, watching her.

Sabine held his gaze, recalling the way it had felt when she'd shared the warmth of her soul with him. Despite his claims, she knew the real reason he wouldn't accompany them to the surface. As long as he held the souls of his people, it was too dangerous to step outside the underworld. If anything happened to him, they would be the ones who suffered.

Just as he had in Akros when he ruled the city's under-belly, he was protecting those who were his.

As she stared into his amber eyes, she realized Vestior was right. No matter what happened, she would do whatever it took to protect the people she loved—even if one of them was now the most fearsome demon in the world.

She walked toward Dax, watching as his gaze sharpened on her. Throwing her arms around his neck, she lifted her head and kissed him. He swept her into his arms with a growl, holding her tightly against himself. She poured all of her emotion and longing into their embrace, telling him without words how important he was to her. When they finally broke away, they were both out of breath and his eyes were silvered with passion.

She leaned back and cupped his face. "This isn't good-bye, Dax. It'll never be good-bye."

"Fuck no," he said, his voice husky as he stared down at her.

She managed a smile, even as her heart hurt at the thought of leaving him again. "I'm going to miss you, King Dax'than Versed." She gave him another soft kiss. "Take care of my demon, will you? Next time I see him, I want him in the same condition I left him."

He pressed his forehead against hers. "Tell that lizard and my worthless brother that I'll flay them both alive if they let anything happen to you."

"Deal," she whispered, sliding her hands down his chest.

"I could kill them both now and keep you," he warned.

"But you won't."

His hands tightened on her hips for a moment before he pulled away from her. "Go, before I change my mind."

She started walking away but turned back. "I forgot to ask; do I get my alliance?"

Dax pretended to consider it for a moment before calling,

"Bring a bottle of Faerie wine with you when you come back, and you have a deal."

Sabine grinned at him. With a small salute, she turned toward the exit and to where her dragon was waiting to fly her off into the sunset.

ABOUT THE AUTHOR

Jamie A. Waters is an award-winning writer of science fiction and fantasy romance. Her first novel, Beneath the Fallen City, was a winner of the Readers' Favorite Award in Science Fiction/Fantasy Romance and the CIPA EVVY Award in Science Fiction.

Jamie currently resides in Florida with a murder of crows in her backyard and two neurotic dogs who enjoy stealing socks. When she's not pursuing her passion of writing, she's usually trying to learn new and interesting random things (like how to pick locks or use the self-cleaning feature of the oven without setting off the fire alarm). In her downtime, she enjoys reading, playing computer games, painting, or acting as a referee between the dragons and fairies currently at war inside the closet. Learn more about her at: jamieawaters.com.

Printed in Great Britain
by Amazon